The Outcast

A NOVEL

D. L. WHIPPLE

Paperback ISBN: 979-8-9922347-0-1

Hardback ISBN 979-8-218-53477-6

Ebook ISBN 979-8-9922347-1-8

Cover design by David Prendergast.

"What doesn't kill you makes you stronger."

Maxims and Arrows section of Friedrich Nietzsche's
Twilight of the Idols (1888)

The Outcast is dedicated to my wife and
lifelong partner, Beverly, who never complained about
the solitary hours I spent at the keyboard writing
and rewriting it, nor did she ever question my sanity for doing so.

Banning, Iowa
Sunday, August 25, 1963

CHAPTER 1

Jim and I watched the rain coming down in torrents from inside the grain shed that connected the silo to the barn. It was supposed to be cloudy with a chance of rain. We should have finished feeding the cattle a half hour ago, but the rain had been relentless all morning, and neither of us wanted to get soaked. We were in rain gear, though it gave us little protection from the howling wind that whipped the rain into our faces like birdshot from a 12 gauge.

My brother was twenty-two, six years older than me, and I thought he knew everything. Still, he rarely said anything of value or gave me helpful advice. The last thing I expected from Jim that morning was concern for my well-being.

"You're not screwing anybody, are you, chump?" he asked. "If you are, you better use a rubber because any girl that would screw you is probably too dumb to know what makes babies."

I thought for a second about this pearl of wisdom he'd tossed my way. "I don't even have a girlfriend, and the girls I date can at least read and write. That's a step above anything you could screw."

The cattle gathered around the feeder bunks, expecting their morning silage topped off with ground corn. A lightning bolt split the sky over the cornfield bordering the feedlot. Seconds later, thunder shook the walls of the grain shed.

"Look, dumbass. You don't screw your girlfriend. Girls like Cathy Mason or Tina Barksdale are the ones you screw. You're going to be a junior this year. That's when things like that start happening."

Hearing that Cathy Mason put out was news to me. I hadn't thought about her since she'd dropped out of school last year. I filed that piece of information away for future reference. It was common knowledge that Tina Barksdale dropped her drawers for just about anyone. She was eighteen, though, and out of my league.

"Yeah, right, Cathy and Tina are both out of school. They're dying to go out with a high school kid. Give me a break."

"I didn't mean them," my brother shot back. "You're such a dumbass. I'm talking about girls like them. What are you, a fairy? You do like girls, don't you, butthole?"

"Yes, I like girls. What do you think?"

"Sometimes I don't know about you, Danny. Did you know you have a little wiggle in your ass when you walk?" He knew he was rattling my cage. I was trying just as hard not to let him get to me, but the ass-wiggle thing was a low blow and made me wonder if it was true.

"You're so full of shit that your eyes are brown." Not a lot of originality there, but he'd struck a nerve, and it was hard to be creative when you were wondering if your ass wiggled when you walked.

"I'm trying to tell you something, little brother, so listen up. If you go just shoving your dick in Sally Slut without a rubber, you're going to end up with a bun in the oven and a future that's shot to hell. What I'm telling you is if you need a rubber, I'll give you a couple."

I studied my brother's face for a few seconds, trying to figure out if he was concerned about me or just messing with my head. It was hard to tell with Jim. "Sure, you never know. Thanks."

"Come to think of it, mine are probably too large for you. I'll ask Mom to pick up the mini size next time she's in the drugstore." Jim fist-tapped me on the shoulder and laughed like a hyena.

"Screw you, Jim. I thought for once you were being nice."

"Hey, I was just messing with you. But I meant what I said. Some girls don't care if they get pregnant or not. They want to get married and have kids. Dad would kill me if he found out I was giving you rubbers. Just don't put your dick anywhere you don't want it to be for the rest of your life. Got that, kiddo?"

"Yeah, tell me something I don't know."

Jim turned back to the rain, seeming to find it more interesting than talking to me, but this subject was more stimulating than the weather.

"Have you done it with anyone?" I asked.

Jim snickered. "You mean the dirty deed, bumping uglies, intercourse, copulation—"

I cut him off. "Yeah, that. Have you?"

"Yeah, I've done it a couple of times. I'm not saying who with. I'm telling you, champ, it means nothing if it's not with someone you care about. It's no different from two dogs going at it."

The wind was dying down, and the rain had started to let up. Jim jammed a shovel into the pile of silage he had thrown down from the silo. "Let's go, butthole. We're already late."

He was about to head out the door when I said, "The bunks are full of water. You can't put silage in until the water drains or it will all float out."

Jim glared at the bunks as if his look could drain the water. "Then get your butt out there and scoop out the water so we can get this done. I told

3

Becky I'd take her to Fairmont today, but I'm already going to be late."

Jim always made me do the crap work. He liked to order me around like a peon.

"Blow it out your ass. I'm not going out there and getting drenched. You do it."

"Get your ass in those bunks, or you'll be swimming in that water." Jim put his shovel down and stepped up next to me. I knew he would do it—I'd been in this movie before.

"Okay, but you have to put the grain on after we put the silage out." It was a poor trade, and my brother knew it. Topping off the silage with grain took much less time than shoveling out the water, but at least it saved me some face.

"Okay, then. Get your ass out there so we can get this done."

My back was to the wind in the first bunk, but I took it head-on from there. Jim threw the silage into the first as I jumped into the second. A powerful gust caught my rain hood and ripped open my jacket, soaking me down to my shorts. I cursed the wind, Jim, and everything else within view. I was finishing the last bunk when my shovel caught a nailhead, sending me out of the bunk face down in half-frozen mud and cow shit.

"Son of a bitch!" I screamed into the wind. I pulled myself up, using the shovel for balance as I shook off most of the mud and shit.

"Smooth move, Ex-Lax. I rate that dive a ten." My brother stood in the doorway, laughing hard enough to make his eyes water.

I considered a straight-on tackle, driving him into the mud beside me, but he still had that shovel in his hand. It wasn't worth the risk. I stomped by him and headed to the pump house, where there was a stove and water to clean up. There was no way my mother would let me in the house smelling like the ass end of a cow.

The temperature hovered in the low fifties. Usually, this early in the morning, that wouldn't have seemed that cold, but soaking wet and covered in mud, it felt like Antarctica. Even my gonads were hiding somewhere up in my groin. The oil stove was on low, but it at least made it bearable as I stripped off my rain jacket and used the hose to wash off the mud. I was as cold as I've ever been. Jim came around the corner as I left the pump house. He was still laughing. I shoved past him, saying nothing, realizing that I'd need a well-thought-out plan before killing him.

I left my muddy jeans and boots on the side porch, put on my dad's coveralls (which he'd left for my mom to wash), and then headed up the stairs to my room. Blood was again circulating through most of my body. I grabbed a clean shirt and jeans and went down the stairs to the bathroom before my brother could get to the house. He'd want a shower before picking up his girlfriend, and if he got in first, he'd be in the bathroom forever. I knew it would piss him off, but I needed a hot shower more than I feared his wrath, and it was simply fun hearing him bitch.

I stood for a few minutes, letting the glorious hot water cascade over me, driving the numbness from my body. It was just what I needed, and the memory of my half-frozen testicles faded into history. I was approaching nirvana when Jim pounded on the bathroom door, hurling me back to reality.

"Don't use all the hot water, you little twerp, or I'll twist you into a knot!" he shouted.

Until then, that hadn't occurred to me, but I appreciated the suggestion. It's nice when one can combine retribution with relaxation. After listening to more of Jim's obscenities and pounding on the door, I leisurely toweled off, put on my clothes, and opened the door. Steam flowed out around me, fogging the mirror. According to my calculation, about three minutes of hot water remained.

My brother rushed by me and slammed the door. I waited in the kitchen, sipping a cup of hot cocoa my mother had made for me. It wasn't long before I heard Jim yell, "You little son of a bitch!"

My mother promptly tapped on the bathroom door. "Jim, don't talk like that in this house."

Sticking around for an encore was unnecessary. With a wink, I handed my mother the cup and headed for my room. I thought I heard a little giggle from her as she turned away. It was an excellent time to make myself scarce until my brother left for his date. An experienced warrior knows when to retreat.

In my room, I put my feet up on the desk, contemplating what Jim had said about screwing. I'd never had sex. My fingers had never even been inside a girl's pants. The most I'd ever done was get under Wanda Greska's bra in eighth grade, and that didn't count either because all she had was bumps. I wondered what it was like to do it. The older guys in school talked about getting laid, but until this morning, I'd had doubts. If my brother could get laid, though, I figured anybody could. Maybe the other guys were telling the truth.

I'd looked through a few magazines, but that was more for older guys like my brother. Having seen pigs, cows, and dogs go at it, the process was no mystery to me. I was curious about what it was like for a girl. Was it just something they put up with if they liked a boy, or did they enjoy it too? My parents had done it because they had kids, but I didn't want to dwell on that. Some things were better left in the murky darkness of ignorance.

I pushed away from my desk, got up, and walked around the room with my palms on the cheeks of my ass. I didn't feel a wiggle. Did that mean I didn't have one? I trusted nothing Jim said, but why would he say something like that? How would I know if I did or not? I couldn't just ask someone at school. I came down the stairs as Jim was coming up. He tried to burn me with a look, which I returned with a big grin. I knew he wouldn't mess with me. He was already late to pick up Becky.

As I entered the kitchen, my dad glanced up from the Sunday paper. "Any of those steers look sick to you this morning? I noticed one yesterday with snot on his nose."

"I didn't see any that looked sick." It was the truth, but I hadn't looked either. For additional cover, I added, "The rain was coming down so hard it was hard to see anything."

"Then check them well when you feed them tonight. We don't want something spreading to the entire herd."

"I will." I was out the door before he could think of something else for me to do.

The rain had stopped, but a light mist hovered near the ground like an afterthought. Dark clouds drifted to the east, leaving a pale blue sky behind. Ranger, my dog, came bounding up to greet me. He ran along beside me as I headed to the barn. A warm breeze pushed out of the south, raising the temperature and my attitude. Puddles shimmered in the sunlight, dotting the gravel yard between our house and the barns. A hawk flew high overhead, scanning the ground for prey emerging from the rain. Ranger ran ahead of me, dashing from one puddle to another, and the joy in his eyes made me smile.

Ranger darted around me, then sprinted after a corn-thieving rat next to the cribs. I needed to feed the calves in the cattle barn and spread a couple of bales of straw for bedding. The two Hereford calves were late births, and with the nights getting colder, we put them in the barn rather than risk them getting sick in the pasture. The calves were in a twelve-by-ten-foot pen, sectioned off from the rest of the cattle barn. As I entered, they rushed up to me. I scattered a pail of grain into their trough and gave them fresh water. Ranger scratched on the door outside, letting me know he was back. He seldom came into the cattle barn. The smell could be overpowering. To a dog, it was a blast furnace of odors.

I scattered straw and played with the calves. They romped around the pen like kindergarten kids let out for recess. I chuckled and addressed them by the names I had given them: Jenny and Benny. Without me noticing, my father had entered the barn. I stopped when I saw him standing beside the pen, his hands nailed on his hips. At six-two, my father was an intimidating figure, and he had a face cut from granite.

"Danny, I've told you several times. Don't name the stock. Cattle are not pets; they're the way we make a living. By naming them, you establish a personal connection, and then it seems wrong to sell them for slaughter, which is exactly why we raise them. You're sixteen; you're not a kid anymore. Start manning up, son. I don't want to tell you again."

I didn't argue the point. I had in the past, and it had only made it worse. It was why I couldn't be a farmer. I could never sell an animal for slaughter that I'd fed and nurtured. I understood it was necessary, but it wasn't something I could do. A farmer had to harden himself, walling off his feelings from nature's kindest creatures. When I looked into the eyes of an animal, I saw feelings, memories, joy, and fear. I'd never seen hate. The way I saw it, if you can cradle a kitten in your arms and not feel a sense of love and compassion, then you've missed an essential part of life.

We left the barn together. Before heading to the house, my father briefly stopped to tweak the old water pump for the stock tanks. This morning, he and my mother were taking Susan to college at the University of Iowa. They wouldn't return until late afternoon, and my brother was taking Becky to Fairmont for lunch. It was too wet to work the fields, and with the cattle fed, I had some downtime. A full Sunday ahead of me and no one to give me orders or bother me.

I went to the house, leaned against the fender of our 1956 Chevrolet pickup, and watched the box-moving procession. My mother opened the porch screen door for Susan, who almost dropped the boxes she was carrying. My sister had the athletic skills of a one-legged frog. A giggle burst out of me. What a klutz. She needed handrails to walk on the sidewalk. My mother steered her and kept her upright until they reached the gate. My father followed with more boxes and loaded them into the trunk. I wondered if there was anything left in the house. I could pack my entire room into two boxes with space to spare.

My mother was jubilant. She'd always wanted to attend college but couldn't afford it, and her parents hadn't felt a girl needed to attend college. It was almost like she was going rather than Susan. When my sister came over to say goodbye, my mother and father were already in the car, ready to go.

"You're on your own now, dimwit. I won't be there to rat you out to keep you in line," Susan said, then hugged me.

I hugged back and replied, "I know. I can't wait to live my life without a snitch."

"You know you're going to miss me," Susan said.

"Not as much as you're going to miss me," I said, then added, "Yeah, I'm going to miss you, sis."

"Keep your head down. The next two years are some of the best you'll ever have."

"That's damn depressing."

"Bullshit. Hug me again. I've got to go."

I hugged her, then opened the car door for her and watched as they drove down the lane and out onto the road. I was going to miss her, although she was a pain in the ass most of the time. As sisters went, I'd gotten a pretty good one, but there was an upside. There was one less person to share the bathroom, which was no small thing when there was only one for five people.

I played catch the ball with Ranger for a while. My arm was tired after a few dozen throws, but Ranger was just warming up. When he brought the ball back and I didn't throw it, the look in his eyes always made me feel guilty. I was feeling lazy. Rainy days did that to me. Maybe I just needed an excuse to do nothing. I whistled for Ranger, then headed up into the loft of the straw barn.

Our farm had three barns, but the straw barn had been my favorite since

I was a kid. I opened the outer door to the loft, letting in a stream of sunlight. You could see most of the farm from the loft's height. The higher view made the farm look almost magical. All that remained of the storm was a gentle breeze. A murder of crows cawed somewhere in the woods, heard but unseen. A stray cat skittered between two of our five corncribs, probably chasing down a mouse scavenging our corn. Jim hustled out of the house to his car. Before getting in, he scanned the farm buildings, probably for me, and drove off.

Ranger settled into a sunny spot in the straw, and I joined him. I was feeling less jubilation now about my brother's cold shower. It was a cheap shot. Why did I act like a jerk sometimes? Now, there was a question my mother would have liked answered. My sister always said it was my way of getting attention. That might have been the case because I'd get plenty of attention for the hot water stunt when my brother got home.

I had the whole day ahead of me, no supervision, a driver's license, and a pickup sitting with the keys in the ignition. It was a hard temptation to resist. I rubbed Ranger's stomach. He rolled onto his back, his eyes completely joyful, saying *more, more, more*. I lay back in the straw, watching small bits of chaff float in the sunbeams, rising and falling with each movement of air. I moved Ranger's head off my lap, letting him sleep. It was just after ten. A few puffy white clouds floated overhead. It was turning into a beautiful fall day. Only a few puddles remained, and the thermostat on the side of the barn read sixty-eight.

A gentle puff of breeze ruffled my hair. It was longer on the sides than usual, but I liked it that way and was stalling on getting it cut before I started back to school. It was almost long enough to comb the sides together in the back—a look that some called a duck's ass. My brother thought it would be a natural look for me.

The nearest town to us was Banning, twelve miles from the farm—too far to ride a bike. I'd gotten my driver's license a month earlier, but I didn't have a car of my own. If the corn crop was good and the prices increased, my dad might buy me a car. Still, until then, I had to ask permission to drive the pickup and, on rare occasions, my folks' 1962 Pontiac Bonneville.

Banning was a small town of about 1,800 people living within the city limits. The people here had a strong connection to the land. You either tilled it or sold things to people who did. Roots ran deep, generations buried in soil nurtured by decades of memories. Two other towns in the county, Granner and Rowan, were even smaller than Banning—neither had much to offer, mainly gas stations and bars. Madison's county seat was in Fairmont, which was about four times the size of Banning. There'd always been a rivalry between the two towns. People in Fairmont thought they were more important because they had the county courthouse, the sheriff's office, and the place where we went to vote. Apart from that, Banning people believed Fairmont was unnecessary.

Most people I knew thought Banning was a great place to live but compared to what? Most had never been out of the state. I wasn't speaking from experience—I'd only been over the state line once, and that was to Austin, Minnesota, for my aunt's funeral when I was seven. When I graduated, I planned to live anywhere other than Banning, preferably a long way from Iowa.

There was nothing I hated about Banning. There were nice things, such as a city park beside the Iowa River. Our school had a new gym and a cafeteria. We had three churches: Methodist, Presbyterian, and Lutheran. The Catholics went to Fairmont to attend services, but only a handful were around Banning. People stayed put around here. My dad liked to say that our babies were born with glue on their asses, and he might have been right. The *Des Moines Register*, the only paper people read other than the *Fairmont Weekly*, once reported that over 80 percent of people born in Iowa were buried within fifty miles of their birthplace. It sounded right to me. In the

Lutheran church graveyard, the Prescotts had a family plot. My grandfather, grandmother, and many relatives already rested in peace there. My dad had plots for all of us, but the only way I was to be buried there was if they shipped my body back. I would not be one of the *Register*'s statistics, buried within walking distance of my birthplace.

That year, I would be a junior at Banning High. Most of my classmates planned to stay in Banning after graduation or go to a college close enough to come home on weekends. Once, as a joke, I brought a road atlas to school to prove there were other states outside of Iowa. Only my best friend, Steve Wiederman, thought it was funny.

Mostly, I wanted to leave because Banning was small. There were no hiding places, not for anything, at any time. Most anyone here could recite your family history, including every lousy thing your relatives ever did. There was no need for a town archive. There were four or five gossips who could tell you who got knocked up fifty years ago, by whom, and the name of the child. My family's garden had a few bad seeds; too many people knew where they were scattered. People still talked about my uncle Earl, a former bootlegger in the thirties. A rival shot up Earl's Model T and left him for dead. There were still those who referred to Earl as "Possum Earl." My dad said the best thing Uncle Earl ever did was play dead, and he wished he'd continued to do it.

More recently, my cousin Darwin stole two cows from a neighbor's pasture but got caught while trying to sell them to another neighbor. The judge allowed him to join the army rather than sentencing him to jail. A year later, they flew his body back from Korea. People seemed to remember the bad things but forgot that my dad came back from the Philippines with a piece of shrapnel in his leg and a box of medals.

My father drank heavily during those first years he was back from the war. When he quit drinking, I was about six or seven. I recalled him stumbling around, asking Mom where she hid his booze. There were several occasions when neighbors or his brother brought him home stumbling drunk. He looked stupid, singing and telling everyone how much he loved us. Most of all, I remembered my mother crying.

My dad's drinking bothered Jim more than me. Maybe it was because he was older and cared more about what people thought of him and the Prescott family. When someone implied they were better than me, I was more prone to say "fuck you" than my brother. I wasn't ashamed of who I was, that my father had been a drunk, or anything else about my family. Everybody had something hidden in their closet.

Becky's family, the Kesslers, always thought they were better than everyone else. John Kessler had inherited 1,200 acres from his grandfather, who bought the land during the Depression at low prices from farmers unable to pay their mortgages or feed their families. I preferred relatives like Possum Earl.

Jim had been dating Becky since high school. Whenever we were around the Kesslers, I could tell they were none too happy about it. Becky herself was okay. She would never enter a beauty contest, but she wasn't homely. My brother was borderline handsome, making some think he was only dating Becky because of the Kesslers' wealth. That wasn't who he was, though, and it pissed me off to hear it.

All my brother wanted to do was farm. He said to me many times it was all he knew, and he was probably right. Becky was their only child; he was probably set for life if they got married. I hoped it all worked out for him. Regardless of our constant bickering, I loved my brother. If my butt were ever on the line, he would be there for me, and in return, I would be there for him.

Jim was a puritan compared to me. Not once had he been in any trouble. I was more adventurous, but overall, I considered myself a decent guy. My face had never appeared on a wanted poster. I avoided hurting anyone's feelings if I could because I knew how it felt to grab the shitty end of the stick. Many of my friends and I had started kindergarten together, and an easiness had always remained when we were together. I couldn't remember a time we exchanged angry words among us. I'd called my friends about every demeaning and disgusting name I knew, and they had returned the favor. It was what guys did when they liked each other—and to show that you weren't a pussy. None of it meant anything. I was pretty sure that my friends didn't think I was an ugly, dim-witted blow job. Nor did I think my best friend, Steve, was a perverted dick-wad.

I didn't have a steady girl, nor had I ever been in love. I didn't know why. My ability to clean up was quite impressive. I didn't resemble Quasimodo, but I wouldn't be mistaken for Tab Hunter or James Dean. I was six feet tall, muscular, and I had wavy dark hair. Without breaking a sweat, I could press 150 pounds and complete the quarter mile in not much over a minute. You would think all that would count for something, but it only impressed the guys.

School was starting in a week, and I was ready to go back. All I'd done that summer was work. The hay was in the barn, the beans and oats were in the bins, and the corn was almost ready to harvest. Then, in the spring, the cycle would start all over again. Sometimes, it seemed to me the only reason farmers had kids was for the free labor.

Farming meant hard work and long hours. There were no vacations on a farm. In the spring, summer, and fall, fields were prepared, planted, cultivated, and harvested. In the winter, the stock had to be watered and fed and bedded, eggs had to be gathered, and something always had to be repaired. As far as I could recall, my father and mother had never taken an entire weekend off, let alone a real vacation.

I was isolated on the farm, my little island twelve miles from town—it might as well have been a thousand. Jim had gotten his car when he turned eighteen. That felt like a lifetime away. Other guys at school already had their own cars. I'd only driven my father's prized possession, a 1962 Pontiac Bonneville, with my father sitting beside me. Two guys at school had already gotten convertibles, but my mom said I could rule that out. Said they were unsafe if they rolled over, not to mention cold in the winter. I told her I didn't plan to roll the car over or even dent it. As far as freezing, I'd put the heater up a notch. Problems solved.

In the interim, Dad said I could drive our seven-year-old pickup, a real chick magnet. I couldn't wait to pick up a girl in a rattling red-and-white six-cylinder. Take that to a drive-in theater and you wouldn't be able to hear the movie because of the laughter. If a girl got in, she'd probably scoot down in the seat so nobody would see her. My dating future was dim to nonexistent, and my ride wasn't helping.

Our three hundred acres of corn had turned light brown, replacing the sea of green I'd enjoyed all summer. The trees encircling our house were changing color as well. In mid-October, the leaves would peak, ushering in another winter. I loved the fall, but I wasn't a big winter fan. Twenty below zero took the fun out of everything except sitting in front of a stove.

Last winter, the temperature had dropped below zero for three weeks. At anything below ten degrees, riding the school bus was brutal. If the below-zero temperatures weren't enough to satisfy any masochistic tendencies, then Iowa always had a ton of snow to make you happy. We'd had three snow days last year. Staying out of school just added to my misery. Town kids could sit in their warm houses watching TV, while I was busting ice out of the water tanks or clearing snow out of our feeding bunks. The cattle required food, water, and a dozen other chores, regardless of the weather. Fuck a bunch of snow days.

CHAPTER 2

It was a beautiful Sunday, and I was bored. Jim wouldn't be back till night chores, and my folks wouldn't be back till late afternoon. I could drive over to see Steve, but I hadn't asked if I could use the pickup. Steve's father might mention it to my dad, and then I'd be shit up a creek. Since it was so nice, some of my friends might be hanging out in Banning. It'd been three weeks since I'd seen any of them. If my dad found out I'd driven to Banning, the next few weeks would not be enjoyable. Then again, how was he going to find out?

Just after eleven, I was behind the wheel, all cleaned up, wearing my favorite Green Bay Packers T-shirt and jeans. Ranger ran around the passenger side, expecting me to open the door so he could hop up beside me. I always took him with me when I drove to the field or to check the cattle in the river pasture. He would bounce around the pickup, enthusiastic for a ride. It made me feel like a royal turd taking him back into the yard. I opened the gate. His head lowered, and his eyes took on a look that drilled into my heart. He trudged past me and into the yard, then dropped to the ground like his heart had stopped. That dog was a pro at working me.

"Stay," I said again as I shut the gate.

I flicked the key over, and the Chevy's mighty six cylinders roared alive. The gas gauge read half a tank, which was plenty for what I needed. I cranked both windows down and then turned the radio volume to blast status. Ricky Nelson's voice pounded my eardrums with, "Hello, Mary Lou."

Fifteen minutes later, I was over the river bridge at the stoplight on Main Street. Several cars were parked diagonally along the curb. Small towns closed up like a book on Sundays, a day of rest for all except farmers. The only businesses open were the two gas stations at the other end of town, the A&G Grocery and Glen's Hardware on Main Street. Two women, my mom's age, loitered outside the A&G. Old man Foster, who once ran the Six-Pack Bar on the edge of town, sat on a wooden bench in front of Glen's. A typical, exciting Sunday in Banning. Mike's Café was generally open at eleven on Sundays, but the *closed* sign was still hanging on the door. Mike served a great hamburger. It was a kids' hangout after school and on Saturday nights.

I drove down Main, hung a U-turn at the fire station, and drifted by the city park. Three kids, junior high age, played catch with a football, and some grade school girls sat at a picnic table near the river. As I swung back, I spotted Brent Arrington sitting on the curb and Rick Deter leaning against the light post in front of Mike's. They were an odd couple to be together. Brent was Banning's football star, and Deter was a complete loser. It was like seeing Marilyn Monroe and the town drunk together. I was heading down to the school to see who was hanging around the ball field when Brent raised his arm, flagging me down. I hit the brakes and nosed into the curb in front of Mike's.

Brent was a year ahead of me in school and cool as ice. He rode a Harley-Davidson motorcycle that was always within arm's length, but today, he was sitting on the curb with a bottle of Coke and without the bike. It was starting off to be a strange Sunday. Deter gave me a little wave, which I ignored as I got out to see what Brent wanted.

Brent was the closest thing Banning had to a celebrity. He'd made the all-state football roster two years in a row, and this year would be no different. He had an excellent chance of becoming a pro. Everybody said so, especially Brent himself. He had two athletic scholarships in his back pocket and was the undisputed king of Banning High. Being a buddy of Brent's would be like walking in the sunshine. As one of the town's minor minions, I envied how girls looked at him and how guys hung on everything he said. Despite having known Brent since grade school, we weren't friends. I didn't swim in the inner circle; I floated around the periphery without being too intrusive or notable.

"How's it hanging?" Brent asked as I climbed out of the pickup. A comeback came to my lips—*like a bugle; you want to blow it?* I kept it to myself. Brent didn't take lip from anyone and certainly not someone he considered a lesser human.

"What's up? Where is everybody?" It wasn't one of my best, but I hadn't expected to run into Brent, much less hang out with him.

Brent was an inch shorter than I was but had tree-trunk legs and broader shoulders. He worked out on weights and ran every day. I was always too tired after doing chores to do much more than change channels on the TV.

I glanced inside Mike's. "Why isn't the café open?" I asked, trying to keep the conversation going. Just being seen talking with Brent Arrington could add points to my reputation.

"Brilliant observation, Sherlock," Brent replied. Rick Deter laughed like Red Skelton had just cut a fart on TV, so I gave him a glaring stare, and he turned away. I may have had to take shit from Arrington but not from Rick the Dick. Deter was a hanger-on, a bona fide parasite who, if not swatted, would latch on and stay with you forever. I slumped against the pickup fender, expecting Brent to take off, leaving me with Rick. Being seen hanging with a dork was the opposite of standing here with Brent.

"Where's the bike?" I asked.

"My asshole father took the keys. That fat bitch who lives across from the school saw me doing a wheelie down Main Street and told my mom, and she squealed to my dad. I'll get that old bitch back, wait and see."

Since Brent had stayed put, I sat beside him on the curb, stretching out my legs, hoping someone would drive by and see us together. Brent and I, best buds, hanging out on a Sunday afternoon. How cool was that? Where was a photographer when you needed one? As I was about to say something brilliant to Brent, Chad Wilson turned the corner onto Main Street in his new red Ford convertible, top down, radio blaring. Franny Gardlin and Tina Barksdale were sitting with him.

Brent yelled, "Are you getting any of that, Wilson?" I sat tight, waiting to see the reaction. I wanted to be Brent's buddy but not a crippled one. Chad was no dude to mess with. He had a reputation for carrying a lead pipe under his seat so his knuckles wouldn't get bruised as he beat you to death. Chad threw a third-finger salute behind the girls' heads as he drove by. Brent returned the sign with double birds of his own, but Chad was long gone.

"Your old man's letting you take the truck now?" Brent asked, setting the empty Coke bottle down between his legs.

I shrugged as if to say, of course, what else was new?

Brent combed his fingers through his hair, laying the errant strands behind his ears. His hair was a wavy light brown, matching his eyes. Some guys had it all. My dad said Brent strongly resembled his dad, Ron Arrington, who was infamous in Banning for his sexual escapades and admired for impregnating two sisters in high school. Brent's dad married one of them—the better-looking one. You put a bun in the oven, you marry the baker. The girl Brent called his cousin was his half-sister. Rumor was that Ron Arrington would fuck anything that moved and didn't moo. My father said that wasn't exactly accurate—that he would never leave Ron Arrington alone with a cow.

Mike flicked the sign over and pushed up the shade on the door. Rick started across the street and then turned back toward us. "I'm going to get a Coke. You want anything, Brent?"

I thought, *What the fuck am I, chopped liver?* But I said nothing. I'd make sure Rick paid for that in the future.

"Some gum if you're going into Mike's," Arrington shot back.

"Sure," Rick said with a grin, "you want Dentyne?"

"You got it!" Brent shouted back. "What a fucking blow job." Brent sat back on his elbows and shook his head.

Rick smiled as he came back across the road. One hand held a Coke, and the other held out the pack of Dentyne to Brent. He sat beside Brent, taking a good swallow from the Coke bottle. Brent gave a little moan and shook his head again.

"What's shaking, man?" Rick said, mimicking Brent by lying back on his elbows. His high voice sounded more like that of a cartoon character than a seventeen-year-old boy. Red blotches from a morning of popping zits sprinkled the left side of his face.

"Not much," Brent said, getting to his feet. "Danny and I were just taking off." Brent jerked his head at me and headed toward the pickup. I glanced at Rick, shrugged, and got up, leaving him alone on the curb. Rick waved as we backed away, dejection written all over him. I felt sorry for the guy, even if he was a pest. I knew all too well what it felt like to be one of the unchosen.

We were just about to leave when Rick called out to us.

"Hey, Brent, you want to get that fat bitch that squealed on you? I'll do it."

"How are you going to do that?" Brent asked.

"Oh, I don't know. I could throw some eggs at her house."

"Yeah, why don't you do that? We'll drive around and come back for you."

"You're not going to help?" Rick asked, disappointed.

"No, that would ruin it. She knows me, and I'd be the first person suspected. You're not chickening out on me, are you, Deter?"

"Well, no. I said I'd do it, and I will," Rick said, straightening up and pushing his chest out.

We watched him walk past old man Foster and into A&G. He came out with an oblong box containing a dozen eggs. He glanced at us, then turned and headed up the street.

"What's shaking, man? Can I hang out with you guys? Maybe we can all pop zits together," Brent said mockingly. "I can't stand that jerk-off."

"Rick is harmless. He'll get in a shitload of trouble if he throws those eggs," I said.

"Who gives a shit? It's Rick Deter, for God's sake. He's a total loser."

Brent pulled the pack of gum from his pocket, tossed a stick up in the air, caught it in his mouth, and then offered one to me. I took it, though I was thinking that if we went someplace my dad could find out about, I would be screwed. The thrill of hanging with Brent was wearing thin.

"Where are we going? I don't have much gas."

Brent leaned over to my side, eyeing the gauges. "Half a tank—you're golden. You've got plenty. Let's go."

"Plenty for where?" I should have felt the ax dropping on my neck right then.

"You know where Loretta Tinsley lives?"

"Yeah, I know. She was on my bus route when I was in grade school. Why do you want to go out there?"

"What do you think I'm going out there for?"

"Man, she's an eighth grader," I said.

"She's going to be a freshman this year. What does that have to do with anything?"

"Little Loretta Tinsley?" I asked, surprised. "You're beating on the wrong drum there, Brent. She's still riding a three-wheeler."

"Bullshit, just drive. You'll see," he shot back.

I remembered Loretta as a sweet kid who'd ridden the bus with me. She was cute in that farm girl way. Shy. Even her smile was innocent. A wink would make her giggle. I didn't understand why a guy like Brent Arrington would have any interest in someone like Loretta. I knew both her parents, Evert and Ester. Jim and I had helped her father put up hay two years earlier when he'd broken his leg. My father held a low opinion of Evert, considered him henpecked and timid as a little girl.

"Little young, isn't she?" I asked.

"She's got a body half the senior class girls would trade for in a minute."

I hadn't seen Loretta in a couple of years. The girl I remembered had little nubbins on her chest and skinny legs. "Where did you see her?" I didn't think her folks would let her date, much less see someone as old as Brent.

"I saw her at the city pool last Wednesday. She was telling her friends about some kittens she had, and her folks were going to Mason City today. I told her I loved cats and might come to see them."

"You like cats?" I asked.

"Fuck no, but I do like pussy. Man, have you ever seen her in a bathing suit? What a beautiful set of tits. Nipples that point right at you. I got a hard-on just talking to her. Luckily, I was standing in the water, so she didn't see my dick trying to bust out of my trunks." He threw his head back and laughed. "Can you imagine if it would have jumped out, swishing around like a shark in the water?"

"I don't think that's possible."

"You don't know how well I'm hung," Brent replied.

He was wrong. After football practice, in the shower, I had seen Brent's dick plenty of times. He had no more to be proud of than I did, but with Brent, what he had was always better and bigger.

Cornfields shot by on both sides of the road. The sun beat down like it was a summer day. A few random puddles remained in the fields, but by late afternoon, you'd never have known it had rained. I cranked my window down a few more inches, letting the wind flow over me. For several minutes, Brent stared out his window. An uneasy feeling gnawed at me, like I was doing something wrong. I shoved the feeling aside. Instead, I thought about what Steve's envious face would look like when I told him about hanging out with Brent Arrington. I imagined walking into the morning assembly at Banning High with Brent and his friends. Everyone's eyes would be on us—a bunch of guys chilling and being cool as an iced-down beer keg.

Brent's eyes pulled away from the window and locked on me. "You fuck that Greenly girl?"

I'd gone with Karen Greenly for several weeks, doubling with a friend, Remy Fettler, who had his license and his own car. At the start of school, Karen had dropped me for Bruce Fuller, one of Brent's classmates. Bruce's dad had given him a new Dodge convertible. I hoped that was the reason rather than because I sucked.

"Nah," I replied. "I never got that far." Who was I kidding? I'd never even tried. I'd liked her and thought she was too nice of a girl to let me feel her up, much less pork her.

"You're not a virgin, are you?" Brent asked.

I didn't answer. Brent laughed, giving me a shoulder tap. I didn't need to answer. The answer was apparent from the stupid look on my face. I turned left from the blacktop onto a gravel road about six miles out of Banning, then took a right onto another that went by the Tinsley's farm. Gravel clicked and banged off the underside of the pickup, leaving a rising dust cloud behind us. I was hoping Brent was right about Loretta's parents being gone. If Evert saw me out there, he'd sure as hell mention it to my dad, and then my ass was grass in a world of lawn mowers. I turned down a narrow lane and dodged the potholes that plagued any farm lane after a rain. Missing my aim on one, I bounced over a deep rut.

"Shit, you'd think Tinsley would grade their lane now and then," I said, dodging another.

"You drive like old people fuck." Brent tightened his grip on the armrest. "Is this it?" he asked.

"No, I just thought it looked like a nice place to visit. One farm is the same as another."

"Nobody likes a smart-ass," Brent said, hammering a fist into the side of my arm. I tried not to flinch, but it damn well hurt.

"Fuck," I said, rubbing my arm.

"Don't be a pussy. I hardly touched you."

The lane ended beside a large yard with a two-story house on the right and a white barn with several sheds on the left. A John Deere diesel with a mounted corn picker stood sentinel outside a metal equipment shed. Evert Tinsley's new red Dodge pickup was parked just outside a white picket fence surrounding the yard. Maybe her parents weren't gone after all.

I parked next to a side gate that opened onto the well-kept yard. Rose bushes ran along the foundation of the large two-story brick house. Four massive round columns guarded a front porch overlooking the front yard. We sat for a minute, studying the windows.

"Maybe she went with her folks?" I said, hoping that was the case. We waited a few minutes, and then I slipped the gearshift into low.

"Hold it a minute," Brent said, grabbing my hand. "I'll go up to the door. Maybe she's napping or didn't hear us drive in."

A curtain on the left side of the porch pulled back, and I saw Loretta's face peering out.

"There she is," Brent said.

He jerked the door open and dropped to the ground. I turned off the engine. If her mom or dad were here, I was utterly screwed. As a preventive measure, I'd have to tell my dad I took the pickup rather than face the "Wrath of Khan" when he learned it from Evert Tinsley. I got out and leaned against the fender as Brent sauntered to the front gate. Loretta disappeared from the window and reappeared on the front porch a second later. She was all smiles, with a ponytail that swished back and forth with each bouncy step. Brent was right. She had changed. This was not the Loretta Tinsley I remembered from grade school. This girl had a long, flowing ponytail instead of pigtails and was much taller. But the most significant difference was the breasts that stretched out the red-striped tank top she wore above red short shorts that emphasized a gorgeous set of getaway sticks. Little Loretta Tinsley was a knockout, but the innocence was still there in her eyes and her smile.

"I didn't think you meant it," she said to Brent as she pushed open the gate, giving me a wave.

"Hey, would I break my word to you?" He glanced over at me. "You know Danny, don't you?"

"Sure, we're old bus mates. How are you, Danny?"

"If I were any better, I'd be dancing," I replied, shooting a wink in her direction.

Loretta giggled and held the gate open for me, so I shoved off the pickup, trying to look as cool as Brent, and strode over to where she stood.

"Your dad or mom around?" Brent asked.

I held my breath.

"Why? Did you need to see my folks?" Loretta asked, disappointment coming to her face.

"I thought perhaps your dad could give me a tour of your farm," Brent lied.

"Oh, no. They went to Mason City. They'll probably be back about five."

"That's a shame," Brent said, digging his shoe into the dirt.

I looked away, thinking Brent's line of bullshit was like watching a bad school play.

"I can show you around," Loretta bubbled.

"Are you sure you don't mind?" Brent asked, throwing me a look.

"Oh, I don't mind. Do you like cattle? We have some new calves. You can come too, Danny."

"Danny's an old farm boy. You've probably seen all the farms you want to, haven't you, Danny Boy?"

The moniker pissed me off. I wasn't his fucking stooge. If he expected me to chauffeur him while he paraded Loretta around, he could shove that thought straight up his ass.

"No, you come along too, Danny," Loretta said, beaming. "It's great that you came by. I was getting bored trying to think of something to do."

"Oh, come on, there's a million things to do on a farm," Brent said, then turned and winked at me. I didn't have a clue what that was supposed to mean. He continued to chat up Loretta as I looked on like an admiring fan. As we walked toward the barn, Brent kept up his stream of bullshit. I nodded at his chatter like one of those bobbleheads that dorks put on their car's dash.

"It must be great to have all this land around you. All we've got is a front yard about half the size of yours," Brent said, then gave an *aw-shucks* look as if he were some country bumpkin. He dug his shoe into the dirt again. If the bullshit got any deeper, I was going to need wading boots. No wonder I didn't have a flock of girls fluttering around me like Brent. I was getting dumber just listening to him, but Loretta was eating it up. She was thrilled to have two high school boys out to see her. It amazed me she didn't ask Brent for his autograph.

It was Brent's confidence and his ease around Loretta that I envied. I'd never considered myself a loser, but no girl had given me the attention Loretta was showing Brent. She hung on his every word, giggled and laughed at every stupid thing he said. She was the same little Loretta, just in a woman's body. Her shyness only added to her attractiveness, but I still saw the silly, naive girl I'd joked with on the bus. I didn't understand why we were even out here. Brent could have dated any girl he wanted to—and he did.

"Do you guys want anything to drink? My mom made some lemonade before they left."

"Nah," Brent said. "We just had a couple of Cokes in town. Why don't you give me the nickel tour?"

Brent may have had a Coke, but I would have loved some lemonade after standing in the sun for ten minutes listening to Brent talk and Loretta giggle. Brent nudged by me, his shoulder so close to Loretta's that they were rubbing. I followed a few steps behind like a well-trained dog, thinking that I'd rather be pitching shit out of the henhouse.

Loretta's ponytail swung back and forth as she bounced along beside Brent. She seemed happy with the attention. Maybe I was a spoilsport. I should have been thankful I was along for the ride. Even if Brent was an insincere asshole who just wanted to stare at her tits for a while. What could that hurt? This was not the Danny and Brent show. There was only one star here, and my presence was no longer required. I fell back a few steps, thinking that sitting in the pickup and listening to the radio might be less boring.

Loretta pointed toward a field off to her right. "Our farm is 440 acres. It's not the biggest around here, but Daddy says we have some of the best land. Last year, we got 135 bushels to the acre, and Daddy said that's more than anyone else."

Brent turned back toward me, grinning like a kid who had just found a super prize in his Cracker Jack box. I gave a knowing wink back like I was part of whatever was happening. Loretta was becoming more animated as Brent egged her on with questions and stupid comments. She was oblivious to his fixation on her bouncing breasts. I felt sorry for her. Brent was making a fool of a sweet, innocent girl who could have been on the cover of a teen magazine.

A red-tailed hawk circled above the cattle yard, watching pigeons feed on corn left in the feeder bunks. A flock of sparrows darted in and out, grabbing what they could from the bigger birds. As we neared the barn, the hawk dropped like a stone onto the feeding birds, sending them into the air. It skimmed the ground and, in a burst of feathers, grasped a pigeon in its talons before rising back into the sky. Feathers drifted down. Loretta and Brent didn't pay attention to any of the show as they walked toward the barn.

"You're going to love it in high school, Loretta. There's the harvest ball, homecoming, and prom."

"Oh, I don't know if I'll be going to any of that," she said with a giggle.

"Why, any guy in school would love to have you on his arm," Brent said.

"Now I know you're putting me on." A light blush came to her cheeks.

He was overplaying it. I didn't think any girl could buy into that bullshit, but that didn't seem to be the case as Brent took Loretta's hand. It seemed to surprise her, but she smiled rather than pulling her hand back.

"What's in there?" Brent said, pointing to the large white barn.

"That's our hay barn."

"You milk cows in there?" Brent asked.

"No, silly. No one milks cows anymore—unless you have a big dairy. We raise beef cattle. Most of our breeding stock is in the pasture. We used to raise pigs, but my dad says it's not worth it anymore because the big hog farms can do it cheaper. We only have a few calves in the barn now; the rest are in the pasture. Mostly, it's used to store hay for the winter."

Brent had wasted his talent playing football when he could have won an Oscar for his performance. I was near convinced of his passion for farming, but I remembered what Brent said on the way and knew it was bullshit.

"Hey, I'd love to see the kittens you were talking about at the pool," Brent said with a boyish laugh.

"They're up in the loft. We'd have to climb a ladder," Loretta replied, at last showing some reluctance.

"I don't mind. Lead the way." Brent gave me a glare.

I got the message. *Make yourself invisible.*

Loretta turned and faced me. "You can come too, Danny."

Brent stood slightly behind her so she couldn't see him throw me the finger. Brent and I wouldn't ever be best buddies if I continued to tag along.

"I'm more of a dog guy. You two go on up. I'll look at those calves you were talking about," I said.

Loretta opened the door, and Brent and I followed her inside. He gave me a look that would have frozen water as I entered. What did he expect me to do, stand outside cuffing my carrot? At least inside, I could relax in the hay.

Barns were mostly the same. Some were bigger, some smaller, but basically, they were dark and smelled like cow shit and hay, and this one was no different. It could have been our barn. Two center aisles divided the interior, with pens along the sides and two large doors on each end for the cattle to enter and exit. A ladder ran up to the loft on the front wall of the barn. Even though Loretta had flipped on the lights, creating a dim glow, I opened the door to allow more light in and remove the stale air. As we neared the ladder, Brent stumbled into Loretta, shooting his hands out to regain his balance. His left hand brushed over the front of her shirt. She stumbled back against the wall, looking embarrassed.

"Oh, crap, I'm sorry. My eyes haven't become accustomed to the dim light. Did I hurt you?" Brent said apologetically.

Loretta forced a smile. "No, I'm fine."

He pointed his finger up. "Is that where the kittens are?"

"Yes, they're up there behind some hay. Are you sure you don't want to see them, Danny?"

I was always up for playing with kittens and puppies. Why did Brent have to be such an asshole? He could still look at her tits while I played with the kittens.

29

"Yeah, Danny, do you want to come up and play with the kittens?" Brent asked, his voice friendly, but his eyes threatened to beat the shit out of me.

"Nah, you two go ahead. I'll look at your calves."

Loretta seemed disappointed but gave me that little smile she always had available. "They haven't been fed yet. I usually give them a can of shelled corn in the afternoon. You could feed them if you want to."

"Will do," I said with a mock salute.

Loretta was a sweet kid and no match for the charms of a football idol. I felt a pang of regret for bringing Brent out to see her. He was toying with her. She'd feel like a fool when she realized Brent would never take her to a prom or anywhere else. I was seeing Brent in a different light. Knowing what he thought of Loretta Tinsley, I wondered what he thought of me. Was I just a dork, unworthy of the great man's friendship?

Brent extended his arm, gesturing like Sir Galahad welcoming a fair lady to his castle. "Ladies first."

Loretta giggled and started up the ladder. Brent stepped directly under her. As I passed him, I saw the reason for his grand gesture. He stood beneath her, staring up as she climbed. Now I wasn't a prude, but trying to see up Loretta's shorts was disgusting. I walked down the aisle to the calf pen and saw the can on top of a burlap bag of corn. I filled it, spread the corn in the feeding trough, then found a comfortable place on the hay bales and lay back. This was fast becoming a horseshit Sunday.

I could hear them up in the hayloft. Their voices were muffled, but I could still hear Loretta giggling. I wondered if he was feeling her up and kissing her. They were definitely doing more than petting kittens up there. For several minutes, I heard nothing. Then I heard Loretta say "please," followed by more silence, and then Brent's voice rose, but I couldn't understand his words.

One calf pushed its head into the hay manger and bunted me playfully. I sat up, stroking the side of the calf's face. She was going to make a beautiful cow someday. The calf nudged me again, enjoying the petting, and then I heard Loretta scream, "No!"

Their voices grew stronger and louder. Brent sounded angry. I didn't have to understand the words—Loretta sounded scared. But the words became clearer anyway. "Please don't. I don't want to," then she said it again louder, followed by her muffled scream.

I jerked myself upright, pushing the calf away, and listened. An icy chill gripped me. Time stopped, and my breath froze in my chest as my heart tried to pound its way out.

"Stop! No!" This time, Loretta's scream brought me to my feet. I ran to the ladder and climbed the steps two at a time. I stopped halfway up, listening, not wanting to accept what I believed was happening. My heart was thumping wildly in my ears. Brent said Loretta's name softly, and then she sobbed. I swung off the ladder onto the hay.

"That was nice. I told you it would be. You were fantastic," Brent said.

I couldn't see Loretta. I took several steps forward until Brent no longer blocked my view of her. She lay mostly naked in the hay, curled into a fetal position, her back to me, shaking with sobs. Hay matted her hair, her red shorts lay beside her, and her tank top had been pushed up over her breasts. Brent was buckling his belt.

"What happened, Brent?"

Loretta turned her face up toward me, then turned away as she attempted to cover herself.

Brent twisted around, a grin spreading over his face. He saw my eyes go from him to Loretta. "Go ahead, sport, get some of that if you want to. It's all yours. I'm done."

I tried to absorb his words, understand what was before my eyes. What had he done to her? Had they really had sex while I lay below, and why was Loretta crying? Every muscle in my body tightened instantaneously. It was as if an intense pressure was pushing down on me, making me smaller. I forced myself to breathe. She was trembling as she lay exposed to our eyes.

"What did you do to her?" I asked.

"I didn't do anything to her she didn't want. Get a grip, Prescott. Don't turn into some fucking wimp on me."

"She's crying."

"So, what the fuck? It's her first time. They all cry the first time."

He walked to the ladder, glanced over his shoulder at me, and then went down. I kneeled next to Loretta. I touched her shoulder. "Are you okay?"

Her head jerked up toward me, and her eyes locked on mine. They were vacant, distant, not the Loretta who'd joyously welcomed us. She pulled at the tank top, trying to cover herself.

"Are you okay?" I asked again.

She sat up, reached over, took her shorts, and covered herself. Her right hand shot forward, slapping me hard across the face. She turned back to the wall, curling back into a ball. "Get out," she whispered. "Please leave me alone. Please, Danny, I don't want you here."

I climbed slowly down the ladder, not wanting to leave Loretta yet not knowing what else to do. I stopped halfway down, feeling like I was drowning. I couldn't go back up, yet I didn't want to leave. I wanted to run, vanish into the air, disappear, and never look back. My heart pounded as if it wanted out, and my legs felt too weak to support me. I moved down to the bottom of the ladder and dropped to the barn floor. Brent had shut the door. Only a dim light lit the way. I wanted the darkness to swallow me so I wouldn't have to face what had happened to Loretta.

Now Brent yelled my name from outside the barn. He was angry and wanted to leave. I stepped outside into the bright daylight. Brent was waiting in the pickup, the door half open, a smug look on his face, eyeing me as if I carried some stench. Why did I think we came out here? It haunted my brain.

Was I that stupid not to have known? I'd brought a wolf to the door of a lamb.

I asked myself again if I was going to leave Loretta crying in the loft. I turned back toward the barn and then stopped. If we stayed, would it only make it worse for her? What would Brent do if I didn't take him back to Banning? I didn't know what to do, so I did the easiest thing—the cowardly thing. I did what Brent wanted.

"Climb your ass in, Prescott. Let's get the fuck back to town. Do you want to wait until her folks come back? Let's get the hell out of here."

No, I didn't want to be here when her parents returned. It would be a disaster for Brent, me, and Loretta; it would only make things worse. I climbed in the pickup, taking a last glance at the barn. That vision would stay with me forever. The thought of Loretta's father finding us here terrified me. He would kill both of us after seeing what had been done to her.

We were halfway to the road when Brent rolled up his window and looked at me. "You better get your shit together, Prescott. You could have screwed her just like I did, so don't go taking an attitude on me."

"I didn't know you were going to do that."

"Do what? Fuck her?" Brent threw his head back and laughed. "What did you think I was going there for, to pet her kittens?"

"She's still a kid."

"Not with tits like that." Brent chuckled.

"What if she tells her parents?"

"Give me a fucking break. What is she going to tell Mom and Pop? 'Oh, Daddy, I invited two boys out here while you were gone, and one of them fucked me.' She doesn't want her folks to know any more than I do mine."

We rode in silence for several miles. Brent acted as if this had been a date to the drive-in. Girls didn't cry like that after necking at the passion pit. This was something else. Something terrible.

"It didn't look to me like she wanted to do it," I said.

"What do you know about it? You're still a virgin. Forget it. Nothing is going to happen. She'll get up and get dressed, and that's that. Heck, she may even call me for another bouncy-bouncy."

"I doubt that. It didn't seem like she enjoyed it. She was crying."

"Don't play the innocent bystander with me, asshole, because you're not. You knew what we were going out there for, and she knew what I wanted when she invited me out. She was all for it—and then she got a little scared."

"It didn't seem that way to me."

We drove for several miles without speaking. Brent turned on the radio and hummed along to a song by the Shirelles. My mind raced through the probable outcomes that might happen because of today. All of them were disastrous. Brent turned off the radio. He was silent again for several miles. The only sounds were the gravel hammering the undercarriage and the wind whipping through the side window.

"You're like a worried old lady. Here's what happened. We went to the farm, and she showed us around. Then, she took us up to the loft to see the kittens. We started to fool around with her. Nothing happened, and then we left. That's our story. You got that?"

I stared out the windshield. All I wanted was for him to get out of the pickup and let me go home. What he said no longer mattered to me.

"Hey! I'm talking to you, asshole." Brent slammed his fist into my ribs, knocking me against the driver's door. My right arm dropped instinctively to my side. The truck veered to the left, nearly into the ditch. Gravel pounded against side panels as I whipped the steering wheel in the opposite direction to control the slide. A second blow caught me high on my shoulder, sending me against the door latch. Pain shot from my ribs to my head. I shoved down hard on the brake pedal. The pickup skidded sideways, stopping less than a foot from the ditch.

I winced in pain, pulling air into my lungs. My hands gripped the wheel as if it were a lifeline. "What the hell, Brent! Are you trying to kill us?" Another foot and we would have ended up nose-down in the ditch.

He glared at me, his body rigid, his hands gnarled into fists. His words came slowly and threateningly. "I don't want this getting around. If my girl hears about this, she'll get pissed, and I don't need the hassle. You start to jack your jaw, and this thing could get blown out of proportion. It was just a roll in the hay. Let's leave it at that." He turned away and closed his eyes. "I swear to God, Prescott, I'll kill you if you ruin my chances for a Big Ten scholarship."

Then his demeanor changed as if we'd just been discussing the latest movie. "I've got a good chance of breaking the state yardage record this season. I missed it by fifty-two yards last year—can you believe it? Fifty-two measly yards. With recognition like that, I'm sure to get an offer for a full ride from Illinois or Iowa."

I dropped Brent off in front of his house. He said nothing more as he got out and walked halfway up his walk, then turned and looked at me for several seconds. It wasn't a glaring look or even an angry one, but I felt like I was a mouse being eyed by a cat.

I was near home when, despite having both windows open, it felt as though all the air had been sucked out of the cab. I couldn't draw enough air to breathe. Tears streamed down my cheeks as I pulled to the side of the road. I threw open the door, and my vomit splattered the ground. I fell back into the seat, my body quivering like a leaf in the wind. How could I have left her lying alone in that barn? What was wrong with me? Was I that afraid of Brent, or was I a monster just like him?

I just sat there, staring into a bleakness I'd never known before. I wasn't sure how long I remained still. Eventually, a car pulled alongside, breaking my stupor. A man I didn't recognize asked if I needed help. I replied I didn't, and he pulled away. Even as he was talking to me, I couldn't shake the memory of Loretta lying in the hay, sobbing. The image tied my stomach in knots.

Pulling into our yard, I prayed I wouldn't see a Pontiac in the garage. There wasn't. I was fortunate not to have to face my dad and answer for driving to Banning. I parked the pickup exactly where he had left it and laid my head on the steering wheel.

Ominous, dark clouds were building in the north again. A breeze changed from gentle to cooling gusts, sending dirt devils scurrying across the gravel in our yard. Sporadic drops of rain tapped the windshield as the temperature dropped and lightning filled the northern sky. A storm was coming.

Ranger greeted me as I walked through our front gate. I gave him an incredibly long hug and went to my room. I needed time to think and figure out what I would do if Loretta's parents called mine, but I was hoping I wouldn't need to do anything. My mother and father arrived forty-five minutes later. Dark clouds had gathered overhead, and thunder rumbled in the distance. I stayed in my room until my father called me for chores. During chores, I avoided him as much as I could. I didn't want to further my sins with lies if he asked what I'd done all day. A drizzle was falling as we returned to the house.

Mom was chatty as she made supper, describing Susan's dorm room and how much she liked her roommate and the beautiful campus. Usually, I would have been chiming in with questions, but nothing penetrated the fog in my head that night. She dropped a dollop of lard into the frying pan. "Is everything okay, Danny? You seem preoccupied. Did anything happen today?"

Mothers have a sixth sense about their children. The only way to combat it is to hide from it, which I did. "My stomach is a little queasy. Maybe it's a bug going around."

She placed her palm on my forehead, a mother's automatic reaction to any mention of illness. If I'd said I busted my leg, she would immediately have checked to see if I had a temperature.

"You don't feel warm," she said, taking her hand away.

"I think I'll skip supper and lie in my room until I feel better."

"You should eat something. What did you have for lunch?"

That one caught me off guard. "I fried a couple of eggs," I lied. I was never good at coming up with immediate lies, but I could sometimes pull it off with preparation. Somehow, my mother usually knew when I was not forthcoming with the truth. It was best to get away from the human lie detector.

A minute later, I lay in the dark, trying to push away thoughts of the afternoon and think of something more pleasant. The image of Loretta lying in the loft tore at my guts and dug away at my conscience like a badger after prey. If I felt this way, how did she feel right now? What had happened when her parents came home? A dozen possibilities ate at me, all disastrous.

I told myself I had done nothing wrong. That was the problem, though. Not doing anything was wrong. I knew that now. I pictured Loretta telling her parents. Instead of running away from the trouble it would bring, I should have stayed and made Brent walk back to town. I should have done something, anything.

Sleep was elusive, and I found myself hungry after having vomited the remains of my breakfast onto the road. I switched the light on. The entry music for *Bonanza* played on television—my parents' favorite show. I snuck down the stairs and into the kitchen. I was quietly making a peanut butter sandwich when my mother entered the room.

"Feeling better?" she asked.

"A little. Maybe it's one of those twenty-four-hour bugs."

"If you're hungry, I can fix you something," she offered.

"This sandwich is fine. You're going to miss *Bonanza*. I think I'll read for a while, then get some sleep."

"Okay, you're sure you're going to be okay?"

"Mom, everything is okay with me. I'm just not a hundred percent yet."

I trudged up the stairs to my room. Each step was an effort. Back in my room, a copy of my brother's *Sports Illustrated* lay on my dresser. I skimmed through it, pausing at an article about boxer Cassius Clay, now known as

Muhammad Ali, but I couldn't distract myself from thoughts of the afternoon. Somewhere around eleven, Jim stomped up the stairs and into his room. Ten minutes later, I heard his light snoring. I desperately tried to sleep, wanting to erase the day from my mind. During the night, exhaustion allowed me to escape my thoughts.

I awoke as the first vestiges of light seeped through my bedroom window. My first thoughts were that I had only dreamed about what had happened. In the dim morning, it didn't seem real. I swung my feet over the side of the bed and sat up, holding my head in my hands. The clock said six fifteen. My dad would be up soon. I pulled on my work clothes and slipped downstairs and outside into the cool of the morning.

It had turned colder since the rain. Ranger came running from the woodshed. I clapped my hands, and he jumped into my arms. I buried my face in his fur, and he licked at it as he placed his paws over my shoulders. If the world could be like a dog's love, I would never be sad.

"Something terrible happened yesterday, boy," I said to him as I gently lowered him to the ground. He looked up at me. He didn't care. There was nothing I could do to lose his love. I stroked his head one more time and headed to the barn, and soon Jim and my father joined me there as I put hay in the calves' manger.

"You can do that later, chump," Jim said. "You fill those bunks with silage. I'll throw down some more while you're doing that. We have a ton of work to do today."

"Who made you king?" I said, but my voice lacked my usual sarcastic ring.

After feeding the cattle, I saw my dad coming out of the equipment shed and remembered that he planned to work on the corn picker. He and Jim had already mounted the picker on our best tractor, a John Deere 8010 diesel. However, we still needed to repair the picker heads before corn harvesting.

"I want you to pick up some parts for me at the John Deere dealership later this morning. I'll call them after breakfast and have them put aside for you. You take the pickup, but do it before lunch. I want to pull those old bearings out this morning and put the new ones in this afternoon, so get caught up on your chores. You neglected to clean out that calf shed yesterday."

I stubbed the toe of my boot into the dirt. "I know. I got to fooling around at the river and then felt sick."

My father nodded. "Yeah, we don't have time to be sick. You okay now?"

"Yeah. I'll get to that calf shed after I finish chores." He picked up a wrench and began loosening a bolt on the picker's feeder chain. I walked back to the barn. Jim had pulled a load of corn up next to the hammer mill for grinding. It was a job both of us hated, and I was surprised he hadn't asked for my help.

I filled the bunks with hay and hooked the WD-45 tractor to the manure spreader. By eleven, I had hauled three loads of manure to the field and spread the new bales of straw over the floor of the calf pen. Jenny and Benny jumped and rolled in the fresh straw. I laughed, enjoying their antics, romping playfully and butting one another. The animals were what I loved most about the farm, and I felt a sense of accomplishment looking at a field of corn, its stalks reaching eight feet into the sky, laden with ears that would fill the cribs. I understood why my family loved it, but there was an enormous world past our fences, and I wanted to see every corner of it.

Near noon, I drove to Banning to pick up the bearings for the picker. Sitting behind the wheel, the feelings I'd fought off all morning came tumbling back on me. I couldn't shake this sense of doom that hovered over me like circling vultures. No one had come to the farm, and there were no angry phone calls from the Tinsleys. Maybe I was overplaying it.

Later that afternoon, I helped my father install the new bearings. Sunday was becoming a distant memory, a bad dream that had never happened. My best option was to forget and keep my mouth shut.

CHAPTER 3

Jim and I spent most of the day grinding corn and putting new blades on the stock cutter. After feeding the cattle, we unloaded a wagon of ground corn into the grain shed. I was beat, and not only from working—Sunday stayed in the back of my mind like a pesky fly. We'd just finished our chores when Sheriff Brennan's cruiser came down our lane and parked next to the farm's pickup.

"I wonder what he wants," Jim said. "I heard someone stole a trailer from a field near Rowan."

"I don't think that's it," I said, my mouth turning to cotton as we stood there. "He's here for me."

"For you, sport? What did you do, steal a candy bar?"

We stood at the corner of the barn, watching as my father got into the sheriff's cruiser. Jim continued with his questions, but I said nothing. I could hardly breathe.

"What the hell, Danny? Say something. Have you gotten yourself into some deep shit?"

I could hear my brother's voice, but it was distant, though he stood right beside me. My focus was on the two men inside the cruiser. A few minutes passed, and my father got out of the car and motioned to me. Jim walked with me to the car.

"Sheriff Brennan wants to talk to you, Danny. He says you and that Arrington boy were at the Tinsleys' yesterday. I told him that wasn't possible, and he said you'd taken the pickup into Banning. Is that right, Danny?"

"I'm sorry."

"Be sorry later. Now, tell the sheriff what he wants to know. He's got some questions for you. I don't know what's going on, Danny, but whatever it is, it's serious. I want you to tell the truth. This is no time for lying. I think that Arrington boy has gotten into a load of trouble, and I hope you're not involved."

My father got in the back seat as I entered the front seat with Sheriff Brennan. There were no preliminaries, no chitchat as I slid into the seat. Sheriff Brennan studied me briefly, then placed a notepad on the steering wheel. His pen hovered over it as he said, "Tell me what happened Sunday at the Tinsleys' farm. Let's start with when you met Brent Arrington in Banning. Leave nothing out. You lie to me, son, and it will go harder on you. Know that right up front."

I looked over my shoulder at my father's stone face and wondered if he could ever love me again after he knew the truth. There was no downplaying what had happened to Loretta, and I didn't try. I couldn't look at my father again. I didn't want to see the shame and disappointment on his face. Sheriff Brennan listened intently, seldom interrupting, occasionally jotting down a note. When I finished, my throat was dry. He didn't speak for several seconds, his eyes on me as if searching for a lie.

"Is there anything else you want to tell me?" he asked.

"I don't think I've forgotten anything."

"Did you take part in the attack on Miss Tinsley?"

"No! Like I said, I didn't go to the loft until I heard her scream."

"Did you do anything to stop the attack?"

"It was over when I climbed up to the loft."

"If you had no part in this, Danny, why didn't you say something to your father when he arrived home?" Sheriff Brennan's eyes narrowed on me.

"I wasn't supposed to drive the truck without permission. I guess I hoped nothing would happen."

"Nothing would happen," the sheriff repeated. "You hoped 'nothing would happen' despite your friend attacking an innocent child?"

"Brent said he didn't." My words sounded like a lie, even to me.

"And you believed him. Even though you said she was lying there crying?" Sheriff Brennan took a deep breath and regarded me with contempt, as if he considered me something that should be flushed down a toilet. "Why would you think the girl consented?"

"It was what Brent said."

"And you believed him?"

"I wanted to," I said.

"She's lying naked and crying, and you were unsure what happened?"

He made my words sound like lies. I hadn't lied, but how could anyone believe anything I said?

"You said you'd heard her scream for Brent Arrington to stop?"

"Yes, but I didn't think that he would hurt her. Girls say 'stop' even though they don't mean it. I don't know. Loretta felt excited that Brent had come out to see her, and Brent didn't want me to go to the loft with them."

"What did you think Brent was doing to her if he wasn't assaulting her?"

"Maybe feeling her up. Something like that."

"A girl ever told you to stop, Danny?"

I shrugged. "I've never done anything that a girl would have to say stop. Brent said he didn't force her to do anything she didn't want to. I wanted to believe him."

"Do you believe him now?" the sheriff asked.

"No."

"It doesn't make much difference if she consented or didn't. Loretta Tinsley was two days shy of fourteen. She is underage in Iowa, so she can't legally give consent. Regardless, she told her parents she tried to stop the assault but couldn't. Either way, it's little difference to the law."

I hadn't looked at my father, who sat quietly in the rear seat. Sheriff Brennan had occasionally glanced back at him, gauging his reaction. I knew if I looked, all I'd see was shame and disappointment.

"What's going to happen now?" I asked.

"Is my son being charged?" my father cut in.

"At this point, your boy is being charged as an accessory to the assault, but that may change at the arraignment. It's up to the county prosecutor."

"I didn't do anything to Loretta. I didn't know what Brent was doing, or I would have tried to stop him."

"Were you standing guard, ensuring no one came to the farm or that her parents didn't return early?" the sheriff asked.

"No. How can you say that? I just gave him a ride, that's all."

"That's enough questions, John. My son has answered truthfully. We need to talk with an attorney." My father sighed. "Now, what happens next?"

"Evert Tinsley has filed charges against both Brent and your son for rape. He believes Danny was acting as a lookout and an accomplice. There will be an arraignment tomorrow morning, where the judge will determine whether there's enough evidence to justify charges. I would suggest you have a lawyer there tomorrow morning."

In the meantime, it turned out, I would spend the night in the county jail. Sheriff Brennan instructed me to get in the back seat for the ride to Fairmont as my father got out of the car. Ranger ran beside the cruiser partway down the lane, and then I watched him slowly disappear through the back window. I'd never been away from him overnight. He wouldn't understand why I had left him. I watched our farm recede into the distance, my future disappearing along with it. Farms and fields slipped by the windows as the sky darkened. The worst had happened, and my fears were justified. The world had slipped from my hands and busted into pieces that I might never put back together. Whatever was going to happen. I knew my life had changed.

Sheriff Brennan didn't speak once in the thirty-five miles to Fairmont. I watched familiar terrain flick by the window in a blur, remembering little of the ride. I was thankful that Sheriff Brennan didn't continue to ask questions. Resting my face against the side window, I watched the fields, light posts, and farm buildings sliding by in an infinite kinetoscope. A whole world was slipping past, a world I no longer felt a part of. As we approached Fairmont, I asked, "Did they arrest Brent?"

"They took him into custody and booked him into jail about three hours ago. He will attend his arraignment in the morning as you will."

We turned off the highway onto Tylor Street and then right onto Baxter past the courthouse, then turned in behind, to a parking lot that said it was for official vehicles only. I'd been to the Madison County courthouse several times with my father but never in the sheriff's office. Sheriff Brennan parked next to the entrance in front of a curb painted with *Sheriff Only*. He walked around the car and opened my door. As my foot touched the ground, he grabbed my arm and yanked me out of the seat.

"You don't do nothing unless I tell you. You got that, boy?"

"Yes, sir, but I didn't . . ."

He pulled me into a front waiting room with benches and a partition in the center. A deputy sat on a high stool on the other side of the partition. He pulled a clipboard off the wall as we approached. I recognized him as someone who had been at our farm many times—Fred Nolte was our mail carrier till he'd joined the sheriff's department four years earlier. My father said he'd gotten the job because his uncle was a state senator and the former mayor of Fairmont. "Worthless as tits on a boar," my brother had said.

He'd put on at least fifty pounds since he'd run a rural mail route. His shirt stretched over his stomach, pulling at the buttons, and his duty belt was on its last notch. My brother referred to him as Fat Freddie. Someone said he'd developed a bowel problem that'd caused his weight gain. My father said it was because he was a total asshole. Deputy Nolte pried himself off the stool and eyed me with his hands on his hips.

"You got a notorious outlaw there, Sheriff?"

"Name is Daniel Prescott, rape and trespassing. He's got an arraignment tomorrow."

"Yeah, I know the little fuck. Why so quick with the arraignment?"

"Judge Neely is leaving on vacation and going fishing again. He didn't want this to wait until he came back."

Nolte's primary responsibilities were in the office, where he dispatched and served as the jailer. I'd heard it was because he had to stay near a commode because of his problem. My father said that he was the only person in the sheriff's department who wasn't full of shit.

"Do you want me to put him down there with the other one?" Nolte asked.

"Different cells," Sheriff Brennan said, pushing me into a chair beside a desk. "Book him, photo and fingerprints, the works."

"Want me to make out a request for a records search?" Nolte asked.

Sheriff Brennan put his hand on my shoulder. "You robbed any banks, killed anyone, or jerked off on Main Street?"

"No, sir," I said.

"Don't worry about the record search, Fred. I believe he's clean. We probably wouldn't get a report back till after the trial anyway."

Nolte took me to a small room with a table, two chairs, and a filing cabinet. He inked down a pad, rolled my fingers in the ink, and pressed them on a card. He raised the card close to his eyes, studied it, and then dropped it into a box with a stack of others.

"Stand over there," he demanded, pushing me toward a wall with a white screen. Then he snapped several photos with an Instamatic camera as I turned left and right. He had this insipid grin on his face as he took each one.

"They'll send you to the big house, not reform school," he said, shaking his head. "Especially for raping a thirteen-year-old. You're going to be prime meat in there. How was she? At thirteen, she was probably a virgin, right? Was she tight? I'll bet she was."

He wetted his lips again, then swallowed hard. "Was it worth it? I mean, you're going up for a long time. You probably beat off last night thinking about it." A bulge rose in his pants.

"You're disgusting. I never touched the girl, and I wouldn't," I shot back.

In two quick steps, he was on me. He was surprisingly agile for a fat man. He grasped my arm at the elbow, leading me out of the room. "We've got your buddy downstairs, Prescott. Hopefully, the judge won't grant you bail. I would love to have you spend a few months here with me. I'll teach you respect for an officer of the law."

"You don't need to editorialize, Frank," said Sheriff Brennan. "Just take him down to his cell."

We walked side by side past several rooms and into the dimly lit hallway. His grip intensified with each step. At the end of the hall, Deputy Nolte inserted a key into a steel door that opened to steps going down into the basement. Down there, Nolte pushed me into a small room about the size of our bathroom. One wall had a built-in concrete bench, and there was another steel door at the end, identical to the one at the top of the stairs. On the bench were a pair of orange coveralls and a stack of bedding. Deputy Nolte ordered me to remove all my clothes except shorts and socks, fold them neatly in a pile, place them on the bench, and then put on the coveralls.

After I dressed, he unlocked the second steel door and directed me to bring the blankets and the beat-up pillow. Inside, four cells lined each side of a narrow corridor. Gray paint covered the walls, floor, ceiling, and cell bars. Anything not gray would have stood out like a pimple on Elizabeth Taylor's nose. Only the middle cell on the left was occupied. Brent stood at the cell door, hands on the bars, watching as I walked by. He laughed when Deputy Nolte shoved me into the end cell opposite him. I stumbled and fell against a steel bunk built into the wall. Fortunately, the blankets had taken most of the impact. In the cell's corner was a stainless-steel commode below a sink with a metal mirror bolted to the wall. There was a small window high on the wall, too high to see outside, applicable only to know when it was daylight or night.

I spread a blanket over a thin mattress smelling of urine and unwashed bodies. It was fitting for the environment. The pillow was nearly as flat as the blanket, but at least it appeared to have a clean pillowcase. I doubled up the pancake pillow, shoved it under my head, and closed my eyes. I was in jail. I was in jail. That kept going, over and over in my mind. It was a nightmare I couldn't wake up from. If I hadn't gone to Banning, I would be looking forward to starting school, playing football, being an upperclassman, having a license, and hanging out at Mike's. It was supposed to be the best year of my life, and I'd screwed up everything. If they sent me to jail, even the army wouldn't take me.

"Hey, Danny! Can you believe this shit?" Brent shouted at me.

I said nothing. There was nothing to say.

"Hey, come on, Danny. Say something. Let me know you're alive."

I took a deep breath and rolled onto my side, faced the concrete wall and hoped he'd shut up. I didn't want to hear his voice. Sunday was the last thing I wanted to talk about.

"Look, man, I know I fucked up. It was wrong to give you a ration of shit on the way back to town. I'm sorry. I was all hyped up about what happened in the barn."

I got up and gripped the bars. Brent stood across from me, doing the same. A dozen times, I'd seen this scene in the movies. "What happened in the barn, Brent? This time, the fucking truth."

"It was like I told you. We went up to the loft. One thing led to another; you know how it is. She let me strip her. She even took her bra off. When I was putting it in, she panicked, went batshit on me, and started screaming. She told me to stop, and I did."

He was never going to tell me the truth. It wasn't in him. "Go tell your bullshit story to someone else. I'm not interested in listening to anything you have to say."

"Danny, I mean it when I say I'm sorry. I know you're super pissed at me, and you have every right to be, but if we don't stick together, you'll be cutting your throat too. We're in this together, buddy. I'll be straight with you, man. The possibility of losing my scholarships has got me scared shitless. You know how hard I've worked to get into a Big Ten school."

I returned to my bunk and curled up with the blanket. It was quiet for several minutes. The small rectangular windows at the tops of the cells let in just enough light for me to know that the sun was setting. In the back of my mind, I had hoped that someone would come and say we could go home, but no one was coming.

"Hey, say something, Prescott. We have to talk, or else we're in deep shit. What did you tell the sheriff?" He waited a few seconds until it was clear I wouldn't respond, then added, "Didn't your lawyer tell you to keep your fucking mouth shut? Don't be an asshole, Danny. Answer me."

His voice trembled with the same fear I felt. I might've even felt sorry for him if I hadn't been there. But the memory of Loretta lying in the hay crying pushed any empathy for Brent out of reach. Everything he said was self-serving. He didn't give a shit whether I lived or died.

"They can't prove anything. You don't have to lie. Just say nothing, and we're home free. Just talk to me, Danny. What can that hurt?"

I didn't answer, and he was quiet for a while. I welcomed the silence as I drifted into a twilight sleep, aware of my surroundings yet not fully awake. The evening light from the windows vanished, leaving only a solitary overhead light that gave the cells a foreboding and depressing grayness.

It was pitch-black outside when Brent's voice woke me. "Hey, Prescott, just answer. Let's talk. Look, man, it's for both our good. You know damn well that she wanted it. She invited me out there and took me up to that hayloft. Don't forget that. If we stick to our story, it's our word against hers— two to one. According to my dad, they need to corroborate a charge of rape, and she took a bath, so they didn't use a rape kit. That means somebody has to verify her story, so if you keep your mouth shut, we're home free. Remember, it's our word against hers. No one is going to believe that bitch against me if you say nothing."

My whole body tightened into a hard knot. I wanted to scream at him to shut up, to go somewhere and die, but I said nothing.

A second ticked by, then a minute. Brent's voice was pleading. "Danny," he said softly, "I know you don't have a lot to lose. I do. If we don't shake this thing, they'll take back my scholarships, which will blow my chances for the pros. You be a standup guy on this, and I won't forget it, and neither will my dad. I'll even tell the coach to let you run the ball more. Shit, together we can be a force on the team. Good night, buddy."

I pulled the blanket tighter around me, pressing my forehead against the cool concrete wall, praying that I would go to sleep and never wake up. I fell asleep but awoke as tired as if I hadn't slept at all. I lay there, listening to the sound of the jail awakening, metal striking metal, and the echo of footsteps above. Crime must have been down in the county, as they didn't bring anyone else in all night. Not even Jeffery Candella, the town drunk, was in residence. The noise level above increased, and then the steel door at the end of the cells opened. Deputy Nolte wheeled in a cart with two meal platters. He stopped at Brent's cell and slid a tray into the slot in the cell door.

"How are we doing today, Brent?"

"We're doing just fine," he replied cheerfully.

I leaned against my cell door to look at Brent, but all I could see was Deputy Nolte's broad ass and the cart.

"Do you think you'll kick Pepperdine's ass this year? I hear they've got this kid on defense who just grabs opposing players and knocks them on their asses until he finds the one with the ball."

"We'll smoke them—just like we did last year."

"That was some game you had last time against them. You tore the fucking field up. What did you make, four touchdowns?"

"Five," Brent answered.

"Yeah, that's right, five. I remember I lost ten bucks on that game."

"You bet against us?" Brent asked.

"Hell no, I'd never bet against you. It was my bet on the point spread didn't work out."

Despite the fact that I wasn't feeling hungry, any beverage sounded more appetizing than the awful swill I had consumed from the cell's tap. I was tired of waiting for whatever was on the cart.

After another minute of blathering, Nolte pushed it to my cell door and placed a tray into the slot. "Take this, or it's going back to the kitchen."

I picked up the tray and went back to my bunk.

"I'm supposed to tell you that your arraignment is at ten o'clock. Be ready to go by nine forty-five. The judge is in a bad mood. I heard some hammering outside—I think they're building a gallows." His stupid grin widened as he broke into a horsey laugh. He scooted the cart in a U-turn and left.

There wasn't a clock in the cell block, and I didn't have a watch, so I didn't know what time it was. Returning to my bunk with a tray of bacon, scrambled eggs, and fried potatoes, I had no desire to eat. I nibbled at the crispy bacon and ate a forkful of eggs but left the rest on the tray and slipped it back on the shelf. I tried to clean up as best I could in the sink, with only a towel that felt more like sandpaper. I ran my fingers through my hair, wishing I'd gotten a haircut like my dad wanted. A few minutes later, Nolte and another deputy escorted Brent and me to the second-floor courtroom. Brent walked just ahead with Nolte, while the other deputy escorted me.

Brent swaggered up the steps. I'd seen that confident gait dozens of times going out on the football field. It was just another day at the beach for this asshole, while I was struggling to keep my breakfast down. Brent joked with the deputies about the upcoming football season and Banning's chances of keeping the regional title. I said nothing to either deputy.

We entered the courtroom through a side door and went up to a waist-high wood railing to the side of the judge's bench. I stood behind Brent, waiting for the judge to appear. Suppose the judge said to hang both of us? I was all right with that. At least it would be over. I stared straight ahead, not allowing myself even a glance around the gallery. It felt as if my body were shimmering with shame and humiliation. What did my parents feel as I stood waiting? Brent waved to someone near the front and smiled at everyone. It was like he was here to accept an award. I wanted to rip his head off and toss it to his admirers.

Nolte and the other deputy stood just behind us, whispering about a planned hunting trip as the last seconds of my life slowly ticked away. After several minutes, District Court Judge Edward Palmer appeared from a side door opposite us. He glanced at the nearly packed courtroom, then pulled out a high-back chair from behind the bench, nodding to the bailiff to call the court to order.

I recognized the county attorney sitting with another man to the left of the judge's bench. He'd been to Career Day at our school, discussing jobs available in the legal system. He'd forgotten to include that of a prisoner. Across from him were two men in suits seated at a table to the right of the judge's bench. Having watched *Perry Mason* on TV, I guessed one was probably Brent's, and the other attorney was mine. Behind them sat my mother and father. My father's eyes remained fixed on Brent, and they were not friendly.

"What's on the docket this morning, Bob?" Judge Palmer asked the bailiff.

"I got four this morning, Judge." Bob handed him several manila folders. While the judge studied the folders, the courtroom was still like a church in prayer. He glanced up several times, looking at Brent and me. After several minutes, he nodded to the bailiff, who read a case number and Brent's name. Feet shuffled, and the murmur of whispers cut through the courtroom. The judge's gavel came down hard on the bench, and the courtroom again took on the silence of a library.

"Does this boy have representation?" Judge Palmer asked.

One of the suits stood up. "Attorney Anthony Miller, representing Mr. Arrington in this matter."

"Fine, Counselor, sit down," the judge said. "I just wanted your name. And you?" He nodded to the other suit.

"Attorney Merle Shagger. I represent Mr. Prescott."

"Fine. Proceed, Mr. Steward."

The county attorney rose and read the Iowa Code 702.17, 709.4, 902.9. "Sexual abuse is a third-degree felony. In Iowa, third-degree sexual abuse is a sexual act with a twelve- or thirteen-year-old, punishable by up to ten years imprisonment and a fine of $1,000 to $10,000. Your honor, the victim, Miss Loretta Tinsley, is thirteen years old, and the defendant, Brent Arrington, is eighteen."

There were audible gasps throughout the courtroom. The judge looked sternly at the spectators and then nodded at the prosecutor to continue.

Brent's mouth dropped open. He seemed to have not been aware that Loretta was thirteen. I looked at his parents, sitting just to the left of my mother and father. Mrs. Arrington looked startled as she grabbed a handful of her husband's shirt sleeve. Fear filled Brent's eyes as his confidence and scholarships disappeared. Any hope I harbored for myself drained away with Brent's.

"On the afternoon of September 1, Mr. Arrington attacked and raped a thirteen-year-old girl that he barely knew. He claims it was consensual, but the evidence refutes that. He enticed the victim up into the loft of her family's barn on the premise that he wanted to see the newborn kittens there. His accomplice, standing behind him, kept watch. Mr. Arrington forcibly stripped the girl of her clothes and then assaulted her. Whether she consented is essential only in the severity of his guilt. There is ample evidence based on the defendant's statement to bind this defendant over for trial. The other defendant, Daniel Jeremy Prescott, assisted Mr. Arrington in the assault on Miss Tinsley and acted as a lookout during the attack."

"Prosecutor, one case at a time. We'll get to the other defendant. Right now, we're addressing Mr. Arrington," the judge admonished.

"I'm sorry, Your Honor. I thought it might speed things up a little."

"The court appreciates your concern, Counselor, but I'll decide on the speed at which this court operates. Now, what else?"

"The prosecution requests to hold Brent Arrington for trial on the charge of child sexual abuse, sexual assault, and trespass based on the victim's testimony and statements by the defendants. Iowa law states explicitly that it is an abuse of a child below fourteen to engage in sexual intercourse, whether or not the act was consensual."

"Fine, Counselor. I'm familiar with the law. State the facts of this case; you can review the law's fine points with Mr. Arrington's and Mr. Prescott's attorneys later. Let's hit the highlights; this is an arraignment, not a trial. I've got a jury to pick before noon."

53

"Right, Your Honor. I'll keep it concise. The defendants drove out to the Tinsleys' farm uninvited on Sunday. Miss Tinsley came out to see what they wanted. The defendants told her they were there to see her father for a farm tour. Since her parents were not present, Miss Tinsley offered to show the two boys around. They entered the hayloft at Mr. Arrington's request, while Mr. Prescott stayed below to stand watch for her parents. Mr. Arrington then forcibly raped Miss Tinsley. Afterward, he called his accomplice, Daniel Prescott, to attack Miss Tinsley. Miss Tinsley's resistance prevented a further attack. Both these young men are equally accountable for this unspeakable act."

Every muscle in my body stiffened, and my knees weakened as the prosecutor's words cut into me like a saw blade. I swayed backward against the deputy. Darkness closed in around me, and I felt my stomach try to come up into my throat. I prayed again that I wouldn't lose what little I'd eaten for breakfast. The deputy gripped my arm, holding me upright against him.

"Take a deep breath, you piece of shit. I'm not going to have you passing out on me," he hissed, his lips brushing my ear.

The prosecutor sat down, pleased with his performance, as murmurs rose in the courtroom. The judge's gavel again came hammering down.

"Mr. Miller, how does your client plead?" Judge Palmer asked.

"Not guilty. It is correct that my client first stated that their sexual relations were consensual. Still, he did not mean that he penetrated this young woman. Miss Tinsley had told him at the city swimming pool that she was fifteen. He had no way of knowing her actual age. Mr. Arrington admits he kissed and fondled Miss Tinsley, but it was entirely consensual between them. Miss Tinsley remained in the loft with Mr. Prescott after Mr. Arrington left. He does not know what happened between the two after he left. Miss Tinsley took a bath and didn't inform her parents of the alleged attack until the next day, making a rape exam impossible. The prosecution has no direct evidence of the alleged rape by either of the individuals. I request the dismissal of all charges against my client because there is no evidence to suggest that any crime has occurred."

Arrington's attorney sat down, waiting for the judge's response.

"There is ample evidence based on the testimony of the victim, her parents, Mr. Arrington's earlier statements, and those of the other defendant. Mr. Arrington is bound for a trial. Next."

Brent's attorney promptly rose to his feet and requested that his client be released into his parents' custody.

"Do I hear any objections from the prosecution to have bail decided now?" the judge asked.

The two men at the county attorney's table held a brief conference, then answered. "We can proceed with bail if you'd like, Judge."

"Then let's get it out of the way."

Brent's attorney described Brent as a talented young man with a bright future who had never been in trouble with the law or at school. He and his family had an excellent reputation and a long history in the community. Brent was no flight risk, he explained, and his family would adhere to any rules the county imposed.

"Any objections from the prosecution?"

"No, Your Honor," the county attorney answered.

The judge nodded to the bailiff, who briefly conferenced with the judge. "The court releases the defendant into the custody of his parents to appear in court on November 11," the judge announced. "Next case."

Brent shoved his elbow into my ribs as he walked by. My legs trembled inside the orange coveralls as the deputy pushed me forward to where Brent had stood. I felt everyone's eyes on me now that the spotlight had shifted from Brent. My parents' attention, however, was on Merle Shagger.

"Mr. Prescott pleads not guilty, Your Honor."

"Okay, that figures. Let's hear the prosecution."

The prosecutor picked up a folder, his eyes wandering over to me like ants feeding on spilled syrup. Again, he recited Iowa law, concluding that although I was not directly implicated in the assault on Miss Tinsley, my assistance was crucial for the assault to have taken place, aiding and abetting the attack, thus making me equally responsible.

"Mr. Prescott provided the means for Mr. Arrington to travel to the Tinsleys' farm. He took his father's truck without his parents' permission or knowledge. He stood watch below the hayloft, fully knowledgeable of what Mr. Arrington was doing. He did nothing to stop the attack, even though Miss Tinsley screamed throughout the assault. Despite witnessing Miss Tinsley's injuries, he failed to assist her. His actions remove any doubt of his guilt in this unprovoked attack. Further, even though he claims his innocence, he did not report the assault to authorities or anyone else. Instead, he drove Mr. Arrington back to Banning and said nothing to his parents. This demonstrates his guilt through his actions before and after the rape of Miss Tinsley."

"Counselor?" the judge said, nodding to Mr. Shagger.

Merle Shagger stood and cleared his throat. "My client did not know Mr. Arrington's intentions when he drove Mr. Arrington to the Tinsleys' farm. He gave a friend a ride. Mr. Arrington informed my client that Miss Tinsley had invited him to the farm, but his father took his motorcycle keys, so he needed a ride. Mr. Prescott could not hear what was occurring in the loft, and when he heard Miss Tinsley scream, he immediately climbed up there. My client was not present during the alleged attack, nor did he do anything to harm Miss Tinsley. The only interaction between my client and Miss Tinsley was when he went up to the loft after becoming concerned about the sounds he was hearing. He asked Miss Tinsley if she was okay, and she told him to leave, which he immediately did. Your Honor, my client is an honor student at Banning High School. He has never been in trouble with law enforcement or at his school. His parents are third-generation Madison

County residents with excellent community reputations. I request my client's immediate release and the dismissal of all charges against him. He is entirely innocent of these allegations, and there is no evidence to support the charges against him."

"That will not happen, Counselor. The prosecution has provided ample evidence of your client's involvement to bind the defendant over for trial. A jury will decide how much, if at all, he was involved. The court orders Prescott to appear at a date to be determined. It releases him into the custody of his parents."

The judge brought his gavel down. "Next."

Deputy Nolte's fingers tightened on my arm, pulling me toward the door. For a second, I panicked. Didn't the judge say that he released me to my parents? Why was I being taken back to the jail? When I resisted, he opened the door and yanked me toward him. I stumbled through the doorway with the deputy gripping my arm in a vise.

"The judge said I was being released," I protested.

He didn't answer, just continued pulling me down the hallway and into the tunnel leading to the cells. I stumbled along beside him. The deputy's intense grip both held me upright and pushed me forward. At the bottom of the stairs, he opened the door and shoved me into the room. He picked up a bag from the floor and threw it at me.

"Your clothes are in there. Put what you have on in the bag." He stood over me, leering, as I pulled off the baggy coveralls.

"You don't have to fold those. Just shove them in the bag. Let's go, move it."

I dressed in a hurry, not bothering to tie the laces in my work boots. Nolte seized the plastic bag from the bench and again clutched my arm as he shoved me against the door. He moved close to me, the stubble on his face brushing my cheek. I felt the wetness of his breath on my neck, smelled the staleness of his breakfast. "You're going to be coming back here, Prescott. Pieces of shit like you always do. When you do, I'll be waiting. You raped that little girl, and now you're trying to blame it on a buddy. That's about as low as you can get."

He pushed me up the stairs in front of him. Halfway down the hall, he opened a side door and shoved me inside. I felt all hope fade as the door slammed shut behind us. The room was small, barely a ten-by-ten. A small table with chairs on each side was all it contained. I feared what might come next. I'd already had enough—whatever was going to happen, I would not make it easy for Fat Freddie. He stood with his back against the door. I moved a few steps back and braced myself for an attack. He scoffed at my reaction and took a quick step toward me. I raised my fists in defense. Nolte glared at me, and a smirk emerged on his face.

"If I wanted to beat you bloody, I would have already done it. Sheriff wants a word with you before you're released, so sit the fuck down, or I'll pull this billy club from my belt and put you down."

I pulled out a chair just as he struck me in the back, driving me forward onto the table.

"Not that one, you dumb shit. The other side. The sheriff sits there."

I stumbled around the table, pain shooting across my back and shoulders, and dropped into the nearest chair. Deputy Nolte opened the door, turning to me before he left. "I know that little girl you raped. She is a sweet little thing, and you ruined her life. I hope they send your ass up for the full ten, and when you come back here—" he winked at me "—I'll be waiting."

The door slammed shut behind him. I crossed my arms on the table and laid my head down, forcing myself not to cry. Still, a few tears came. I was getting a taste of what my life would be like if I was convicted.

After five minutes, Sheriff Brennan entered the room and sat opposite me. I wiped my eyes with the back of my arm. He pulled a handkerchief from his pocket and tossed it across the table. I wiped away a dribble of snot from my nose.

"Keep it," he said. His gesture showed no kindness. "You don't have to talk to me, but I'd highly recommend it. I know what you told me in front of your dad. Now it's just you and me and these walls. I won't use anything you say against you because you already have an attorney, but I want the truth, boy. I don't want any bullshit. This is not the time for that. What happened on Sunday? Why did you take your dad's truck without permission? Did you and Arrington arrange to go to the Tinsleys' farm on Sunday?"

"I didn't know Brent was going to be in town. We're not really friends and never have been. He was just there on the street when I drove by. I only wanted to see who was around Banning and show off that I had my license."

"Who else was there?"

"A guy named Rick Deter."

"The little egg-throwing shithead?"

"I guess so."

"Is he a friend of yours?"

"God no," I said.

"Whose idea was it to go to the Tinsleys' farm?"

"Brent said Loretta had invited him to come out. It was his idea."

"What did you talk about on the way to the farm?"

I looked closely at the sheriff, trying to determine if he believed me, but his face told me nothing. "Nothing much. He talked about Loretta some."

"What exactly did he say?"

I was ashamed, ashamed I'd been part of that conversation. "He talked about Loretta's breasts and how sexy she was."

"He's eighteen; she's thirteen," he said. His jaw tightened and his eyes hardened. I saw his disgust for me.

"I knew she was too young, but I thought she wanted to be with him. You know . . . he's Brent Arrington."

"Did he give you any sign that he was going out there to have sex with her?"

I'd hardly thought about what he'd said on the way to the farm. The vulgarness of his words. Brent had been clear on what he wanted, but I'd thought nothing would happen. "He said he'd like to fuck her, but guys talk like that all the time when they have no intention of doing it or even a hope of doing it. I thought it was just more of his bullshit."

"What did he tell you on the way back to Banning?"

"He said she wanted it and that he did it but he didn't force her, and then we got into a fight."

"A fight over what?"

"I didn't believe him."

We sat for several seconds, not speaking. Sheriff Brennan's eyes never left me. Then he cleared his throat. My eyes pulled away from the empty wall I'd been staring at and locked on his.

"One last thing. You said in the car that you asked if she was okay. You could well see she wasn't. Why didn't you help her?"

I'd asked myself that hundreds of times and still had no answer I could accept. "I didn't ask to help her. When I kneeled beside her, I asked her if she was okay. She slapped me and told me to leave, and I did."

Sheriff Brennan pushed his chair back from the table and stood up. "All right, Danny, you can go. Your folks are waiting outside to take you home. If you've lied to me about any of this, I'll see that you spend the rest of your teenage life in the Anamosa State Penitentiary. We understand each other?"

"Yes, sir."

I got up and went down the hall to the doors the sheriff had brought me through the night before. My parents were waiting on a bench just outside the entrance. As I came through the door, my mother rushed to me and hugged me. My father stood a few feet away, saying nothing. "Let's get you out of here," my mother said, and we followed my father out the door.

My dad opened the car door for me, and I got into the back seat as my mother turned to look back at me. "Everything's going to be okay."

No one ever believed that when they said it, and my mother didn't either. We knew our lives had changed, but we thought things would seem better by saying the words. They never were. As my father pulled away, I saw the small windows close to the ground that had been my only view of the outside world. I hoped I'd never see them again. I waited until we were on the highway, then said, "That prosecutor thinks I'm as guilty as Brent. Everyone must hate me."

My mother shook her head. "Danny, everyone doesn't hate you. They don't know you. You can't let what people think and say bother you. We know you did nothing wrong."

"But I did, Mom. I took Brent Arrington out there."

My dad finally spoke. "You didn't know what he was going to do. You're not responsible for what the Arrington boy did."

"Why do I feel like I am?"

"Because people treat you that way," he said. "Look inside yourself, Danny. I don't believe you can hurt someone the way Brent hurt Loretta. Don't let anyone, that prosecutor included, convince you that you're the same as him. You're not."

As we drove, cornfields and farms swept by constantly as they had in the sheriff's cruiser. I'd seen them all my life, but today, they were different. It was a foreign landscape, an alien planet I no longer belonged to. Even as we drove down our lane, it didn't seem like it was my home anymore. I stayed in the car as my father drove into the garage. My mother had gone into the house. I wanted to talk to my father but didn't know what I was going to say. Still, I couldn't leave what was unsaid hanging like a guillotine's blade between us. I felt there was something he wanted to know or tell me.

He looked at me in the mirror. "How well do you know this Arrington boy?"

"I guess like everyone else. We're not friends, but we've always gotten along fine. He hangs with the cheerleaders and the other seniors. He's really popular. I'm not part of that group."

My father dropped his eyes from the mirror, staring into the darkness of the garage. He didn't speak for several minutes. We sat together alone in our thoughts, neither knowing exactly what to say but wanting words to close the gap between us.

"I knew his dad, Ron. He's younger than me and was a few years behind me in school. His parents ran the sale barn and owned two farms. Ron Arrington was that way, too—popular, arrogant, and entitled. There was a girl back then who said that Ron raped her too. She was a nice girl, but old man Arrington and Ron ruined her reputation. They spread rumors she was charging guys for sex and that Ron's only mistake was not paying her. People believed the Arringtons and not the girl. It changed her. Over time, she became what the town thought she was. She died a drunk and a used-up woman."

"Ron's parents did that?"

"Parents will do a lot to save their children, even to the point of destroying someone else's."

"Did you know the girl?" I asked.

My father didn't answer for several seconds, and when he did, it shocked me.

"Yes, she was my sister. Your aunt. Alice."

"She was the one who died in a car accident, wasn't she?" I asked. I'd heard snippets about her from relatives, but they talked about Aunt Alice away from children and in hushed tones, and now I knew why.

"I was never sure if she was drunk or meant to hit that bridge. Either way, it ended up the same. Some in our family were relieved—the family's reputation and all—as if we were pillars of the community. Ron and his father ruined her reputation; in a small town, that's all you have. Getting that back is hard. Maybe impossible. I can testify to that. That's not what is going to happen this time or ever again. I want you to know I believe you, son. I never doubted you. You're stronger than Alice, stronger than even you think. Don't react to what someone might say. I want you to stand tall. You're my son.

You're a Prescott. Stand your ground regardless of what they throw at you. Will you do that?"

"Yes, sir, I will."

He opened up his door, hesitated for a moment, then opened mine. As I got out, he pulled me into a hug. I couldn't remember my father ever hugging me before, and I'd never forget it. It meant more to me than anything he could have said. We walked out of the garage together. My father wasn't a demonstrative man, but his hand was on my shoulder. I'd never felt closer to or loved him more than at that moment.

Ranger waited outside the garage and jumped on me as I walked out. I clamped my hands and opened my arms, and his total weight hit me in the chest as I hugged him close to me, his tongue lapping at my face.

"That dog was whimpering all last night. If you ever leave, take him with you or we'll get no sleep. Right now, we have chores to do. Jim could use some help with the cattle." My father looked down. "And can you lace up those boots before you trip over them?"

Jim was filling the last bunk with silage as I picked up a shovel to help. He said nothing as I spread ground corn over the silage. It was like candy to the cattle, who nudged me, eager to get a mouthful. I didn't know what to expect from Jim—maybe a sermon or maybe he'd just be pissed off. Becky Kessler and her family would not have received the news well of his little brother being in jail, especially for this.

I'd finished with the last bunk. Jim was still there, leaning against his shovel. "What've you been up to, sport?"

"Took the night off. I was tired."

"Anything interesting been happening in your life?"

I took a few seconds, then said, "No, nothing special. Why?"

"What's going on? Dad told me you drove the pickup to Banning and then out to the Tinsleys' farm the day Loretta was assaulted. What did you and that arrogant prick do? Mom told me you didn't touch the Tinsley girl; you just gave the turd a ride. There's nothing funny about this. This isn't some prank, some teenage stupidity. You've got serious troubles, so don't bullshit me. Maybe there's something I can do." He stared at me, waiting for an answer.

"I didn't hurt Loretta. I could never do anything like that." I bit my lower lip, something I used to do as a kid. Until now, I hadn't considered what this would do to Jim. Now, he was potentially the brother of a rapist. I wondered what he'd said to the Kesslers. They were such prudes, worried about their sterling reputations.

"You probably took a ration of shit from the Kesslers over this. I'm sorry it happened, but I would have never taken Brent out to see Loretta if I thought he would do anything bad to her."

"The Kesslers are nothing I can't handle, and they're the least of our worries. Becky understands." Jim studied me briefly, then put his arm around my shoulders. "There is one thing, sport. Be careful what you say around Dad about the Arringtons. There's a history there, and the old man has a short fuse regarding Ron."

"You mean about Aunt Alice?" I asked.

"You know about that?"

"He just told me."

"Then you know how he feels. Let's not light that fuse, okay?"

"Sure, I understand." I didn't really. I didn't understand the depth of my father's hatred for Brent's father. Family ran deep with him, and he'd passed that on to his sons. I would do anything for my parents, and for Susan and Jim.

"Danny, I know I give you grief all the time, but I want you to know that I'll always be in your corner. You might be a poor excuse for a brother, but you're all I got, and I'm stuck with you."

"Those words, Jim, will forever stay in my memory." I gave my brother a sincere look. "So that I never say them to anyone else."

"I'm glad you understand." He laughed and pulled me into a shoulder hug. Regardless of what he said, I'd let him down, but I loved him for not saying it.

I spread an extra layer of straw for fresh bedding in the calves' pen. Benny and Jenny romped around in pure joy. It was the simple things that brought the most pleasure to the young. As bad as I felt, their antics made me laugh. There were so many beautiful things around me on the farm if I only looked, and I wondered why I hadn't noticed them before. As I left the barn, I heard a banging in the equipment shed, followed by a few choice swear words. My father was working on the picker and evidently skinning his knuckles.

"Need an extra set of hands?" I asked, stooping to where he sat with his legs under the picker.

"I've got the rollers almost adjusted. Those ear snappers are a bitch. You can grease her up."

I started greasing the bearings with the pressure gun and found two grease fittings requiring a replacement. It was another knuckle buster. The fittings were small and in tight places; add a dab of grease, and you had a series of "son of a bitches," "fucks," and "shits," along with bleeding knuckles. It all went with the joys of farming.

My father had a smirk on his face as I pulled myself out from under the picker. "I guess you are a Prescott after all. You can certainly swear like one."

"I told you someday I'd make you proud. I learned from the best."

He laughed. "I can't argue with that," he said, wiping down the wrenches before putting them away. "Two of those steers looked a little peaked yesterday. Did they eat their grain?" he asked as he put a wrench back into its place on the wall.

"I didn't see any of them hanging back. They were all at the bunk."

He wiped a smudge of grease off his chin. "We need to separate any that are showing signs of watery eyes. One might have a touch of pinkeye, which is contagious. I don't want them infecting the rest of the herd. They should still be in the lot if Jim hasn't put them in the pasture. If you see any, we'll pen them up for the vet to check in the morning."

I followed my father to the feedlot. We separated three from the herd and put them into a separate pen. It looked like pinkeye, but we'd caught it early enough that all would keep their vision. Jim let the rest of the herd out into the river pasture. Ranger ran behind the herd, driving them out of the gate. As the last cattle cleared the gate, Ranger ran full speed to me, circling until I patted him on the back for a good job. "I see you enlisted my dog to help you," I told Jim.

"Couldn't have done it without him. Maybe I could have done it faster if he hadn't chased two of them in the wrong direction," Jim said as he walked up.

"He's a work in progress. I'll have him counting and separating them by weight in a few months," I replied.

He passed by me. "A work in progress, just like you."

"You think I'll ever amount to shit?" I asked, hurrying up beside him.

"Not a chance," he said, tapping the back of my head and knocking my hat off. "Not a chance in hell."

We headed toward the house for lunch. It was a good feeling knowing some things hadn't changed. Sarcasm was our way of saying "I love you," even if no one else understood the language, or maybe that was the point.

CHAPTER 4

The next afternoon, my father asked me to check the fence in the river pasture. A neighbor called to say that he thought one of our steers was munching grass on his side of the river. After I stacked fencing material in the pickup bed, I opened the passenger door, and Ranger eagerly jumped in. He loved the river pasture with all its exploration of frogs, turtles, and squirrels. Every trip was a new adventure for him. The world would be outstanding if everything we did felt like a fresh and wonderful experience, regardless of how repetitive.

Sitting behind the wheel of the pickup brought back that Sunday with Brent and ate away at me. Ranger laid his head on my lap, looking up with eyes that said he understood. I stroked his head and wished I could forgive myself as quickly as Ranger could. I pushed the thoughts away and was about to leave when Steve Weidman drove down our lane. Ranger looked disappointed as I turned off the engine and left him in the pickup. Steve did a U-turn in the yard and drove up beside the pickup.

"Where you going, dude?" he asked. Steve had been my best friend since before kindergarten. We'd played cowboy and Indian together, gone trick-or-treating, and doubled on our first dates. No one was closer to me or knew me better.

"Dad wants me to check the river fence. George Gretzky told him he thought our steers were crossing the river."

"I'll come along and help."

"Free labor. How can I turn that down?" I said. "Would you mind sharing the seat with Ranger?"

"The more the merrier," Steve said.

I hoped my dog felt the same. Steve got in, and Ranger slid to the middle. We bounced down the rutted cattle path, Ranger's head ping-ponging to whoever was talking. Steve watched the fence line as I drove slowly beside it, dodging the occasional stump or downed tree limb until we reached the river. The brush and trees were too heavy along the riverbank to drive the last hundred yards of fencing. Steve carried the hand tools, while I brought the wire puller and extra wire. Ranger ran ahead, scaring up grasshoppers and a dove.

If the cattle were getting out, I thought I knew the place. It was a constant problem in any dry season, when the river pulled back from a marshy area that provided water for the cattle. Dappled sunlight flickered through the canopy, giving the river a storybook feel. Steve hadn't asked about or even mentioned Brent, the arrest, or Loretta. I knew he must have been aware— the whole town of Banning was aware. I dropped the wire and stretcher and sat down on a large log. Steve joined me as Ranger dashed after a frog.

"Are you taking the bus on Monday or driving in?" I asked.

"Neither. I have a dental appointment to take these off." He parted his lips in a lopsided grin, showing his braces. "No more metal mouth."

"Congratulations. I know how much you wanted to get rid of them. Now you have no excuse for not French kissing me."

"I'd rather suck pig shit through a garden hose," Steve shot back.

"How long have you had them on? It seems like eons."

"It's been three years. Three years of cleaning crap out of them every time I ate. Three years of people looking oddly at me when I open my mouth. You're lucky you have perfect teeth."

"If they're perfect, it's the only thing I have that is. My life couldn't be less perfect right now."

Steve wasn't going to bring the subject up—that was Steve. Even now, he wouldn't respond to that. He'd wait until I was fully ready to talk about it. We sat for a few minutes more, enjoying the river and the cool shade; a crow called out to others from somewhere in the canopy. Butterflies flickered over a patch of mud as a frog leaped from the water, barely missing a dragonfly.

"What have you heard about me, turd bird? What are the jungle drums saying?" I asked. I figured we might as well get the boogeyman out from under the bed, and I wanted to know what people were saying about me.

Steve was always smiling and laughing, but that all dropped away. "Man, you stepped into some intense shit."

"More like a shit storm," I said.

"What were you doing with Brent Arrington? I had the impression that the dude only socialized with royalty."

"When I got to Banning, he was sitting outside Mike's on the curb. I gave him a ride."

"What was wrong with his Harley?"

"His dad took the keys, so he didn't have wheels."

"How did you end up at the Tinsleys' farm?"

"He wanted to see Loretta."

"How did he even know her? She's in junior high."

I repeated what Brent had told me about his meeting Loretta at the pool and how she'd invited him to the farm. Steve had the same reaction as I had.

"Brent is dating the most gorgeous girl in school. What's he want with a kid like Loretta?"

"She's not a kid anymore. She'll be a freshman this year and . . ." I was hesitant to describe Loretta's body. It seemed like a further violation of her. Instead, I said, "She's a beauty now. Taller."

"I heard she told him she wasn't a virgin."

"Who told you that?" I asked, anger jumping into my words.

"Donnelly."

"Rick Donnelly? He's a good buddy of Brent's."

"He said you did it too after Brent screwed her, but you were the one she didn't want to do it with. That's why she got mad when he told her to fuck you too."

All breath left me for a second. Did people believe that? Did my best friend think I would do that?

"Do you think that's what happened?" I glared at Steve.

"What do you think of me, man? Do you think I'm that kind of asshole? I know you, Danny. I know you better than I know my parents. You'd never do something like that."

I watched the river for several minutes, the current slapping over rocks near the opposite bank. A blue jay chattered on a branch overhanging the river as a breath of breeze shifted the petals of wildflowers under the trees. I took a deep breath. I owed my best friend an explanation.

"She seemed happy to see us when we arrived. Then Brent started laying it on thick, telling her how great she looked. He fed her a line of bullshit. She didn't even suspect what Brent wanted or how he thought of her. I didn't think he would do anything bad or do anything she didn't want to. Brent told her he wanted to see the kittens. They went up into the hayloft. I didn't go up until after it was over."

"So you weren't there, and you didn't see Brent rape her?"

"I didn't see him do anything. Loretta was lying naked in the hay when I climbed into the hayloft. Brent was buckling his belt and told me they'd done it." I didn't want to tell my best friend that Brent had asked me if I wanted to do it to her too or that she had slapped me. Those were things I was afraid even a friend would not understand.

Steve looked puzzled. "So, he was up there raping her, and you were down below?"

"I know what you're thinking. It's all I've been thinking about since then. Why didn't I go up into the hayloft with them? Why didn't I hear it? Why didn't I do something after I saw Loretta naked? I don't know, man. How can I expect anyone else to if I don't understand it?"

"She must have done something. Was she acting sexy or making Brent think she wanted to screw? Why would a guy like Brent Arrington have to force a girl? I hear he's screwed half the girls in the senior class."

"You don't believe that, do you?" I asked.

"No, but that's what the guys say."

"And most guys don't know shit."

The river was peaceful, almost like it wasn't part of the real world. A few fallen leaves floated by on the slow-moving current. A turtle sunned on a rock nearby as a carp flashed in the sunlight, taking something off the water's surface. Something that died so the carp could live. Nature's rule. Was rape natural? What did a girl have to do that would justify rape—wear clothes that reveal too much, French kiss, and talk dirty? What was it that justified raping someone like Loretta? There was nothing.

"She did nothing, Steve. Nothing but be Loretta. She was innocent, vulnerable, naïve, just like when we rode the bus with her."

"Then I wonder what made him do it."

"Maybe he did it because he's a son of a bitch and because he could. Why are you taking Brent's side on this?"

"I'm not."

"It sounded like it to me."

"I would think you want that too. It gets you both off the hook."

"You think I'd railroad Loretta just to get off the hook?"

"No, man. I didn't mean that. What's your problem, Danny? You're all over me. I'm your friend."

"Shit . . ." I shook my head and turned away. What was I doing? I was driving away the only friend I might still have.

"Steve, don't pay any attention to me. I'm not sure what I think anymore. There's no justification for what Brent did. None. I should never have left them alone in the loft. Brent wasn't at the farm to look at kittens. I knew that." I took a deep breath. "There's something I'm ashamed of. But I'll tell you. I didn't go up into the loft because I didn't want to piss him off. I wanted to be one of his buddies, just like Donnelly and Zimmerman. That makes me a genuine piece of shit, doesn't it?"

"Probably, but who doesn't want to be the great Brent Arrington's friend? I would have probably done the same thing. That makes me an asshole too."

"So everyone thinks I'm a piece of shit?" I asked.

"Danny, I don't know what they think, but I'll tell you what I think. I think I've got to get back home. If you want me to help you with that fence, we have to move our asses. My dad thinks I'm taking a book back to Stephanie Martin."

"Why didn't you tell your dad you were coming here?"

Steve dropped his eyes to the ground. I waited, feeling anger build inside me. Was he ashamed to tell his parents he was coming to see me, or had they forbidden him from seeing me?

"You know how parents are," he stammered.

"No, Steve. Tell me, how are they?"

"My dad thinks I should stay away until all this gets sorted out."

"Sorted out," I repeated.

"Yes, sorted out. Danny, you can't blame me for what my dad thinks. I'm here, aren't I? What the fuck do you want? I won't run out on you. What kind of friend do you think I am? Shit, you've always played on my team. I'm on your side. Man, this is payback time for me. When we were in second grade and I had to wear that brace on my leg, you were the only one who played with me. In sixth grade, when those junior high guys bullied me, you stepped in. You got the shit beat out of you, but at least you tried." Steve chuckled, and the smile came back on his face, bringing one to mine as well.

He stepped toward me and opened his arms with a dopey grin. I hugged him, and we slapped each other's backs like a swarm of mosquitoes were attacking us. Then we both pulled away, somewhat embarrassed. Neither of us was the hug-it-out type, but that hug took away much of the pain I was feeling.

"Let's fix the fence before you propose," I said, grabbing the barbed wire and walking down the fence line as Ranger scouted ahead. The fence was fine until we approached the marshy area near the river. As I suspected, a section of fence was down halfway across the slew. The cattle tracks went both ways, so the errant steers may have returned. We wouldn't know until we counted them at feeding time. Jim and I would have to get them tomorrow and bring them back if they were still across the river. Steve stabled the last strand to the post while I pulled it tight. We didn't mention Sunday again, but it was on both of our minds, just like I knew it was on Loretta's and Brent's. We were each isolated yet bonded together, which gave us no choice but to continue until we found an end.

It was almost feeding time, so I brought the steers up, herding them with the pickup and Ranger picking up any strays. Steve left right after we unloaded the fencing material and tools. I waved as he drove off, hoping it wasn't goodbye. I understood the pressure Steve faced in high school and disliked putting him in that position, but I was grateful he'd stayed on my side.

Jim was throwing down the silage from the silo into the grain shed as I fed the calves their corn and oats. I scattered a half bale of straw into their pen, then started filling the bunks with silage as Jim came down the silo ladder.

"Was that Steve or his dad just here?" Jim asked.

"Steve."

"What did he want?"

Normally, I would have mouthed some smart-ass answer, but Sunday had changed that between us. "I think he wanted to boost my morale. He helped me fix the fence that runs along the river."

"Did you find where the steers were getting out?"

"There were tracks in that marshy area. We ran a couple of extra stands where they were getting out. The tracks were coming and going, so they might have come back. We need to count them to be sure."

After counting the steers and ensuring they were all there, we headed to the house. As we came into the kitchen, my mother was preparing supper. She had changed from the dress she'd worn to the courthouse into the flowery one she liked to wear around the house. She turned to me as I entered and tried to produce a smile. Nothing worked for anyone today.

"Dinner will be ready in half an hour. Is your dad coming in?" she asked.

"He's probably checking those sick steers," Jim said. "The vet is going to look at them tomorrow. One looks like he has pinkeye."

"Then I better call Doc Snider right now," she said, drying her hands and going to the phone.

She was on the phone as I finished washing up. It sounded like Doc Snider asked about me, and my mother told him I was fine and we were hoping to get this all cleared up. As I entered our living room, I switched on the TV and browsed through our five channels, yet all I came across were news and commercials. I stopped at KGLO as my photo flashed on the screen, followed by Brent's. I turned up the sound.

The local news anchor reported that authorities had arrested two local Banning boys for assaulting a thirteen-year-old girl on Sunday. The girl's name was being withheld because of her age, but sources said the assault took place at a farm outside Banning. One boy, Brent Arrington, was a Banning Raiders football team star athlete. It was unclear whether he would take the field this season because of the pending charges. School officials hadn't responded to requests for comment. I felt my mother's presence behind me, and I turned. She stood like a statue, her mouth frozen open. The weather map appeared on the screen, replacing Brent's photo and showing various temperatures around the state.

"Oh dear," she said, placing her hand over her mouth.

"I'm sorry, Mom."

"You did nothing bad, Danny; there's nothing to be sorry for," she said, still staring at the TV screen. Then she turned and went back to the kitchen.

I went to my room and tried to read, but my mind kept forgetting the words as soon as I passed them. I heard my dad come in, and then my mom called me for supper. The conversation at the table felt forced, with everyone using meaningless words to fill the air with sound. My dad said little besides asking me to pass the salt and pepper. There was no kidding or insults between my brother and me. Our once raucous meals had changed into something joyless. I ate quickly and left the table.

After supper, I watched TV with my parents. Jim and Becky went to a movie in Fairmont, *To Kill a Mockingbird*. It was my favorite book and a movie I wanted to see. Fairmont was my only chance to see it, but I couldn't ask Jim to take me along. At ten, my father shut the news off without watching it and got up from his recliner. He and my mother always watched the evening news at ten—it was a farmers' ritual. It left a heavy silence in the room as we wondered what a family did at ten if they didn't know the weather or the hog prices. I turned the TV back on and flipped to channel 13, WHOTV, where we always watched the news.

"We might as well see what they're saying about me, Dad. Not knowing is worse." I stood in the doorway as they first covered the local news. They didn't mention Banning. I silently thanked the powers that be for the small favor and went to my room while my parents watched the weather forecast.

Unable to sleep, I lay awake, staring into the darkness, remembering the times I'd teased Loretta on the school bus. I'd told her I wanted to adopt her as my little sister. She'd always blushed, but she'd enjoyed the attention. What was it like for her tonight? Was she able to sleep? Was she staring into the dark? Did she also wonder what the people of Banning were saying about her?

I woke early. Outside, the darkness was giving way to a rising sun. I heard stirring downstairs. I glanced at the clock on my dresser, its luminous hands ghostly in the emerging light. It would still be another half hour before my dad would be up. I thought it might be Jim, so I dressed and headed down. No lights were on. My mother was sitting at the kitchen table, her hands circled around a cup of coffee. I poured a cup as well and sat down with her.

"What are you doing up so early?" I asked.

"I was thinking about that poor girl and how she must be suffering tonight."

"I know. I've been thinking about her too, Mom."

"Did I ever tell you that her mother, Ester, told me Loretta had a big crush on you? It was several years ago. She told her mother that she hoped to marry someone like you. I remember being proud that someone would say that about you."

"Not so proud of me today, though."

"You're a fine young boy, Danny, and I'll always be proud of you."

We sipped coffee, waiting for the morning light to fill the room and begin our day. I finished my coffee and placed the cup in the sink. "When Dad and Jim get up, tell them I'm out feeding the cattle."

A light freeze with a drizzle coated the silage with a thin layer of ice. I broke the silage free and tossed down enough for the morning feeding. As I came down the silo ladder, I heard Jim scooping the silage into the feed bunks.

"What got into you this morning, champ? You haven't gotten up ahead of me since Mom pulled you off the bottle."

"Morning to you too. I was eager to feel the cold morning air on my face and smell the silage, the cow shit, and your morning breath."

"Well, here, let me give you another smell to remember when you're sitting in that nice, warm classroom." Jim lifted his leg and cut a fart that lasted at least five seconds, sounding as if a flock of turkeys had flown out of his ass.

"Jeez," I said, backing away from him.

He fanned his ass with his hand, sending more my way. "Someday, with practice, you too might be able to do that." Jim laughed.

I backed away another step. The smell around him was worse than standing over a rotting animal carcass. "What the hell, Jim? Did something crawl up your ass and die?"

"Just hold your breath, but let's feed the cattle in the interim." Jim jammed his shovel into the silage I'd thrown down. I picked up a shovelful and followed him to the bunks, amazed that my sense of smell was still functional. Jim and I checked the herd for sickness and counted them before leaving the grain shed.

"You better hope that doesn't get into the groundwater, because it's going to make the cattle sick," I said, moving beside him.

"It was just a fart," Jim said, quickening his pace.

"Oh no, you're selling yourself short, Jimbo. That was a monumental fart, and you should be proud of it. I think people in the scientific community should know about this."

"Give me a break, you little shit, or I'll crumble you up and use you for wiping paper."

"What are you going on about?" my father asked as we entered the equipment shed. Parts of the picker lay in an orderly pile beside the workbench.

"Nothing. Danny is just jacking his jaw for exercise."

"Jim, do something useful and start on the west eighty. Next week or the week after, I want to pick corn. Danny, I want you to check the elevator to ensure none of those links need replacing. I don't want to be doing that in the middle of the harvest."

I helped Jim hook the disk to work the soybean field west of the house, then went to work on the elevator. After replacing a half dozen links in the elevator chain, I returned to the equipment shed and watched my father tighten the snapper rollers that pulled the corn ears off the stalks. He scooted out from under the picker and dusted off the back of his overalls. I handed him a shop rag to wipe the grease off his hands. He cleaned them, dropped the rag onto a worktable, and sat beside me on the bench. I tried to decipher the concerned look on his face. Was it disappointment, disgust, or shame? All were up for grabs.

"Danny, these next few weeks are going to be a real bitch for the whole family and especially you."

"I know, sir."

"No, you don't. You don't have a clue what it's going to be like." He hesitated, his eyes moving away from me. "You need to grow up. I wish it were different, but it's not. Having Jim here, I probably treated you too much like a kid. I'll try not to do that anymore. If you're not strong, this thing you're facing, that we're all facing, will break you and change you in ways you'll regret."

"Yes, sir. I'll try."

"The people here mean well. They're well-intentioned, but they can be as mean and unforgiving as a junkyard dog. They'll be watching you, judging you every minute, and many of those judgments won't be fair or correct. You'll have to be stronger than a steel anvil, or this town will chew you up and spit you out in pieces. It did it to my sister, and I can't let that happen to you. I believe in you, son, but it's more important that you believe in yourself. I know you told the truth, but that doesn't mean people believe you. Your mom and I will be there right beside you. You let them get to you, and they win. You strike back, and it proves to them they're right."

"Dad, I'll do my best. I'm sorry I'm putting everyone through this, but I don't know how to fix it. I don't know how to make it better."

"That's not your worry. I'll handle that end of it. We've got an excellent lawyer. We have to let this thing play out and not do anything stupid. Don't talk to people about this—it could come back to bite you in the ass. And stay away from that Arrington boy."

Jim continued to disk the bean field until dark. My father and I fed the cattle and had the chores all done as my brother pulled the tractor into the shed. We all walked together to the house for supper. The dust clung to my brother like a coating of paint, and the whites of his eyes looked out through a mask of it.

"You go into the house like that, and your mother will take a broom to you," my dad said as we neared the side porch.

Jim dusted off his coveralls as best he could, then joined us on the porch. He tossed them to me to hang on the hooks we used for our work clothes. I carefully checked the back of the coveralls as I hung them up.

"What are you doing?" my father asked.

"Just checking to see if these things have a reinforced ass."

Jim grabbed me around the shoulders as we walked into the kitchen, laughing. My father was still looking oddly at his two sons as we went to the bathroom to clean up. There were some things no parent could or should understand.

After supper, I went to my room. John Steinbeck's *The Grapes of Wrath* lay open on the chair beside my bed. It seemed a year ago I'd left it there. Then, the Joads' troubles had seemed overwhelming compared to mine, but now it was a toss-up.

We seldom received calls at night. For farmers, the night was for relaxing and for family. Since Susan had left for college especially, our phone had rarely rung after dinner, but that night was an exception. The phone on the kitchen wall rang several times as I tried to read. After my mother hung up, I heard her crying. My dad said something comforting to her, something I couldn't hear. After that, no one answered the phone. They just let it ring. We were on a party line with five neighbors. Private lines were available only in Banning, so we couldn't simply take the receiver off the hook to stop the calls. It would keep the line open for all five neighbors and prevent anyone from receiving or making calls.

My mother always answered the phone at night by the third ring. Night calls were important, and long-distance calls foreshadowed tragedy. The calls were clearly about me and what had occurred at the Tinsleys' farm. Any remaining joy I carried vanished as the black hole surrounding me sucked it in. I wanted to jump from the bed with every ring and rip the phone off the wall. At around ten, the calls stopped. The cruelty my dad described was happening—and not only to me but to them.

I thought of a book I'd recently read for Lit class, *The Prince* by Machiavelli, and the famous quote, "What doesn't kill you makes you stronger." If I came out of the other end of this, I would be a piece of Damascus steel. It was unfair to punish my parents, and I hated everyone in Banning for doing it. How had a minor act of driving to Banning resulted in such a catastrophic consequence?

After the local news, my mom and dad came upstairs. I wondered if there'd been anything about Brent or me on the news that had fostered all the calls. Since *The Fairmont Herald* published only on Wednesdays, the attack on Loretta Tinsley would probably be in the next edition.

At twelve, I was still awake. In the moonlight, the luminous hands of the alarm clock were a constant reminder of my life ticking away. I felt useless and weak, not the man my father said I should be. At close to one, I was still awake. Before Sunday, I'd anxiously looked forward to returning to Banning High on Monday. Now, I dreaded the start of school. Would they see me as a pariah? Would anyone talk to me? Would the kids I'd known all my life remain my friends? Would their parents even allow them to be?

The following five days passed in a fog. My father, Jim, and I replaced boards on the storage cribs, ground enough grain to feed the cattle for the duration of picking, and completed a dozen other tasks to ensure that all our efforts could focus on getting the corn picked and in the cribs.

CHAPTER 5

It was Monday—the start of school. I waited at the end of our lane for the twenty-year-old school bus, which everyone called the Yellow Rattler. I hoped Hank Donaldson would be behind the wheel of the rattle-trap. Hank was a retired farmer, his face grizzled from years in the sun. He had a gravelly voice from decades of Camel cigarettes. The man was in his late sixties and drove the bus to supplement his meager savings, accumulated from fifty years of busting his ass on a rented hardscrabble farm. All Hank had to show for that hard work was a busted-up leg and arthritic hands. It wouldn't be long before he couldn't wrap his fingers around the steering wheel. When that happened, Hank would be done—no reason to get up and no reason to go on.

The cheap false teeth supplied by the county that Hank seldom wore did not help his appearance. Some kids referred to him as Mr. Sourpuss. A few made fun of him behind his back, though they always announced a cheerful hello as they entered the bus. Hank knew what was going on. Being old didn't mean being stupid. He had a job to do, and he did it, never smiling or saying hello. I felt sorry for him. I treated him with respect because he'd never taken a handout or asked anyone for anything.

The Yellow Rattler came down the road, leaving a trail of dust billowing in its wake. It was a few minutes early. The squeal of worn-down brakes stopped the Rattler as the door screeched open. Old Hank was behind the wheel. I nodded to him, and as our eyes met, I knew he was aware of the heap of shit I was in.

With a dozen kids on the bus, it usually sounded like a Ladies' Aid meeting. Today, silence and stares accompanied me down the aisle. It was as if the body snatchers had replaced everyone I'd known all my life. It shouldn't have surprised me. I was the alien, the curious monster that had crept out of the sludge. Matt Prader looked down as I walked by his seat. We had started kindergarten together and were close friends in the fourth and fifth grades. I thought at least he would say hi, but he looked the other way as I passed. Last fall, we had hunted pheasants together, and now he didn't even see me.

The conversations started again after a few miles, but I stayed invisible. Wasn't that what I'd wished in the jail cell, to be invisible? The Yellow Rattler continued to screech and rattle as Hank continued his stops toward Banning. Kids would board the bus, stealing glances at me, the new untouchable. The boy who would taint them by any association. They feared that what was happening to me might happen to them—safer to avoid me. Hank screeched the Rattler to a stop outside the large double doors to the high school. I waited until everyone filed off and then got up. Hank touched my arm as I passed. "Did you do what they said?"

"No, I didn't." Not old Hank too. Out of everybody, I would have thought there'd be some compassion in this old man. Some level of understanding. I waited for him to tell me what a piece of shit I was.

"No, I didn't think so. We've been riding together for five years, and I know you. I've seen a lot of bad ones in my time, and you're not one of them. Good luck to you, Danny."

I stopped just outside the bus, then turned and looked up at him. "Thank you, Mr. Donaldson. You don't know how much I needed that."

He nodded and pulled away. I was in the middle of thirty to forty kids yet alone. Half a dozen stood outside the school doors, staring in my direction. I knew each of them. They were my friends. They said nothing, gave no reaction, just stood and looked.

I gazed up at the largest building in Banning for a few seconds. The three-story brick structure and two-story gymnasium took up the entire block. I'd never thought much about the building, but today it was cold and unwelcoming.

I walked past a group standing by the doors and went inside. One wide expanse of stairs led to the assembly halls and classrooms, while the other led down to the cafeteria, music, and equipment rooms. Grades seven and eight were on the main level, along with the administrative offices and teachers' lounge.

I climbed the steps to the second floor, where I had spent the past two years. Each morning, all high school students met in a large assembly hall that doubled as our homeroom and study hall. We each had a locker and an assigned desk there. Principal Larson took morning attendance as we gathered in the space. At the back was a small library with windows that overlooked the room.

During the first two weeks, each of the classes sat alphabetically. Students could swap desks if both agreed to switch the following Monday. Switching Day, as it was called, was the day you grouped up with your friends. The girly cliques grouped in the middle, while the guys hung to the back seats. Athletes claimed the back corners of each of the four class sections. The front, known as the ghetto, was where the brains and the dweebs congregated—not a desirable location to spend a school year. It was that way in my father's time too. Why change unless there was a damn good reason?

I headed toward the middle of the junior class section, per my last name. Sitting alphabetically made it easier for teachers to place names with students.

It wasn't difficult, with fewer than two hundred students in the whole high school and less than half of those being juniors and seniors. Everybody knew everybody within two weeks. It was the teachers who were new to the school. Banning was a spot where you started and moved on to something better. This year, there were only three new students in our class: one guy and two girls. The guy was easy to spot. No one was talking to him. We could have been twins.

The first day always followed the same routine—teachers introduced themselves; Principal Larson welcomed everyone to the new school year and then introduced any new students. This day did not start as usual for me. I should have been joking with friends, exchanging war stories from the summer and glad-handing everyone. While waiting at my desk, I pretended to read *The Grapes of Wrath*, but it was difficult to avoid hearing the whispers or noticing the side glances. Until now, I hadn't known what it felt like to feel eyes burning through your skin, to be an object of interest and scorn. I had expected some attention, maybe exclusion from the high and mighty, but not this feeling of isolation. No one spoke to me. There were no "welcome backs" or "how the fuck have you been?" No one was curious about what I'd done all summer. I expected more from my friends. My worst fear had been a confrontation with Brent. I scanned the desk rows for the seniors, but he wasn't there.

His little group of loyalists were gathered in the jocks' corner, though, talking and looking directly at me. Instead of hiding their loathing, they displayed it openly. Brent should have been near the front of the senior section, but no one was sitting at the second desk. Katy Anderson sat in the first seat, talking with two other girls.

Others noticed Brent's absence. Sherri Burton, a cheerleader, gestured at the seat, then shifted her gaze toward me and whispered something to her friend. I closed the book and stared directly at them. Their eyes darted away. I shoved down the anger I felt. Maybe I would have done the same in their position. I looked around, hoping to see Steve or a friendly face. Matt Prader came down the aisle.

"Hey, Danny. Good summer?" Matt said, sliding into the seat in front of me.

"It was okay," I replied.

Did anything interesting happen to you, Matt? How about having lunch? I think there's going to be a lynching party for me in the afternoon. It's BYOR, so bring your own rope.

As I continued searching the assembly for Brent, I felt a tap on my shoulder. Principal Larson's secretary, Mary Paulson, also known as Typhoid Mary because she always carried toxic news, asked that I come with her. I slipped my book into my desk and followed her out of the assembly as conversations stopped and faces turned, following us like a spotlight. It was like walking out of a tomb. I heard my footfalls on the tiled floor. Nothing good ever came from following Typhoid Mary out of a room.

A slow, simmering rage built in me as we walked down the stairs toward the principal's office. It was humiliating enough to be an outcast in school, to have my photo on TV, and now I was being escorted out of assembly like a circus animal. She ushered me into Principal Larson's office.

"Wait here. Mr. Larson will be with you presently. He had to talk with a teacher first."

I sat facing Larson's desk and waited for him. Initially, I'd felt anxious about the meeting, but soon, my anxiety simmered into anger. Why did he have to see me now when he could have waited until after the assembly? No one cared to hear my side. They accused me; therefore, I was guilty. I'd known these kids most of my life. That should have accounted for something.

I waited several minutes, feeling every second dragging by. The clock behind Larson's desk kept ticking, adding to my anxiety. After waiting for ten minutes, the principal finally arrived in the room. He only acknowledged me after he sat down behind his desk. He looked at me for a moment before speaking. His lips pursed as he formed a steeple with his fingers, his fingertips touching his chin. "Good morning, Danny."

"Good morning, sir."

"How was your summer?"

Are you shitting me? How was my summer? Oh, overall, sir, it was okay. There was that thing about Loretta, then being arrested and spending a night in jail. You might have seen me on the news. I'm infamous, or is it notorious? *Not bad for one summer, huh, Mr. Larson? Anything interesting happen with you?*

"It was okay," I answered.

"This trouble that you're in, ah . . ." He took a deep breath and exhaled slowly through his nose, sounding like a leaking tire. "This has presented us with a problem."

No shit, Sherlock. Then we both have a problem, don't we? I could see the shitstorm building. I'd never caused him or anyone else at this school one ounce of trouble, yet here I was in his office. Some kids sat in this chair about as much as I had ridden the school bus. But that was old news. Now, I was something they didn't want around.

"What kind of problem is that, Mr. Larson?"

"I'll be straightforward with you on this matter. Loretta Tinsley's parents don't feel comfortable sending their daughter back to school under the circumstances."

"What circumstances are those?"

"Don't be coy with me, Daniel. You know what I'm getting at. You're a smart boy. It's your presence at this school."

"What about Brent's presence?"

"Brent is not coming back to school. His parents feel it would be better for Brent to live with his aunt in Fort Dodge. He'll complete his senior year there. Although the school is losing a great asset, it's the best decision for everyone."

"Well, you're luckier with me. You're not losing anything, are you?"

"I didn't mean it that way, and you know it. I only meant that Brent contributes a lot to our football team."

"Yes, it's a real loss. Now it only leaves me for you to embarrass and humiliate." I wasn't sure where that had come from. I'd never sassed or talked back to anyone in authority, especially not Principal Larson.

"Danny, there's no reason to get smart-mouthed. If you can't conduct yourself appropriately, I'll send you home right now."

"Appropriately? That's not the way I'm being treated."

"What did you expect after what you did?"

"What I did. You don't know what I did, Mr. Larson. You may think you do, but you know nothing. Everyone out there in the assembly thinks they know too. Well, no one does. They weren't there, and neither were you. I thought civilized people waited until a person was tried and convicted before lynching them. I guess that's not the way you run a school."

"You are not being punished or lynched, as you described it. Under the circumstances, this school must decide for the good of everyone. I had hoped that you and your parents would be cooperative about this. The school requests that you not attend Banning High School until this matter is resolved."

"I did nothing but give Brent Arrington a ride, and you're kicking me out of school?"

"You are not being kicked out of school. Let's be clear, I'm not kicking you out of school. I'm asking you to attend school elsewhere until this matter is resolved. The Arringtons were cooperative in this. Why can't you be?"

Principal Larson's jaw clenched and unclenched; his hands white-knuckled the arms of his chair. He wasn't used to being challenged, but at this moment, I didn't care. They were kicking me out of school—I had nothing to lose. My father had told me not to react, and I had. He was right. This was the most challenging thing I'd ever faced. I pushed the anger down. I was losing this battle. It was time to regroup.

"Mr. Larson, I apologize. I meant no disrespect, but this is a difficult time for my family and me. I did nothing to Loretta Tinsley. All I did was give Brent a ride to the Tinsley farm. If they haven't convicted me of anything, this school cannot expel me or prevent me from attending."

Principal Larson steepled his fingers again and swallowed hard as he glared at me. This was going differently than he had planned. If he'd thought I would make this easy, he was mistaken.

"I am not voluntarily going to a different school. You will have to expel me, and I want to know why."

His jaw clenched shut, and his eyes narrowed in anger. He did not speak for several seconds. Then his hands relaxed from the arms of the chair, and he folded them in front of him on the desk. He took in a large breath of air, letting it out slowly through his nostrils. It reminded me of a bloated hog we had, but that sound came out of its ass. His words were slow and calm. "Danny, we've got to respect the wishes of the Tinsley family in this matter. You, more than anyone, should understand that."

"Why are my rights any less than someone else's?" I strained to remove the emotion from my voice. After all, weren't we both civilized people?

"I told you why. It is because of what you and Brent did to their daughter. You can't expect her to see you every day in this school. It will be hard enough for this young lady without you being here as a constant reminder." His voice dripped with his loathing of me.

"I did nothing to Loretta Tinsley. I was only there at the farm. Don't mix me up with Brent Arrington. Although I'm sorry about what happened, I did nothing to her. I wish it had never happened to her, but what should I do? I don't have an aunt in Fort Dodge, Iowa."

Principal Larson's fist slammed down on the desk. His eyes bored into me. This would not end well for me if it continued. I had to control my mouth and my anger. *Don't react*, I told myself. *Don't react.*

Larson wetted his lips. "We have worked out an arrangement with Fairmont High School. They have agreed to take you in as a student until this matter is resolved."

"That's thirty-five miles from here."

"Yes, yes it is. Two teachers have graciously volunteered to take you to and from Fairmont. They will pick you up in the mornings and drop you off after school. I have authorized them to use the driver's ed car." He pursed his lips, waiting for my response, his hands again forming that fucking steeple.

Gracious, my ass. What fantastic people there were in this school. Which weak-kneed assholes had he browbeat into graciously volunteering to sit in a car with a rapist for an hour a day? No way was that going to happen. *Fuck you very much, but no thanks.* Nothing was going to be gained from sitting here any longer, angering him further. It was time to get out of Dodge.

I stripped all the anger from my voice and said, "I'll discuss this with my parents. I can't make that decision without their approval." After a moment's pause, I asked, "Am I allowed to leave now?"

"Yes, Danny, I can understand that. If your parents have questions about the arrangement, have them call me, or I'll be glad to meet with them." He took another of those deep breaths. I fought the urge to leap across the desk and pinch his nose until his head exploded.

"You can return to assembly now. Please let me know the results of your discussion with your parents by tomorrow. It is only fair to the Tinsleys. I'm confident that your parents will understand."

"Yes," I said, "we want to be fair to the Tinsleys." I didn't wait for a response. I opened the door, walked back to the assembly hall, and took my seat.

Someone had written *rapist* on the top sheet of my tablet. I covered it with Steinbeck's novel. So, this was the way it was going to be. I looked over at Remy Fettler, sitting in the next row and looking back at me. We'd played football together in junior high and high school. Next to Steve Wiederman,

90

he was my best friend. He shrugged, but he hadn't smiled or waved, just turned away, like "what do you expect me to do?"

I wanted to yell, "Remy, thanks for your support. Now go fuck yourself!" but I thought my father might consider that to be a bit reactionary. I sat back, closed my eyes, and waited for the next bucket of shit to hit me in the face.

As the assembly waited for Principal Larson to give his welcoming address, attention turned away from me. Even when you're a monster, people tire of looking at you. I affected a stoic look, or maybe it was more of a don't-give-a-shit look. Either way, people ignored me, an improvement from being stared at like a carnival freak.

At nearly eight thirty, Principal Larson appeared in the assembly hall. A few seconds later, Brent Arrington entered. The murmuring gave way to a shuffling of feet as everyone turned to look at him. Brent strolled to his seat, his gaze dramatically sweeping the entire assembly. He smiled and nodded to several people, who smiled back. I resisted the urge to rip my desk from the floor and throw it out the window. Principal Larson rapped his knuckles on the lectern, instantly dropping the noise level to zero.

Larson cleared his throat as everyone waited, some stealing glances at Brent. One benefit of Brent being in the room was that I was no longer the center of attention. Larson welcomed everyone, naming the three new students and asking them to stand, which they all did to the forced welcoming applause—standard bullshit for the first day. I looked over at Brent from the corner of my eye. He was glaring at me. This would be one of those days I would not note in my diary. Larson tapped his hand on the lectern. All attention shifted back to him. "As some may know, this is Brent Arrington's last day with us. He's asked to say a few words. Brent?"

Brent rose from his desk and faced the group like a politician seeking votes. He dropped his eyes to the floor, and a sad look came to his face as if he'd been told his dad had died. "I just wanted to say goodbye to everyone."

There were *oohs* and *aahs*. He dutifully waited for the disappointment to subside. "I'm going to miss everyone here, especially all the guys on the team."

Again, a spattering of nods and murmurs. Brent glanced away as if emotion had overtaken him. "Some of you may have heard the accusations made against me. My parents and I feel it would be too distracting to Banning High and me, so I'm transferring to another school until this is all resolved. I'm going to miss everyone here."

Brent took his time walking from the assembly, his eyes low, as if he'd just lost his puppy. The scene would have been complete with a funeral dirge playing. There were a few more goodbyes: "See you, Brent!" and "Take care."

Larson cleared his throat and again tapped on the lectern. "Again, welcome back. Please go quietly to your classes."

The morning dragged by as if there were an anchor attached to my ass. I'd preselected my courses and skipped registration, giving me a break from ten to twelve. Most of my classes, except chemistry, were on the second floor. The labs for chemistry and biology, as well as the advanced courses attended by seniors preparing for college, were on the top floor.

All morning, my chest tightened like an invisible belt was notching up as I went from classroom to classroom, enduring stares and whispers. It was the same routine: first the stares, then avoiding my eyes if I looked their way. A few kids uttered a nervous "hi" when trapped with me.

Mark Davis, who was called Skeeter, talked to me as we waited in the hall between classes. Skeeter was five-four, relatively small for a boy in his junior year. He tried out for all the sports: football in the fall, basketball in the winter, and baseball in the spring. He'd made the traveling squad in baseball but played very little. That didn't stop Skeeter from giving 100 percent every time he was on the field, and everyone liked and respected him. I did too, and my respect grew tenfold when he stopped and talked with me. The exceptionalism in people comes out at the worst of times. I hoped, given the opportunity, I would have done the same. It took courage and compassion.

I had underestimated the hurt, embarrassment, shame, and anger I would feel standing alone or sitting at my desk. Having a smallpox sign around my neck would have made me more popular. I thought about skipping lunch, but what would I do the next day and the days after that? It might be easier going to Fairmont, but would it really be any different there? I would be the new kid. I had never been a new kid anywhere. In Banning, everyone knew you from birth. The only difference there would be that the people turning their back on me wouldn't be friends.

At lunch, I went through the line like anyone else. Jerry Reinhart, a douchebag and a senior, cut in behind me, stepping on the back of my shoe. He was bigger than me at six-two and nearly two hundred pounds. He was a blocking force for the football team and a relatively good tackle but too slow for much more. We had always gotten along at football practice and off the field. I turned and faced him.

"Something I can do for you, Jerry?" I asked.

"You ratted Brent out, didn't you, fuckface?"

Two other seniors stood to the side, watching intently but not joining in. At least not yet. This seemed to be my next bucket of shit.

"I didn't rat anybody out. You've been watching the wrong channel for your evening news."

"I talked to Brent. That bitch invited him out. He said she was all over him at the pool. All he did was give her what she wanted. You didn't back him up. You wussied out. If he doesn't play for Banning this year, you're the reason. He's five times the player you are, you fucking snitch, and you've ruined his chances for a full ride to ISU."

I pushed his hand away. "Don't believe everything Brent says. He wanted a ride, so I gave him one. I didn't see what happened in the hayloft. I wasn't there, but I saw Loretta Tinsley afterward, and she didn't look like she'd just been to a prom. That's what I told the sheriff. If you have a problem with that, Jerry—tough shit."

"I've got a problem with you, Prescott. We're going to lose the regional title because of you."

This would only get more heated, and no one would be in my court if it came to blows. It could only go one way, giving Larson a reason to expel me for fighting. I walked away and took a place at the back of the line. I looked like a chickenshit, but it was hard to know what to do when every alternative sucked.

Jerry was showing himself to be a loyal friend of the great Brent Arrington. That was what he wanted, and he'd made his point. I hoped that would be the end. I set my tray with a hamburger, bowl of chili, and french fries down at a table occupied by two sophomores. Both shot me a disgusted look and sat at another table. Another kid, a freshman farther down, stayed. I didn't know him—he probably felt he wasn't close enough to be contaminated by my presence. I was almost finished eating when a tray slid onto the table across from mine.

"Want company?" a female voice asked.

I looked up from my hamburger to see Wendy Warner, known as Weird Wendy because of her loner status and unique fashion choices.

I looked around the cafeteria. There were several open tables. "You sure you want to sit here?" I asked.

"Why not?"

"I'm a leper."

"I've had my shots," she said, biting into her apple as she sat down across from me.

Although Wendy and I had known each other since grade school, we'd never been friends. I'd probably said fewer than fifty words to her. I saw her around at football games and school dances. She was generally alone. I figured that was how she wanted it because she was a mini beauty queen at five-foot-four, petite, and perfectly built for her height. Her hair was black, long, and gorgeous, but she wore it in odd ways, sometimes like girls in the 1930s. Her large black eyes reminded me of Natalie Wood. Today, she wore an outfit that would have been perfect at a hootenanny, with her hair in side braids. Wendy Warner danced to a unique set of drums.

After being scorned most of the morning, I was suspicious of her motives. She had never shown the slightest bit of interest in me.

"Why are you sitting here when no one else will talk to me?" I asked. "You lose a bet, take a dare, or maybe it's just that you want to shock your friends by sitting with the loathsome Danny Prescott?"

"Huh," she said, a quizzical look shaping her face. She smacked her lips and pressed her index finger against her chin. "That's a hard one. Now let's see, I can rule out the last one because I have no friends, and let's see, that leaves me with only two other choices. I don't gamble, and I never take dares. Dares are stupid and infantile. Got any more?" A brief grin formed on her face as she took a large bite of her apple and then set it down. She was enjoying my discomfort.

I took a good swig of my Coke and held her gaze. "Your cheeseburger is getting cold," I said.

I pushed her tray toward her. The grin turned into a big smile.

"Not much for table manners, are you, Danny Prescott?"

I laughed. I tried not to, but I did. "Sorry, I've been having one of those days. How's yours going?"

"Oh, I don't know. I decided not to run for homecoming queen, so I guess okay."

"Oh, why is that?"

"I think the election is rigged. You have to be popular to win, and people have to like you. Having a lot of friends is also important. So, it's all rigged against people like me."

I laughed again. This time, Wendy joined me. I liked her bantering and her weird sense of humor. Maybe she was taking pity on the oppressed. I no longer cared about her reasons; I wanted someone to talk to me, and laughing felt good. Wendy brought both to the table.

"What do we talk about?" I said, pushing my tray to the side.

"Well, Danny Prescott, anything interesting happen over the summer?"

"Same old, same old. How about you, Wendy?"

"Nah, nothing changes around here. I had hoped for some uprising among the townsfolk, but the vampires were more accepted this year."

"You like being weird, don't you?"

"Yeah, you ought to try it."

"Nah, I'm afraid it might draw attention to me, and I want to be homecoming king."

She laughed again. I loved that laugh.

"Why did you sit with me, Wendy? You're a senior, and I'm a low-life junior."

She finished her cheeseburger, wadded the wrapper, and dropped it on her tray. Her eyes shifted away momentarily, and I was afraid I'd somehow insulted her. "You looked like you could use a friend, and we've known each other since grade school, so I thought, why not? You got a problem with that?"

"I'm glad you did, Wendy. Thank you."

"Jeez, if you're going to get all mushy and stuff, I'm going to leave. In fact, I really need to. I've got to check with Mr. Reddick before I can switch classes." She picked her tray up, hesitated, and bent closer to me. "If you ever want to talk, I'm around. Okay?"

"Okay, Wendy."

As she walked away, I wondered again if I could trust her. I wanted to. Was it pity that brought her to my table or that she had few friends and I was up for grabs, a stale sandwich nobody wanted? I didn't want anyone's pity. But sitting with her was like basking in the sun after a week of rain, even though we'd only spoken briefly. It felt good. She made me feel like I had before, and I wanted to feel that way again. I stored my tray in the rack as I left the lunchroom. For the first time, it didn't seem like everyone was staring at me.

I didn't have to hurry to get back to the assembly hall. I had two back-to-back classes scheduled for the afternoon, the first at two and the next at three, which left my schedule open for football practice starting in two weeks. I'd preregistered all my courses during the summer thinking that I stood a good chance of making first string. After World History, I walked to Coach Esker's office in the basement. His door was open, and he was sitting behind his desk. I tapped on the doorframe, and he looked up from the book he was reading and motioned me into his office.

"Danny," he said, clearly surprised to see me.

I was just as surprised to be there.

"Coach Esker, can I talk to you?"

"Sure, come in. Please shut the door."

I took a minute to gather my thoughts. Coach Esker had always treated me fairly. I wanted to tell him what had happened, to explain that I was not part of the attack on Loretta. If anyone would believe me, I thought it would be him. "This morning, I had a conversation with Principal Larson," I began.

"I heard."

Of course he had. Principal Larson would ensure that Coach Esker adhered to the party line. If the coach turned against me, I was done with this school. I tried to read him, but his face remained impassive. "He doesn't want me to come back to school. He said I should transfer to Fairmont." Again, I waited, hoping for encouragement, but he remained silent.

"I wanted to tell you in person what happened," I continued.

"Danny, you may not want to do that. You're in serious trouble, and maybe you shouldn't be speaking about it to anyone. You don't owe me an explanation."

I shook my head. "I want you to understand what happened. It's not how Brent is telling everyone. I gave him a ride to the Tinsleys' farm. Her parents were gone. Loretta and Brent went up into the hayloft, and I stayed below. I don't know what happened in the loft, but I'm being blamed the same as Brent." I took a deep breath and waited.

The coach clasped his hands together, leaning forward on his elbows. "Danny, I don't know what to tell you. I didn't think either of you was the type of young man who would do that to a young girl, but I'm not the decision-maker here."

"Will they allow me to play football if I stay here?"

"Danny, this is between you and me." He placed particular emphasis on the words. "The school can't prevent you from attending, and I can't keep you from attending practice. That's the law. The school cannot take any action one way or the other unless you're convicted of something, but they can create substantial obstacles for you. You're going to have to decide if it's worth it."

He leaned back in his chair. "If you play, there will be more pressure to keep you off the traveling squad. The other players may not accept you. Brent was the captain—and an extraordinary player. If a coach is lucky, he may have one or two players in his career like Brent. I've been coaching for almost thirty years, and Brent is my first. Teams have a rhythm. All teams peak. There's one season when they're at their best. This was our year to go all the way. Understandably, some people will have strong feelings about you playing ball this year."

"Does that mean you don't want me to play?"

"You were a solid player last year; you're back, two inches taller, and fifteen pounds heavier. I expect you'll be as fast as you were last year. With the defense focusing on Brent, you'd be our double threat. I want you both to play. I was hopeful Brent's parents would change their minds, but Brent came in this morning and told me he was going to play for Fort Dodge. Nobody is better than Brent at busting through the line, but you're faster, with better hands. You and he destroyed that for everyone on the team—and me. This could have been the year we won the state title. You can see why I'm not sympathetic to your situation."

"I'm sorry, Coach. I won't push it if you don't want me to play. I know I'm putting you in a difficult position."

Esker took a few seconds before answering. His gaze lingered on me for what felt like an eternity. I thought of myself dangling on a spider thread.

"Let's see how it goes. You come to practice next Monday, and we'll go from there. That's the best I can do."

As I was about to leave, he said, "Danny, have you ever heard of Brent doing anything like this before?"

I shook my head. "No, I never have."

Something about how he asked me left me feeling like he wanted something confirmed. There were few secrets in a small town, and almost nothing happened in the school that Coach Esker wasn't aware of.

My last class was Trigonometry. I heard very little of the lecture other than that the assignment had to be completed by Friday. I was finishing an assignment in English Lit when Wendy came into the assembly hall. She passed the junior class section. As she came down the aisle, she looked at me and smiled, then took her seat in the senior section. I found myself wondering why I'd never noticed her before. She was a natural beauty—if you looked past the frumpy clothes and pigtails. She had a weird sense of humor that I found endearing and funny. Maybe I liked her because I was as weird as Weird Wendy Warner.

The four-o'clock bell rang, signaling the end of the school day. Books slammed shut as the noise level jumped from quiet to riot level. Students streamed out of classrooms and assembly and down the stairs to the line of yellow buses parked double in front of the school. I spotted bus number six, nodded to Hank as I passed, and dropped into the rear seat of the Yellow Rattler. My first day at school was over. I had never wanted a day to end more than this one.

Compared to this morning, the kids on the bus paid little attention to me. There were a few long glances my way that I ignored. So far, I had yet to identify one benefit to being an outcast. I had survived the first day and had approximately 150 more to go. What a cheery little thought.

Outside the Rattler's windows, the Iowa landscape slipped past in a blur. As often as I rode this bus, I cared little about what was outside the windows. A sea of undulating cornstalks and barren bean fields interrupted only by the occasional trees around the farm buildings flowed by in a constant stream. This was the world I knew—not skyscrapers, traffic lights, and more people than one could count. I wondered how I would feel in a city surrounded by thousands who didn't know my name or anything about me. It had to be better than this.

The squeal of the Rattler's brakes tore me from my thoughts as we jerked to a halt at the end of my lane. I said goodbye to Hank. Halfway down the lane, Ranger bounded toward me. He came full speed; I bent down, stretched my arms, ready to catch him, and almost got knocked over. I fell to one knee, holding him against me. He snuggled his nose against my neck. All I needed was his hug and love to make the day better.

"I got through that one," I said to Ranger as he padded beside me. Ranger looked up, his eyes telling me I'd made his day just by coming home. I hurried up the walk and onto the front porch. The smell of freshly baked bread filled the house. My mother was a fantastic cook, but baking was her specialty. Since that terrible Sunday, she'd hardly baked anything. It gave me hope that maybe, somehow, we would get back to the way we were.

I plastered butter over a hot bun and ate while I changed into my work clothes. Jim was in the field disking but had thrown down enough silage to feed the cattle. As I came out of the barn, I noticed a red Dodge pickup in our yard. My father sat in the truck, talking to the driver as I loaded corn in the wagon for Jim to grind. I couldn't see the man inside, but the pickup looked familiar. I knew I'd seen it before.

As my father got out, I saw the driver was Evert Tinsley. A few minutes later, the pickup was gone. I felt I was shrinking into myself and breathing like the air lacked oxygen. It was becoming an all-too-familiar feeling. I finished loading the corn and then checked the three sick steers in the cattle shed. Their breathing sounded clear, their noses were dry, and their pinkeye was improving. We could probably let them out in the pasture tomorrow.

I fed the chickens and laid down fresh straw under the roosting platforms. The pungent ammonia odor of the chicken excrement caused my eyes to water. I spread oyster shells in their feed trays to harden the eggshells, then went to the house. As I zombie-walked through my chores, I could only think about Mr. Tinsley and why he was talking to my father.

My parents were sitting at the kitchen table talking when I entered.

"What did Evert want?" I asked, taking a bottle of Pepsi from the refrigerator.

"Don't spoil your supper, son; we're having beef burgers tonight," my mom said. "Your favorite." And it was. She made the best beef burgers in the world, and her fresh buns were delicious. I put the Pepsi back. I didn't mention we'd had hamburgers at school.

"He said he wanted us to know he and Ester did not hold what happened against the Prescott family. It was nice of him to stop by and say that," my father said.

"Daniel . . ." my mother said.

When she called me Daniel, it was serious. The name always made me feel smaller.

"When Loretta told Sheriff Brennan what happened, she said that she slapped you but not why. Evert thinks it was because you were going to do something to her. It's why he swore out the complaint against both you and Brent."

My whole body tightened as if I'd been submersed in ice water. I should have told the sheriff that when my dad was in the car. Now it was like a lie.

"When I bent down to see if she was okay, I touched her shoulder. That's when she slapped me. I don't know why. Then she asked me to leave, and I did."

My father said, "We know you didn't do anything or have any intent to harm her, but you should have told the sheriff. Now there's some doubt as to what you said."

My mother dabbed her eyes with a tissue and looked away.

"Do you believe me, Mom?" The breath caught in my throat as I waited for her to answer.

She turned toward me. "I never doubted you for a second. I know my sons. I know you could never do something like that. It's not in you."

"Does Loretta blame me for what happened? Does she think I knew what Brent was going to do? Maybe she thinks that's why I brought Brent out there—that I was in on this all along."

"I don't know. She's very confused right now."

My father cut in. "Loretta is having a difficult time. She won't go to school or even leave her room. Some kids called her yesterday and said some very hurtful things to her. I don't understand what is wrong with some people. That Arrington boy attacks her, and people are upset that he won't be playing football for Banning this fall. Where the hell are their hearts?"

Bad news traveled at the speed of lighting in Banning. Everyone in town knew Brent wouldn't be leading the Raiders to victory this year. That evidently ranked above a girl being attacked on her farm.

"I don't understand how anyone could be so cruel to that sweet girl, especially not after what she has been through," my mother said.

I felt sorry for Loretta too. It was difficult to fathom that someone would bear a grudge against her for what had happened. "Why would they do that to her?" I asked.

"Evert thinks the Arrington boy may be behind it," my father said. "Was he in school today?"

I dreaded adding more timber to the fire. I had caused enough problems for them, but I had to tell them about Principal Larson asking me to change schools.

"Brent was in school today, but he's not coming back. He was just there to say goodbye. He's transferring to Fort Dodge. Until he graduates, he will stay with his aunt. The school doesn't want me to come back either. They want me to go somewhere else."

My father's face flushed with anger. "Who the hell told you that?"

Despite knowing better, I added fuel to my father's anger by throwing on another log. I wanted to get back at Larson and the school. "I got it straight from the horse's mouth. Principal Larson called me into his office. He wanted me to transfer to Fairmont High School. He said a teacher would drive me back and forth in the driver's training car."

"Why, Danny?" my mother asked. "Why in the world would they do that? I can see why Ron Arrington would want his son to go to a different school. But you've done nothing wrong."

"Because Larson is a complete asshole!" my father shouted, getting up from the table, his muscles rigid, fists clenched at his side, ready to take on all comers. He had a hair-trigger temper, but it cooled as fast as it heated. You just had to be quiet and wait for the fire to burn out.

My mother and I were silent, waiting to see how this would go. After a bit, he sat back down at the table. "Did he say why they wanted you to leave?"

"He said Loretta's parents didn't feel comfortable with her returning to school if Brent or I were there. Maybe Mr. Tinsley called him."

"I don't think it was Evert, or he would have mentioned it when he was here. Larson must have done this on his own. If he did this without the school board's approval, I'm going to hang his ass out to dry."

"Ray, please. Let's not make this any worse," my mother begged.

"Linda, our son has a right to attend that school." His voice quivered with anger. Addressing my mother by name was her cue to not say more without detonating the dynamite. "We pay taxes, which pay his salary. Danny has not been convicted of anything, and unless they've changed the law, he's innocent and sure as hell can attend that school."

My mom placed her hand on my father's arm. "Ray, please," she said. She was right. Anything we did was going to make things worse.

"What did you tell him, Danny? You disagreed with him, didn't you?"

"I said I'd talk to you and Mom about it. He wants to know tomorrow. He said it wasn't fair to Loretta. Dad, maybe he's right."

"Well, it isn't fair to you either," my dad said. "Evert is not behind this, nor is the school board. It's that asshole Larson. He thinks he's God. Well, he sure as hell isn't, and it's not that prick's decision."

"Ray, please," my mother said.

My father took a deep breath and let it out. "I'm sorry for what happened to Evert's daughter. Danny bears some responsibility, but Evert said she didn't want to go to school, and he didn't mention Danny as the reason."

"The girl has been through so much, Ray. Maybe we can do this for a while until she's better."

"I said I feel sorry for the Tinsley girl too. Who wouldn't? But it's not Danny's fault what that boy did. It was that piece of garbage they need to throw out, not Danny." He turned to me. "Did he tell you that you can't return to school tomorrow?"

"He asked me to tell him what we decided."

"I'll go talk to Evert again in the morning. Maybe we can work this thing out. I can't believe it's at his request. He's the fairest man I know. Then we'll see what happens." My father got up from the table and went into the living room. I followed him and sat next to Jim on the couch. He was watching the news.

Susan called after I'd finished three of my mom's beef burgers on freshly baked buns. Mom talked to her first and then handed me the phone. For several seconds after I said, "Hello," she said nothing. I was afraid she was sharpening her teeth to chew my butt out.

"How are you holding up?" she asked.

Her opening salvo caught me by surprise. Was this actually my sister? "It's been hard on everybody," I said. "Do your friends at college know I'm your brother?"

"I told them. It was in the *Des Moines Tribune* and the *Register*. A few asked if I knew you."

"You should have said no."

"You haven't lost your sense of humor. That's good."

"I'm sorry if this has embarrassed you, Susan."

"You did nothing but give that egotistical prick a ride."

"Whoa. This can't be my prissy sister that we sent off to college. Could I get some identification?"

Susan laughed. "Your first few weeks will be the worst. Remember Wanda Furring? She got drunk and passed out at a party after the prom. I think it was the first time she ever drank hard liquor. Some creep took off her bra, wrote her name on it with a Magic Marker, and hung it on the school's flagpole. It was terrible for her for a couple of weeks, but it all calmed down, and people found something else to gossip about. It's not a big deal today."

"You remembered it," I said.

She chuckled. "Touché, little brother. I've got to go. This is a long-distance call and costs a fortune. I just wanted to say hang in there. We're all with you."

"Susan . . ."

"Yes."

"Thank you."

We said goodbye, and I went into the living room, where my brother was watching TV. Susan had put on a front for me. I knew my sister, and I knew she was embarrassed to have a brother accused of rape. It wasn't like having your bra hanging on a flagpole. It wasn't worth the fight. I was a pariah. Coach Esker wasn't ever going to let me play football, so why go back? I sat down next to Jim on the couch. "I'm going to quit school. It's not worth what it's doing to everyone. No one will talk to me, and no one wants me to be there."

"That's my boy. Roll over and let them kick the shit out of you. What are you going to do? Go to Fairmont, like they told you to?"

"You have ears the size of Dumbo," I said.

"Dad was talking loud enough for the neighbors to hear."

"I'm not going to Fairmont either. It was on the news and in the paper. They'll all know about me at Fairmont, so what's the point?"

"Oh, that's smart, Danny. Yeah, throw your future away. They win, you lose. You've proven them right. You're a coward. What then? Drive a truck all your life, or maybe you could get a job at the slaughtering plant."

"Who invited you into this conversation, dipshit?"

"Both of you shut up," my father said as he slumped into his recliner.

My mother came into the room. "Please stop. We're a family. Don't talk to each other like that."

"Mom, you don't have to go to school every day. You don't have to see them looking at you like you're a freak."

"You've got to give them some time, Danny. They don't know what to say either. It'll get better. These kids know you. Show them you are the same boy you've always been. You've known these people all your life, Danny. You'll see."

"Like all the people who have been calling you on the phone, Mom? I heard the phone ringing last night. You stopped answering it. Are those all friends?"

"Danny, what the hell is wrong with you, talking to your mother that way?" my father growled.

She turned to go.

"I'm sorry, Mom. I'm sorry I said that. I didn't mean it."

She put her arms around me. "I know you didn't. This is hard for all of us, but we've got to stay a family. If we lose that, we lose everything. You're right, Danny. Some people were cruel, but many of the calls weren't. Many said they knew you and us and didn't believe what the Arringtons were saying." She brushed away a tear from her cheek and sat down on the sofa next to me.

I poked my brother on the shoulder. "Know what?" I asked.

"What?" he asked, irritated.

"You're right. I'm not going to let them win. Tomorrow, I'm returning to school, and your advice, despite coming from a dumbass, was helpful."

"I take it back. School won't do you any good, and it will ruin everything for everyone else. Stay home and pitch shit out of the chicken house."

"You boys. I give up," my mom said, heading back to the kitchen.

Dad said nothing as he walked up and changed the TV channel.

"Hey, I was watching—" Jim protested.

"*Gunsmoke* is on," my father said as he dropped back into his recliner, and that was that. Nothing came before my father's favorite program. Matt Dillon was holstering his gun, so we'd missed nothing important. As I watched Matt Dillon and Chester with my dad and brother, I wondered if what was happening to our family drew us closer or pushed us apart. We were under attack by friends we'd known all our lives, the law, the school, and the Arringtons. We had each other. Whatever direction this took us, it would take us there together.

After *Gunsmoke*, our parents went to bed. Jim and I watched a rerun of *The Andy Griffith Show*. Opie didn't report a boy who had stolen candy from a store, but he did the right thing in the end. Sheriff John Brennan was no Andy Griffith, and I was no Opie. I would have to write my ending. After all, this was my series, and there were no reruns.

CHAPTER 6

Rather than wait for Principal Larson to summon me out of the assembly, I went to his office early on Tuesday morning. Typhoid Mary wasn't guarding his door, so I walked right past her desk and stood in the open doorway to his office. He folded the newspaper he was reading and motioned me toward a chair.

"Danny, how good of you to just stop by." His words had the ring of sarcasm. I sat in the chair he'd indicated.

"I thought you'd want to know what my parents and I decided."

"And that is?"

"I won't transfer to Fairmont, and I won't be dropping out of school."

He glared at me over steepled fingers as if using them to sight in on me. He gritted his teeth, and his face stiffened as he slammed his fist on the desk. His words spewed out like venom from a snake's fangs. "Who do you think you are? I'll tell you what you are. You're an embarrassment to this school and your family. Having sullied an innocent girl and ruined her, you continue to sit there as if you have a right to be here. You are scum, a pissant in this community, and you don't deserve to associate with other students. At least

Brent Arrington had the decency to leave. This institution bent over backward to accommodate you, Prescott. I went out of my way to organize transportation for you to and from Fairmont at extra expense. Well, sir, that's off the table. Next Monday night, when our school board meets, I will insist on your expulsion, not just suspension. Now, get the hell out of my office."

I rose from the chair; Larson's eyes bored into me. I glared back as I opened the door. He'd lost all leverage with the threat of expulsion. I wanted him to come around the desk. Then we'd see who walked out of the office. Typhoid Mary was still not at her desk as I passed. I'd missed the chance to kill the rodent without witnesses. Maybe next time.

The next three days at school were more tolerable, or maybe I was just getting used to it. People treated me as less of a pariah, more like an unwanted relative. My former friends ignored but tolerated me. Seldom was I called upon in class by teachers, and there were still students who shunned me, a few who wouldn't sit near me. That was all right. I'd have to learn to hate their guts. The guys I had played football with were still standoffish around me, but they no longer avoided me. Remy Fettler told me he and some football players didn't want me coming out for practice. I could do nothing to change their opinion other than blow my brains out in front of the morning assembly. That might provide some relief to the student body.

At my locker, I collected the few personal items I hadn't taken home for the summer. I stripped the Banning Raiders pendants from the locker door, where I'd taped them during my freshman year, and tossed them with my letterman's sweater into a trash can.

The one bright spot in my day was Wendy Warner. I counted the minutes until noon. At lunch on Wednesday, I sat at the table staring at a hot dog beside a lump of macaroni and cheese. Eugene Farrow, a sophomore, sat down at our table next to Wendy. He was new to Banning and didn't fully grasp the severity of sitting with an outcast and a weirdo. Wendy and I gave each other a *what-the-hell* look as he picked up his hot dog, shoved a quarter of it in his mouth, and smiled.

"Is this a private meeting?" he asked.

"No, the public is invited. You're the new kid?" Wendy asked.

"You say that like it's an accusation."

I liked this kid already. If you could hold your own with Wendy, you scored high in my playbook.

She offered her hand with a smile. "I'm Wendy Warner, and you might be?"

"I might be Eugene Farrow, the new kid. My folks just moved here from Mankato, Minnesota. My dad is the office manager at Farm Bureau."

"Hi, Eugene, son of the Farm Bureau manager. Welcome to Banning." I didn't feel an introduction on my part was necessary.

Eugene was an excellent audience. He laughed at our jokes and played along where he could. He seemed like a good kid, and I was glad he'd joined our little lunch group.

On Friday, after leaving my eleven-o'clock sociology class, I was feeling lower than whale shit. If I'd thought things were improving, I'd been dead wrong. In sociology class, Ms. Butzine gave me a *C* on a report I'd researched carefully and knew fulfilled every assignment criteria. Every other grade I could see handed out was a *B* or an *A*. I was never once called on in her class. The message was coming in loud and clear.

I didn't go down to the cafeteria to eat lunch with Wendy. Instead, I took a walk, ending up on the bleachers. I didn't think I'd be good company at lunch anyway, and being alone seemed a grand idea. As I sat staring at the football field, I decided to say piss on it and not return to school on Monday. I was considering what I would say to Wendy, when she stomped up the bleachers wearing blue-and-white-striped bib overalls over a red checkered flannel shirt. She wore her hair in a severe bun at the back of her head. The look was both quirky and gorgeous.

"Missed you at lunch, butthead."

Wendy put far too much emphasis on it—I hoped that would not be her pet name for me going forward.

"I needed some alone time."

"Did it cross your feeble mind that I might have waited for you? I sat there all alone, munching on my apple and potato salad. No hash, thank you. Surprising, huh? Luckily, when I was almost finished, Gene, the new boy with a father who manages a Farm Bureau store, kept me company."

She sat beside me and slammed down the two textbooks she was carrying to make it clear that she was pissed. "What's got you down, bozo? You look like you've lost your best friend, but that couldn't be because I'm here to cheer you up."

"It was that stupid sociology class."

"All sociology classes are stupid. What happened?"

I shook my head and took a good breath of air. "It's not important."

"It is if it made you not want to see me. Tell me."

"First, Bitch Butzine gave me a *C* on a paper that deserved an *A*. Then, as the class was discussing the American jury system and its effect on society, Karen Tanner asked if a jury that knew the defendant could be impartial in a small town where people knew everyone. It went from there to what if they knew the victim and if the crime was despicable like rape? Ms. Butzine let it go on. She could have stopped and guided the discussion another way, but she didn't."

"You sat there and took it?"

"Yes, I sat there and took it," I said, more forcefully than intended. Wendy turned away from me and shifted her gaze to the practice field, where a few students had gathered.

"I'm sorry. I didn't mean to snap at you. I should have done something, said something. I just sat there and took it."

"I think you did the only thing you could." Wendy put her arm over my shoulders, and I slipped my arm around her waist and pulled her closer to me. We sat quietly for several minutes, just enjoying being together.

"Did you know it was Friday the thirteenth?" she asked.

"Then I guess that's fitting, as this is my last day. I'm not coming back on Monday. They'll expel me at the next board meeting on Monday night. On Tuesday, Principal Larson will walk me out of the school, and everyone will watch. I won't let him do that."

Her smile disappeared. She dropped her arm from my shoulders and pulled away. "Are you going to go to school in Fairmont?"

"No, what's the use? It will be just as bad there. At least here, I know all the kids who despise me."

"'What's the use? Oh, poor old me. Everyone is so mean to me. I'm going to crawl in a hole and never come out.'"

"Why are you being this way, Wendy?"

"I thought you were more of a fighter than this. You're just going to curl into a fetal position and let them beat on you?"

"Well, I surprise some people. Sometimes even myself." I could see the disappointment in her eyes, and it hurt. This wasn't a time to be glib. I added, "It's not you who's getting beaten on."

"You think it's been easy for me? You don't think I've taken shit from everyone? Do you think I enjoy being called 'Weird Wendy'?"

I didn't answer immediately because, actually, I did. It had never crossed my mind that she cared about people's opinions of her. She sometimes dressed like a hobo. She was prettier than most of the girls in the school, yet she tried to look frumpy.

"There's a difference," I said. "You could be popular if you wanted to be. If you wanted to, you could be beautiful."

"Oh, thanks a lot. Do you believe that I willingly choose to be Weird

113

Wendy? You think I enjoy being a lone wolf?"

"Maybe you like being different. You could fit in. You're a straight-*A* student. No one looks at you with disgust. I didn't choose to be an outcast. I didn't decide to be a pariah. No one gave me a choice."

"Everyone has a choice. You made yours coming back to school. You knew it would be hard. Brent is damn near a god here. I respect you for that. I thought, *now there's a kid I could warm up to.* Now you're going to throw that away and us along with it."

I turned and looked into her eyes—those big, gorgeous, dark eyes. If there were an *us*, I would not throw that away. In those eyes were caring, compassion, and sadness. Just my luck, I was falling in love with the weirdest girl in school. "If I don't quit, will you be here for me?"

She put her arms around my neck, bringing me closer to her. I leaned forward, meeting her kiss. It was long and terrific. I think she felt it too. When we drew away from each other, she smiled, the sadness gone from her eyes.

"That was nice," I said.

"I thought so too," she whispered back. "If you're here, I'll be here, but what will you do if they expel you?"

"I don't know. Maybe I'll join the service when I'm eighteen. They have a program where you take your GED."

"That's your plan."

"Well, it's all I've got so far."

"It needs work."

"You think? Look, Wendy. It's not like I have a choice. What's the purpose if I return on Monday and they expel me Monday night?"

"What happened to 'I'm going to make Larson expel me. I'm not going to make it easy for him. They'll have to drag my dead body out of assembly, and then I'll come back and haunt them,'" Wendy said in a mocking falsetto.

"I don't think I was ever quite that dramatic."

"I added a little something to make you more interesting."

The 12:55 bell rang, summoning all inmates back into lockup. "I guess we had better get our butts back in," I said.

"Why?"

"Why what?"

"Why do we have to go back?" Wendy asked. "If this is our last afternoon together, I have a better idea."

"What?"

"You'll see." She took my hand and led me down the bleachers. All the little ants were rushing into the school building.

"We can't do this, Wendy. We can't skip school."

"Why?"

"Because by the end of the day, everyone will realize we're both gone. They're going to know that you're with me."

"You don't want to spend your last afternoon with me?"

"It's not that. I don't want to give them anything to use against you. I like you, Wendy, and I don't want you to get in trouble because of me."

She clasped my hand as we walked toward the school. Everyone had scurried in, leaving us alone. As we neared the doors, I stopped and pulled her to me. This time, it was my kiss, and when we pulled apart, I took a long look into those dark eyes and knew that whatever this was, it was real.

"You're sure you want to be with me? They could send me to prison. When I come out, all I'd be is a high school dropout with a criminal record."

"No one's perfect—" she laughed "—and no one will send you to prison. I won't let them. It's you and me, Wendy and Butthead, against the world."

"You really have a way with words, but you could use some help in motivation. Maybe take a philosophy class."

"I was quoting Plato."

"Who's Plato?" I asked.

"He lives next door to me. Let's go in. We'll be late, and you're the one worried about what people think."

It was hard to focus on the American History lecture about the Civil War when a war was happening in my head. I noted the assignment on my tablet, wondering if I'd be around to hand in the paper. If I stayed in school, would Loretta ever come back? That didn't seem to be fair either.

Ranger met me as I stepped out of the Yellow Rattler. I swore he could tell time. I sat with my back against the mailbox post, holding him in my lap. Ranger enjoyed the stroking and occasionally offered a tongue lick in appreciation. I recounted my shitty day to him, and as we walked down the lane, I told him about the kiss and Wendy. He seemed interested until he spotted a rabbit close to the fence and sprinted under the barbed wire in pursuit. My love life ranked way below a rabbit.

The smell of freshly baked bread hit me as I opened the door. I was surprised that my mother was baking bread on a Friday when her baking day was usually Monday. She dabbed a bead of sweat from her forehead with her apron. "There are some cinnamon rolls in the oven," she said as I picked up one of the bread rolls. They were hot from the oven. I broke it apart and slabbed a generous amount of butter between the halves.

"When?" I asked eagerly. She knew all my favorites, and her cinnamon rolls were at the top of my list. She rolled each strip of dough in sugar and cinnamon, not simply sprinkling it on top. Caramel virtually dripped off of them. No one could duplicate those rolls, even with her recipe. Neighbors and a few relatives had tried. One cousin even accused her of leaving something out of the recipe. The thing was, my mother never went by a recipe. It was just a little of that and a little of this based on years of cooking and secrets passed down from her mother and grandmother.

"I was thinking about maybe not going back to school on Monday," I said tentatively.

"Why? What happened?" My mother dropped the dish towel she held on the table and brushed her hands over her apron, a sign that she was preparing for war.

"Principal Larson will expel me after the school board meets on Monday night, so why suffer the humiliation of being walked out of the school by the principal? No one wants me there—not the teachers, not the students. I don't think Coach Esker is thrilled about having me back either. I'm a constant reminder that the great Brent Arrington will not win the state championship for Banning. It's a foregone conclusion now that we would have won this year if not for that asshole Prescott leading him astray."

After my passionate monologue, I expected my mother's support, but she looked at me disapprovingly. "You're going to throw it all away because it's getting tough for you at school?"

I was about to answer, but she wasn't through. "Well, Daniel Prescott, it hasn't been a cakewalk for anybody around here either, but no one here is complaining or throwing their hands up in surrender because we know our Danny is out there every day showing everybody that he's done nothing to shame himself or his family."

I was so wrapped up in myself that I hadn't considered what my family was going through and how they were going through it because of me. "I'm sorry about what I've put everyone through."

"No one's complaining, Danny. We're your family, and we love you. I won't make you return to school if that's what you decide, but your dad won't be happy. It's not something he would do."

I took a bite of the bun I'd forgotten was in my hand. My mother's words sank into me like the butter on the bun. "Okay, Mom, I'll think about it. Maybe I'll go back on Monday, but I won't make it easy for Larson. I'm not walking out like a whipped dog."

She hugged me. There were tears in her eyes as she smiled. "You wouldn't be my boy if you did."

"Mom, sometimes I just need a kick in the ass to do the right thing."

"My foot is always available," she said with a chuckle, and I didn't doubt that one bit.

"The pickup is not by the garage. Did Dad take it?" I asked.

"He's at the sale barn in Fairmont. He was thinking about getting some feeder pigs for the winter. Before you start chores, he wants you to check the amount of shelled corn left in the small bin. He didn't get a chance this morning."

I changed into work clothes, pulled on my boots, and went to the barn. Jim was plowing the west eighty. I fed the cattle, then counted heads as they ate. They were all there, so the fence over the slew was holding. A half hour later, Jim pulled into the yard, disconnected the plow, and backed the tractor into the equipment shed. He greeted me with, "Don't we look all clean and neat, schoolboy?" He had enough dirt on his coveralls to plant an herb garden.

"Would you mind if I took the first shower?" I asked as we walked toward the house for supper.

He skipped ahead of me, then turned around, walking backward. "I would suggest you not go near that bathroom, not to get an aspirin, not to take a piss or do any other bodily function. See, little brother, you're a turd, and it will be easy for me to flush you down the toilet into the septic tank. No one will ever hear from you again."

"Mom will miss me," I said.

"I'll take that risk."

I caught up beside him. "Jim, can I ask you something?"

"You just did."

"No, I mean something serious?" We stopped just inside the gate. "How do you know when you've found the right girl? How did you know with Becky?"

"You're serious," he said. He studied me briefly, seeing if I was putting him on. "You just know. You think about her all the time. When you wake up, you wonder if she's awake. You want to be with her and no one else. Most of all, you want to protect her, and there's nothing you wouldn't do or give her."

"Thanks," I said.

"You have someone in mind?" he asked.

"I was just wondering."

"Yeah, right. I've got to shower." As he entered the house, he turned in the doorway and looked back at me. "This isn't about that stuff I told you about wearing a condom?" Jim whispered.

"No, not even close."

"Good," he said.

My dad returned from the sale as we cleaned up, and my mother was preparing supper. He removed his jacket and went into the living room to watch the news.

"Did you buy anything at the sale?" I shouted to get above the chatter on the TV. I was hoping he took a pass on the feeder pigs. They were a pain in the ass in the winter. Give me a herd of cattle any day.

"No, the prices are too high right now."

The local news had just finished when my mother called us for supper. A large dish of cinnamon rolls sat in the center of the table, making my mouth water. As she placed a beef burger on everyone's plate, she asked, "Danny, your father and I were wondering if you'd like to celebrate my birthday next Saturday night. Jim, Becky, and maybe Susan can join us. After next weekend, corn picking starts, and then there are the holidays. So, next Saturday night looks like it if I want to celebrate my birthday."

"Sure, my social calendar is wide open. Happy birthday, Mom."

"It's not till Friday, but thank you."

"Where is Dad taking you?"

"To the finest restaurant in Iowa." My dad laughed.

After grinding a load of corn for the steers on Saturday, Jim and I cleaned out the calf pen, laid down fresh straw, and then started on the chicken house. I took a brief break, while Jim hauled the manure out and spread it on the alfalfa field. The pasture grass and everything else was going brown and dormant, which meant more silage, corn, hay, and work for everyone.

A flock of blackbirds grouped in the trees around the house, taking a break before heading south. I sat on the ground next to the chicken house and rested my back against the straw bales to be spread under the roosting benches. I laid my head back and closed my eyes, feeling the sun's warmth on my face. A lone eagle flew lazy circles above me in a cloudless sky, floating gracefully on outstretched wings. God must have loved the eagles to gift them with that kind of freedom. I chuckled as I watched Jim in the field, the spreader throwing a cloud of straw and chicken droppings into the air. Not everything in farming had grace. It was a side never shown on TV, but it was as natural as that eagle floating on an airstream. Jim made a final loop, shut down the spreader's beater bars, and headed back toward the house. I connected a garden hose to the bib. As Jim unhooked the spreader, I sprayed the interior, flushing out any remaining manure.

"That's it for me for the day, sport. I'm going to clean up and go over to Becky's."

"It's not even three o'clock," I said. "We've got to spread straw under the roosts."

"You can do that. It'll take less than a half hour. Do you want me to stick around? I can find something for us until Dad returns with an entire list of things to do."

"Have fun with Becky," I said quickly.

"Hey, maybe all the brain cells in that head of yours aren't dead," Jim said with a chuckle.

My dad drove in a half hour after Jim left; I had just spread the last of the straw. Mr. Tinsley's red pickup followed him down the lane. Evert stayed in his pickup as my dad parked by the garage and walked over to where I was standing. "I ran into Evert in town. He asked to talk with you, Danny. I told him it would be up to you."

"What does he want?"

"I don't know what he wants, Danny. He said he wanted to speak to you about what happened that Sunday. I know what the lawyer said, but this isn't the city and Perry Mason. We're still people here, and Evert is our neighbor, and he's hurting. Son, you don't have to, but we owe him the courtesy of hearing what he wants."

"Okay."

"He's waiting in his pickup. I'll be right here."

Evert opened the passenger side door for me, and I got in. "Hello, Danny." Nervously, he moistened his lips with his tongue. He didn't look at me. He didn't want to be here any more than I did. I felt sorry for him—he'd always seemed to me to be a nice man.

"Loretta is having a difficult time since this happened," he said.

"Yes, sir, I'm sorry."

"I'm not here for that. There's nothing I can do about that right now." He paused again, still not looking at me. "She thinks she must have done something that caused this, and I keep telling her she did nothing wrong. We no longer answer the phone because some kids have said as much to her, asking her to drop the whole thing."

"She didn't," I said.

"I don't care what you and that monster think," Evert growled. He took a deep breath. "I'm sorry. This is hard for me. Loretta said she slapped you, and I told the sheriff I thought she did so to fend you off. I may have misunderstood. Loretta said that's not what happened. I don't know why you did what you did, and at this point, I don't care. My only concern is Loretta getting better. Whatever you did will be dealt with later."

"I would never do anything to hurt Loretta, and I would do anything to reverse what happened, sir. I didn't know what to do that day. She wanted me to leave, and I did. I shouldn't have." His eyes went to something far in the distance. When he turned back to me, hatred filled them.

"Why didn't you help my little girl? They say you're a good kid. Why didn't you help her when she cried out? She looked up to you, and you didn't do a damn thing to help her. She doesn't understand why. She doesn't understand that, and neither do I. Why would someone she considered a friend bring a monster to our farm? She seems bothered by that as much as by what . . . what he did."

Tears glistened in his eyes, but he shook them off and pulled a handkerchief from his pocket. "Would you write a note to my daughter telling her she did nothing wrong and that you didn't know his intentions when you brought him out? Ester thinks it might help."

I nodded in agreement but said nothing more.

"Give it to your mother. She'll see that Ester gets it."

I got out of the pickup, and Mr. Tinsley drove off. I told my father what Evert had asked me to do and what I had said. His only reply was that he was proud of me for talking to Evert. What choice did I have?

CHAPTER 7

The temperatures dropped each week as frost laced the leaves and flat surfaces each morning. It felt like the end of something, not a renewal. Fewer birds greeted us each morning. Only the pigeons, starlings, and sparrows remained. I was up early Sunday morning and had already thrown the silage down for the cattle when Jim came into the grain shed. He yawned and leaned against the side of the door.

"Rough night?" I said.

"There are no rough nights with Becky," he said. "She doesn't enjoy drinking."

"That's a bummer. You won't get any if you can't get her drunk." I laughed.

"Don't talk about her that way, or I'll shove this pile of silage up your ass." There was no humor in his voice. I'd pissed him off. It would have been wise for me to think about that comment before shoving it out of my mouth. Joking about Becky had not been my most brilliant move. Sometimes, it was best to keep a thought to yourself and enjoy it in the privacy of your mind.

It was in my best interest to change the subject quickly. "I'd have to lease a warehouse to store everything you've threatened to shove up my ass."

"Okay, next time, I won't threaten. I'll promise."

"And I always keep my promises," we both said in unison.

As Jim filled the last bunk, I spread a layer of ground corn over the silage. Before we left the barn, we checked the sick steers we'd separated earlier from the herd. All three looked better, with no signs of sickness. We gave them one last feeding in the barn and then released them into the yard with the other steers. Outside, my father was removing the side of the water pump that provided water to the two stock tanks.

"Is the pump acting up again?" Jim asked.

"The seal isn't holding. It's leaking water. When the temperature drops to freezing, we'll have ice all over the place, and if this pump freezes up, we'll be hauling water to the cattle with pails. Glen's Hardware is open on Sunday afternoons during the harvest season, so I'll run in and pick up a new seal."

"I'll ride along with you. We could stop at Mike's for a hamburger," I suggested.

"I guess we could do that, but you'd better mention it to your mom so she's not fixing lunch for us. What about you, Jim? Do you want a burger?"

"I'm going to the Kesslers' for lunch."

"You're spending more time over there than here," my father remarked.

"That's a crock. It's just the weekends."

"And the nights," I added.

"Little brother, you know what I said about the promise."

It was nearly noon when Dad and I parked in front of Glen's. Half a dozen people were milling around the aisles of the hardware store. Glen himself was behind the cash register, and his son, Rodney, was stacking oil filters and spark plugs on a display rack. My father went to the counter and waited, while Glen boxed some small tools and a package of bolts and screws for the Fuller brothers. The two were in their late forties. Both looked scruffy, even after a bath. Some people just didn't clean up very well. Jess Fuller turned, rolled his eyes, and scoffed as my father and I walked up.

"Is that your boy who raped that Tinsley girl? You got some balls bringing the little bastard in here," Jess said with a sneer.

"There's no reason to talk like that, Jess," Glen said.

"I'll handle this, Glen," my father said, stepping directly in front of Jess with a glare. He moved closer until their noses almost touched, forcing Jess to take a half-step back. "You have something you want to discuss with me? I'd be glad to talk about it outside."

I saw Jess's brother Jake take a hammer off the counter and slip it down along his side. I stepped around my father, took a crescent wrench off the counter, and glared at Jake.

"Unless you picked up that hammer to build a barn, I'd put it back on the counter and step away, Jake. Otherwise, I'm going to be forced to beat you to death with it," my father said without looking at him. Jake held the hammer for several more seconds, then returned it to the counter.

He turned to his brother. "Let's get the fuck out of here. The air in here stinks."

"What about the stuff?" Jess asked, reaching for the tools and sack of bolts.

"Leave them. And fuck you, Glen, for sticking up for this scum. You don't give a shit who you do business with."

"Yes, I care very much, Jess. Don't come back here again. You can take your business to Fairmont," Glen said.

The brothers stomped down the aisle, shoving the doors open as they left. An elderly farmer and his wife nearly collided with them on the sidewalk.

"It's getting bad when the Fuller brothers call you scum," my dad remarked.

"I'm sorry about that, Ray. That was uncalled for. What can I get for you?" Glen asked.

He returned with the seal a few minutes later, shoved it into a bag, and handed it to my father. As we walked by the elderly farmer, he said, "Ray, not everybody feels like the Fuller brothers do."

I no longer wanted a hamburger, and my father didn't stop when we drove by Mike's. We were almost home when he said, "You're going to encounter people like that all your life. I appreciate you stepping up in there, but it wasn't necessary. I've known the Fuller brothers since they were kids. They're both cowards and bullies. They've always been that way, and I shouldn't have offered to step outside with Jess. It's not the way to handle things. All I've done is give the town something more to talk about. I'd appreciate it if you didn't mention this to your mother. She's got enough on her plate as it is."

"I won't, Dad, but I don't care if it wasn't the right way to handle it. I'm proud of you, and I'd have gladly busted that bastard's head with the wrench if he'd raised that hammer."

My father smiled as he got out of the pickup. We took the seal and a bag of tools and went to the pump. I handed him the tools he needed and held the new seal in place as he tightened the cover. He flipped the switch, and the pump motor whirred, sending water into the pipe without a leak.

"Sorry about the hamburger. We should have stopped. It's a while till we eat supper," he said as he gathered up the tools.

"I was thinking about Mom's cinnamon rolls and all that caramel on top."

"I'll put these tools away. You save at least one of them for me."

In record time, my father and I finished two of my mother's cinnamon rolls each and a glass of milk. We talked about the upcoming corn harvest and beef price, which he'd usually do with Jim while I listened. Things had changed between us—for the better. It seemed impossible that something good could come out of something so terrible. Maybe I hadn't been looking hard enough.

Just after three o'clock, my father left to visit a neighbor. Ranger and I watched a fox chasing something in the hayfield. The fox bounced and zigzagged, then stopped. Ranger watched intently, wanting to join the chase, but I held him back. He was bigger than the fox, but it had sharper teeth and had been born in the wild. I wanted Ranger to avoid the battle scars he was bound to bring back from the skirmish. I'd opened a Pepsi and was relaxing on the front porch when Steve and Matt Prader drove into the yard.

Matt Prader looked a little sheepish as he walked up to the porch. He was a better friend of Steve's than mine. Matt and I had known each other since third grade and hung out at the beginning of summer until he left to visit his cousin in Utah. He'd made it a point to keep his distance from me at school. Steve came up on the porch, while Matt stopped at the porch steps.

"Hey, Danny, what are you up to?" Matt asked.

"Six foot, one inch, but you knew that," I answered.

He laughed. "Same old Danny."

"Yep, just a barrel of laughs. It's been a while, buddy," I said. If Matt thought this was going to be easy, he was mistaken.

"Yeah, I'm sorry about that. What can I say? I'm an asshole."

"Are you expecting an argument from me?"

Matt shrugged and dropped his eyes to the ground.

"Coming over and saying hi at school would have been nice," I said.

"I know. Things just seemed to be all screwed up. We were all trying to figure out what the fuck was going on, you know. Brent was telling everyone what happened, and you were nowhere."

I made him sweat a few seconds longer. He looked sorry. More accurately, he looked like one sorry asshole. "Come up on the porch, dipshit. I'll get you a Pepsi." I went to the refrigerator and brought back two more bottles. "What brings you two here to darken my door?" I asked, dropping back into a chair.

Steve looked at Matt. "Some mothers are starting a petition to keep you out of school. They think even if you didn't actually do it, you and Brent were in on it together, and he wouldn't have done it if you hadn't taken him to the farm."

I turned the Pepsi bottle in my hands as I absorbed Matt's words. Wasn't it ever going to stop?

"My mother is one of the people behind this," Matt said. "She's good friends with Brent's mom. If they quit spreading lies about you, this whole thing would die down. She keeps telling everyone that you were the instigator, not Brent. If it weren't for you, he would never have gone to the farm. I know it's bullshit, but I can't help what my mom does. Danny, I didn't want you to think I was part of it. I don't agree with all the shit that's going around. You're still my friend, even though I know I haven't been acting like it."

"People are going to believe what they want to, but we think it's a crock," Steve said, "and we thought maybe some of us would go to the school board meeting Monday night to support you."

"Who's some of us?" I asked.

"Jessie Phillips, Mary Pittman, Bess Fuller, Tim Westbrook, the two of us, and some others. That's if you thought it would do any good."

Ranger dropped his head into my lap, giving me an excuse to think a minute before I answered. "I thought everyone wanted me gone."

"Some kids feel that way but not all," Steve said, and Matt agreed.

"The kids that know you, the juniors, are mostly on your side," he added. "Some football players think you're getting a raw deal too."

"I appreciate you taking my side," I said to Steve. "And Matt, I was hoping I hadn't lost you as a friend. Some people think I was Brent's lookout while he did it, and others can't understand why I didn't stop it. I'm guilty either way in their minds. I'm tired of saying that it's not true. Loretta told her father that I didn't hurt her and I wasn't there when Brent did it. Our attorney is going to ask the judge to drop the charges. Maybe that will change things."

"That's great, Danny. Man, that's fantastic," Steve said.

"Yeah, then maybe all this bullshit will stop," Matt added. "We were on our way to Banning to see who was around. We might pick up a few more who want to attend the meeting. Do you want to come along?"

"I wish I could, but my brother's gone, so I've got to do all the chores alone tonight. You guys have fun. Thanks for stopping and volunteering to take my side at the board meeting. It means a lot to me. Maybe it will even help."

When my father came home, I was unloading ground corn into the grain shed. Feeding the cattle was Jim's and my job, but my father filled the bunks as I threw down the silage. I told him about the petition and that Matt, Steve, and others planned to attend the board meeting. He didn't think it would matter much but agreed it was a friendly gesture. It deflated my bubble of hope that their support might change the board's decision.

After supper, I went to my room and tried to write the note that Mr. Tinsley had requested to Loretta. An hour later, at least a dozen sheets lay crumpled in the basket. I couldn't find the words to convince Loretta that nothing that had happened was her fault. Everything I wrote sounded like it came from a cheap paperback. I didn't have the words to say what I felt. Saying sorry seemed meaningless, but I said it anyway several times. None of this would have happened if I hadn't left her alone with Brent. I didn't ask for her forgiveness. I didn't deserve her forgiveness. I put the paper aside, deciding to try again later.

That night, the phone rang while my dad and I watched *Law Man*. Next was one of our favorites, *Bonanza*, at nine o'clock. My father and I were both fans of Westerns. It matched our idea of what a man should be. The Old West would have been our time—no bullshit with petitions or school board meetings. If you had a problem with someone, hang or shoot him. The way my life was going, in the Old West, I'd have been lucky to make it to sixteen without a noose around my neck.

Eight thirty was an odd time to be calling on a Sunday night. Good news by phone seldom came after dark. My mom rushed to the phone. She was going to miss the big gunfight. I half listened to her end of the conversation as Marshall Troop killed the wannabe gunfighter. My mother hung up the phone, but after several minutes, she hadn't returned. The commercial came on, and my father went to see who had called. They were whispering in the kitchen. It had to be bad news. I hoped it wasn't about my sister. This family had had all the shock it needed.

Five minutes after the commercial ended, they came back into the room. My dad walked to the TV and shut it off. We never missed *Bonanza*. The bands around my chest tightened. I could think of nothing that I'd screwed up so severely that would cause him to shut it off. My mouth went as dry as if I'd stuffed a spoon of flour in it. I prayed it wasn't about Jim or Susan.

"Danny, we just had a call from Martha Dobs," my mother said. She twisted a pale yellow handkerchief into a knot. She'd been crying. "You might remember her, Danny. She's a member of the Lutheran Ladies Aid at our church and lives near the Tinsley farm."

I remembered the old gossip from Sunday school. She loved being the carrier of bad news. It was her specialty, and I knew my mom did not care for her either. "She told me that Loretta attempted to kill herself this morning. Her parents wanted her to return to school on Monday, and I'm afraid it was just too much for her."

"Is she . . ." I couldn't finish. I didn't want to hear the answer.

"According to her mother, she will be okay. She cut herself but not deep enough to sever a vein. She's in the hospital now, but they're taking her to a place in Mason City where she can get the help she needs. I feel so sorry for that girl. If only there were something we could do to help."

I went up to my room. My concern for Hoss Cartwright's well-being had vanished with the news about Loretta. The note I'd been writing lay on my dresser. A note wouldn't matter now. I somewhat understood her feelings, but the isolation, guilt, and rejection had to be far more intense than my own. How could her friends assure or help her understand the fierce feelings crushing her? How could they know when even I didn't? She needed someone to turn to, someone who could understand what it was like in the hayloft with Brent. I had Wendy and Steve to grab onto when I felt like I was drowning. Loretta didn't have someone she could confide in, someone who wouldn't judge her. I'd left her in that barn, left her to deal with the most horrific thing that could happen to a girl. I could not walk away again. I couldn't stand by and watch her destroy the innocent girl who'd come bounding out of the house to greet Brent and me. I had to do something.

Loretta,

You must be feeling so alone now. I'm sorry I was part of it. I didn't know I was bringing a monster to your door. Your father said that you think I betrayed you. In a way, I did, but I never thought he or anyone else I knew would do something so terrible. I should have never left you alone with him and never left your farm afterward. I have no excuse.

You're the only innocent person. You trusted two boys you knew. You did nothing wrong. Nothing you did led to what happened. I was naïve; I wanted to be Brent Arrington's friend, and he used that. I never thought someone that evil could be in Banning. I realize that saying I'm sorry is not enough. You may not want me as a friend, but I will do whatever I can to help you.

Danny

The words seem so meaningless as I read them. I had to do something more than write a few words. I owed Loretta Tinsley much more than that.

CHAPTER 8

In the early morning hours, sleep overtook my thoughts. I opened my eyes to sunlight streaming across the room. I sat up and dropped my legs over the side of the bed. My body felt like I hadn't slept at all. It was after seven—I should have been up at five thirty. My father hadn't awakened me for chores, and I'd slept through the alarm.

It was too late to help with chores, so I dressed for school. The Rattler wouldn't show for another half hour. It hardly seemed natural that this would be my last day at school. I realized how much a part of me it was to walk into assembly, play football, to do all the things that made up my daily life. If today was going to be my last day, I'd make the best of it.

My mother was putting away the breakfast dishes. My dad and Jim had already eaten and were putting a new drive chain on the picker. She put away the dishcloth that she'd been drying dishes on, opened the oven, and took out a plate of bacon and eggs.

"Sit down and eat. You don't want to miss the bus."

"Why didn't Dad wake me up this morning?"

"We thought you needed the sleep. We heard you tossing around into the early hours. I know you're bothered by what happened, Danny, but worrying doesn't help. I talked briefly with Ester this morning. They were preparing to drive to Mason City to be with Loretta. Ester thought she was doing better. She'd even gone outside and played with her cat. Evert thought that if she went back to school and saw her friends, it would help, but it was a little too much for her. Yesterday, she went to her room and wouldn't come out. Ester said she acted like she was eight and wanted to sleep with her doll. Then they were watching TV, and Loretta took a bath. It was just fortunate that Ester checked on her and found her before she lost too much blood."

"Everyone in school will be talking about it," I said.

"Going in today won't be easy, but you're doing the right thing by facing this and not running from it. I am very proud of you."

I held the letter out to her. "It's the letter Mr. Tinsley asked me to write to Loretta. I didn't seal it because I thought they'd want to read it first. They may not want her to have it now, but I promised."

She held the envelope and carefully laid it on the table as if it were breakable. "I'll call Ester and take it over if they still want it. You'd better get heading down that lane. The bus might be there already."

Ranger tagged along as I walked, preferring my company to the clamor of the hammer mill grinding the corn. Five minutes later, I sat at the rear of the Yellow Rattler as Ranger trotted back. A somberness permeated the bus. There was no laughter, and the conversations were muted. Wendy was waiting for me as I stepped off the bus. Her usual smile was absent.

"You've heard," I said.

"Yes, I think everyone has. There were police cars and an ambulance. Everyone was phoning everyone. I wanted to call you. I know this must hurt you too, but my mom had the phone tied up gossiping."

"I've got to help her. She doesn't have anyone to talk to. I think she's keeping it all inside, thinking that she's to blame. I know what happened. Perhaps I'm the only one who can speak to her about it. Her father said she'd received calls accusing her of lying about Brent. They blamed her for him leaving school. I can't believe people are like this."

"You talked to her father?"

"He came to our farm. He asked me to write a letter to her to help her understand it wasn't her fault, and that I didn't bring Brent out knowing what he intended to do. He thinks Brent or his family might be behind the calls."

"I talked to a few of the freshman girls. They said she was the most popular girl in their class, but she didn't act like it. According to one of them, boys used to surround her when she was at the pool. I think some of these girls are jealous, but it could be Brent's doing too. He's a vicious person. He doesn't care who he hurts as long as it isn't him."

"If he's responsible for the calls, it's as good as putting the knife in her hand," I said, stopping outside the assembly hall. "I want you to stay here until I'm at my desk."

"What are you talking about?" Wendy asked.

"I don't want you to walk in with me. It will be like being on the bus or the first day of school, and I don't want that for you."

"Do you think I'm ashamed to be with you?" she asked.

"Wendy, please. There's not much I can do for anybody, so let me do this one thing for you."

I walked into the assembly, leaving Wendy in the hall, and sat at my desk. It was like a ripple spreading from a rock thrown in the water as eyes turned to me and conversations stopped. I placed my books on the desk, then turned, looking directly at those who were staring. A minute later, Wendy entered the room and walked down my aisle toward me. As she passed, she hesitated, looking down at me, and smiled as she gently touched my shoulder. How could I not love a person who would do that?

Steve and Matt entered the hall a minute later and came to my desk. Matt stood next to me as Steve dropped into a desk beside me. "Man, we heard about Tinsley. What happened?" Steve asked.

"I don't know. Her parents thought she was doing good. Her father thought it might have been some phone calls she was getting or that they wanted her to go back to school."

"That's tough." Matt looked around the assembly. "Just when the tide was turning your way. The board meeting tonight will probably be a disaster."

"Way to go, asshole. Cheer him up," Steve said.

"He's right, Steve. I don't think you should go to the board meeting."

"Are you sure? I mean, of course, if that's what you want."

I saw they both were relieved. It would have been unpleasant for them, and the good it did would be like a fart in a tornado. Whatever support I'd garnered was gone. I was being forced back under my rock. Even if the charges were dropped, there would be those people who would believe the worst. It was just the way small towns were. Where there's smoke, there's fire, and there were many in the town who believed I had been the lookout for Brent. At least I wouldn't be around to take their abusive bullshit. There was a good side to everything if you looked hard enough. The school board would vote to expel me tonight, and I no longer cared. Let them do whatever they wanted.

Wendy and I ate lunch together as usual, but no one, not even Skeeter, joined our table. Although a nipping cold was in the air, we went to the bleachers. A few grade-school diehards played on the merry-go-rounds, while a couple of older boys played catch with a football. The playground was relatively quiet. Wendy told me her father had asked if she would like to invite her friends over for a homecoming party, as they'd done for her brother during his senior year. I grinned, wondering if I would be invited.

"I told my dad it sounded like a great idea, but first, he would have to find me some friends."

"What did he say to that?" I asked with a laugh.

"At first, he laughed, and then he asked if I was serious. It's sad when you think about it, Danny. 'Weird Wendy.' I wonder if they'll put that under my yearbook photo?"

"Do you care?" I asked.

She didn't answer at first, just looked out at the kids playing. "I didn't think I did, but I do, really, and that's sadder yet."

"I know," I said. "It hurts and keeps hurting, no matter how often you say to yourself that you don't care."

"Birds of a feather," she said, squeezing my hand and putting on a weak smile.

"And such a pretty bird at that," I said, squeezing back.

Wendy appeared sadder today than I had ever seen her. I worried I might lose her too. I didn't think it was just Loretta—it was a tough job being friends with Danny Prescott.

"I know how Loretta must have felt." Tears came suddenly to Wendy's eyes. "I should have called her. I knew how she felt, but I didn't. Now, God knows what will happen to her."

"I don't think a call to her would have helped," I whispered.

"That's not it, Danny," she said, leaning against my shoulder. "Brent tried to do the same thing to me, but I was able to fight him off." She hesitated as if regretting what she'd just said, then dabbed away a tear. "When we were freshmen, there used to be a string of trees where the new baseball diamond is now."

"I remember," I said, finding that my breath had deserted me. This wasn't the first time. Brent Arrington had done this before. Despite wanting to hold her and reassure her, the rage brewing inside me was overpowering. I wanted to kill him. I wanted to pull off his legs and arms like one would a fly. I wanted him to suffer the way Wendy and Loretta had. "Wendy, I . . ."

"Over there was where he attacked me." She pointed to a fence at the end of the athletic field, where the trees used to be. "I gouged his face with my fingernails. That's why he stopped. He cursed me, called me the vilest names, and said I would pay for what I did to him. Then he just walked away, leaving me there, my clothes dirty and ripped."

"I'm so sorry, Wendy. Why didn't your parents or the school do something?"

Her voice was low and hollow. "I didn't tell anyone. I was ashamed and didn't want anyone to know. I don't want anyone to ever know. Back then, I was flirtatious, and I thought maybe my actions had given him the impression that I would do things like that. I just wanted to forget and never think about it again, but he didn't let that happen. He told everyone I'd asked him to come to the woods and offered to do it, but he didn't want to because I was on the rag. His words, not mine. He told everyone that instead, I gave him a blow job."

She broke into tears, and I held her close to me, feeling each painful sob. She buried her face in my chest, her tears wetting my shirt. I didn't care who saw us or what they thought. She pulled a tissue from her pocket, straightened up, and wiped her eyes.

"Of course, I denied it to anyone and everyone, but they believed Brent. The boys called me BJ and laughed. It hurt so much to know my friends didn't believe me and thought I was a slut. I must have plotted a hundred ways to kill that bastard, but in the end, I just drew into myself. The turtle, Weird Wendy. He didn't have to spread all those lies about me. I never told anyone that he tried to rape me. Maybe if I had, Loretta would be okay today."

"You can't know that. You did nothing to bring any of this on any more than Loretta. It was Brent and no one else. And if he ever comes near you again . . . I'll kill him."

She tried to smile but failed. "I told you this because I didn't want you to hear the lies from someone else and look at me and wonder if they were true."

"I heard the rumors. Wendy, it's a small school in a small town."

"Did you believe them?"

"I believe little of anything I hear in the locker room."

"Did you wonder if they were true?"

"I did. I did until you sat down across from me in the cafeteria. Then, I knew they were all lies."

She looked at me for the longest time, gauging if what I had said was true. People believe what they want and not what's right before their eyes. Anyone who knew Wendy Warner knew she would never do what the rumors described.

"The worst thing was when boys started calling me and asking me out. The humiliation was unbearable with every call—I knew exactly what they wanted. I refused them all. I've never dated anyone. The girls avoided me. I wanted to be a cheerleader and be in the school plays, and he ruined all of it. Maybe I should have reported him, but I didn't. I was afraid to go out with anyone. Instead, I became Weird Wendy, the oddball no one wanted to date or hang with. It worked, until I met you."

"You're stronger than me, Wendy. I couldn't have done what you did, not alone. I wouldn't be here if you hadn't sat across from me. You saved my life that day. You gave me a reason to keep going."

"Maybe we're stronger together." She brushed my cheek with her fingertips and smiled.

The five-minute bell rang, and the few remaining diehards on the playground, including Wendy and me, moved toward the school. She blew her nose as we walked, throwing me a big smile. "Did I cheer you up? That was my objective."

"Your technique needs a rework, but . . . ." I stopped and looked deep into those big, dark, beautiful eyes. "I think you're the most wonderful, bravest person I have ever met. Anyone who doesn't see that is an idiot."

"You're sweet, Danny Prescott. I'm glad I set my tray next to yours too."

We had just made it to our desks when Coach Esker came to the front of the assembly, announcing that football practice would begin Wednesday and all interested students should attend a meeting in the locker room to sign up and be assigned a locker. Several former teammates glanced at me, wondering if I would be there. I was one of three possible running backs. I had backed Brent up at the halfback position and played wide receiver toward the end of the season. Whether or not they liked me, they needed a good running back, and that would be me—if there weren't a board meeting tonight. I half listened to the rest of the announcements. They didn't affect me.

Later that afternoon, Typhoid Mary motioned to me as I left for class. I followed her to Principal Larson's office. The son of a bitch couldn't wait until tomorrow to deliver the knockout punch. Well, I'd gone the distance, for whatever that was worth.

The principal was behind his desk, steepling his hands. It was a habit I now despised. I fantasized about leaping over his desk and breaking every one of his fucking fingers. I slumped into my usual chair as Mrs. Paulson gently shut the door behind me.

He sat there as if it were my meeting, waiting for me to start. I wouldn't do it. My intention was only to listen and then leave, nothing else. I was determined not to react and to walk out with my dignity intact.

"The school board has informed me that they have removed my recommendation for your expulsion from the agenda tonight. I received a call from a board member a few minutes ago. Unfortunately, Miss Tinsley will not be returning to school, which negates the need to transfer you to a different school, at least for the interim. Also, I understand that Mr. Tinsley contacted several of our board members, advocating for you to remain at Banning High School. You owe the Tinsley family; they deserve a heap of gratitude. I think it's a mistake to keep you here with all these impressionable children, but it's the school board's decision at this point. If you step out of line, Daniel Prescott, it will be my decision, and you'll not be coming back."

It took me a few seconds to comprehend what Larson had said. I was not being expelled. "Does that mean I can play football?"

"I can't speak for Coach Esker."

I tried to keep a smile off my face as I saw the disgust rise on his. They probably never could have expelled me. The prick had been playing me. Legalities my ass—he'd hoped he could force me to quit. He was on his own little crusade. Well fuck him. I'd stood my ground, and I'd beaten him.

"Can I go now, sir?" I asked.

"You can go when I say you can go."

"May I speak openly, sir, or will you continue demeaning me?"

"Go ahead, Danny. Say what's on your mind. Give me a reason to boot your butt out of this school."

"You don't know me. You don't know what occurred at the Tinsleys' farm. You're a closed-minded, mediocre man, or you wouldn't be the principal in this grease spot on an Iowa map. You think you're a big fish because you're swimming in a small pond. You can watch me all you want, but I'm staying." When he said nothing, I stood. "Are we done, sir?"

"Get out of my office," Larson said, hardly hiding his rage.

I did. I closed his office door as gently as Typhoid Mary as I left. The anger was gone as I walked back to my desk. I felt like skipping and doing somersaults. I was eager to tell Wendy—hell, I was eager to tell everybody. My mother was right. If you wait long enough, even shit turns to applesauce. Well, not exactly her words but close enough.

I went to my World History class, sat near the back of the room, and opened my text. The teacher said nothing even as I walked in late, and I wasn't asked a question. Being invisible had its advantages. It was hard to feel joyous about remaining in school with Loretta in the hospital. After what

Evert Tinsley had done for me, I thought I owed the Tinsleys far more than my gratitude. I needed to help them get their daughter back.

That afternoon, I jumped off the steps of the Rattler and raced Ranger down our lane. He stayed ahead most of the time but fell behind as we turned into the yard, allowing me to save face. I burst into the house with the news. My mom and dad were standing in the living room, waiting for me with giant smiles. They already knew. Banning's news network was faster than the Rattler.

"Now we can finally breathe a little easier," my mother said as she hugged me.

Jim leaned against the wall as if it were no big deal.

"What did Adolf Larson say?" Jim asked.

"He said it was a great day for Banning High and that if he ever had a son—"

"Bullshit," Jim said, unsticking himself from the wall.

"He wasn't happy. He said he'd be watching me, and if I stepped out of line, I was gone for good."

"An asshole till the end," my father replied.

"Ray, that's why the boys talk like that."

"No, Linda, they talk like that because they're boys."

"Your father is taking me to the Oasis Restaurant in Fairmont," my mother said proudly. "What do you think of that? Susan can't make it. She's got a test, but I want my two boys there."

"I think that's nice of the old penny pincher," Jim said. "The Kesslers took us there for Becky's graduation from Fairmont Junior College, but I'm sorry, Mom. I wished you'd said something sooner. The Kesslers are having a family thing, and Becky is their only child. They want me there to introduce me to the grandparents."

"That's all right, Jim. This is a special time for you. It's not like I won't have another one."

"I'll be there, Mom," I said. "You can count on me when everyone else lets you down."

"Well, we've messed around enough here. We've got chores to do," my father said and headed for the door.

As Jim and I fed the cattle, my dad walked among the herd, counting them and checking each one for pinkeye or signs of sickness, finding none. On the way out of the barn, he motioned us into the pump house, reached into the water tank, and pulled out three beers hidden in a black plastic bag. He opened each with an opener we kept for Pepsi and handed one to Jim and me.

"This is the first beer I've bought in ten years, but it's a special occasion. Jim asked Becky last night to marry him, and she accepted."

I gripped my brother in a headlock, giving his head a knuckle rub. "You son of a gun, you did it. Congratulations. When's the wedding?"

Jim shrugged me off, but he clearly enjoyed it. "We haven't set a date."

"That's not all," my father said. "The lawyer called today and said the judge granted a hearing to review Danny's arrest and the charges. He said there's a chance that since Loretta corrected her statement that all the charges may be dropped against Danny and his entire record expunged. They made it clear to Mr. Shagger that they expect Danny to testify against Brent."

Jim and I slapped each other's backs. Things were turning better for the Prescotts.

"Wait," my father cut in. "That's not all. I sold half the corn crop this morning at the high annual price. Even if the prices slip some, it will be the best year we've had in five years." We clicked bottles, and I took my first swallow of beer with my father. Jim looked at me with raised eyebrows, and my father caught the look.

"Don't worry, boys, I'm not going on a drinking binge. I'm having a beer with my sons." He took a long swallow, and so did we. "Danny, if I catch you with a beer in your hand and one is not in mine, you can kiss getting a car goodbye."

"Does that mean I'm getting a car?" I asked.

"You don't need a car. You have a perfectly good pickup," Jim piped in.

"Shut up, Jim, or I'll open the next beer bottle with your teeth," I shot back.

"Oh, I'm scared." My brother grabbed me in a headlock and returned the knuckle rub I'd given him earlier.

"If you two don't settle down, your next drink will be from the hose outside," my father said and chuckled.

We left the pump house after a second beer and a vow not to tell my mother—one of those men things that women wouldn't understand. As we approached the house, I quietly asked my dad, "Do you think Mom would be okay if I invited a friend to the restaurant for her birthday?"

"Who did you have in mind?"

"Well, this girl has been nice to me at school. I want to do something nice for her."

"Like take her to a fancy restaurant?" my father asked.

"Yeah, I mean, I know it would be expensive."

"Well, let's see," my dad said as we walked. "Considering we just sold part of the corn harvest at a good price, and if we had to, we could trim your allowance, we can probably swing it."

"What's Peter Pan asking about?" Jim asked, coming up beside us.

"Or we could cut Jim's salary back to what he's worth and go to restaurants every night," I suggested.

"Look, you mental dwarf. I don't know what you're talking about, but it's got my veto," Jim said.

"I think we can swing it without endangering your brother's salary. He's about to become a married man with additional responsibilities."

We stripped out of our coveralls, stored our boots in the rack on the side porch, and went inside. Supper was on the table: pork chops, mashed potatoes, green beans, and a pumpkin pie. We washed up quickly and took our usual places at the table, with my mom and dad on the ends and Jim and me across from each other.

After passing the food around, my father said, "Danny has a friend he wants to invite to your birthday dinner on Saturday night."

"So that's what you two were mumbling about. Who's your little friend? If it's Steve, he'll ruin everyone's meal and get you kicked out of the restaurant." My brother laughed.

"It's not Steve, you dimwit," I said.

"Your brother is not a dimwit, and Jim, you could be less insulting to your brother. We're at the table. I've taught you boys better. Now, who is this friend? Is it someone we know?"

I looked across at Jim, who was eagerly awaiting my answer. His fork of mashed potatoes stopped halfway to his mouth.

"Wendy Warner."

My mother looked at my father, giving him a look that puzzled me.

"What? You know her?" I asked.

My mother grinned. "No, though I know who she is. Her mother was my best friend in high school."

"In Banning?" I muttered.

"No, I was going to Fairmont High School then. We moved the summer before I graduated. Your father and I met during my senior year at Banning."

While I knew my parents had gone to school at Banning together, I didn't realize that my mother had also gone to Fairmont. I knew hardly anything about what they were like when they were my age. It didn't seem fair that they knew virtually every detail of my life. "You and Wendy's mom were best friends?"

"I'm just surprised Danny knows any girls, at least well enough that one would eat with him," Jim remarked.

"Please, Jim. This is important to Danny," my mom said.

Jim got up from the table. "I've got people to see anyway, but Mom, I'd encourage you to meet this girl and ensure she's sane before taking her to a restaurant."

My mother looked over at my father again. He had a curious look on his face. "You got yourself into this, Linda."

"I don't exactly know her mother. I was friends with Wendy's birth mother. Her name was Terra Jurgenson."

When Wendy mentioned she was adopted, I'd never thought about her having a birth mother. Now, I wondered if she knew her birth mother or even knew who she was. "Was her real mother not married?" There were stories about girls leaving town and returning after having a baby. The gossip biddies could recite every name.

"No. Terra married a boy named Harvey Bartelson not long before he joined the army. Wendy was born while he was away in France. The war changed him. When he returned from Europe, he was mean to her and couldn't hold a job. Terra died of a brain aneurysm when Wendy was less than two years old." My mom sighed and shook her head. "I shouldn't be telling you these things, Danny. It's not my place."

"But why didn't her father take care of her?" I asked.

"He tried, but it was too much for him. He left and didn't tell anyone he was leaving. He left Wendy alone in an old, dilapidated farmhouse where they lived. If it had been in the winter, she would have died. No one knows where he went or what happened to him. He just disappeared. A family from our church took her in until the Warner couple later adopted her."

"Do you think Wendy would be uncomfortable at dinner because you were friends with her birth mother?"

"I'm not sure she knows who her birth mother is. Some adoptive parents don't want their children to know. Please don't mention any of this to Wendy. I shouldn't be talking about such things myself. It slipped out."

"I won't. Then can I ask her?"

"I think it would be delightful having her join us."

After dinner, my father and I watched *Cheyenne*, another of our Westerns. Then I did a trigonometry assignment on the kitchen table until *Surfside 6* came on. Cookie Burns was one of the coolest dudes on TV. When the local news came on, I went to my room to do an English Lit assignment. Since I wasn't getting kicked out of school and my social calendar was blank, I completed all my assignments and even did extra-credit work. Studying kept my mind off the shitshow my life had become.

The next morning, I climbed on the bus without worrying about being dragged out of the assembly and marched out of the building. It probably wouldn't have been that dramatic, but the more dramatic I made it, the more relieved I felt. The entire day was nothing to write about in my diary—besides a kiss from Wendy. Tuesday morning meant Trig class. Several guys complained about the problems the instructor, Windon Swenson, had assigned over the weekend. One had taken me over three hours to solve, and even then, I was unsure if the answer was correct. We handed in our homework and then waded through a pop quiz while Mr. Swenson graded the assignment.

He retrieved the pop quiz, returned the papers, and instructed me to bring my homework to the front. I immediately went on guard. I grabbed the homework off my desk, wadding the paper. Despite busting my butt on this assignment, I was being dragged to the front of the class to be ridiculed. I pushed down the anger rising in me and repeated to myself, *Don't react, don't react.* But there was a point where enough was enough, and I was close to reaching it.

I went to the front and turned, facing the class. I wanted them to see and appreciate the pissed-off look on my face. With my best *fuck-you* expression, I stood tall, my back erect and shoulders back. Tammy Wexler and Annette Herstein shared a whisper, followed by a giggle, and then looked away. As I was about to ask them to share their remarks, Mr. Swenson grabbed the assignment from me and displayed it to the class. I braced for the onslaught of laughter.

"This object in my hand, ladies and gentlemen, is a perfect paper—Danny is the only person who solved every problem. I don't doubt that he spent considerable time and effort solving these problems, especially the last one. Most of you gave up; others didn't even try."

A girl in the front row, a real suck-up, raised her hand, and Mr. Swenson nodded to her. "I worked on the last problem for three hours, Mr. Swenson."

"Then you should have made it four," he replied.

"There's nothing in the text about which formula to use. I tried using the Pythagorean Theorem and the cosine double angle formulas," she protested.

"You didn't find it in your text because the problem is from my college textbook. It's one you'll face if you take a course in college trigonometry. While I didn't expect any of you to solve it, I expected a stronger effort. I'm disappointed in this class, but I'm proud of Danny for not giving up. I would like him to explain his logic in approaching and solving the problem."

He handed me my homework. I went to the blackboard and began jotting down the steps I'd used to solve the equation. I started by stating the problem: "Construct three circles inside an acute triangle, tangential to two sides of the triangle and externally tangential to each other."

For once, the eyes on me didn't make me feel like crawling in a hole. Standing before the blackboard, I knew I would get through this. I was going to persevere. I was standing my ground, just like my father would have. I went to lunch feeling like I'd just won the Irish lottery. Wendy was waiting at our usual table in the cafeteria. I dropped my tray beside hers, and my smile revealed the news I was eager to share with her.

"Okay, smart-ass, what's the big grin about?" Wendy asked.

"I thought it was more of a smile."

"Don't correct me. It's a smart-ass grin, so what's it all about? Someone give you a goose while you stood in the lunch line?"

"Nothing that exciting," I said, sitting across from her. I told her about the Trig class and how I thought Swenson would tear into me. As I went through my story in excruciating detail, she laughed. It was exhilarating to share something positive with her. I had been climbing out of my hole since Loretta had tried to end her life. Sitting and talking to Wendy was the high point of my day.

"That's fantastic, Danny. I wish I could have been there. That has to make you feel great. Maybe you could help me with my Algebra II assignment?"

"That won't be possible this weekend because I'm taking you to the finest restaurant this side of the Mississippi."

"What are you talking about?"

I told her about my mother's birthday dinner and that my folks wanted to meet her. While my heart was doing triple beats, she took her time responding. As that little grin came to her face, both sexy and beautiful, she said, "This is like a date?"

I hadn't thought of it that way, but I said, "Yes, it's a date, like with Troy Donahue and Sandra Dee."

"And that would make you Troy Donahue?"

"Is that a problem?" I asked.

"No, I can use my imagination."

"So, does that mean you're going?" I asked.

She hesitated, and my heart climbed somewhere up in my throat.

"What if they don't like me?"

"Why wouldn't they like you? You're gorgeous, smart, funny . . ."

"Now you're making fun of me."

"I'm really not. You're all those things."

"Then why haven't you asked me out before?"

"I never asked you out because I only have our farm pickup to drive."

"Pickups are nice."

"I guess I could clean it up some."

"Cleaning it up would also be nice," she said.

"It would be our first date," I said, trying to find an argument to convince her to go.

"It would be my first-ever date."

"You're kidding."

"I'm not."

"You've never been out with anyone on a date?"

"Why does that sound so profound to you?"

"Well—" I stammered.

"I'm waiting."

"You're one of the best-looking girls in high school. You're intelligent, funny, sexy . . . You have Natalie Wood eyes."

"How can I refuse with an answer like that? Of course I'll go on Saturday night. Which restaurant is it, so I know what to wear?"

"It's the Oasis in Fairmont."

"That is fancy. We took my brother there for his graduation. I was only ten, but I remember it had white tablecloths, and I had to sit quietly and use a napkin."

"You'll have to be quiet this time too—and use a napkin."

"Look, Buster, I let you off once, but you're making it a habit."

Wendy and I walked outside into a beautiful fall day. Earlier, the sky had been overcast, but now the sun blazed, warming our skin as we walked to the bleachers, this time hand in hand. Several other couples dotted the bleachers. Maybe what Wendy and I had was contagious. We went to the very top and sat away from the others.

Wendy seemed excited and talked about the first date being special to girls, one they always remembered, like their first kiss. I thought she might think I was picking her up in the pickup, not riding with my parents. Going to a restaurant was one thing. Being trapped in a car with them was another. "Would you mind if we rode with my parents?" I asked timidly. "We could pick you up at about six."

She looked at me, that smirk coming back to her face. "You are so easy to get to." She laughed. "You're worried that when you said it was a date I thought you'd pick me up but not with your parents in the car."

"Yeah, kind of." Sometimes, it was difficult to know when Wendy was putting me on. "We can still neck in front of them. My parents are okay with that," I said. "Before I got my license, they used to take me and my date to the drive-in." Two could play this game.

"You've necked with a girl in front of your parents?"

"Sure, doesn't everyone?" I remained serious even though my chest hurt, attempting to keep from laughing.

Wendy stared at me for several long beats, then kissed me on the lips. "I'm up for it if you are."

When would I learn? The apprentice does not take on the master. We eyed each other for another few seconds, then burst into laughter. I loved the little smirk before she laughed, and I wondered again how someone with such a laugh could harbor so much hurt inside.

That night was one of the warmest we'd had in days. After supper, I wore a light jacket and walked outside with Ranger at my heels. Another cold front was approaching, and I wanted to enjoy the last summer night. Plus, I needed to be alone to think. As we approached the grove at the back of our house,

Ranger shot ahead. A rabbit darted out from under a fallen log. He sniffed around the log, then darted back, feeling very proud. Moon shadows cast the woods in a mystical light as the quiet amplified each night sound. I braced myself against a large sugar maple my grandfather had planted, its canopy bursting in brilliant reds that floated down with each breath of wind. Leaves in reds and golds lay in masses around me. Ranger lay beside me, his head gently resting on my leg.

So much had happened in such a short time. Our attorney felt confident that all charges against me would be dropped, but I felt the weight of the debt I owed Loretta hovering over me like gathering storm clouds. The darkness I felt surrounded her, too, the helplessness, the feeling of isolation and abandonment. If the next time she succeeded in killing herself, I would carry that with me all my life. I had to do something.

My mother said they had taken Loretta to the Iowa Community Mental Health Center in Mason City. It was a forty-five-minute drive, and I could easily make it there and back in one afternoon. My parents would never let me go if I asked. I would have to lie to them to take the pickup, but it was the lesser of evils. Whatever I had to do, I would do it. I couldn't walk away again.

CHAPTER 9

The Rattler was a few minutes early on Wednesday. Hank was waiting at the end of our lane, so I ran full out, panting as I climbed on board. He glanced at his pocket watch as I came up the steps. "No bad. A little over a minute."

"I had these books," I said, holding them up. "With a football, I could knock off five seconds." I laughed.

The news had circulated that charges might be dropped against me. Two football players came up and asked if it was true. It might have been just me, but it felt different. At just after three, I shoved my books into my locker, then went down the stairs to the locker room. Inside, it sounded like a jailhouse riot, locker doors slamming and echoing off the concrete walls. Everyone was talking and joking, waiting for Coach Esker.

Esker exited his office with Assistant Coach Terry Bailer following behind, and the room quieted. He instructed everyone to take the benches to his right and left. I took a seat near the end. The musty smell of the locker room brought back wonderful memories of last season. It reminded me of how much I enjoyed playing and practicing with my teammates. I remained apprehensive. I could stay in school, but would they let me play?

"Gentlemen—and I use that term loosely," Coach Esker began. The group responded with forced laughter. "You all know that the Banning Raiders have a regional title to defend, and this school, this community, and your parents have high expectations of each of us. We will measure up to those expectations and exceed them." He paused as his eyes scanned the room, stopping momentarily on each of us.

"We have some challenges ahead." The coach took a deep breath, his eyes moving above our heads, then settling back on the group. His voice strengthened. "But gentlemen, none we can't meet. I'm depending on you. Assistant Coach Bailer is depending on you, and this school is depending on each of you to bring back that regional title to Banning. And—" he paused dramatically "—what are we going to do this year?"

The group responded firmly. "Bring back the regional title!"

"That's right. And we can only do that if we all give it 100 percent and play as a team." Esker was on a roll. His eyes again wandered around the locker room. To think I had eaten this shit up a year ago. I didn't want to let the coach down, but as far as the town and this school, they could kiss my ass. I would give 100 percent on the field for myself, my parents, and to win.

"This year, all positions are open, as they are every year," Esker continued. "Don't feel that because someone played a position last year, it's not up for grabs. Everyone will give everything at practice to show that they deserve to be given a uniform. If you don't do that, you don't play. Is that understood?"

Yeah, right. Good luck with anyone beating out guys like Rodger, Dave, or Jerry. They were seniors, first string, and outweighed most anybody in the room, and if you challenged them, you'd end up in a little puddle on the field. Yet I responded, as did everyone in the locker room, with a resounding, "Yes, sir," proving I could suck up with the best of them.

Then Coach Esker brought up the challenge of the Banning Raiders playing without the great Brent Arrington, the elephant in the room that no one had mentioned until now. I received a few glances, but I wouldn't have been surprised if everyone had turned toward me and yelled, "Yeah, and everyone knows it's Prescott's fault."

At the end of the talk, Esker instructed us to line up outside his office. Everyone formed a line in front of his office to sign the practice roster and be assigned a locker. Later, when it became clear who would be on the team, the coaches would fit and assign helmets and pads. I was eighth in line. Coach Esker treated me like any other player, welcoming me back and encouraging me to do my best, then handed me a locker key. I was three lockers down from Brent's old locker, which went unassigned.

I was halfway up the steps to the main floor when Jerry Reinhart shouted my name. He was one of several who had always been at Brent's side, a faithful lackey. "You're really going to try out for the team again, huh, Prescott?"

I knew I should keep walking, but I turned back to face him. "I don't see why not. Last year, I played in several games."

"Well, no one wants you to play this year. You're an embarrassment to the team and the school."

"You're the spokesman for the team now? I must have missed that announcement."

"I speak for myself, you lying sack of shit. You're why Brent is playing for Fort Dodge and we're left with half a team." Reinhart played linebacker on defense and sometimes a tight end on offense, and he played both well. He was as tall as me and fifteen pounds heavier. I knew this would end badly if I kept mouthing off, but my mouth again overwhelmed my common sense.

"Arrington isn't here because he's a scumbag. Now I suppose you'll have to find another person's ass to kiss." I turned to leave. I had nothing to gain by continuing this hissing contest with a snake.

He came up the stairs until he was standing one step below me. "Brent said he thought you were a straight-up guy, then discovered you're a yellow, lying piece of shit. You think we don't know why you lied about him?"

"No, please do tell."

"It's because you think you'll get the halfback position. You're fed up playing second fiddle to the top running back in Iowa. If Brent was here, you knew you would never play halfback. You're not good enough to carry his jockstrap."

"Jerry, you've always been his lap dog, Brent's little puppet. He pulls the strings, and your mouth moves." I took a step up, trying to leave. This would have only one outcome, and I didn't want to wait for the conclusion.

"Hey, Prescott. Is Weird Wendy playing your skin flute now? Brent said she gives a great BJ."

I spun around to face him. My fist was already coming at his head as I turned. I caught Jerry solid in the side of the jaw. His head jerked backward, and then he swayed and went down on one knee before falling backward.

Several kids kneeled beside him at the bottom of the stairs. Reinhart's eyes rolled back, showing white as he tried to get to his feet. My breath lodged in my throat as I watched. I stepped slowly down the stairs and stood on the bottom step, watching him as his eyes regained focus. For a second, I thought he might not get up. Rodger Zimmerman and David Lockmier helped him to a sitting position against the wall. Reinhart shook his head, trying to clear his vision. A trickle of blood oozed down his chin from a split lip as he glared up at me with more surprise than anger.

"I'm sorry. I didn't mean to do that, Jerry." I sat down on the bottom step as more kids gathered around. I waited for Coach Esker to come and shorten my football season to one day. Someone handed Jerry a handkerchief to wipe the blood from his face just as Coach Esker worked his way through the group gathered around Jerry.

"What happened here?" he asked, looking at me.

"I slipped on the stairs, Coach. It was just a little horseplay with Danny." Jerry nodded toward me. "I lost my balance."

One of Jerry's sidekicks, Richard Donnelly, stammered something, and Zimmerman cut him off. "Shut up, Dick. You weren't even here." Richard looked confused but shut his mouth as commanded. Reinhart's eyes locked on me. I was as confused as Richard about why Jerry had lied. He knew that hitting another player would fry my ass. Esker would kick me off the team, and Principal Larson would kick me out of school.

"Well, stop the horseplay. Stop messing around on the stairs. People can get hurt," Esker said as he assisted Jerry in getting up.

The group moved up the stairs. As I watched from the top, Coach Esker inspected Jerry's eyes for a concussion. This was not over; Jerry Reinhart would not let me walk away from this unscathed.

I went to the assembly hall and tried to finish the chapter for Sociology II. Still, my mind kept returning to the encounter. When he had foul-mouthed Wendy, I'd lost it; I could have blown everything I was trying to accomplish. I would have let my folks down and let myself down. My father had told me not to react, and I had. This was not the first time I'd heard a similar remark about Wendy, but I hadn't known her then. Now, I knew how mean and untrue those words were.

I went back to the assembly hall and sat at my desk. As some football players filtered in, they shot me unfriendly glances. Most didn't know precisely what had happened on the stairs. I was thankful Wendy wasn't in the assembly hall—she had a creative writing class that period.

Neither Jerry nor his buddy Paul were around. That bothered me. Jerry was probably waiting until after school to administer my ass-kicking. When several other players didn't show, I wondered if the entire first string might form up for a payback for what they thought I'd done to Brent. It was a half hour till the four-o'clock dismissal bell. Time for a lot of things to happen.

I considered my alternatives. Running like hell was not an option, however desirable. They knew I had to take the bus, and even if I could make it onto the bus, it would just delay the inevitable. It would be better to get it over with and out of the way. After all, they wouldn't kill me. I had taken a good ass-kicking before and survived. I didn't look forward to nursing a bruised body, but being called a chickenshit was no great shakes either.

The ending bell rang, and on cue, desktops slammed shut, followed by a general uproar as everyone filed out of the building. I picked up my chemistry book and a Hemingway novel and headed down the stairs to wait for the Rattler. Outside, several players gathered around the bike stand next to the buses. Sometimes, being paranoid had its advantages. I stopped just inside the doors. The Rattler wasn't there yet, and the run-like-hell option looked much better. I opened the door and walked out, stopping near where the group of players had formed. Rodger Zimmerman, Dave Lockmier, Jerry Reinhart, Richard Donnelly, and several other players stood in a semicircle. I was surprised to see Rodger there. He was a senior, one of our best players, and along with Brent, a team captain. I thought he would stay neutral, and he had stopped Richard from ratting me out to Coach Esker. He motioned me closer.

I hesitated, although I saw no other way out. A hopeless feeling came over me, not because I was about to get my ass handed to me in front of everybody but because these guys had been my friends, my teammates. I had grown up with them and liked every one of the boys who stood around the bike stand. The Yellow Rattler still hadn't shown. I waited to see who would step forward—I was sure it would be Jerry. He stood off to the right, glaring at me. I walked over to where he stood. His jaw had turned dark orangish, and his lower lip had swelled to twice to its normal size.

"Why did you cover for me?" I asked.

"I didn't do it for you, Prescott. If Coach Esker knew what happened, he'd probably suspend both of us. Don't think this gives you a pass with me."

"Just the same, I'm sorry. Thanks for not telling Esker." No one else said anything, but I knew this couldn't be all that was coming. I heard the Yellow Rattler's brakes squeal to a stop behind me. It was time to make an ungraceful exit, so I turned to leave.

"Jerry wasn't through. He's got something else to say," Rodger interjected. His eyes bored in on Jerry.

Jerry swallowed hard; his tongue ran over his swollen lip. "I'm sorry about what I said about Warner. It was out of line, but—"

Rodger stepped in front of him. "That's all he wanted to say, Prescott. Your ride is here. See you at practice tomorrow."

I got on the bus even more confused, thinking maybe I had just entered the Twilight Zone. Jerry Reinhart had apologized to me for giving him a swat to the head. There was something wrong with this picture, but whatever was going on was far better than getting pounded into the ground like a fence post. Rodger was behind this, but I didn't understand why. I thought he was Brent's friend, and I had never been real buddies with him. He was friendly to me, but so were most of the guys on the team, before all this.

As I entered the yard, my mother was digging up her tulip bulbs for winter storage. A jagged row of dirt lay along the side fence that separated our front yard from the farm. She stored the bulbs in the basement for replanting next spring. Ranger hadn't met me on the lane as usual, electing to dig in the dirt with my mother. He quit digging long enough to greet me now, though, jumping up for a pet and putting a smear of dirt on my jeans.

She grinned at Ranger. "He's been a big help."

"Then tell him to clean my jeans."

"Just throw them in the hamper. I was going to wash a few things anyway. Did everything go okay at school today?"

"I signed up for football. If they let me play, I have a good chance of making the starting squad."

Last year, I'd run a few plays and had several good runs, averaging six yards per carry—though nowhere near Brent's hundred yards a game. Esker used me more to take the heat off of Brent when they double-teamed him. I realized it was easier running when they had to key in on him. Brent was our superstar, so I had little opportunity to show how good I was. I accepted I wasn't as good as him, but only a few players in the state could match his running.

The rest of the week was a breeze compared to Wednesday. At football practice, we ran laps, did wind sprints, and tried to get in shape for regular practice beginning Monday. The coaches didn't mention the dustup with Jerry Reinhart, but most of my teammates now knew what had occurred. I suspected even Coach Esker was aware of the facts.

Thursday and Friday, Wendy and I strolled around town after lunch. I found it easy to be with her on those walks. We talked about everything and nothing. She was funny, intelligent, and easy to talk to about anything. She told me about her childhood and her parents' protective nature. She hadn't told them about the assault because she was afraid of what her father might do and how they might look at her. Her mother sensed something terrible had happened that year, but Wendy denied it. It was just something she wanted to forget, and now this with Loretta had brought it all back.

We talked about her birth mother too. Her parents had told her before she started school, knowing someone else would if they didn't. I didn't mention that my mother had been friends with her or that I knew anything about how her birth father had left. If she wanted me to know those things, she would tell me. Yet, it seemed to me that knowing and not telling her in itself was a lie.

CHAPTER 10

Saturday afternoon was a hustle to get chores done early so everyone would have time to get cleaned up and dressed for dinner. It was challenging, with one bathroom and four people attempting to leave simultaneously. My mother had showered earlier to conserve the hot water for our three quick showers. Surprisingly, Jim stepped aside and allowed me to go after my father.

I imagined all kinds of disasters happening that night. Images of my dad making stupid jokes as Wendy forced laughter, my mother quizzing her about her adoption. By late afternoon, butterflies were doing the mambo in my stomach. I wished I had kept my mouth shut and gone to the restaurant with my parents. Wendy would have to like me a lot to survive this night. I snickered, thinking about my mother's face if Wendy walked out in one of her hootenanny outfits or wore her hair gathered in a bun like an old matron. I had enough experience with girls to know you did not tell them how to dress. It didn't matter to me. Wendy was Wendy, but it might surprise my parents if she came out dressed like a 1930s flapper. It would be a birthday my mother would remember for a while.

As we scurried around getting ready, my mother continually remarked about what a great evening it would be and how much she looked forward to meeting Wendy. She was far more excited about meeting Wendy than the dinner, it seemed. Dad chuckled at all the commotion, but I noticed how he shaved close and used a ton of cologne along with the Old Spice aftershave. I hoped the heater in the car might dull the scent by the time we picked her up.

At just after six, we climbed into the Pontiac. My mother wore the pretty red dress she'd bought last year for my cousin Ellen's wedding. She seldom dressed up, although I think she enjoyed it when she did. She looked elegant with her hair done, and I told her so. My father wore his only suit, which he called his funeral suit because he never planned to buy another one. They'd reduced the size of the lapels since he purchased the suit, but I doubted if he knew or gave diddly squat about it. Fashion wasn't high on my father's list of essential things, but he still looked sharp in his white shirt and tie.

As we drove to Banning, I could've sworn someone had jammed steel bars up our butts. I was also in my only suit, shoulders pressed back against the seat, sitting ramrod straight. It was hard to explain, but there was something about putting farm people in suits that caused their backs to straighten and their shoulders to pull back. Dad said he looked like a man ready for his coffin. Now I understood why they referred to a corpse as a stiff. It wasn't rigor mortis but the suit.

We parked along the curb in front of Wendy's house at about six thirty. A large pair of elm trees guarded a well-kept lawn in front of their two-story white clapboard house. A long porch stretched across most of it. I had never been inside her house and worried this would be the night she introduced me to her parents. Meeting a girl's parents ranks up there with being chased through a graveyard by zombies. I stood in front of the screen door for a second, taking a deep breath, hoping her dad wouldn't answer. My hand had hardly touched the doorbell when Wendy opened the door.

"Don't we look sharp, Mr. Prescott?"

She took my breath away. This girl was not Weird Wendy. No sloppy sweater, no baggy slacks, and her wild hairstyles were gone. Poof. Standing in for her was a gorgeous girl in a pale blue sweater over a beige knee-length skirt stressing curves that, until now, I'd never known she had. Her hair, which had reached past her shoulders, was cut short in a pixie style, framing her face tightly and highlighting her large dark eyes. I could only stare in wonderment.

She looked disappointed. "You don't like it. I told my mom—"

"Wendy, Wendy," I cut in. "You're gorgeous. I love your hair that way."

"Are you being sincere, Danny? Don't feel you have to compliment me. If—"

"I don't have to make things up. I always thought you were pretty, but tonight, you're beautiful."

"You said exactly the right thing, Prescott. My mom talked me into it. She used to work at a salon in Des Moines," Wendy said as she twirled around once, giving me the full impact of her new look. She pushed her arm through mine and closed the door behind us. I breathed a tremendous sigh at not having to meet her dad.

As I walked Wendy to the car, my mother's face appeared plastered on the Bonneville's side window. I opened the door for Wendy, went around the other side, and got in. My mother and Wendy were already talking as I scooted into the back seat. Later, my mom would claim my feet weren't touching the ground as I walked beside her.

"I love your hair, Wendy," my mother said. Her arm was on the seat as she turned toward us. I prayed she didn't do that all the way to the restaurant.

"Thank you, Mrs. Prescott," Wendy said shyly.

"Oh, call me Linda. Danny tells me you're a senior. Do you plan to go on to college?"

I whispered to myself, "Please spare her the interrogation."

Wendy hesitated, then said, "I haven't decided what I want to do. I may attend a two-year college in Mason City, but I'm unsure. I'd rather start at a full four-year college like Drake or the University of Iowa."

"Well, you have plenty of time. How are your parents?"

"They're fine. Mom's doing some canning from our garden. My dad's not hot on canned peas and stuff. He'd rather have them right out of the garden."

"Oh, I'm the same way. Raymond and Danny prefer the garden over the store-bought, but I like my canned veggies better than what Piggly Wiggly sells."

I hoped Wendy didn't see me cringe. My mom always called my dad Ray, but now it was Raymond. Next I'd be Daniel. *Someone just shoot me and end my misery.*

"I understand the Ralston Purina plant is running an additional shift. Is your dad putting in much overtime now?" my dad asked.

Oh, great. Now my dad was adding to it. *Lord, if they stop talking, I'll be good for the rest of my life.*

"He comes home late most nights, but recently, he was promoted to a manager, so we're hoping that after a while, he can reduce his hours," Wendy said.

"Well, give him my congratulations. That's great for him."

My dad didn't know her father, maybe wouldn't even recognize him if he passed him on the street, but now he was congratulating him? Oh God, when were we going to get there?

"I will," Wendy said.

Thankfully, that was the extent of it. My mother turned back to face the front and said something to my father. Wendy and I whispered in the back. My dad asked if we'd like some music, and we both answered yes in unison. He lowered the volume and pushed a button for a station playing something from the early fifties. I hoped it would keep my mother from hearing every word we said in the back seat. Wendy took my hand, giving it a little squeeze. We exchanged grins as if we had just pulled off a major coup.

I could not get over the way Wendy looked. She was beautiful, a cross between Elizabeth Taylor and Natalie Wood. Wendy had been concealing her knockout figure with all those unflattering clothes. I wondered, not for the first time, what she saw in me.

Dad parked away from other cars in the restaurant lot, making us walk from the very end corner of the lot. I asked him if a bus would pick us up. He said he didn't want to park where people could smack their door into ours and chip the paint. I took Wendy's hand as we followed my parents but dropped it when we neared the door. No use risking my mother turning and saying, "Look, Raymond, the kids are holding hands. Isn't that just the sweetest thing?"

As we neared the Oasis entrance, a man dressed in a black suit opened the large wooden doors for us. Heavy velvet curtains adorned the windows that overlooked the parking lot. A large oil painting that I guessed to be Paris in the early 1900s covered one wall in the foyer. Dark wood paneling covered the others. Overhead, crystal chandeliers added a dim glow to the interior.

The maître d' escorted two couples ahead of us to a booth along the wall before seating us in the center of the room. It was one of the worst tables in the restaurant. Still, my father said nothing, even though several booths were vacant along the wall, which would've given us more privacy. I felt like a spotlight was on us. My father saw me looking at the other tables and booths.

"Probably reserved," he said.

"Mom called for a reservation, didn't she?" I asked. Then I gritted my teeth. Who was I to be complaining about where we sat? I'd hardly been to a restaurant other than Mike's Café.

Before I could say something to redeem myself, a waiter interrupted us by pouring water into our glasses. My mother sat with her back rigid, not touching the back of the chair. She looked uncomfortable, as did my father. I noticed Wendy sitting the same way. I straightened up like a soldier waiting for his orders. We all had our hands cupped in our laps, speaking in hushed tones as if we were in church, not celebrating a birthday. I wished again that I'd never brought Wendy here. I wanted to impress her, but this was phony. This was not who we were. Wendy must have thought we were all jerks. I wanted the evening to end.

My mother turned to her and said something inane as the waiter returned. He handed us each a leather-covered menu three times the size of an encyclopedia and stood watching us as if we would steal it. There were things on the menu I couldn't even pronounce, much less know what they were, and most cost more than my entire month's allowance. I caught my mother's eye and gave a shrug. She glanced at Wendy and said, "Would you kids rather go to another type of restaurant?"

"Oh yes," I blurted out.

Wendy nodded her head in agreement.

"Ray?"

"Up to you. It's your birthday. What would you two kids like to eat?"

I looked at Wendy, and she grinned back at me. "Pizza," she said.

My father got up, folded his napkin, and placed it on his plate. "Pizza it is, then."

My mother laughed, got up, and followed Wendy and me toward the door. She was laughing as much at herself as at the situation. She would have referred to the whole shebang as "putting on airs" had it been anyone else. On the way out, the waiter rushed up, asking if something was wrong. My father answered that there was not but that something had come up, and we had to leave. The waiter turned, giving us a "harrumph" as we left.

My mother said, "Do we think we should have tipped him?"

"For what?" my dad said. "He didn't do anything."

As we got to the car, he asked if we knew a pizza restaurant nearby. Wendy and I said in unison, "Tony's Pizzeria."

"It's on State Street, just off the main," I added. I had been there twice with Steve and loved pizza from the very first piece. In Tony's, it was called pizza pie. I liked cheese and hamburger but would eat anything Tony put on it. The tomato sauce was spicy, and the mozzarella was thick.

When we got there, we quickly found a seat. My father joked it was his kind of place when he noticed the waiter had tomato stains on his apron. "Must have been the maître d's night off," he remarked as the waiter left. Wendy thought it was funny, and I laughed too.

Tony's was not a quiet place. It was one large room with red-and-white oil-clothed tables scattered randomly around a terrazzo floor. The concrete block walls displayed posters of Italy and movie stars. Our voices competed with the low roar coming from a dozen other tables. Wendy thought my father was funny and my mother charming. I agreed 100 percent. We ordered a second round of Cokes and thick chocolate brownies to top off the night. It was a grand birthday celebration—and the night I officially fell in love with Wendy Warner.

On the way back, we convinced my dad to play our favorite DJ station from Chicago. We listened to Elvis, the Everly Brothers, and Brenda Lee. Wendy laid her head against my shoulder, her eyes closed, listening to the music. On the way back, we barely spoke. It was enough to be together, holding her hand, her body next to me. It was a feeling I'd never had before, and I didn't want it to end. My father turned off the highway onto the blacktop toward our farm when we were about eighteen miles from Banning. I was about to remind him we had to take Wendy home when he said, "It's been a big night. You don't mind driving Wendy home, do you, Danny?"

"No, sir, not at all."

I would have jumped up front and kissed him if my seat belt hadn't been on. At home, my parents told Wendy how much they enjoyed meeting her, and she thanked them for the pizza and the fun night. At ten thirty, I parked the Pontiac next to Wendy's house. The lights were on in their living room, and I could see the TV's reflection in the big bay window that faced the street.

"I had a great time tonight. I think your parents are super, Danny." She slid closer to me, her body molded against mine, her hair lying softly against my neck.

"My parents adore you. If you break up with me, they'll probably disown me."

"Do you think there's a chance of that?" Wendy asked.

"If you were smart, you would."

"Would I now. Why is that?"

"You think I'm stupid enough to explain why you're too good for me? Not a chance. You're going to have to figure that out for yourself," I said.

"I just saw my dad look out the window, so I better get inside. I had a great time tonight."

When I walked her to her door, she kissed me lightly, pressing her body against mine. I felt like yelling and laughing and doing backflips all at the same time. I returned to the car, thoughts of Wendy still filling my head. As I opened the car door, a hand grabbed my shoulder and spun me around. A fist, feeling like a sledgehammer, slammed into my chest. All the air burst from my lungs. My knees folded as I gasped, trying to get my breath. A second blow struck me hard in the ribs, sending me to the ground. Another blow caught me in the side of my head, and I crumbled onto the pavement alongside the car. I struggled up onto my hands, but a knee slammed into the middle of my back and forced me back onto the pavement, face down.

"You are a slow learner, Prescott, so I'm giving you another lesson. I tried to be reasonable with you. We could have been friends, but you had to go spill your guts to the sheriff. I can't let you screw my life up. Now, you can correct this by just saying that nothing happened. The little bitch just wants to get back at me."

Brent grabbed my hair and forced my face into the concrete. "I'm not asking you to lie. They'll dismiss the charges against me if she can't make the trial and you don't testify. This is good for both of us. I don't want to hurt you, but I want to play pro ball, and right now, those two are in conflict." He hammered a fist into my left side, sending a bolt of pain pulsating through my body. I moaned and tried to draw in a lungful of air. "What do you say, Danny? Are we a team now?"

"I hear you," I moaned. Brent's weight shifted off me. I rolled onto my side, and he slammed his boot into my stomach, sending pizza and Coke spewing from my mouth and onto the street.

"Shit, you fucking creep," Brent said, attempting to kick the vomit off his boots. He leaned down inches from my face. "You heard what I said, Prescott. Next time, I'll kill you."

I lay on the ground next to the car for several minutes until my head cleared and I could sit up. I did my best to dust off my clothes. My suit had traces of vomit, but it wasn't torn. At least I could be thankful for that. I slipped behind the steering wheel as the lights went off in the Warners' living room. I left the radio off as I drove home. There was no music in the world that I wanted to hear. I imagined several ways I could kill Brent Arrington. Still, none was painful or brutal enough to satisfy the rage that burned in my guts. I had lain there like a baby while he beat on me. There was no pride left in me. He had beat that out of me too.

Running to the sheriff was no good. Brent would lie his way out of it—say I started it or deny it was him. All the gossip would start up again, and maybe more lawyer expenses. Brent might even be more of a hero around the school. A hero defends his good name or when attacked, defends his honor. Brent could twist the truth 180 degrees. It wasn't worth it, and it wouldn't change the bruises and cuts on my face.

The house was quiet. I softly shut the bathroom door to make as little noise as possible. I was too tired to explain how I looked. I took off my suit. It had only one small tear on the elbow that my mom could repair. My only dress shoes had severe scuff marks, but I hoped to remedy that with shoe polish and some hard rubbing. My face was another matter. The left side looked as bad as it felt. I had done most of the damage myself as I tried to get up and he forced my face back into the gravel.

The deeper cuts were red and raw, with bits of gravel and debris embedded in them. I used a tweezer to pick out the debris. There were jagged scratches above my eye and along the side of my face, running to my chin. A tiny wedge of flesh stuck up from the top of my ear, which I cut off with a toenail clipper. The swelling was already closing my left eye, but what worried me more was explaining why I looked this way. I discovered a new threshold of pain as I used a cotton ball and alcohol to sterilize the scratches and cuts. I waited a couple of minutes for the blood to clot. A bandage would make it seem worse and do little more than prevent the injuries from healing faster. I took a hand towel to lay on my pillow in case the cuts bled during the night. I took off my shoes and carried them up the stairs. Each step seemed to creak louder than it ever had before. I hung my suit in the corner and hoped my mother wouldn't notice the dirt until I brushed and cleaned it. As I fell asleep, I counted all the painful ways that I could end Brent's life.

At just after six, my brother pounded down the stairs—the only person in the house with lead boots. I slipped my legs over the side of the bed, holding my head in my hands. Even the slightest movement was painful. I felt like I'd been run through our hammer mill. I got up and studied myself in the dresser mirror. A purple bruise covered the middle of my chest, and another went down my left side, extending from my hip to my armpit. The left side of my face was a mass of scratches and minor cuts, and it had turned a yellowish-black color. There was no way I could hide the injuries on my face.

As I entered the kitchen, where Jim and my father were sitting, Jim asked. "What hit you? A semi?"

"Did you have an accident?" My dad was more worried about the car than me.

Jim stared at me as he laced up his boots. "I think the girl did it. He probably asked her for another date."

"Jim, that's not helpful. You can see your brother's hurt."

"Yeah, I'm hurt, dumbass. Dad, the car is fine," I said, trying to turn my face away from the light. *I tripped walking down the sidewalk* flashed into my mind. That was about as plausible as a carload of thugs trying to steal the car but me fighting them off. The only thing available to me was the truth, maybe with a bit of window dressing.

"Brent was waiting for me when I dropped off Wendy. He doesn't want me to testify. We got into it."

"Brent did this to you?" my father asked. He gripped my jaw, forcing my face to turn into the light, inspecting the jagged cut that ran from below my eye to the corner of my lip. "I'll see that little bastard in jail—and his father too."

"No, Dad. I don't want that."

"Why, for God's sake? You're not afraid of him, are you?"

"No, it's not that. Things are getting better at school. Getting the sheriff involved will make things worse. He's probably back in Fort Dodge right now anyway. It will only stir everything up again, and Brent will deny it or lie and say I started it."

"He's probably right," Jim said. "They've won the PR battle so far. Maybe I should visit the little slimeball the next time he's in town—maybe take the cattle prod with me."

"I don't want you getting involved in this. The Kesslers would not be happy to see your name added to the list."

"Please, just let it go, Dad. Maybe this will be the end of it."

We all knew that wasn't true, but we also wanted this to end. Feeding the flames with more gasoline would not put out the fire.

"All right, Danny, but if he as much as spits in your direction, I'll drag the little bastard down to the sheriff myself." My father rose from the table. "Let's get at it. We've got chores to do. Are you okay to work, Danny?"

"He doesn't have to feed the cattle with his face," Jim said, walking past me.

I was with my brother on this one. I would rather do chores than explain why my face looked like a hamburger patty to my mother. That could wait until later, when I could put a better story together. She had a way of getting the truth out of me. It wasn't right to lie to my parents, but sometimes, little lies were necessary to do the right thing, and bringing more problems into our home didn't seem right. I needed time to work this out myself.

Jim climbed up and into the silo and threw down the silage as I filled the bunks. I couldn't have made it ten feet up that ladder this morning. Jim said nothing; he just climbed the ladder like it was his job. I was filling the last bunk when he climbed down. He stood leaning against his shovel. "Are you going to help fill the last bunk, or is that shovel stuck in the concrete?" I said, taking another shovel full of silage.

"You're hurt worse than you're letting on. He must have really beat on you. Every time you shove that scoop in, you wince."

There was no use trying to hide this from Jim. "He did a real job on me. If Dad knew how bad, he may have gone ballistic. I don't think he meant to screw up my face. I did that trying to get up. He meant to hit where it wouldn't show."

"You can't just let him walk away after doing this."

"I'll handle it."

"You'll handle it, little brother? How?"

"I don't know. I'll figure it out."

"Here's an even better idea. You and I will find him, and I'll talk with Brent Arrington."

"What good will that do? He'll laugh in our face."

"Not if I have a baseball bat and you have a cattle prod."

My brother was serious, but that wasn't going to happen. We'd both wind up behind bars. However, the cattle prod, well, that might be an alternative for me.

"You know, little brother, you don't have to testify against him if you don't want to."

"What would you do, Jim?"

"This isn't about me. This is about you. I don't want anything to happen to you. You're not much, but you're my only brother, and Mom's too old to have another kid."

"You'd testify, and so would Dad. I couldn't face any of you if I turned tail and ran. Deep down in your black heart, I know you like me."

"Okay, we'll give him a pass this time, but if that son of a bitch as much as dials our number, we get the cattle prod and bat."

"Deal," I said.

CHAPTER 11

By Monday morning, the swelling was down, but the dark bruising and scratches looked like I'd placed the side of my face against a grinding wheel. I'd made several decisions as I lay studying the cracks in the ceiling in my room. I had to take control of what was happening. Hoping everything would have a fairy-tale ending was not working for me. I was an outcast at school, my brother wanted to bounce a baseball bat off Brent's head, and a girl I should have protected had tried to kill herself.

In junior high, we had all been friends and were pretty much the same. Why was it so difficult now? Why was my life so complex? In junior high, riding the Rattler was a joy and a time to spend with friends, joke, and laugh. I remembered Loretta giggling if I winked at her or told her she looked pretty. That was the same Loretta who had walked with us toward the barn that Sunday, laughing and smiling as she had on that bus. Hers was an innocent, sweet laugh, and that Sunday had changed everything.

I had to see Loretta. Other than that, I didn't have a plan. Whatever they were doing for her wasn't working. After that, I'd face Brent. One thing was for sure: he'd never beat me like that again; next time, he wouldn't walk away unscathed. I was certain of that.

I boarded the Yellow Rattler with half a face but determined to see this thing through, whatever the outcome. The glances I received on the bus didn't bother me. They were curious rather than condescending and malicious. I'd settle for that. This may have been how Quasimodo felt; the thought made me smile, which puzzled the two freshmen girls sitting across from me. I gave them a wink, and they turned their attention back to the window.

There were curious looks during morning assembly, but I hardly noticed them anymore as I attended class or studied at my desk. Wendy stopped me in the hall. She'd missed assembly and was hurrying to her next class. She touched the side of my face and asked what had happened. I begged off an explanation and told her I'd meet her for lunch. We needed to be alone when I told her about Brent.

After History class, I went to the library. I found the Methodist Mental Health Center address in a listing of psychiatric facilities in the Midwest. They described the health center as a moderate psychiatric care facility. The photo showed a large building behind a large expanse of lawn. There were no fences or guards. I had been to Mason City a handful of times with my parents. I knew where the principal streets were and how to get there. I found an old service station map in our car's glove compartment. It showed only the main streets in Mason City, but luckily the center was on one. What I was about to do could make everything worse, but it was a gamble I had to take—both for Loretta and myself.

Steve met me as I was coming out of the library. "Dude, what happened to your face? It looks like someone beat you with an ugly stick."

"Thanks, Steve. Way to go, raising a buddy's self-esteem."

"No, I mean . . . what happened, man? That's not a case of acne."

"Come here, loudmouth." I hustled Steve over to a corner of the hall.

"Brent jumped me as I was leaving Wendy's Saturday night. I never saw him coming. He knocked me down and then ground my face into the road."

"Are you going to turn him in?"

"Why is that the first thing anyone asks? No, it would be his word against mine. He might even say I started the fight. My luck with that hasn't been sterling. They would probably arrest me."

"There's a rumor he's coming back," Steve said. "Matt said he saw him in town on Sunday. I heard that he's not the big star in Fort Dodge like he is here. He has to share the stage with another running back that's as good as he is, so he wants to come back here where he's King Kong."

"Who told you that?"

"I heard it around."

"Steve." I stared him down.

"My dad knows someone on the school board. Brent's dad has asked the school board to reinstate Brent so he can play football this season."

"It's bullshit," I said, but it all sounded true.

"Maybe," Steve replied. "I've got to run to shop class. I'll call you tonight. Maybe we can do something this weekend."

"Hey, before you leave, do you still have that combat knife with the push-bottom blade? The one you bought at the army surplus store in Des Moines."

"It's at home. Why?"

"Do you want to sell it?"

"No, man. You can have it. I don't know why I even bought it."

It was an hour until lunch, but my hunger level and my mood had dropped to about minus ten. It couldn't be true. Brent was practicing with the Fort Dodge team—how could they allow him to come back here? There had to be some rule preventing him from playing for Banning, and he would never return if he couldn't play football.

I finished a math assignment in the assembly hall and headed to the cafeteria. That Monday, they served fried chicken with mashed potatoes, peas, and something resembling a piece of bread with a cherry. Wendy was waiting in our spot, but she wasn't sitting alone. Jessie Phillips and Tim Westbrook sat across from her. Both were trying out for the football team. I had hung out with them last year, but they'd been avoiding me like everyone else. I put my tray next to Wendy's and sat down. She wore a dark blue pleated skirt with a blue-and-yellow-striped blouse. Her hair was in the same stylish bob that she'd worn on Saturday night. She looked gorgeous. Weird Wendy no longer existed.

"Whoa, what happened to the face?" Jessie asked.

I touched the undamaged side of my face. "What, do I have a pimple?" I said sarcastically.

"No, man, the other side of your face is all scratched up," Tim said.

"He knows. Don't be an idiot," said Jessie.

"What brings you gentlemen to the land of outcasts?" I asked. Wendy nudged me in the side, sending a stabbing pain rippling through my body, and then she gave me an odd look.

"Wendy's in our art appreciation class. We were talking about the assignment Mr. Reynolds gave us," Jessie said.

"And you're here appreciating art? I assumed you'd be more interested in porn."

"I don't look at porn," he said sheepishly.

Wendy nudged me in the ribs again as I elaborated on Jessie's centerfold art collection, and the pain in my side cut short any further discussion.

"I'll jot down those artists I told you about and give them to you next period," Wendy said.

I peeled off a piece of chicken with my fork and shoved it into my mouth, my eyes never leaving the two invaders.

"We're going to head out. Thanks for the help on the assignment, Wendy. See you in class."

She waited until they were clear, then turned to me. Her eyes blazed with something other than compassion.

"What happened to your face?"

"I don't want to talk about it."

"You don't want to talk about it." Wendy picked up her tray and left.

I took a deep breath, wondering what had just happened. Why was she so pissed that I wasn't thrilled to see two guys jamming chicken in their mouths as they ogled her? What had I done that was so bad? This was our table and our time, not the art appreciation hour. The chicken was greasy, and the mashed potatoes were cold. What else could go to shit on me? I scraped what remained of my meal in the garbage, stacked the tray, and went to find Wendy. After checking some of her haunts, I saw her on the bleachers. The sun was out, but a frigid chill was in the air. Wendy was sitting near the top, her hands stuffed into her jacket. I went to where she sat but stopped two steps down from her so we were at eye level.

"Are you mad about something?"

"What would I be mad about?" Wendy said in an angry tone.

"That's what I asked."

"We can do this all day, but it's boring," Wendy said, her eyes looking past me.

This was the first time I had seen this side of her. "I'm sorry I said that when you asked about my face."

Wendy continued to look past me as if she hadn't heard.

"I may have reacted badly in the lunchroom," I said.

No response.

That removed any doubt in my mind as to whether or not Wendy was super pissed. I tried to explain why I had reacted the way I had, while trying to understand it myself. "That's our place, Wendy, yours and mine. With you, it became my sanctuary. To me, it's almost a sacred place. It was the place where I came back from the bottom because of you. It made me angry that they were there. They looked like they were coming on to you. I'm sorry."

Seconds ticked by, and Wendy still said nothing. I was on the verge of panic. Had Weird Wendy been replaced by a cheerleader with a pixie cut and new clothes? If she no longer wanted me around, then Brent's threat to kill me was meaningless. I would pay him to do it.

Her eyes linked with mine. I knew the look. She was tired of wading through my bullshit. I took another shot. "Okay, I was jealous. You're smart, beautiful, and funny, and I don't know why you even like me. I'm afraid you'll realize that and not want to see me anymore. I wake up each morning and can't wait to see you. Lunch is the high point of my day only because I'll be with you. And then I walk in, and you're sitting there looking like a fashion model with those guys drooling all over the table."

"They weren't drooling on the table," Wendy said.

"That's not the way I recall it."

"Let's skip that for now. What happened to your face?"

"Can I sit down?"

"It's a free country."

"You're not going to make this easy, are you?" I sat next to her. "Okay, let me have it. What do you hate about me, and what must I do to make you like me again?"

"How long has it been since someone sat with me at lunch?"

"There was Mark Farrow," I said.

"Mark was a new kid. He didn't know the rules," Wendy answered.

"Me."

"You don't count, and don't be an asshole. Since you're clueless, I'll tell you. It's been like, never, and today, two classmates are sitting there, two guys that you know, and you do your best to show them they're not welcome. Then, when I ask you about your face, you blow me off like I'm nothing after what I confided about Brent. You have the gall to say, 'I don't want to talk about it.'"

"When you put it that way, I'm a real asshole. I'm sorry. Can we start over and act like I just came into the lunchroom?"

"What happened to your face?"

"It was Brent. He was waiting down the street from your house. Somehow, he knew I'd be there. He jumped me as I was getting into the car. He did a proper job on me. Besides the facelift, he did a pitty-pat on my chest and ribs. I can hardly raise my left arm. It was to persuade me not to testify at the hearing." I figured I might as well tell her everything. "He said next time he'd kill me."

She scooted closer to me. Her eyes gave affirmation that everything was going to be okay. "What did you tell your parents when they saw your face?"

"I had to tell them the truth. What else could I say?"

"Did they call the sheriff?"

"I asked them not to. It would make everything worse. Brent would lie, and even if the sheriff believed me, would everyone else? Brent could say I jumped him and he fought back, and then everyone would choose a side. I don't want to go through that again. I want it all to end, to be like it was. It feels like I'm walking against a windstorm."

"You're going to let Brent get away with this?"

"You, more than anyone, should know how I feel. I tell my side, and Brent would lie and people would choose sides. We've both seen that play and know how it ends. I not going to let him get away with it. Next time, I'll be ready; he won't walk away next time."

"Danny, you're scaring me. I don't want anything to happen to you, and I don't want you to do anything stupid."

"Nothing is going to happen to me. The stupid part, well, we'll see, but I can't sit back and hope everything will improve. Hope isn't working any better for me than it did Loretta. I'm going to drive to Mason City and see her tomorrow. I don't know if it will help, but I have to try."

"Don't go, Danny. I know you want to help her, but it could ruin everything. They might even put you in jail for violating the terms of your bail."

"What if she tries again, and this time succeeds? What then?"

"I don't know, but I know what will happen if it blows up on you."

I kissed her lightly on the cheek. "I've got to do this, Wendy. Are we okay with the jealousy thing?"

"You've got to promise never to piss me off again."

"I'll make it a priority," I said.

"Close enough," she said, kissing me on the lips.

We'd drawn an audience of three sophomore girls below the bleachers.

"It's okay. We're cousins," Wendy shouted, followed by an exaggerated wave.

They laughed and waved back.

Weird Wendy was still with me, albeit more beautiful. I could live with that.

CHAPTER 12

At supper, I asked my dad if he was using the pickup tomorrow.

"I'd like to drive to school tomorrow. Football practice may run late, and the coach wants to review the new plays."

"I thought Steve usually drove to school. Isn't he playing football this year?"

"It's only the offense line that the coach wants to stay late," I lied. I didn't like it, but I was getting better at lying. I could see no other way. My parents wouldn't let me leave the house if I told the truth.

"You can take the pickup. If something comes up, we have the car."

On Tuesday morning, with the illegitimate sanction of my parents, I left for Mason City with the map unfolded on the seat beside me. I went through Banning, then turned off the blacktop onto Highway 65, which would take me through Hampton and on to Mason City. My driving was reminiscent of an old woman's heading to church—I kept at or below the limit. I didn't want to take a chance of being stopped. I noted the streets I'd jotted down earlier as I entered Mason City.

Mason City was not Banning, Iowa, but it wasn't New York City either.

To a farm boy, anything with over two traffic lights was intimidating. My slow, tentative driving solicited horn blasts several times from cars behind me. One kind gentleman in a gray Lincoln gave me a third-finger salute and mouthed a term I was familiar with and often used. I turned on Third Avenue, which became Templeton Boulevard and ran by the Health Center. Five blocks down Templeton, I spotted a large bronze plaque in a high brick wall announcing the Methodist Mental Health Center. The hospital occupied the entire block. In the middle were two large wrought-iron gates. On the other side, stone pavers led to a series of three-story brick buildings. In the center building, windows flowed along its entire length, divided in the middle by large glass entry doors.

A parklike lawn stretched across the front of the buildings to the street. Maples, ash, and elms dotted the expansive manicured lawn. About a dozen people sat or strolled casually among the trees and shrubs. A couple sat on the grass close to where I stood. A white-capped nurse pushed a wheelchair beneath one of the larger trees, left her patient, and returned inside. Loretta was not in the yard. I would have to go inside to find her. The hospital was larger than I'd pictured. I gambled that the middle structure was the main building. I'd read a novel where the main character walked confidently by security, acting as if he belonged and had a right to be there. It worked for him. With no other plan, it was all I could come up with. The glass doors opened automatically as I approached. Inside was a long, elevated reception desk with two people answering the phone and typing. I approached the one who looked the busiest and stood waiting. After several minutes, she replaced the receiver and looked at me.

"I'm here to see Loretta Tinsley."

The receptionist flipped open a binder, scanned down a column of names using her index finger, and then looked at me again. "Your name?"

"Ah . . ." I thought all I'd have to do was ask for Loretta's room number. "Danny."

"Danny Tinsley?" she asked.

"No, it's Prescott," I replied. "My aunt was a Tinsley."

She glanced back at the binder. "You're not on the list, Mr. Prescott."

"Are you sure? I'm her cousin. I've driven all the way from college to see her."

"Her parents were here yesterday. They said nothing about a cousin visiting."

"They probably forgot. I was delayed when I was supposed to meet Uncle Evert and Aunt Ester here yesterday."

"Her parents come every day. You could wait in the guest waiting area. They're usually here by noon."

"It's important that I see my cousin. I've got a long drive back. I can't wait for them. Her doctor said that it was vital that I see her. We're very close."

"She's the girl who cut her wrists?" she asked.

I didn't know if it was a statement or a question. "Yes, she's been through a challenging ordeal."

The receptionist looked around for help, then glanced at the list again. "You said your name is Danny?"

"Yes, Danny Prescott."

"Okay. You can go up, Danny. Make sure your uncle adds you to the list. You know, you look young to be in college."

"I get that a lot from my professors."

"It's room 218, second floor. The elevators are over there on the right," she said, pointing toward a bank of three elevators.

Upstairs, I found that Room 218 was located directly off the elevators, to the left of the nurse's station. I walked by two nurses as if I knew exactly where I was going. My heart was beating wildly. If I had a heart attack, at least I would be in a hospital. The door to 218 was open. A hospital bed lay to the left in the middle of the room. There was no equipment beeping, no IV stand, none of the usual stuff one saw on TV shows. It was a sterile room with nothing on the white walls except a sign that showed an escape route for fires. Next to the bed was a single guest chair. Loretta was sitting in a wheelchair in front of the window overlooking the front yard. I walked halfway into the room and stopped.

"Loretta, it's Danny Prescott. Can I talk to you?"

She didn't react to my voice or my presence in the room. I brought the chair up next to her. Her hands lay folded on her lap, bandages covering each wrist. "Please talk to me. I know this is hard for you. It is for me too." I waited several minutes while she continued staring at the window, her eyes blinking occasionally but not showing that she knew I was there or had heard me.

"They said you wouldn't speak. I'd hoped you would talk to me. A terrible thing happened to you that Sunday. I can't change that. I can't make that better, and I know the future will be hard for you. Returning home and to school may be the most difficult thing you've ever done. You think you're alone, but you're not. The terrible thing that Brent did doesn't change who you are. Nothing you did led to what happened."

All the things I was going to say to her, all the thoughts, abandoned me. I didn't know what else to say if she refused to speak. Still, she said nothing. "Please talk to me, if only to tell me how much you hate me. I should have never left you alone with him. I should have stayed with you until your parents came home. There were so many things I should have done but didn't. I'm sorry, Loretta."

I sat for several minutes, just looking out the window with her. Then I said, as much to myself as to Loretta, "You believe that your life is not worth living. You think everything is ruined, but none of that's true. Your friends miss you. Someone told me you were the most popular girl in your class. You have a lot of friends hoping you'll get better and that you'll come back to school. I know what it feels like to think you're all alone, that there's only darkness around you, and it's not worth going on, but things do get better. I won't tell you everything will be the same. It won't be easy for you, but it's worth the fight, or the bad guys win. It seems unfair to you to go through this, and it is. There are mean, stupid people who are going to blame you, and that's not right, but neither you nor I can change that. They're not worth your time or your effort. So, piss on them."

I reached over and placed my hand on hers. She didn't jerk away. She didn't respond at all. "When I heard you tried to end your life, it was like someone had cut away a part of me. I'm responsible for you being here, and I'll carry that with me all my life. I had to come to tell you that you're not alone."

"Why are you really here, Danny?" Loretta asked. But it wasn't the voice of the little girl I'd rode with on the bus or the girl who had welcomed us to her farm. Her voice was weak, as if all her strength was needed to speak. Instead of being a hero riding in on a white horse to save the day, I was more like a boy on a stick pony.

"I thought I was here to save you, but now I realize I'm here as much for myself as for you. The thought of you hating me and thinking I betrayed you is almost unbearable. I had to tell you that you're not alone, that you have people who care for you, and that I'm sorry."

She turned toward me; her face was a caricature of the pretty, gregarious girl who had welcomed Brent and me to her farm. "I don't hate you." She turned to the window, wiped away a tear, and asked, "Why didn't you come up with us to the hayloft?"

"A thousand times, I've asked myself why I didn't. Why did I do what he wanted? I don't have an answer, Loretta, at least not one I can live with. A part of me wanted to leave, get him away from you. I knew he didn't want me to follow you to the hayloft. I knew he wanted to be alone with you, and I didn't question why. Things like what happened that Sunday don't happen in Banning. He was the great Brent Arrington, and I wanted to be his friend, so I did what he wanted. That makes me as bad as him."

She pulled her hand away. I had admitted something to her I hadn't been able to admit to myself. I knew it was true, and I knew I'd have to live with that knowledge. We looked at each other for several seconds. There was so much hurt and sadness in her eyes, and I didn't know what else to say.

She touched my face with her hand. "You're hurt. What happened to your face?"

"It's nothing," I said. "It was Brent. He enjoys hurting people."

"Why would he . . ."

"What the hell are you doing here? Get out of here. Get away from her." Evert Tinsley's voice thundered, vibrating off the walls. I'd just made it to my feet when he plowed into me. We stumbled backward into the wall. His hands encircled my throat, and his lips parted in a snarl. He wanted to kill me. I pulled his hands free as I shoved him back. He tripped on the overturned chair and went down onto his knees.

Loretta screamed, "Stop it! Stop it!"

Evert got to his feet, righted the chair, and sat down. He took several deep breaths and then dropped his head into his hands. I remained on the floor, my back against the wall, as a nurse rushed into the room. Loretta was standing, her hands covering her ears. She was shaking as tears streamed down her cheeks.

I'd failed. I'd made things far worse than they were and probably affected Loretta's recovery. Everything I touched turned to shit. I didn't care what happened to me now. Whatever it would be, I deserved it. The nurse hurried to Loretta. "What happened, sweetie? Are you okay?"

Evert raised his head from his hands. "Get him out of here before I kill him."

The nurse grabbed my arm. "You have no right to be in here. Come with me, or I'll call security."

I allowed her to pull me to my feet and got up. I'd reached the point where I no longer cared what happened. To gain admission to the hospital, I'd lied to the hospital and my parents. My good intentions didn't make me a hero. I was a stupid sixteen-year-old kid, nothing more. A man twice Evert's size entered the room. His white shirt had *Jacob* embroidered above the left pocket.

"That's him," the nurse said. Jacob gripped me by my shirt, pinning me against the wall. I didn't resist. He was five inches taller than me and twice as broad in the shoulders. One hand gripped the belt on my jeans as the other held tightly to my arm. I was probably going to jail, and all the shit at school was going to repeat itself.

"I want him to stay, Daddy. Please," Loretta said. "He was only trying to help. He's the only one who has, Daddy. Please."

Jacob stopped pulling me from the room.

"He has no right to be here, honey," Evert said.

"We were only talking. Please, I want him to stay."

After a few seconds, Evert nodded to Jacob, who took his hands off me.

"What do you want me to do, sir? I came up to take the patient for her walk outside," Jacob said.

"Danny can do that," Loretta said. "Please, Daddy, it's all right."

"We'll be okay," Evert said to Jacob. "It's what she wants."

"Are you sure?" the nurse asked. "Maybe I should go with them."

"Don't worry, I'll be okay. I want to talk to Danny alone. It will just be for a while. I will be fine. You can watch us from the window."

Evert's shoulders slumped. He seemed to deflate, his anger gone along with his strength. "My little girl hasn't said a word for days and hasn't called me Daddy since— She'll be okay with the boy," he said to Jacob.

The nurse followed Jacob from the room. Evert put his arms around Loretta and hugged her. "Hearing you talk again is like hearing angels sing, sweetheart. I only want you to be okay."

"Can Danny take me outside? Just for a little while." Loretta took her father's hand and held it to her face. "I'm going to be okay now, Daddy. Don't worry."

"If that's what you want, but take the wheelchair. You're still weak, and you haven't walked since we brought you here."

She attempted to smile and sat down in the chair. "If I must," she said with a sigh.

I pushed Loretta into the hall and to the elevator. Evert looked beaten and old as he stood in the doorway, watching as the elevator's brass doors slid shut behind us. We exited and passed the reception desk; the receptionist stood up. "Is everything okay? Your uncle seemed upset when I told him his nephew was here."

"It was a misunderstanding. It's fine," I said as we passed.

"Nephew?" Loretta asked.

"I lied to get in."

"That's not good, Danny."

"Not much I do is."

Loretta pointed to a large maple next to a patch of wilting flowers bitten by the frost. "I like to sit over there. There's a bench on the other side of the hibiscus bushes."

The sky was a pale, cloudless blue, the late-morning shadows receding with the sun's height. A crow sat in the top branches of an elm, eyeing any movement on the ground. Multicolored leaves lay in small piles around us, driven together by a light breeze. A few stubborn ones clung to branches, the last to give up, waiting for the next puff of breeze to release them for their aerial ride to the ground. I pushed the chair next to a concrete bench facing the building.

Loretta ran her fingers through her hair. "I must look a mess," she said.

"You look fine, Loretta. You always do."

"I've never seen my dad that mad. You're lucky he's not a big man like Jacob."

"Yeah, if he were the size of Jacob, there would only be pieces of me pushing your chair. Thank you for saving me back there. I was supposed to be the one saving you."

"You know, I saw you from my window when you came across the yard. I thought about telling the nurse. I'm glad I didn't."

"But you didn't look at me when I came in—or talk to me."

"I didn't know why you had come. And I did hate you just a little bit."

"I've made things worse," I said with a sigh. "It's become a habit with me."

"Like lying?" Loretta asked.

"Yes, like lying, but that stops today. It doesn't help, and it just leads to more lies."

"Everybody lies. Since I've been here, I've had a lot of time to think. I guess that's why they put me here. People keep telling me everything is fine even when it's not. They tell me I'm the same person I was, and I'm not. Dad says all my friends want me to return to school. You said it too, but no one has called or come to see me." She hesitated and looked at me, and her voice grew stronger. "If you won't tell me the truth, if you'll just lie, you can just leave now."

I took a while before I answered. She was right. Everybody lies. "There will be no lies, I promise. You may not like what I say, but I won't lie to you. There's been too many lies already, and I'm tired of lying too."

Then I waited, not knowing what else to say, but I knew whatever I said would be true.

"Why did he pick me?"

I knew, or thought I did, but now, as I faced her, I wondered if the truth was really what she needed. It was difficult to find the right words. I wanted to tell her the truth, at least as I believed it.

"You're very pretty, Loretta—young, innocent, and naïve, but you're not a little girl anymore. You're not the little girl I winked at on the bus. Brent saw that, and he's an evil person. He thinks he's entitled to do whatever he wants, take whatever he wants. That may sound trite, but it's the only way I can describe him. To him, you were someone he could take advantage of, use his charm and do whatever he wanted. It wasn't anything you did but who you were: a beautiful, sweet, innocent, trusting girl he could use."

"Then why did you leave us alone? I thought you were my friend." The words came softly, as if she feared the question and its answer.

"If I had one thing to do over, it would be that. I've asked myself that many times, and Loretta, I still don't know. Or maybe I don't want to accept the answer. I could see he was coming on to you and that it made you uncomfortable. That should have been enough, but I did what I knew he wanted me to; I left him alone with you, but I never thought he would do anything to hurt you. I wanted to be his friend—be part of his group—be one of the popular kids. I'm not sure what that says about me."

She looked away from me for several seconds. I wondered if she hated me now. My words had been the truth, and now I knew it too.

"It makes you no different from me. When he was flirting with me at the pool, I saw that the other girls were jealous. It made me feel good. I flirted back. At least I tried to flirt. I'm not sure if I know how. That might have been why he did that to me."

"I don't believe that, and you shouldn't either. Nothing you did at the pool or the farm led to what happened. You're a kind and sweet person. Don't blame yourself for being innocent and naïve or seeing the best in people. You trusted us. You can't be blamed for that. You didn't see the predator behind the smile, nor did I."

She thought about what I'd said and then asked, "I am what I am now. Why would anyone want a girl who someone else has used?"

"Someone who would think of you that way is a narrow-minded fool and not worth your time even to consider." I took her hand, searching for the words that would help. "Loretta, you can't be accountable for what someone else does. Don't let what he did change who you are. Don't let something that Brent did define you. You're so much more than that."

"Then why do they blame me? They called me saying awful things."

"Because there are people who were born assholes. You should be the last one to be blamed for anything, but you're right; some do. There are people who always believe the worst about others. It must make them feel good. Someone said that you're the most popular girl in your class. Maybe they're jealous. It brings you down to their level. You can't let them be your view in the mirror. Whoever they are, they're a minority. This has taught me that knowing people all your life doesn't make them friends. Genuine friends will be there for you, and you have a lot of friends at school who want you to get better and come back."

"Then why haven't they called? Why haven't they tried to see me like you did?"

"I'm not sure. They may not know what to say, so they say nothing. Remember that boy who rode the bus, the one whose father got electrocuted?"

"Bobby Kiddel," Loretta said.

"No one said anything to him when he started riding the bus again. I didn't. What do you say to someone who lost their father? So I said nothing. I ignored it like it hadn't happened. I never asked him how he felt or said, 'I'm sorry about your dad.'"

Loretta nodded. "I didn't talk to him either. It made me feel guilty that I had a dad while he didn't. I should have said something to him, told him I was sorry."

"That doesn't make us bad people. Maybe it's why your friends don't call or come over. Maybe they're waiting for you to show them it's okay."

Loretta looked out over the expanse of lawn, her eyes settling on something far away. I waited for her to speak, hoping my words were helping. She wanted the truth, and I was answering with the only truth I knew.

She looked up at the building. "My dad is watching us from the window." She waved, and there was a movement in the window of her room. "Thank you, Danny. I'm glad you came to see me. I'm glad you're my friend."

"You need to raise your standards."

Loretta laughed, and I felt a load lift from me.

"If you come home, I'll be there. I know you have other friends, but I'll be there if you ever need me, and there's someone I want you to meet. Her name is Wendy Warner. I think you two will like each other."

"Is she your girlfriend?"

"I hope so, but you'll have to ask her that when you meet her."

"I want to. She must be a nice person if you like her. Please bring her over when I come home. I better go back in. My dad is probably wearing out the carpet, pacing back and forth." She laughed again as she said, "I'm sorry he tried to kill you."

"Maybe next time," I said, joining her laughter.

She got up from her chair, bent down, and hugged me. "I'll push the chair back. I need the exercise. Goodbye, Danny."

I watched from the bench as she walked into the building, and then I left.

It was a few minutes after twelve when I arrived at school. I'd have to tell another lie about why I wasn't in morning classes. What they say is true—one lie leads to another. Wendy wasn't in the cafeteria line or sitting at our table in the corner. I checked a few other places before spotting her in the library, talking with Sylvia Lindell, one of the cheerleaders. After being chastised once, I stayed near the encyclopedias and periodicals until Sylvia left. Wendy was wearing another new outfit, a light lavender sweater with a matching skirt. As always, she looked great.

"Hi," I said, sitting down next to her. "Are we going out for cheerleading now?"

"I'm game if you are," Wendy replied. "She said she likes my new look and wanted to know where I got my hair done."

"You do look great," I said.

"Too late, and I wasn't fishing for compliments. Did you go?"

"Yes. Loretta's father came in while I was there and tried to strangle me."

"Yeah, right. Are you going to tell me how it went or not?"

"Her father tried to strangle me. Loretta screamed and stopped him."

"You're serious."

"As a freshly dug grave. It didn't go quite as planned."

"I didn't think you had a plan," Wendy said.

"It wouldn't have done any good. I had all these inspirational things to say, but sitting there with her, nothing came to me when it mattered. We talked. That's the one good thing that happened. Loretta is speaking again."

"That's no small thing," Wendy remarked.

The student librarian, Romona Bessemer, tapped on the table next to us. "If you two want to talk, you'll have to leave. Others want to study."

"We're the only ones in the library besides you, Romona," I said.

"That doesn't make any difference. This is a library, not a social hall."

"Well then, Romona, a sign on the door should say that," said Wendy. "It's confusing."

Wendy picked up her books and followed me out the door.

"Have you eaten?" I asked.

"No, you?"

"Let's grab a burger at Mike's. We have time. Neither of us has a one-o'clock class."

She dropped her books off at her desk. On the way to Mike's, I filled Wendy in on all the details. Her assessment was far more positive than mine. Five minutes later, we were at Mike's. Steve and Mark Davis, also known as Skeeter, sat in a booth on the right. The Wurlitzer in the back was playing "Then He Kissed Me," one of Steve's favorites.

"You want to join them?" I asked.

"Up to you. They're your friends," Wendy said, heading for the booth.

I slid in beside Steve, while Wendy joined Skeeter on the other side.

"Didn't expect to see anyone down here," I said in greeting.

"It's goulash day, or to me, it's-time-for-Mike's-burger-and-a-shake day," Steve said.

"Sounds good to me." I yelled our order to Mike, who was frying hamburgers behind the counter.

Mike's Café had been a favorite of kids back in my father's time. Back then, it was called Brown's Park and Eat. Mike Fleming had purchased the restaurant shortly after the war. He redid the interior, adding long chrome-and-white laminated countertops with red vinyl booths. In front of the jukebox were a half-dozen tables scattered around, with bathrooms on either side in the back. Neon advertising signs for colas, ice cream, and cigarettes were arranged above a mirror that ran the length of the counter.

Normally, Gladys Mead waited tables, while Mike handled the cooking and cash register. However, Gladys was out sick today, so only Mike was behind the counter. Everyone liked Mike and Gladys. They were as much of a fixture of the place as the neon signs and tables.

"Missed you this morning in Psych," Skeeter said.

"I had an errand to run. Any crazies show up?"

"Only the usual assortment of perverts, deviants, and psychos."

I laughed. "You've been reading the text."

"That's cheating," Steve added.

"Is this the usual intellectual banter?" Wendy asked.

Mike brought over all four burgers and shakes, and we each contributed our share, except I paid for Wendy's over her protest.

After we ate, Steve pulled me aside outside Mike's, held up his palm for me to wait, and went to his car. When he returned, he spoke in a conspiratorial tone. "Here's what you asked for." He handed me a paper bag.

I peeked inside.

"Thanks," I said, shoving it into my back pocket.

As we walked back, Wendy asked, "Are you going to tell me what that was all about?"

"What?"

"Don't 'what' me, Danny Prescott. I thought I covered secrets in my last lecture."

"Oh, that." I pulled the paper bag from my pocket and handed it to her.

"It's a knife. What do you need with a knife?"

"You cut things, whittle, and . . ."

"Can it find you a new girlfriend?"

"If I tell you, you'll get the wrong impression."

"What impression am I going to get? Your little buddy just gave you a paper bag. He looked around as if we were under surveillance. Inside the paper bag is a very serious knife, which is illegal because it's got a little button on the side that unlocks a very big blade."

"You know a lot about knives," I said, attempting to lighten the interrogation.

"Why do you need this?" Wendy said, holding up the bag.

"Brent said next time he was going to kill me. I take him at his word."

"You think this is the answer?" she said, handing me the bag.

"I won't let him beat on me again. I'll only use it if I have to."

"Oh, Danny." She shook her head, looking disappointed in me.

"I'll give it back to Steve," I said, but it didn't change the disappointment in her eyes.

We got back in plenty of time for our two-o'clock classes. Before going to class, I put the paper bag in my locker—just having it in my locker was enough to suspend me. Before going to football practice, I shoved the bag under the seat in the pickup.

Coach Esker ran us through the usual drills, then took a break as he outlined new plays designed to rely more on the passing game since Brent, the human tank, would not be running the ball. There was a general coolness toward me, but the hostility had lowered considerably.

I was home by six o'clock and changed into my work clothes. My father was picking the end rows of the eighty acres across the road. A full wagon was sitting in the field. Jim was at the top of the elevator, running the chain down to splice it at the bottom. I quickly hooked our smaller tractor, an Allis Chambers WD45, to an empty wagon and headed to the field to bring up the next load.

As my father approached the end of the row, I could see the corn mounted up in the center of the wagon. I pulled into the field, did a U-turn behind him, and followed him down the picked rows in case he couldn't reach the end. He stopped after corn ears began falling over the sideboards. I unhooked the wagon from the picker. My dad shouted something, but the picker's clatter made it impossible for me to understand. I signaled I couldn't hear, and my father shut the picker down.

"Since you brought out another wagon, I'll pick another load. Are you okay with doing the chores yourself? Jim's got enough with that chain breaking again."

"You want me to unload the wagon after Jim fixes the chain?"

"Just leave it parked in the crib alleyway in case we get rain tonight. I'll unload it in the morning."

I climbed up on the back of the mounted picker so he could hear me better. "Dad, I have to tell you something."

"Can't it wait?"

"I've done something that's going to make you mad," I shouted over the sound of the tractor.

He shut the tractor off and looked at me seriously. He would be as mad about lying to him as he would be at what I had done. "I didn't go to school this morning. I drove to Mason City to see Loretta."

"My God, Danny, do you know what you've done?" He shook his head as his eyes burned into me. "Do you realize that you've violated the judge's bail order? When Sheriff Brennan finds out, you're going back to jail till your trial. What could have possibly made you do something so stupid and reckless? You were to have no contact with Loretta Tinsley."

"I know, Dad. I know it was stupid, but I was afraid she would try to kill herself again. All of this happened because I left them alone in the loft. I had to see if I could help. I couldn't wait to see if things turned out okay."

"What happened at the hospital? Did you see her?"

"Yes. Evert came while I was there."

"Oh, Christ, Danny. Can this get any worse?"

"At first he was furious that I was there, but he let me talk to Loretta. She seemed to like that I came to see her."

My father's face told me how serious this was. I did not know what Evert would do. I only hoped that he would understand that I'd only been there to help.

"Take the load on up. I'm not going to pick anymore today."

Jim was picking up tools after completing the elevator repair, so I pulled the load alongside and ran the corn up into the storage crib. Jim headed for the barn to feed the cattle as my father parked the loader in the equipment shed and went to the house. When he returned, Jim and I were loading silage into the last bunk. He stood in the grain shed until we were done.

"Did your brother tell you what he did today?" my father asked Jim.

"No. I assume he didn't blow up the school because we would have heard the explosion."

"This is about as bad. He drove the pickup to Mason City and saw Loretta Tinsley."

Jim looked at me as if he'd caught me pounding my pud.

"Mr. Shagger doesn't feel there's anything to be gained from calling the sheriff. They'll arrest Danny if Evert files a complaint. Shagger will come down if they take Danny back to jail for violating his bail. The judge has set a meeting to review the charges against both Brent and Danny. The prosecution will recommend that all charges be dropped against Danny at that hearing. He said the best thing is to wait and see what happens, and then he'll decide what steps we need to take. Jim, give Becky a heads-up on this. There's no sense in letting them hear it from someone else. That's always worse."

"How can they keep holding these charges over Danny's head when Loretta and Evert have both said he wasn't involved in what happened in the hayloft?" Jim asked.

"It's not as simple as all that," my father said. "The judge still has to rule on the charges. The prosecutor still believes that Danny acted as a lookout for Brent. That makes him an accessory to the attack. 'Aiding and abetting' was the term he used. Mr. Shagger thinks if Danny testifies against Brent, it's almost certain all charges against him will be dropped, but until the hearing, nothing has changed. Danny is still under the bail requirements."

I did the chores as fast as possible. It was almost dark when we went to the house to clean up and eat. We hardly talked at supper. Jim seldom looked my way, fed up with the trouble I kept bringing home. We'd almost finished eating before my mother joined us. Then, my father went to the living room to watch TV, leaving Jim, Mom, and me at the table.

"You stepped on your dick this time, didn't you?" Jim said.

"Jim," my mother reacted.

"Well, I'm tired of him screwing everything up. It's like he's too stupid to learn. You and Dad keep making excuses for him when what he needs is for someone to beat some sense into him." Jim threw his napkin down, shoved his chair back, and left the table to join my father in the living room.

"He's right, Mom. I might have made things worse for everyone if Evert reports this to the sheriff, but I know I helped Loretta. We talked for almost an hour. I wanted her to know I was sorry. I wanted her to know the truth about what happened. I think she's accepting that it wasn't her fault and that she has friends who want to help her."

"I know you only wanted to help, but you took an enormous risk and lied to your father. Now he doesn't know if he can trust you. You need to talk to him."

"I will, but not tonight. I'm going to bed. Maybe I'll be lucky and not wake up."

I went to my room and lay on top of the covers, staring at the cracks in the ceiling I knew by heart. I'd gone to Mason City like Don Quixote, my lance pointed at a windmill. Just like Jim had said, I'd screwed up with the judge, with the school, and with Wendy. I shut my eyes, feeling exhausted. Sleep finally came in the early morning hours.

CHAPTER 13

My mother was picking up the breakfast dishes when the phone rang. She spoke for several minutes as Jim and my father were preparing to go back outside. She held up her hand, asking them to stay. Then she hung up the phone and smiled.

"That was Ester Tinsley. She said Loretta is coming home. She didn't say, but I don't think they're going to do anything. She actually sounded like she thought Danny's visit was responsible for Loretta coming home."

"You must have been born with a rabbit's foot up your ass," Jim whispered to me as he passed.

"It's all because of careful planning and an understanding of human nature, you uneducated turd," I answered back.

"I'm going to give you a lesson in human nature when I whip your ass."

"You two," my mother said. "I swear you'd think you didn't like each other."

"And you'd be right," Jim said, laughing.

"Mom, are you sure Jim wasn't switched with another baby in the hospital?" I asked as we headed out to the barn.

"Both of you, get out of here." But she laughed as well.

The Rattler was sitting at the end of our lane, and I rushed onboard. I was met with a wave of laughter and wondered if my zipper was down. I picked up a distinctive scent a second later and realized the laughter wasn't targeting me. A boy near the back farted again, setting up cheers, clapping, and more laughter. No one showed me the slightest bit of attention. I had lost the spotlight to a fart. A bit of a grin came to my face as it occurred to me that that must have said something about my shitty life.

At lunch, a couple of girls from Wendy's Art Appreciation class joined us before I could tell her the good news about Loretta. It was nice to see Wendy with friends, but I missed our intimate lunches when we were both outcasts, when I didn't share her with anyone. I could see how much she enjoyed joking and talking about art and girly stuff, but I missed having her all to myself.

After lunch, Wendy and I walked to the town park. It was a popular place in the spring to get away from school and lounge on the thick grass. However, today was cloudy and cool, the grass brown, and no one but us was in the park. "I have some good news that will replace the bad news from yesterday," I said. I told her about the Tinsleys' visit and that Loretta was coming home and maybe back to school. I had done most of the talking, maybe with too much pride, as I described how Ester had thanked me.

Wendy was unusually quiet. I expected her to be ecstatic about my news.

"Is something bothering you? Is it something I've done? If it's about the knife, that's done with."

"It's not about your stupid knife." She walked away from me.

"Hey," I said, skipping ahead and blocking her path. "What's going on? You're pissed at me."

"I'm glad everything worked out with Loretta. It's wonderful, but it could have gone all wrong, Danny. You're no longer a child. Honestly, sometimes you're an impulsive idiot. You don't think about the consequences. While you're out on bail, you take your dad's pickup to Mason City without asking. It's what got you into trouble in the first place. You risked being thrown back in jail and expelled from school. You risked everything. Now you're elated that it turned out all right, but it could have gone the other way."

It was like she had slapped me. Her words were acid, and it didn't seem fair. I hadn't expected back slaps and handshakes of congratulations but not this either. She said nothing more, just stood looking at me. I dropped my eyes to the ground, away from her. She was right. I hadn't considered the effect on my family, my future, or her. Wendy's life was coming together while mine was pulling apart.

"Are you blowing me off, Wendy?"

When she didn't answer, I left her standing there and walked to the river. I sat on the small dock that jutted into the water, watching the currents swirl around the pilings. I dared not look back for fear Wendy was gone. Everything around me skipped into a haze as if dense fog had descended on the park. I wondered what it would be like to slip into the water and let the river take me. Wendy was the stitching that held my life together.

I sat on the river's edge, my heart pounding as I tried to think of ways to bring her back.

Then I heard her voice behind me. "Can I join you?" I dreaded hearing the following words, telling me I was a great guy and we could still be friends. I had heard them before, but this time, they would cut away my heart.

"It's a free country. Isn't that what you said?" I mumbled.

She sat down next to me on the dock. For several minutes, we didn't speak. What do you say to someone you love when they no longer want to be with you?

"We're not very good at this, are we?" Wendy asked. She reached into the water, letting the current swirl around her fingers.

I didn't reply. Her words hurt too much, and I just wanted the hurt to stop.

"Are you going to talk to me?" she asked.

"I'm afraid anything I say will drive you away, and I know if I do, I'll never find someone like you again. You're beautiful. You make me laugh even when I feel like shit. I wake up thinking about you. I've never felt this way about anyone before, not like this. If I lose you, anyone else would be second best."

"I feel the same about you, Danny, and therein lies our problem."

"But you don't want to be with me anymore. Is it because other guys have asked you out?"

"Why would you say something like that?"

"I see how guys look at you now when you walk into assembly. You don't look or act like Weird Wendy anymore. It's like you want to be noticed."

"And that's bad?" she asked.

"No, it's not bad, but you're slipping away a little at a time."

"We can't be kids all our lives. I do like you a lot, Danny. I love being with you. You make me feel beautiful and wanted. I also think of you all the time, but I don't want things to explode around me, and I can't revert to being Weird Wendy again."

"I fell in love with Weird Wendy and thought she was wonderful."

"And now?"

"Now, I'd love you if you stood on your head at assembly and spit nickels out your butt."

Wendy tried to hold her laughter, but it broke out anyway, bringing tears to her eyes. "Why would you say something like that? Now I can't get that image out of my head."

"I wanted to know if Weird Wendy was still in there."

"I also heard you say you love me."

"That slipped out," I said.

"Do you?"

"I'm not sure what love is, Wendy." I stared into the water, searching in

203

the ripples for the words. "When I think about being without you, I feel empty. Right now, I feel like I'm being ripped apart because I may lose you. I think nothing but love could feel so wonderful and hurt so much. So, yes. I love you." I waited, knowing that her next words might destroy me.

"Before being with you, I don't think I even loved myself. You said I was your lifeline. I never told you that you were mine too. You've made me feel wanted and beautiful. You made me want to be Wendy Warner again. Please don't take that from me, Danny. I'm not breaking up with you. I can't. I love you and need you too much, but next time you plan to do something stupid, don't."

"Deal." I put my arm around her, and she snuggled against me. I wanted to cheer and cry all at once.

"It's peaceful here. When I was a little girl, I used to sit here and watch my dad fish, but now the river is so polluted, and no one fishes in it anymore."

"Everything changes. Not everything for the better."

"I'm sorry that I spoiled your news. I am thrilled that Loretta is coming home. Take me with you when you go to see her."

"Maybe things are turning for everybody. As soon as she's ready, we'll go to see her, but right now, we'd better get our butts back to school."

We arrived just as everyone filed out of assembly for their afternoon classes. Wendy ran to hers, while I went into the assembly to finish my assignment for my two-o'clock class. At three, I was in the locker room. There was tension in the newbie camp as they watched the coaches hand out equipment and practice uniforms. This was the first cut of wannabes. Veteran players like me leisurely waited to receive our pads, helmets, and uniforms. All but me. It was still uncertain whether I would be allowed to play.

The knockout punch for the newbies would be the team jerseys. No jersey, no practice. In two weeks, Coach Esker would tack a list outside his office identifying which players made the team and which were now tackle dummies. I recalled the elation I felt as a freshman when I saw my name and was assigned a player's number.

I dressed, adjusted my pads without help from any other player, and filed out onto the field with the others. The coach assigned a sophomore to Brent's locker. Still, his old uniform remained unassigned in the coach's office, at least for now. After reviewing what was expected of us at every practice, Assistant Coach Bailer led us through thirty minutes of wind sprints, followed by five laps around the field.

The returning players eyed the newbies with a smirk as they gave it their all. The following practice sessions would significantly reduce their number. Rodger and Dave were taking bets on the first three newbies to fall by the wayside. This day would involve a lot of running and workouts to see which players had endurance and strength. It was no use wasting time on someone who couldn't be made into a player. Running was my strength. The track coach had tried to convince me to join the track team, but planting, farrowing hogs, and spring calving would put too much work on Jim and my father. Besides, no one paid any attention to the track team. Football was king in Banning.

Two freshmen dropped on the third lap, with two more following in the fourth and fifth. Dave gave a thumb-up to Rodger. It was clear he'd picked the right three. The coach whistled us over to the bench. We grouped in a semicircle around him. Esker outlined the rest of the afternoon and said this was a good time if anybody wanted to hit the showers. He added that there was no shame in changing one's mind about playing. There was always next year to try out again. There was a low muttering in the back, and two freshmen boys split off and walked toward the dressing room.

We broke into groups of four, the coaches watching who was partnering with whom. Last season's starting players split into defensive and offensive groups, while the rest grouped up however they wanted. No one called my name or waved me over, and I ended up with three sophomores, two of whom hadn't made the travel squad last year.

How I was treated did not surprise me, but regardless, every rejection was another arrow in the back. I had hoped that everyone would treat me like everyone else. I put aside my anger and ensured everyone's pads were correctly adjusted. If that was how it would be, I would make it as rough on them as they were on me. I would funnel my rage into hitting harder, running faster, and doing every drill better than anyone on the field. Coach Esker and the team would know their best runner was sitting on the bench. I would force Esker to look me in the eye as he passed me over for a uniform.

The coaches walked among the groups as we performed various drills on blocking, running patterns, and key plays. With each practice, the drills increased in number and difficulty. Finally, practices ended with scrimmages as the first- and second-string rosters fell into place.

The final whistle blew, and we gathered around the coaches for one last rah-rah talk. The coaches complimented everyone on their effort and rewarded us with a sprint across the field to the showers. We raced to the other end of the field on the coach's whistle, and then again. We were to give everything we had while Coach Esker recorded the times of the fastest players. I wanted my name to be at the top of his list. The only player who could run the two hundred faster than me was TJ Backus, one of our tight ends. I could have beaten him toward the end of last year, but I didn't challenge him. TJ was a senior and tight with Brent. I didn't want to push back. It was not worth it. Let the kings be kings.

Coach Bailer blew his whistle as cleated shoes dug into green turf. I stayed behind the leaders for the first fifty yards, Rodger, Richard, and TJ running side by side. I could beat Rodger on my worst day. He would start falling back after fifty yards, and then I would pour it on. I pulled up closer, and TJ saw me and broke from the pack. He turned at the goalposts ten strides ahead of me. For the last twenty yards, it was just him and me. I pumped my legs harder, but so did TJ. The last twenty yards were side by side until he faltered in the last ten and I broke free to beat him by five yards.

"My shoelaces came untied," TJ said. It was an excuse used by a player when he knew he'd been bested. Both of us stooped over, hands on our knees and fighting for breath.

"You're lucky you didn't trip," I said between gulps of air.

"Let's consider it a draw." TJ laughed as he extended his hand.

"Draw," I repeated, taking his hand.

My legs pulsated from exertion as the invigorating hot water from the shower soothed my aching muscles. Despite coming in first, I knew I had to continually improve my game. I should have been running this summer. More teammates joined me in the shower. There had been no congratulations, no high fives for this victor, and I didn't expect any. I grabbed a towel and headed out to the lockers. A few still sat catching their breath. I dried off, dressed, and packed my workout clothes into my gym bag as Rodger emerged from the shower and began toweling off on the bench beside me.

I picked up my bag, and as I passed him, he said, "Well done, Prescott." It felt as if he'd just bestowed a crown on my head. Those three words were a testament to every yard I'd run and how hard I was trying. The dark mood I'd been carrying lifted.

Practice always ended too late to ride the Rattler. Since I hadn't asked my dad for the pickup, I looked around to see if Steve had left. His car wasn't in the lot, but my mother was waiting curbside.

"I was getting groceries at the A&G. I thought you might need a ride. This morning was so chaotic, no one thought about football practice starting today."

She waited until I stored my bag in the back seat, then said, "I wanted to talk to you about your dad. Things worked out, but you lied to get his permission to take the truck. It's not the truck that bothers him or that you drove to Mason City. You lied, and you need to regain his trust."

"Mom, I'll try," I said. "I messed up. I won't make the same mistake again. I promise."

"Fine. That's all that needs to be said about it. Oh, your sister called. She asked about you and has been very concerned. You should call her."

On the drive home, my mom discussed her call with Susan, mentioning that she had received an invitation to join a sorority and something called rush week. She also mentioned that joining the sorority would be more expensive than staying in the dorm. Pledges had to live in the sorority house. Still, my mom seemed as excited about it as Susan.

"I told her not to worry; your dad and I would find the money somewhere. Corn prices are good, and college is a onetime experience—she should enjoy it and not worry about money. She'll have a lifetime to do that."

I listened and periodically agreed with what she said. My mind was on Wendy. I wasn't even sure we'd had a fight. Whatever it was, though, it left me with a hollow feeling. My mood bounced around like the silver ball on a pinball table. The one thing I was sure of was that Wendy was the best thing that had ever happened to me. Driving past our field, I saw that my father had picked about fifty acres. Fifty down, only two hundred thirty to go. There were four wagons at the end of the field. Only one was empty. I quickly changed into my work clothes and went to the field, hooking up two wagons in tandem.

My dad shut the picker off. "How did it go in practice today?"

"Okay."

"Just okay?"

"Well, I'm not one of the coach's favorites yet,"

"What does that mean?"

The first thing it meant was that my father was not in a joking mood. My father was a faithful fan of the Banning Raiders. He had played both offensive and defense during the same game. In his day, the team was lucky to field enough players to even have a first and second string. He'd never missed one of my games and, in the past, had been an ardent supporter of Brent Arrington.

"I came in first in the two-hundred-yard sprint to the showers."

"Blew 'em off the field, huh?"

"Yeah, then I gave them the old Prescott shuffle. I moved my feet in the dirt like my grandfather when he heard polka music." My father threw his head back and laughed. He remembered my grandfather's jig too, and he'd been the one to name it.

"Take those loads up, or you'll be forever getting in from chores, and we'll both have a cold meal." He started the picker as I pulled out of the field.

It was dark when Jim and I finished unloading the four wagons, feeding the steers, and filling the chickens' feeding troughs with cracked corn and oyster shells. While putting the WD45 in the shed, I saw the picker's headlights approaching from the field. I waited to see if he needed help with the last load. Jim was already in the house taking a shower. He'd said something about looking at a farm east of Banning with Becky.

My father pulled the wagon up close to the elevator and stopped. I unhooked it from the hitch on the picker and gave a wave, and he drove the picker into the shed. Despite being dead tired from the practice, unloading four loads of corn, and the chores, I knew we would only be done once we had the picker ready to go out again first thing in the morning. In the fall, corn was king, and nothing else mattered. I greased the bearings, while my father adjusted the rollers on the picker. When we finished, I climbed up on the WD45 to run the last load into the crib. My father waved his arms, telling me to let it go. It didn't look like rain, and the night was pitch-black. It could wait until morning.

Walking to the house, I saw weariness in my father's stride. Corn leaves and tassel dust reddened his eyes. I slowed my pace to his. How much longer could he work these hours, and who would do it if he didn't? My brother couldn't do everything alone, and if we both left, what would happen to the farm and my parents? It was a thought that had never occurred to me before. My constant chatter about going and getting away from Banning must have been like stabbing him with each word. How had I missed that? Wendy was right; sometimes I didn't think further than my nose.

Jim had already eaten and was leaving as we walked into the house. My mother put food on the table after my father and I cleaned up. Suddenly, I was hungry. She had fixed smoked brisket, garden peas, fried potatoes, and a tapioca pudding. I left the table feeling as stuffed as a turkey. We settled in the living room around the TV. Wednesday nights were *The Beverly Hillbillies* and *Dick Van Dyke*. I didn't stay around for *The Danny Kaye Show*. I went to my room, read a biology chapter, and finished a trig assignment. It was almost twelve when I finished. I fell asleep thinking about Wendy, football, and Loretta.

CHAPTER 14

In the morning, I ran the remaining load of corn into the crib. Another load and Jim would have to change the elevator to a different crib. I signed one more load to him, and he waved, indicating that he understood. I hurried to the house, quickly showered, and sat at the table. Jim and my dad had already started on their bacon, eggs, and fried potatoes. Mom set a plate in front of me.

"I've got to eat fast. Hank might be early," I said as I stuffed a forkful of potatoes into my mouth.

"He won't be stopping here this morning," my father said.

"Is Mom going to take me?" I asked, unintended irritation lacing my voice.

"You can take the pickup."

I tried to make up for my sharp reply by indicating concern. "What if the picker breaks down and you need to run to town for parts? Mom will have the car." Someday, I would learn that the entire world was not against me, maybe just the town of Banning. I needed to rewire my mouth to my brain rather than my ass.

"It's not the best solution, but we'll live with it. You take the pickup but just to and from school. No messing around at Mike's after practice. I need you here," my father said.

"Don't worry. I've had my share of screwing up."

"I'll note that," Jim said with a snicker.

As I passed my brother, I tweaked his ear. I knew he hated that. "If I'd had a better role model, I would be a better son," I said. I was out the door before he could get out of his chair.

I arrived at school half an hour earlier than if I had ridden the Rattler. The town kids were trickling into the assembly hall. It must have been nice to get up, knowing you only had to walk to school. I went to my desk, opened my biology book, and scanned the assigned chapter again in case of a pop quiz. I still had a few minutes before morning assembly, so I went to the library to check out a book I needed for my lit class.

Wendy was sitting at a table at the back of the room. I slipped into a chair across from her and asked, "What's a beautiful girl like you doing in a place like this?"

She hushed me. I looked around. We were the only ones in there, and she looked at me with the old *gotcha-again* grin.

"You're so easy," she said, shutting her book. Her dark eyes were more prominent and beautiful with the yellow sweater she wore, and this morning, she wore just a brush of mascara and eye shadow. I hoped she was doing it for me and not the guys who eyeballed her every time she walked by.

"What are you reading?" I asked.

She moved her hand. It was a copy of *Catcher in the Rye*. "What are you doing here so early?" she asked.

I told her I had driven in but would have to get home after practice to help my father. We were joking around as Romona came in. She gave us a dirty look, sat behind the librarian's desk, and began reading.

"Could we go?" I moaned. "Romona is a real bitch, and I don't need that this morning."

Wendy gathered up her stuff, being as quiet as she could. Romona watched us all the way out, mice scuttling away from the cat. Wendy touched my hand and winked as we walked into the assembly. I sat at my desk; Wendy took a seat across from me. She told me she had applied to Drake University in Des Moines. Mrs. Brennan, the school counselor, felt Wendy might qualify for a scholarship based on her grades. It was the only way she could afford to go. I dreaded thinking about her being at a university without me. Still, I put a joyful look on my face and said congratulations.

As the desks in the assembly hall filled up, the noise increased to party level, then subsided as the clock neared nine. Wendy went to her desk a few minutes before morning assembly was called. I watched her all the way to her desk, as did several others. From any angle, she was beautiful. The black skirt barely covered her knees and hugged her butt a little too much. For not the first time, I wished she would dress as Weird Wendy again. I'd love her just as much, and the competition would be considerably less.

At noon, Wendy was waiting at the cafeteria door, and we walked through the line together. She turned, giving me the silliest look, somewhere between surprise and throwing up. I looked over her shoulder. Today's culinary choice was hash with rice and an unidentifiable substance accompanied by an apple.

"Barf time. I've got a better idea," I said, sticking my finger in my mouth.

"And, pray tell, what is that, Sherlock?"

"Follow me, Watson, and I'll save you from the agony this meal will visit upon you."

Ten minutes later, we were in Mike's, ordering hamburgers and fries. We weren't the only ones to decide that the lunch sucked. A half dozen kids sat at booths and more at the counter stools. We were lucky to get a booth. As we slid into the only available one, the Everly Brothers crooned "Cathy's Clown" on the jukebox. The song selection was a year old but was still great. Mike turned up the volume to accommodate the inflow of students. I put a dime in and pushed the buttons for G4, Elvis singing "Can't Help Falling in Love." The song had far more meaning since I'd met Wendy.

"What'll it be?" I asked her. I couldn't help smiling when I looked at her. She brought out the best in me.

"B7."

I flipped through the selections and found B7: "Will You Love Me Tomorrow?"

"I like that song too," I said, making the selection.

Mike came over and took our order. He said it would be a while; ten orders were ahead of us. The grill was full, but we would be on the next batch. I glanced up at the Coca-Cola clock behind the cash register. We had plenty of time before we had to be back. We listened to a half dozen more songs, then chowed down on the burgers. Wendy and I walked back the long way on Second Street and then cut over to the school.

As we walked, I thought about how good things had turned out for me. The load I'd been carrying was gone. I'd found Wendy, Loretta was coming home, and I had the possibility that the charges would be dropped against me. Maybe the worst was over. It would be hard for Loretta, but I would be there for her as Wendy had been for me. Perhaps that would make the difference. Wendy jumped in front of me, walking backward. "What's on your little bitty mind, Prescott? Something is bugging you. You fall into these lapses of inattention, and may I remind you that you're with the most interesting person in the world."

"I was thinking about Loretta."

"Oh," she replied, and her smile disappeared as if I'd said a nasty word.

"I'm worried about her coming home. I told her about you and promised to bring you out if she came home."

"Of course. I want to see her, Danny. I would have been mad if you hadn't asked me to go with you."

"Maybe we can go Sunday if she's up for it. I have to see how the picking

214

goes. She seemed so fragile at the hospital. She's going to need our support to get through this."

"Banning is not a place to be fragile," Wendy agreed. "When Brent spread his lies about me, being around anybody was hard. Seeing your friends draw away from you hurts the most. Despite wearing funky clothes and acting like I didn't care what anyone thought, I did—I cared a lot. I hated everyone for not understanding. I hated everyone for believing Brent. It took me a long time to let someone get close to me. We can't let that happen to Loretta."

"I think with a friend like you and me beating the shit out of a few people, she should be fine."

"Now that's a plan," Wendy said with a laugh.

"If you like that plan, you'll adore this one."

"You've got me bursting with anticipation."

"The Met in Fairmont is playing *The Hustler*. Paul Newman is my favorite actor. If I can get the car or pickup, we could go to the nine-o'clock show on Saturday night."

"You know, Danny, you remind me of Paul Newman."

"Really," I said, beaming.

"Yes, you're about the same height." Wendy laughed. "Of course I'll go with you."

"I thought you would be nuts about seeing Paul Newman."

"He's okay, but you're better-looking." She grinned. "I would have thought you would want to see your heartthrob, Natalie Wood. *West Side Story* is playing at the Rex in Banning."

"I'm not into musicals. Why do you think Natalie Wood is my heartthrob?"

"You're always talking about her in *Rebel without a Cause* and *Splendor in the Grass*."

"Those are great movies," I protested.

"They are, but you get that little wispy look when you talk about her."

"She's okay," I said, embarrassed because Wendy was dead-on. I loved Natalie Wood.

She stopped walking and looked at me seriously. "You mean I cut my hair off for nothing?"

I stopped in midstride. I was on my best behavior. Despite that, I had screwed up. Wendy enjoyed my reaction and was putting me on, but I played along. "You're far more beautiful than Natalie Wood. I only like her because she reminds me of you."

She giggled. "You came up with the only answer that would save your life, buddy boy."

"Thank God for that," I said. We were almost at school. As we neared the main door, I asked, "Did you really cut your hair because I liked Natalie Wood?"

She gave me her mischievous smile. "I'll let you work that out yourself."

I left Wendy in the hall and headed for my next class. The teacher gave back our latest test in Trig. I received a perfect score. Being an outcast had left me with plenty of time for studying. My science teacher was sick, so they canceled my afternoon class from two to three, and I went to the locker room to work on the weights. I wanted to match my speed with more strength. It was what Brent had on me. You knew it for a week when he hit you in full stride. I wanted to do the same, but I'd settle for five days.

Halfway through my workout, Rodger and Dave entered the locker room. Dave started working the treadmill, while Rodger stood, eyeing my every move. I figured I was interrupting his routine, so I stopped and didn't finish my set.

"You want to use these weights?" I asked.

"You're doing that wrong, Prescott. That way, you'll strain your back and not benefit from the workout. Get up." I did. Rodger lay down on the bench and began doing reps, then stopped and got up. "You're using too much weight for your first workout. You risk overworking your muscles. Take at least ten pounds off."

I did. He motioned me back to the bench and started throwing instructions. "Put your hands wider apart. Now, lift again slower. Feel the strain in your arms. Shit, keep your back straight against the bench." I did everything he said. "Lift with your arms; you're not trying to build up your spine."

As I worked out, Rodger continued to give me pointers on what I was doing right and wrong. I finished another set, then walked over to where he'd started working out on the free weights. "Thanks, Rodger," I said. "I appreciate the pointers."

"No problem." He continued his workout.

I slipped into my practice clothes and went out onto the field. I couldn't understand what had just occurred in the locker room. Rodger was a friend of Brent's, so what was the deal? Maybe my paranoia was overblown, but paranoia could be a good thing if everybody hated you. Rodger wasn't known for his kindness or altruism. He had a reputation of a tough dude you pissed off at your peril. The severe crew cut he wore did little to dispel that impression. Richard had told me he cut his own hair. "That's why it's not always level on top," he'd said. Rodger was a dude who didn't give a shit what anyone thought of him.

Putting thoughts of him aside, I concentrated on improving my speed and endurance by doing double wind sprints before running laps. I felt the burn in my legs during my third lap, so I slowed down and walked the last lap. I sat down on a bench outside the locker rooms. Amid the usual horseplay and chatter, I could hear lockers opening and slamming shut as players changed for practice. I missed the camaraderie and friendly slaps on the ass and good-natured insults. Before I became the school pariah, I had taken it all for granted.

Coach Esker put me with three of last year's starting players for a series of drills. It might indicate nothing, for he switched several players to different positions, but I took advantage of every opportunity. I gave it all I had. One of the better receivers was a junior like myself, Doug Weissenberg. He was also a possibility for replacing Brent, as was Richard. Although Richard was fast, he couldn't withstand a solid hit.

Doug snagged a couple of difficult passes thrown by our quarterback, Ted Ellington. They were good friends and had been working out together. When it was my turn to receive, Ted put extra heat on the ball, slipping the first pass through my hands. I was ready for the following two bullets and pulled them down. Rodger said something to Ted, who nodded in agreement. I expected the next two to be bullets, but they came perfectly aimed and hit me right in the numbers. I walked back, more confused than ever.

After practice, I drove home directly, as per my orders. My father was pulling a load up behind the picker, and there were two more loads in the field. I drove to the field, hooked the two loads together, and brought them to the elevator. "Picker break down?" I asked as he unhooked the wagons.

"No, but the chain busted again on the elevator. It has to be fixed before we run that load up, and it's a two-man job. Jim's disking the eighty acres we picked, so he won't be helping with chores tonight. He put in the new links, so the chain is ready to put back on the elevator. You pull the chain up and drop it down from the top, and I'll reattach the ends. I want to run all these loads up tonight so the wagons are empty tomorrow. Did practice go okay?"

"Coach worked me with some first-string players. I'm hoping it's a good sign."

"Well, it's not a bad one. Let's get started on that chain."

I duck-walked the chain to the top and dropped it over the end, then pulled more up as my father pulled it down from the ground and reattached the ends. I looked at the crib. At least ten additional loads were in the crib, and there was no way he could have picked and unloaded that many by himself.

"Mom is unloading wagons, isn't she? She shouldn't be doing that." I thought of all the things that could happen when unloading a wagon. None of it was pleasant. "I can stay home for a couple of days until the picking is done."

My father's hands went to his hips, his stance going military. "Who do you think was helping me before you were old enough to wipe your ass? She's fine with it. We ran this farm together until I could afford a hired man. What do you think we had you for? But it turns out you cost more than a hired man."

On my way down the elevator, I tried to think of what else I could say to piss off my father. I was only trying to show some empathy. I hadn't expected to face a firing squad because of it. When I was off the elevator, my father turned on the power takeoff, and the elevator came to life. It was incredible how many ways I could piss him off, and none of them was intentional.

It was dark when we finished the last load. Feeding a herd of hungry steers in the dark was not advisable for anyone but a professional. While spreading corn over the silage, a head wedged between my legs lifted me off my feet and slammed me down on the ground. I hit on my knees; the shovel fell away, and my hand was in a patch of fresh cow shit or often referred to as a cow pie. I scrambled to my feet with the front of my pants covered in manure and mud. My language hit a new low. It was pretty impressive what phrases would come to you when you were in a literal pile of shit. Some of my words were nearly poetic.

After cleaning what I could off my pants, I walked to the hog house, where my dad was spreading fresh bedding. He took a long look at me and whiffed the air. "Sitting down on the job, or did you shit your pants? Either way, it's hard to be proud of you, son."

"Good one, Dad. You missed your calling as a comedian." He was still laughing as I walked to the house to clean up. It was hard to find sympathy when you were covered in shit.

CHAPTER 15

My father ate breakfast while I was cleaning up, and then we went directly to the field to pick corn. My mother wore jeans and one of Jim's old flannel shirts. She helped unload the wagons and level the corn in the cribs as they filled up. To prevent further irritation, I kept my opinions to myself, where they were more appreciated. Gradually, I realized the sacrifices my parents made for all of us. I'd just expected to have nice clothes, go to school, and have money in my pocket. I got up from the table and said, "That was a great meal, Mom, thanks." She seemed stunned as I went out the door. Not much, I knew, but wasn't it supposed to be the little things that counted?

It was great not riding the Rattler. Before the morning assembly, I completed an English Lit assignment in the library, while Romona organized books, methodically checking each one to ensure it was placed according to the Dewey Decimal System. I wondered what kind of hell it would be to be married to her and thanked whatever God had put Wendy in my path. I picked up my books and settled into my desk as Principal Larson entered for morning assembly. People were milling around, but one sweep of his eyes over the hall brought everything to a graveyard quiet. He relished the attention standing at the lectern, a dwarf looking over his kingdom. He cleared his throat, then announced a pep rally a week from Thursday afternoon, the day before our first game against our chief rival, Pepperdine. We had a week to prepare—only a miraculous run by Brent, the last minutes against Pepperdine, had given us an unbeaten season last year. The team had carried him off the field on their shoulders. I was sure if we hadn't, the fans would have. I would know Monday if I would play or even if I would suit up for the game.

Friday afternoon was unusually warm, meaning it was a bitch on the field. It was in the mid-seventies as we ran our laps. The coach worked Doug, Richard, and me in the half-back position and then as wide receivers. Maybe Esker was using me to motivate the other two—I knew I was better than either of them. I was fast and had great hands. I could pull a ball down that others wouldn't even try to catch, but that didn't mean the school would let me play.

Sweat was pouring off us as we took a break from nearly ninety minutes on the field. The coaches ordered us to the watercoolers and handed out salt tablets. Halfway through practice, Coach Esker sent two players to the showers for lagging it. Marvin Overby, a freshman, looked like a wrung-out rag and pulled himself out. That was no significant loss. I was bone tired as I came off the field. I had broken through the defensive line three times to go all the way. As I drove home, storm clouds gathered, and the wind picked up. A hard rain would force us out of the fields, and a quarter of our crops had yet to be picked.

I quickly changed clothes. My father had taken the car to Fairmont to pick up a new hydraulic cylinder for the disk while Jim ran the picker. My mother was hooking up an empty wagon as raindrops hit my face. The wind picked up as more drops darkened the ground, and the temperature dropped. I took the tractor from my mother and headed out to the field. Jim continued to pick as I pulled into the field. The rain was pounding down so heavily I could barely see the picker. I unhooked the empty wagon and got under it to escape the rain. I waited as my brother attempted to get to the end of the field. Jim stopped the picker and began waving frantically. I climbed back on the WD45 and sped toward him; it lurched and jumped over the ruts, nearly throwing me off. Jim was unhooking the wagon as I pulled up. The wind was driving the rain sideways into our faces, making it difficult to see.

"You'll have to pull the wagon out. I'll never make it with this picker. The mud is already balling up on the tractor's tricycle's front tires. I've got to get this picker out of the field." He hopped back on the picker. The rear wheels of his tractor kicked mud upward, with most of it falling on me. He drove away, his wheels leaving a deep trench. I had to hook the wagon up alone as the rain pounded into my face, making it difficult to align the tractor hitch with the trailer tongue. I was still swearing at my brother when I finally dropped the pin into the hitch, securing the trailer to the WD-45.

Water stood in pockets all over the field as I slipped the tractor into gear and headed toward the house. I saw the lights on the picker rounding the turn into our farmyard, and I let go of another stream of four-letter words. Hell had no fury like a cold, wet brother. The rear wheels spun, kicking up a geyser of mud and cornstalks, while the tractor's front tires became laden with mud. The rear wheels dug in past the greasy surface and found traction. I dropped the gearshift into a lower gear and crept forward. The farm buildings vanished in the pouring rain. As I neared the end of the field, mud balled up on the front tires so bad they weren't turning but sliding. If it had been twenty yards farther, I would never have made it.

Once on the hard surface of the farm road, I shifted up and picked up speed. Five minutes later, I pulled the load into the alleyway between the cribs and shut down the tractor. Clumps of mud hung off my shoulders and stacked on my head. Muddy water dripped off me like I'd been in a mud

222

bath. I almost didn't make it out of the field because Jim was too much of an asshole to help me hook up the trailer. I was super pissed. The farmyard around the buildings looked like a lake. We must have gotten more than an inch already. There'd be no picking tomorrow, or maybe for several days until the ground dried. I watched the rain pound down from the alleyway. My anger at my brother grew with each raindrop. I was cold, wet, and miserable. I pulled an empty five-gallon can from a hook and tipped it over, using it as a seat. The temperature had dropped into the low fifties, sending a shiver through me. I wanted to get to the house and dry off with a hot cup of chocolate. Fuck Jim; he could feed the cattle alone, just like I had hooked up the damn trailer alone. Across the yard from me, Jim and my father watched the rain from the comfort of the equipment shed. Something streaked from between their legs into the rain. Ranger shook his coat a few seconds later, spraying more water on me. I laughed and kneeled to hug him. Hell, it was only water and mud. I'd live. My anger at my brother melted away. I waited for several more minutes. The sky was a layer of black, and there was no sign the rain would let up.

"Ranger, it's you and me, buddy. Are you ready for another run?"

He looked at me eagerly, not knowing it meant another run in the rain. He was right beside me as I sprinted to the house. My mother met me on the side porch with a towel and a dry set of clothes.

"Oh, Danny. I think you've ruined your new shoes."

"Mom, how can you tell? They're covered with four inches of mud."

"That's how I can tell, smarty."

Ranger was dripping water like he'd sprung a leak. I pulled an old towel off the rack. After a thorough rubdown, he dropped into his bed of old blankets in the corner of the side porch. Tonight, I'd sneak him something special from the table. I hung my clothes on a nail to dry and drew a pail of water from the tap to clean the mud from my shoes. Maybe they could be saved. Jim and Dad shot through the porch door a second later. The cattle would have to wait until we were all dried off.

The rainstorm ushered in a cold front during the night. The temperature hovered around forty degrees in the morning, like going from fall to winter in one night. Bundled up like it was zero degrees, we trudged out to the barn. Ranger followed, then headed back to the porch. He was a faithful dog, but he wasn't any fool. It was nicer on the side porch, curled up on blankets. Jim threw the silage down as I filled the bunks, and then he came behind me with the coating of ground corn. The cattle crowded around the bunks, their breath huffing little clouds of smoke, our fog factories. I fed the calves, scattered a bale of straw for bedding to keep them warm, and then went to the house while Dad and Jim unloaded the corn into the crib. As I walked in, Mom was breaking eggs to scramble. The house was toasty warm. I smelled the coffee and poured myself a cup.

"When did you start drinking coffee?" my mom asked.

"When my toes became frozen."

"It's not that cold out there, is it? The radio said it was in the forties over most of the state."

The phone rang just as I took a swallow of coffee. I should have made myself cocoa, even if I looked like a kid. After I'd washed up and watched the weather forecast, my mother came into the living room. "That was Ester Tinsley on the phone. Since it rained, she wondered if you'd like to come over this afternoon around two."

"Why does she want to see me?"

"Loretta is at home, but Ester said her mood changed the minute she got to the farm. Maybe seeing someone might help. Loretta asked about you several times."

"Tell her I'll come over and bring along Wendy. Loretta said she wants to meet her."

"I did. I knew you wanted to help if you could. That poor girl is having such a hard time."

Jim and Dad came in ten minutes later. I'd changed into better clothes and sat at the table with hot cocoa.

"Dress up nice just to pitch chicken shit into a spreader," Jim said, sitting down across from me.

"No more talk of work at the table. Danny has something he has to do."

"Yeah, clean the chicken house," Jim protested. "I have to grind a load of corn, and Dad has to pull that bearing on the corn auger."

"No can do, Bo-Bo. You'll have to find another peon to do your bidding."

"What does Danny have to do that is so important?" my dad asked. "Pass the bacon. Have some table manners, Jim."

"Yeah, Jim," I said with a chuckle. It was usually Jim taking off while I stayed home doing grunt work.

"Loretta is home, and Ester called this morning asking if Danny could come over at around two this afternoon."

"Do you think that's wise? We have that court hearing next Friday. Maybe we ought to call the attorney first," my father said.

My mother struggled between what was wise and what was right. "I think we have to leave it up to Danny."

"Maybe it will help. I want to do this, and you said yourself—each time we talk to the attorney it's fifty bucks."

"Fifty bucks. You're shitting me," Jim remarked.

"It's not coming out of your pay, Jim. Since they've asked, it's probably okay," my father responded.

"Also, can I drive the car?"

"Why the car?" he asked.

"I'm afraid the pickup might remind Loretta of that Sunday, and I'd like to take Wendy to see *The Hustler* at the Met in Fairmont afterward."

"How are you going to do that and do the chores?" Jim piped in.

"I've done the chores more than once for you while you goofed off with Becky."

"Linda, we should have kept that hired hand rather than have kids. Danny, you can take the car if your mother doesn't need it. I can take the pickup to the farm sale."

"What, you're leaving too? What about cleaning out the chicken house?" Jim said. "Am I supposed to do that while everyone else is screwing off?"

"And people say you don't pick up on things quickly," I said to Jim with a chuckle. "Okay, I'll come back and do the chores. I can take Wendy to the second showing."

My parents conducted an eye conference, communicating without speaking. My father nodded and said, "All right. Go ahead, Danny. It's too muddy in the field to go out with a spreader anyway."

Jim grinned like a hyena. No one would have to clean the chicken house today. I bent close to his ear as I walked by him and whispered, "Have you ever heard the term *piss off*? I believe it's English. Have fun grinding corn, you limp dick."

"You'd best stay out of my way, you little fart, or I'll kick a mud hole in your ass, then stomp it dry," he yelled at my back.

"Jim, for heaven's sake," my mother chided.

"He told me to piss off!"

"What does that even mean?" Mom asked.

"I don't know. It's English."

My father left at about ten for the farm sale. I'd forgotten to take Steve's knife out of the pickup and hoped he wouldn't find it. If he did, I could explain it by saying it was Steve's. I called Wendy. We talked for a few minutes before I asked her to go with me to Loretta's. She said she would but seemed hesitant, but it may have been my paranoia kicking up a notch.

The few puddles that remained in the low areas of our fields were drying up with the return of the temperatures in the fifties and a cloudless sunny sky. A flock of starlings circled overhead the eighty acres we'd picked, then dove en masse to scavenge corn left by the picker. A red-tailed hawk sat on the dead branch of an old oak at the edge of the field, watching. As the hawk spread its massive wings and ascended into the sky, the starlings left their feeding en masse, scattering, then grouping again above another field. Even the birds had to be wary of a free lunch.

After lunch, I finished the few chores I had left. While around the chicken house, I gathered the eggs to save my mother from having to do it. Dad hadn't washed the Pontiac Bonneville for a couple of weeks. Dirt layered the sides, and there was a large smear on the windshield. I got a pail of water, added soap, and in less than an hour, the Bonneville gleamed in the bright sunlight. Taking the Pontiac was special, and I wanted everything perfect for my first actual date with Wendy.

She was on her porch as I pulled to the curb. Before I could leave the car, she came down the sidewalk and slid into the passenger seat. She was crying.

"What's wrong, Wendy? What's happened?"

"Just drive, Danny. Get away from this house."

As we turned off Main Street, she slid against me, took my right hand from the wheel, and clasped it in hers.

"My father doesn't want me to see you anymore." Tears flooded her eyes. She wiped them away, but more came in their place. I pulled off onto a side street and parked.

"Why? What did he say?" My voice was breaking along with my heart.

"He said people were talking. They're saying vile things about me, and he doesn't want me to see you anymore until this is over. He told me I had to break it off today." She laid her head on my shoulder. "I don't care what they're saying, Danny. It doesn't matter to me."

"Maybe it should," I whispered. In my heart, I didn't mean it, but I was hurting her like I'd hurt everyone in my family.

"No, don't say that."

"Wendy, everybody who gets close to me gets stained. I try to make things better, and all I do is make them worse." Tears welled up in my eyes. We were both crying.

"It's not your fault, and it's not mine. Screw this town. I won't be bullied by snaggle-toothed gossips whose lives are as bitter as their tongues. You did nothing wrong, and we have done nothing wrong. I'm almost eighteen. They can't tell me what to do."

We sat on the side street beneath a red maple that had lost its leaves. Its leaves lay around us in piles of brilliant reds and golds, as tiny rain droplets on their surface glistened in the afternoon sun.

"We can see each other at school, Wendy. This is Banning. Your reputation is who you are. Maybe your dad is right. I saw how happy you've been this week. Friday, I saw you walking with Marge Bristol and Karen Jennings. You were talking and laughing just like old pals. Until this is over, people will associate you with me, and the old rumors will resurface."

"I didn't have that much of a reputation left anyway. Weird Wendy, remember?"

"Weird Wendy is a hell of a lot better than the girlfriend of a rapist."

"What's wrong with you, Danny? Are you giving up now? Are you quitting? Is that who you are? The guy who's going to make it tough for the coaches not to let him play. The guy who would make Principal Larson walk him out of the assembly hall. Where's that Danny at?"

"That Danny is causing problems between you and your parents."

"It's only my dad. My mother thinks you're good-looking."

"Yeah, that softens the blow," I said.

She leaned forward, kissing me. "You're going to have to get over this, Jocko. We're not breaking up."

"Do that again, and maybe I'll believe it."

She did.

"Once more," I said, pulling her close to me. When she pressed her body against me like that, I felt like I could do anything. She kissed me again, this time longer. "I'm a believer, but I may need constant reassurance."

"You got it. Now, move it down the road. Loretta's waiting."

Wendy turned the radio to a rock station as I pulled back onto the road. It wasn't right to put her through this, to be a wedge between her and her dad, but I wasn't strong enough to let her go.

CHAPTER 16

My chest tightened, and my mouth went dry as I turned onto the Tinsleys' lane. The hay barn seemed larger and more prominent than I remembered. Wendy must have noticed a change in my demeanor, for she squeezed my hand and smiled encouragingly. Maybe she, too, was seeking assurance. We were entering unfamiliar territory. I parked outside the gate next to Evert's red pickup. A gust of wind scattered leaves across the grass, sending more cascading down from the oak and hickory trees. I stared at the house, wondering if they'd heard us drive in. Even with the invitation from Ester, I felt unwelcome, an intruder.

"You look like you want to leave," Wendy said.

"I don't know what we're doing here. What can I say that I haven't said already?"

"She asked to see you. Maybe just being here and showing you care will help."

The screen door on the porch opened. Loretta stood on the porch but without the smile and friendly wave there had been that Sunday. Wendy followed me up the walk, and Loretta met us at the bottom of the porch steps. She was thinner than I remembered her being at the hospital. She wore a plain floral dress with a white lace collar and sleeves. The large columned porch stretched across the house, looking out onto the front yard. A partially picked cornfield across the lane went past the hay barn as far as we could see. Chairs sat on each side of a large outdoor sofa with fluffy cushions. Wendy and I sat on the couch, and Loretta sat in a side chair. She had a light jacket on and a sweater underneath. Her hair was loose and falling past her shoulders.

"Hi, Danny. I wasn't sure you'd come."

"Why would you think that?" I asked.

"People say they'll do things and they don't."

"That's not me. Loretta, this is Wendy Warner. I told you about her. I hope you don't mind that I brought a guest."

"No, I wanted to meet her. Welcome, Wendy. I thought we'd sit outside. It's such a nice day; we may not have many more before winter."

"Are you doing all right, Loretta?" I asked. "I've been thinking about you since I left the hospital."

"Some days are good for me, while others are not so great. Sometimes the same day." She giggled. "It's driving Mom nuts."

"Have you changed your mind about coming back to school?" I asked.

"I'm not ready yet. Maybe after Christmas. My dad arranged for a tutor, and the school allows me to take tests at home so I won't lose a semester."

"Loretta, are you concerned about what the kids will say or ask?" Wendy asked.

She looked away. I was concerned that Wendy might have pushed too hard since Loretta didn't know her. Loretta took a deep breath, then looked at Wendy for several seconds. "I'm afraid of what they think."

"You can't control what people think. Believe me, I know."

"How would you know how it feels? You're beautiful. Danny looks at you like you're a movie star," Loretta shot back. It was unlike her. I'd never heard her say an irate word to anyone.

Wendy turned to me. "You never told her about Weird Wendy?"

"No, only that we were friends."

"How would you feel if the same thing happened to one of your friends, Loretta?" Wendy asked.

Loretta seemed close to crying. We were playing way above our league.

"I would call," Loretta whispered. "I would try to see them. I wouldn't do what they've done to me."

The screen door banged open as Ester Tinsley carried out a pitcher of lemonade and several glasses. Loretta put her finger to her lips, silencing any further conversation.

"I thought you kids might like some lemonade. Loretta's been cooking all morning. Try some of her gingersnaps. They're delicious."

"They're just cookies, Mom."

"Let's let your friends decide."

Loretta poured lemonade as Ester brought back a large plate of gingersnaps, set them between us, and turned to Wendy. "I don't think anyone has introduced us."

"Mom, this is Wendy Warner. She's Danny's girlfriend."

"It's nice to meet you, Wendy. I best get back inside. I have a pie in the oven," Ester said as she opened the screen door.

"I wish I could make things like this. My mom's just a so-so cook," Wendy said.

"They're effortless once you know what and how much. For a simple cookie, gingersnaps have a lot of ingredients: ginger, of course; brown sugar; molasses; cloves; eggs; and stuff like that. It's easy once you've made them."

"Sometime I'll come out, and you can teach me," Wendy said.

"Oh, I would love to do that, Wendy. Any time," Loretta said excitedly.

"Okay, how about next Saturday?"

"That would be fantastic. I'll go tell my mother so she can buy everything."

Loretta jumped out of her chair and dashed into the house. The screen door slammed shut behind her. A second later, she stuck her head outside the door. "Are you sure that it's no bother?"

"A hundred percent."

I told Wendy she was the most wonderful person in the world.

Wendy shrugged. "Because I like gingersnaps?"

Loretta busted out of the door. "My mother said she'll make sure we have everything. We can listen to my new Beatles album. I've listened to 'All My Loving' a hundred times."

"I'll bring my Roy Orbison *In Dreams* album," Wendy said.

"Oh, I like him too. Well, not as much as the Beatles, but I think his voice is dreamy."

"Oh, barf," I said. I liked Roy Orbison okay, but the Beatles should have stayed in England.

"What? You don't like music?" Wendy said.

"Sure, the Beach Boys, Elvis, the Chiffons—and they don't look like Moe from *The Three Stooges*," I said in defense.

The girls gave me a round of *boo*s. Just before I was about to be attacked, this time for mentioning Johnny Cash and Ricky Nelson, Evert came into the yard looking haggard and upset.

"Sorry to interrupt the party, but I was wondering if I could ask a huge favor."

Loretta went to the edge of the porch. "What is it, Dad?"

"Yesterday, the hired man accidentally backed into the hopper on the elevator, and I'm struggling to align the chain with the sprockets so I can reconnect it to the elevator. I was wondering if Danny could help me. It will only take a few minutes."

"What's wrong with Len helping you?" Loretta asked. "He did it."

"Honey, I gave him this weekend off. We'll work every weekend from now until we finish picking the corn. He needed some time with his family."

"I'll give you a hand," I said. "I've reinstalled the chain in our old elevator twice. If you've got some old baling wire around, there's an easy way without skinning our knuckles."

"Too late," Evert said as he held up his right hand. His knuckles were raw and bleeding.

"Dad, let me put something on your hand or you'll get infected," Loretta said.

She ran into the house and within seconds was back out with an armful of gauze and tape. Loretta carefully wound the gauze and taped her father's hand. I followed Evert down to a line of double cribs, much like ours. A hopper lay in pieces at the end of the elevator. Holding the chain and reconnecting the hopper to the elevator required two people, but with the baling wire, it took us barely fifteen minutes to finish.

"That went much smoother than the way I was trying to do it," he said. "Thanks for helping and coming out to see Loretta. She needs to be around people; she won't talk to us."

"Kids have difficulty talking to their parents," I said.

"My dad had no problem talking to me. He talked with his hands."

"He was deaf?" I asked.

"Deaf, no." Evert chuckled. "When he wanted my attention, he'd slap the shit out of me."

"I guess that's one way of getting your message across," I said.

"It worked on me," Evert said, cleaning the grease off a twelve-inch crescent wrench. "The inventor of this wrench must have been a sadist or a psychopath, but it's useful when you don't know the size of the bolts."

"I know I've scraped my share of knuckles using one."

"Before you go, I want you to know something. I don't want you coming out to see Loretta anymore. This was Ester's idea. Having you here dredges up bad feelings for her, and you've done enough to hurt her. That monster you brought out here took away her childhood, made her a woman far before her time, and took something she should have given to her husband."

"She's the same girl she was," I said.

"No, she's not; look at her, for God's sake!" Evert said, his voice rising with each word. His arms stiffened at his side, and he clenched his fists. I stepped back, expecting another attack, but he suddenly deflated, shoulders drooping and voice barely audible. "She used to smile all the time. Now, I seldom see her smile or laugh."

"She was today, sir. Loretta needs to see other people, other people her age."

"They'll just hurt her, just like they've already done. Don't come out here anymore. It won't be pleasant for you if you do. You best go on up."

I walked back toward the house. I didn't see Loretta or Wendy anywhere, so I sat on the porch, poured another glass of lemonade, and munched on a small stack of gingersnaps as I waited. It was another half hour before the girls reappeared from a farm path between two cornfields. Loretta led a bay-colored mare, and Wendy rode a chestnut gelding bareback. They walked past the house, waving as if riding in a parade. I waved back. They laughed and talked as they approached the house, and it was not the Loretta her father had described. Loretta was smiling and animated, just like she'd been that Sunday when she came down the sidewalk to greet Brent and me.

"You missed a great time. Loretta took me for a ride on her horses. I love horses but never get to ride," Wendy said.

Both looked slightly disheveled from the ride but also relaxed, like two old friends. I hadn't foreseen this outcome, but it pleased me. I'd been worried about helping Loretta when the solution had been right beside me in the car. We sat on the porch for another hour. Loretta brought out her portable record player, and we listened to the Beatles. It was close to five when I pried Wendy away.

"If we're going to the movie tonight, we should probably leave now," I said.

"Do you have to go?" Loretta asked.

"I'll come back again. Think about what we talked about, and call me anytime. I mean that—anytime," Wendy said.

Loretta held Wendy's hand as we walked down the sidewalk. She was reluctant to let it go when we got to the gate. "I'll see you next Saturday!" she yelled as we drove away.

Wendy remained unusually reserved as we drove toward Banning. I waited, hoping I wouldn't have to probe, but as we neared the blacktop, I asked, "What did you two talk about when you were riding?"

"Girl stuff mostly."

"How about the stuff that's not girl stuff?"

"I don't know if I helped," Wendy said.

"What do you mean? Loretta was smiling and laughing when you came back."

"It's not that. Loretta enjoyed our visit, and she needed that. But she's not confronting what occurred. She thinks what happened . . . I don't know, made her dirty. Somehow, she feels it was her fault, and she doesn't understand why he hurt her like that. She said he was so friendly, then just turned on her. She thinks she may have given him the idea that she wanted him to do that. I told her about what Brent did to me."

"Why?"

"I thought it might help her understand it wasn't her. It was Brent. Nothing she did caused it to happen. She asked me if he'd penetrated me. Those are the words she used. I said no, and then she said, 'Then you're not a slut.' I almost cried." Wendy wiped a tear away. "She didn't want to talk about it anymore. Then she just smiled as if everything was fine and asked me if I thought the Banning Raiders would keep the regional title without Brent playing."

"I think her father is responsible for some of that."

"Why do you say that?" Wendy asked.

"It's just things he said like that Brent took away her childhood, made her a woman far before her time, took something she should have given to her husband."

"That's terrible."

"He also told me not to come back. He doesn't want me to see Loretta again."

"Why? You're the reason she came home."

"He thinks that seeing me dredges up everything that happened that Sunday."

"I think he's more concerned about you than his own daughter. What are you going to do?"

"I can't go to the farm if he doesn't want me there, but you can. I can go with you after all the legal stuff is over. Until then, it would just cause more trouble." I turned the radio up a notch for the Chiffons.

Wendy sang along with the melody, looking at me when she sang the words, *He's so fine*. As I pulled to the curb in front of Wendy's house, her mom came out on the porch and stood looking our way.

Wendy said, "I'd better go in."

"I'll pick you up at seven," I said as she hurried up the walk.

I arrived home ahead of my father, changed clothes, and was doing the chores when he pulled into the yard and parked next to the equipment shed. He started unloading tools from the truck's bed. I walked over to help and see what he had bought.

"I got a good price on some tools we need to work on the equipment," he said as I walked up.

"And some we didn't need," I added, looking into the truck bed.

"Some we didn't, but we need not tell your mother. Isn't that right?"

"Right on, it's you and me, Pop. Your secret is safe with good ole Danny."

"Have you been drinking?" my father asked, only half kidding.

He was a poor judge of comedy, but I lightened up all the same. I wanted to take the Pontiac tonight rather than the pickup. He gave me an odd look, then dropped the tailgate and pulled a large air compressor to the back.

"Do you think my smart-aleck son could grab hold of this and help store it in the shed?"

237

"I think that's entirely possible," I said, taking hold of the compressor's frame.

After we stored the remaining tools from the sale, we drove to the field to check if it was dry enough to pick. There was still water standing in the low areas in the south corner of the field, but most of it looked pretty dry. My father kneeled, taking a handful of dirt and letting it run through his fingers.

"I can pick Monday afternoon if there's no more rain and we get some sun. All except that low spot over there," he said as we walked farther into the field. "How's Loretta doing?" he asked as we walked back.

"She seemed better. She still blames herself for what happened."

"That's a shame, but it's understandable. Women react to that sort of thing differently than men."

"Why?"

"You're asking the wrong person."

"You mean Mom? No way."

Even with Jim helping, chores seemed to take forever. He even let me take the first shower. I was out before my brother could bitch about all the time I was taking. He wouldn't have to worry about running out of hot water tonight. I thought it was unfair of my parents not to have a younger sibling that I could lord it over and complain about. Where was the justice in being the youngest kid? I wore my favorite, a red-and-white pullover, with navy-blue corduroy slacks and brown loafers. After a last look in the mirror, I descended the stairs three at a time and popped out into the living room. Jim came out of the bathroom with a towel wrapped around his waist.

"I'll trade you outfits," Jim said as he passed.

"Not my color," I shot back. Based on his comment, I suspected I'd passed his inspection. It was time to boogie on out of there. Either Jim or my dad had filled the Pontiac with gas, and someone had vacuumed the interior. I suspected it was Mom since no one except Susan could touch her new Kirby vacuum. Even driving at the speed limit, which seemed like a snail's pace in the Bonny, I was ten minutes early picking up Wendy. I didn't want to sit in their living room with her dad since, from all indications, he hated me. I spent the time fiddling with the radio, trying to find a station that played mostly love songs. When "I Can't Stop Loving You" began playing on WLS, there was a tap on the window. I looked up and saw Wendy smiling back at me. She looked stunning, as usual. She hurriedly opened the door and slid in beside me.

"You looked surprised to see me, Yo-Yo. Were you expecting someone else?"

"You look different," I said, studying her face.

"You don't like it. I told my mom not to put the liner on my eyes," she said, looking away.

"No, I didn't mean that. You're pretty enough without it, but it makes you look . . . I don't know, sophisticated."

"Sophisticated? It's too much. Ever since we went shopping, I've felt like a doll she dresses up. I'm washing this stuff off when we get to the theater."

"I think it looks great," I said, trying to make her feel better.

"You're a poor liar."

"I don't get much practice. You look beautiful with no makeup."

"You're lying again."

"Not this time," I said. I gave her an elbow nudge, which made her laugh.

I dialed the radio to 97.3 KDMI out of Des Moines. We listened to the top ten. We both loved a new singer, Bob Dylan. Wendy scooted closer, her head on my shoulder as we listened to "Don't Think Twice, It's All Right." I parked about a block from the Met Theater. It was cooling down from the sixties. Wendy wore a pleated beige skirt with a matching jacket. She was shivering as I bought tickets at the window inside the theater. We passed an older man and woman reading a lobby poster. It was toasty warm inside. Two couples came in behind us, laughing and talking loudly.

"Hopefully, we won't be sitting by them," I said as we walked to the concession stand. "Do you want some popcorn?"

"Not unless you do."

I took that as a yes and bought us both a bag. I turned around to hand Wendy the popcorn as two boys, one bigger than me and one slightly smaller, stepped in front of me, blocking my path. The larger of the two knocked the popcorn from my hands as I attempted to step around him. Then, smirking, he squared himself, ready for a fight.

"Clumsy shit, isn't he?" the smaller one said, and the big brute laughed. I stooped to pick up the half-empty bags, but he kicked them out of my reach. I stepped back, preparing for what was sure to come next.

"What's your problem?" I asked as Wendy came up beside me.

"You're my problem, shit for brains," the big one said, coming a step forward.

"Shit for brains," the smaller one repeated and laughed.

I clenched both fists. If the big bozo took another step toward me, one of us was going down. The older couple and two teenage girls came into the lobby.

Wendy yelled, "Help! Help! We're being robbed."

"Shut up. We don't want your money, but I'm going to kick the shit out of your boyfriend."

She yelled again, "Someone help us! We're being robbed."

The man who had been reading the poster came over. "What's going on?" he asked.

Others congregated around us.

"They said they would hurt us if we didn't give them money. That one just got out of reform school," Wendy said, pointing to the larger one.

"No, no, I didn't," he protested. "I go to Fort Dodge High School and play football there." The two boys turned to leave, but the man who had sold us our tickets came out of the office. He blocked them at the door. I watched the spectacle and wondered what Wendy was going to do next.

"This young lady says that these two tried to strong-arm her," the man said to the theater manager.

Both boys again denied that they were trying to rob us.

"Let's see your tickets," the manager demanded. I held out our two.

"We've already seen the show," the smaller one said.

"Then what are you doing in here?"

Both stammered out an answer that made no sense. The manager grabbed the larger boy's arm. "We'll let the police take care of this."

They both looked as if they were going to fill their pants.

Wendy stepped forward. "We don't want to cause any trouble. We'll forget everything if they apologize and buy us two fresh bags of popcorn. We just want to see the movie."

"I think you're two lucky boys," the manager said, letting go of the larger one's arm. "Now, buy this lovely couple their popcorn, and never come into this theater again."

"I'll take mine with double butter," I said.

The smaller one bought the popcorn and apologized, while the bigger one glared at Wendy and me.

"Sorry about all that," the manager said. "If you need Cokes with that, it's on the house."

By the time we got our drinks, the boys and the manager were gone.

"I could have taken them both," I told Wendy as we munched popcorn.

"Yeah, but we wouldn't have gotten free Cokes, and you'd have no teeth to eat the popcorn." She giggled.

"Reform school? Did you know those two?" I asked.

"Never seen them before in my life."

"You're amazing."

As the theater darkened and the previews of upcoming movies came on the screen, Wendy said, "I am. Never forget that."

I laughed and squeezed her hand. That was my Wendy, and I loved everything about her. I should have felt good about what had happened at the concession stand, but I didn't. I felt smaller. Wendy had made fools out of the two assholes while I'd done nothing. As I concentrated on the movie, the irritating buzz of my cowardice resisted all attempts to push it away. I loved Paul Newman. He could star in a musical, and I'd still go. Wendy seemed entranced by Fast Eddie as he cleared the table on Minnesota Fats. Newman was the hero I wanted to be. It wasn't what I'd been tonight.

We walked out with the crowd and crossed the street to the parking lot. Two figures stood talking by a white car near where I'd parked. One was bigger than the other. Wendy saw them too.

"Let's go back," Wendy said, gripping my arm.

"Not this time, Wendy. You go back to the theater. I'll pick you up out front."

"No, I'm not leaving. You don't need to fight them."

"Go back to the theater, Wendy. I'll pick you up out front," I said again. There was no way I was going to run again. This time, Wendy's antics wouldn't stop whatever was going to happen.

"I'm not leaving. They're here because of him, and they're here to hurt you. Fighting them is exactly what he wants you to do. Why else would two boys from Fort Dodge be in Fairmont?"

"How would they know we were here?"

"I figured that out while we watched the movie—my mother. She's friends with a woman who lives next door to the Arringtons, and she likes to talk. Please, let's go back."

"And then what? We call the police to walk us to the car? I won't do that. Let's go to the car. If they walk toward us, then you can run and get help.

Until then, I'll do as much damage to these bastards as possible."

We strolled toward the car, my eyes locked on the two. Our footsteps echoed off the walls of the surrounding buildings. The dim light in the middle of the lot cast the two in deep shadows. The larger figure turned toward us as we approached. I couldn't make out his features. Wendy stayed at my side, clutching my arm. As we neared the car, the smaller of the two stepped into the light and smiled at us. She had a pleasant smile.

"I think I can take the girl if you can hold the boy off," I said, opening the car door for Wendy.

"Don't joke about this. You did another impulsive, stupid thing."

"Come on, Wendy. Give me a break. Am I supposed to run at the slightest sign of danger? What kind of person would that make me?"

"A smart one."

"No, that would make me a coward. I did nothing in the theater. You stepped in. You were the one who yelled for the manager, while I just stood there with my finger in my butt. Then, you made them apologize. Do you know how that made me feel?"

"Nothing happened. No one got hurt. It should have made you feel good."

"Well, it didn't, but that's not the point. Is that the guy you want to marry? A guy who cowers because he could get hurt, a guy who lets someone else do his fighting? I don't want to do anything that will cause me to lose you, but I can't be someone I'm not. I look at you and think, how can she respect me when I run from anyone who threatens us? That kid could have probably beaten the crap out of me. So what? I'll heal. I have before. Wendy, I'd rather lose a fight than run from one. That's not impulsive. That's who I am."

We sat with the car running, keeping us warm, each in our own thoughts. I was afraid anything I said would be wrong. Wendy broke the silence. A tear glistened in her eye. "I don't want to fight with you, Danny. For so long, I've been angry with everyone. It's like I've been walking uphill for three years.

Meeting you made me realize how unhappy I truly was. I was on the outside looking in and forgot what it was like to be accepted and wanted. Being with you has been the difference, but I'm afraid something will happen and bring Weird Wendy back."

I pulled her close, and she rested her head against my neck. "You're the only thing that matters to me. I don't care if you're Weird Wendy, Gorgeous George, or Ole Wendy Warner. I never want to be without you."

We kissed with a depth I'd never felt. Her body melted into mine. I looked into her beautiful eyes and was lost. I knew this was love. It couldn't be anything else, for nothing else could feel this wonderful. She snuggled close on the drive back to Banning. We sang along to songs, talked about life after high school, and argued about whether Paul Newman and Jackie Gleason were actually making the pool shots. It was just after eleven when we arrived at Wendy's house. I scanned the street for any movement or cars that shouldn't be there. There would not be a repeat performance of the beat-the-shit-out-of-Danny movie. It felt so natural to have Wendy's body next to me. According to my brother, the real thing was when you wanted to be with her only, protect her, and do anything for her. I felt all those things for Wendy.

"I have to go in. If I stay out here much longer, my mother will interrogate me about what we were doing. Parents don't believe that two teenagers can just talk."

"I know. I wonder what they were doing at our age to be so suspicious." I walked Wendy to the door; she gave me a peck on the cheek and went inside. I was about to pull away from the curb when a single headlight flicked on behind me, and then an engine roared, piercing the night's quiet. A motorcycle engine. The low throb of a Harley-Davidson. Seconds later, Brent Arrington moved slowly by my side window, glaring at me as he passed. He formed his index finger into a pistol and pointed at me as he passed, then sped up and was gone.

I started the car. A Harley wasn't a match for a '62 Pontiac Bonneville. At the stop sign, I could still see the dot of red from his taillight. The Bonneville had a 389 V8. I could be behind him within two to three minutes. A slight tap on the Harley's rear tire at sixty miles an hour and Brent would threaten no one again. I watched the red dot disappear after a few seconds, then turned left toward home. There would come a day when I would not turn the other way.

CHAPTER 17

My mother went to church on Sunday morning. My father and I cleaned out the chicken house, while Jim and Becky attended a church thing in Banning. I was feeding Ranger table scraps from lunch when a black '62 Chevy Impala came down our lane, dodging the potholes created by the recent rains. As the car turned into the yard, I spotted Steve behind the wheel, grinning like a Cheshire cat. The driver's side window receded, smooth as butter.

"Power windows," Steve said. "Get in."

"I can't. I have to help my dad with some things. Is this yours?" I asked. I hoped my face was not turning green with envy. The sleek Impala with its SS logo was the coolest piece of iron Detroit had ever produced.

"Don't rain on my parade. Get in and let me gloat."

I went to the passenger side and slipped into the red bucket seat. The car was knockout beautiful. A four-speed chrome shifter protruded from the console. "She beautiful, Steve. What's under the hood?"

"She's got it all—327/300, four-barrel carb, dual exhaust." Steve could barely contain himself, and I didn't blame him. This was a Super Sport

Impala—the car I dreamed of having.

"Did your folks die and leave you the farm?" I asked, running my hand over the padded dash.

"Pretty nice, huh? I would appreciate it if you didn't come on the bucket seat."

"I might just do that. She's so cool. When did you get it?"

"Yesterday, Dad and I went to Des Moines to pick up my aunt from the airport. The plane was four hours late, so we stopped at a dealership and walked around the lot to kill time. This baby was sitting there. Someone had traded it in for a new one with not even five thousand miles on it. I got in and sat behind the wheel, wishing it was mine, when the salesman came out and started bending my dad's ear. Shit, I wanted this car so bad that I was drooling all over the steering wheel. The salesman talked to my dad for a while, and then they went inside. I stayed in the car, plotting ways to get my dad to buy it for me. When they came out, my dad handed me the keys and asked if I could find my way home."

"No shit." I shook my head. "Steve, you're my best friend, but right now, I would kill you for this car."

He laughed and started the engine. It purred in a deep, muscular growl. "Glass packs. Can you believe it? Let's go to Banning. I want to show this sucker off."

"There's nothing I'd like to do more, but—"

"But nothing. It's Sunday. Hell, just for an hour. I'll have you back before your dad even knows you're gone."

Jim drove in and parked his '60 Chevy next to the gleaming Super Sport. My dad came out of the house to see what all the fuss was about. I opened the door to leave as Jim and my father walked around the car, admiring it as I had.

"Mr. Prescott. Can I take Danny for a ride?" Steve asked. "I'll have him back in an hour, and then you can work him till dark or till he dies, whichever comes first."

I didn't chime in, thinking it was a lost cause, but I tried for a disappointed look on my face.

"Half an hour," Jim said. "Then we come looking for you."

My dad gave my brother a *who-put-you-in-charge* look, but he relented. "Ah, go ahead. Half an hour."

We did a quick drive to Banning. Halfway there, Steve dropped a bomb on me. "Have you heard that Brent's coming back and will play football?"

"No fucking way," I said. I didn't want to believe it. I'd heard rumblings at school, but I'd thought it was more of Brent's bullshit.

"Nope. Brent's dad, Ron, sent a request to Principal Larson, asking for his readmission to school and permission to play football."

"That's bullshit. He hasn't been here all season. Why should he get to just walk in as if not a fucking thing has happened?"

"Hey, man, don't shoot the messenger. They're saying that Brent was originally registered and attended the first day of school, making him eligible. Doesn't he have a trial or something coming up? Maybe that will fuck their plans up."

"It's a hearing next Friday to review the charges. Brent's trying to get the charges reduced or tossed. Our lawyer thinks they may drop all the charges against me."

"That would be great, man. You might skate on this one."

"I'm not skating on anything, dickhead. I did nothing but give that son of a bitch a ride. Fuck him. Run this thing up through the gears."

Steve stopped in the middle of the blacktop, looked to see if anyone was coming, then jammed the four-speed into low and popped the clutch. The Impala squatted as it dug in, leaving two rubber strips as the tachometer climbed to five thousand rpm. With a chirp from the tires, Steve pulled the shift down to second. We were just two miles from Banning when he eased up on the gas at over a hundred miles per.

"This thing is a rocket," I said. "You're one lucky little shit."

"You know it, Buddy," Steve said, all smiles. We circled Main Street, waving at whoever was on foot or in a car, and then headed back to our farm. I was happy for Steve, even if he had the car I had wet dreams about. I enjoyed seeing him so ecstatic and happy. As I got out of the car, I said, "You know you had a hard-on as you went through the gears."

As he left, Steve yelled out the window, "That was a jackknife in my pocket!"

The next morning, Jim and my father were changing a tire on a wagon that had gone flat as I walked up. Ranger ran up beside me, expecting a pet. I held out my arms, and he leaped up to my chest. He licked my face as I carried him halfway to the equipment shed before putting him down. I may not have had a cool car, but I had the most incredible dog in the world. Jim was able to pick corn in the late afternoon, while I hustled the loads to and from the field. There were some damp ears, but the cribs were louvered to dry the corn. By shelling time, they'd be as dry as the tassel dust on the stalks.

Jim was picking as my father hauled loads in and ran them up the elevator to the cribs. I was left to do the morning chores alone; it was nearly seven o'clock when I finished feeding the cattle. When I came in for breakfast, my father and Jim had eaten and were back in the field. If the weather held, we'd finish picking by mid-October. My father said to take the pickup to school for the rest of the football season. They had Jim's and my father's car if they needed to go somewhere.

I arrived at school about fifteen minutes before morning assembly and was at my desk talking with Steve and Wendy when Brent came in. He paused at the front of the assembly for several seconds before walking down the aisle to join Jerry and TJ at the back of the seniors' section. Conversation dropped to a hum, then someone whistled, another clapped, and it seemed half the assembly was standing and clapping. Three of the cheerleaders joined his group in the back.

Wendy, Steve, and I nailed our butts to our seats and did nothing. Brent was glad-handed and backslapped by everyone he passed. The king was back; long live the bastard. I grabbed my books, and although my first class wasn't for ten minutes and I'd miss the morning roll, I walked out of assembly and sat in the empty classroom. Half the high school had welcomed Brent back. All that I felt was anger. In my history class, someone had written on the blackboard *Banning Raiders 1963 Regional Champs*. The hero of Banning was back to put our little grease spot back on the map. I dreaded attending football practice. His return changed everything for me.

At lunch, Wendy, Steve, and Matt Prader were waiting at our table. I hadn't talked to either of them since Brent's royal entrance. I set my tray of roast beef, mashed potatoes, and carrots down next to Wendy and across from Steve and Matt.

"That was quite a reception Brent got," Steve said, picking at his roast beef.

"Where did you go so suddenly?" Wendy asked.

"Any place but the assembly."

"I guess we all need to get used to having him around again," Steve said.

"At least we have a shot at keeping the region title now," Matt added.

Wendy and I glared at him. "Is that what's important to you?" she asked.

"No, not me. I'm just saying . . . you know, that's why people welcomed him."

"We must have misunderstood. I thought you were starting a fan club," I said.

"I can go to another table," Matt said.

"Then we'd have to take our anger out on Steve, and that wouldn't be fair because he hasn't said anything," I said. "You can stay if you don't say another word."

"Okay, I can live with that." Matt shoveled a spoonful of carrots into his mouth.

I didn't feel much like hanging around the cafeteria. Wendy and I finished in record time but didn't leave the cafeteria fast enough. As we dumped what remained of our lunch, Brent and several teammates came in. His eyes followed us out.

When I entered the locker room for practice, Brent was already in his practice gear, talking with Dave and Rodger. I went to my locker, put on my practice gear, and laced up my cleats as Brent broke from his group and came over to where I was sitting. He said loud enough for all to hear, "Hey, Danny, they tell me you have been doing a great job filling in for me. I know things have been chaotic since everything happened, but I want you to know it's all behind us. Let's let bygones be bygones for the sake of the team. What do you say?" He was towering over me with his hand thrust out toward me. There was no compassion or friendship in his eyes, only contempt. I stood up, and we were toe-to-toe.

"I'd rather swallow a bucket of snot and have a corncob shoved up my ass. We may be teammates out on that field, but in here and every place else, Brent, you can go fuck yourself."

As I walked away, he said, "Sorry to hear that, Danny boy." He laughed and turned back to his conversation with Dave and Rodger, giving them a shrug and saying, "Well, I tried."

In three seconds, he had made me into a grudge-holding asshole. I'd responded precisely as he wanted, but I didn't care. I walked out onto the field. We did our wind sprints and a round of calisthenics, then broke into two squads: defense and offense. Esker moved me from halfback to wide receiver, alternating me with Richard Donnelly, while Brent took his old halfback position. Brent took several snaps from Ted. He was as good as or better than he had been last season. Brent pounded the defensive line, breaking through half a dozen times. Twice, he took a kickoff and went all the way. Once he broke into the secondary, there was no stopping him. As a football player, Brent was the best on the field, but where we had all been a team, we were now just supporting players.

After running several plays featuring Brent, we gathered around Coach Esker for his daily rah-rah talk, but Principal Larson and Superintendent Adkins came onto the field and signaled Coach Esker to join them. We stood speculating what catastrophe might prompt interrupting a practice. Guesses ranged from someone dead to Coach Esker being fired.

Whatever the two wanted did not sit well with the coach. He was waving his arms, and his face reddened with anger.

Assistant Coach Bailer returned from the huddle as Larson, Adkins, and Esker left the field. He told us to run three laps and hit the showers. I was taking off my shoulder pads when Esker and Larson entered the dressing room and took Brent into the office. All of us milled around, waiting to find out what was happening. A few minutes later, Brent came out of the office and slammed the door as he left. He threw off his practice gear as he walked, rammed his shoulder pads into a locker, and sat on the bench in front of his locker. Several asked what had happened, but Brent was no longer in the mood to talk. He pulled his clothes from the locker and jammed them on as if there was a fire.

Dave sat down beside Brent. "What's going on, Brent?"

He stood up. "Fucking Pepperdine complained to the High School Athletic Association. They say I'm ineligible to play for ninety days because I transferred from Fort Dodge. Larson said they'll fight it, but I can't play Friday night or maybe at all." Brent kicked a bench across the room, barely missing Ted. "It's going to totally fuck my chances for a scholarship at Michigan. I don't want to play for some pissant college. I'm too damn good for that. The motherfuckers," he shouted as he shoved his way past several players until he was face-to-face with me, contorted with rage.

"This is all your fault, Prescott. All because you're a pansy-assed snitch. All you had to do was shut your fucking mouth, and we'd both have been home free. You're not fit to hold my jockstrap. I'll make you pay for what you've done to me."

He spit in my face.

"What's it take to make you fight, Danny Boy?"

I wiped the spit from my face with my forearm and took a step back to slam a punch into his fucking face just as Rodger stepped between us and shoved Brent backward. "You need to leave now, Brent. You said your piece. Danny is not responsible for what's happened to you. You are."

Rodger was the only guy in school who could come out of a fight with Brent in one piece. If bets were taken, I'd have put my money on Rodger. No locker doors shut, no one spoke, no one even twitched as the two titans stood nose to nose. Everyone waited for the explosion.

Brent smiled and laid his hand on Rodger's shoulder. "Sure, Zimmerman, whatever." He shrugged as if it didn't matter. "Good luck winning the district title, much less the regional one." He stepped toward the door, then turned to face the group. "Every one of you fuckers has ridden on my back for years. Now you stand there like fucking statues, a bunch of chickenshits. I'm the only reason you ever won a fucking game—you could go in there and tell Coach Esker that if I don't play, you don't play. That's what I would have done for you, so now fuck every one of you."

Brent flung open the door, hammering it hard against the concrete wall, and was gone. The locker room had never been this quiet. It was like we were all frozen in time until Ted Ellington said, "The guy is a fucking asshole. Did you hear what he said? Well, fuck him. If they bring Brent back, I'm out of here. They can find another quarterback."

"Same here," another said.

TJ added, "Yeah, fuck that egotistical asshole. He didn't win shit. The team did, and we'll win without him now."

There were shouts of agreement as players headed for the showers.

I sat down next to Rodger. "I appreciate your stepping in, but next time I'll handle it. I'm not afraid of him."

"No one thinks you are, but don't be stupid. If you'd fought him, both of you would be out, and the Raiders would be out a halfback. I did it as much for the team as for you. Look, dude, I'm going to share something with you. Most of us were on Brent's side initially, but that's changed. We've all watched you bust your ass and work twice as hard as Brent ever did. He left the school and transferred to Fort Dodge. He didn't give a shit what happened to the team. You do. Just hang in there. Don't let him manipulate you into doing something he can use against you, and don't turn your back on him."

I stripped off my practice gear and hit the shower. I took what Rodger had said seriously. Before leaving the building and walking to my pickup, I made sure Brent wasn't around. There was no sense in tempting fate. Yet again, someone had saved my ass. I should have pushed Rodger aside and had it out with Brent, but *should-haves* didn't make you any less a coward. On the way home, I reviewed what had happened in the locker room. I'd let him spit on me. Most of all, what Brent had said played repeatedly in my head. What did it take to make me fight? What would it take for me to stop making excuses and be a man?

I didn't mention what had happened to Jim or my parents. I didn't want to lose my brother's or my father's respect. Neither would have ever stood there and let someone spit in their face, and Jim had cautioned me on further inflaming my father's anger at the Arringtons. After supper, I lay in my room, wondering what was being said about me and if Wendy had heard. Were they saying it was my fault that Brent couldn't play? Were we going to play that movie all over again? Now that Wendy had entered the mainstream, what was she being told about me? What was she thinking? How could she respect someone who continually allowed himself to be shoved around? I didn't like any of the answers I was coming up with.

CHAPTER 18

I'd gotten up a half hour early to feed the cattle alone while my father and Jim picked corn. As I pulled into a parking spot next to the athletic field, Steve swung his Chevy Super Sport into the spot beside me.

"Do you want to park somewhere else? Your car makes my pickup look bad," I quipped.

"The only thing that would make that pickup look better is a tow truck." Steve was grinning like he'd just pulled a fart off in church.

"What's got you so happy? Your rich aunt die?"

"First, I don't have an aunt, and if I did, she wouldn't be rich, but I did take someone to the drive-in."

"No shit. You put a goat into that new car?"

"No, asshole, but I'll tell you anyway, Sylvia Lindell."

Sylvia was a sophomore and a cute one. She'd just made the cheerleading squad. I couldn't believe that Steve had had the nerve to ask her. He was a good-looking guy but shy as a meerkat. It was great that he was going out again after being dropped by Pam Desett. That had put him back several years on the dating maturity scale.

"Good for you, buddy," I said as I shoulder-bumped him.

"That's the good news," Steve said as we walked, but he stopped just short of the main entrance doors to the gym. "And some bad news."

"Okay, I'll bite. What's the bad news? You have a pimple on your dick?"

"Brent's parents are petitioning the Athletic Association to review his status next week and allow him to play."

"Where did you hear this?"

"Pam is friends with Matty McMullan. She got it straight from Brent."

"Thanks for making my day," I said. "I'm going to look for a new best buddy."

"I may be the bearer of bad news, but I'm accurate."

"That you are, Walter Cronkite."

We walked through the gym and up the stairs to the assembly hall. No Brent. Wendy was at her desk, holding her chin in one hand, deep in a chemistry book. Her mother must have bought out the department store because she was wearing another outfit I hadn't seen: a tight skirt and a red sweater. A pang of jealousy touched me as I worried that every male above the age of five would want to put his arms around her. It was ten minutes before Principal Larson's morning announcements, so I split off from Steve and sat down opposite Wendy.

"You look great as usual," I said.

"You like it? I thought it was a bit much, all red. If one more person calls me Little Miss Riding Hood, I will rip their throat out."

"Did you hear Brent is ineligible to play football for ninety days?" I said, trying to determine how much of my skirmish she'd heard about.

"Yeah, he blew up at Coach Esker and Principal Larson. It's all anyone is talking about. I'm surprised it wasn't on the national news. No one talking about what he did to Loretta. It's like they all forgot. Rah, football. I'd like to shove that pigskin up their noses."

"Wow!" I said.

"Yeah, wow," she said, dropping her eyes to her chem text, then raising them back to me. "I also heard about your tête-à-tête with Brent."

"Is that all over the school too?"

"You did the right thing, Danny."

"You mean letting Rodger protect me?"

"No, I mean keeping your cool and not stooping to his level."

"We disagree on that. It's almost assembly time. I need to get back to my desk."

I felt like an asshole leaving Wendy that way, but my pride was sitting low enough to look up at my manhood. She followed me to my desk and stood over me until I looked up.

"I wasn't through yet, dumbo. Last night, I called Loretta. We talked for over an hour. She's a big fan of the Banning Raiders. I hoped she'd come to the game, but she said she wasn't ready yet. Speaking of which, you didn't call me last night."

"Yeah, I ah . . . I didn't feel like talking, and my mom has ears that stretch to every nook in the house."

"Which is it?"

"Which what?" I asked, confused.

"Your mom or the thing about you not wanting to talk?"

"I knew you'd asked about what happened at practice."

"He's not here this morning. His personal cheerleader, Matty, said the school board is petitioning the IHSAA to reconsider his eligibility since he initially registered for school in Banning. I would have thought the entire cheerleading squad would be mourning and wearing black today."

"I know. Steve filled me in. Did you know he took Sylvia Lindell to the drive-in?"

"I think Steve can do better."

"What? She's really cute."

"Is that what's important? She thinks she's something now that she made the cheerleading squad. She'll need a stronger neck to hold up her big head."

"You're usually not this nasty . . . this early," I added.

"Watch it, buddy; you can be replaced." Wendy laughed.

The bell sounded for morning assembly as she returned to her desk. Principal Larson entered the hall and took his exalted position at the front of the assembly, encouraging everyone to attend the pep rally. We shuffled on to our assigned classes to fill our heads with facts and figures we would never use or remember. At lunch, our private table had grown from two to six. Steve and Sylvia sat across from Wendy and me, with Matt and Ted beside them. Wendy nudged me. She smiled as if we'd just received an award, and maybe we had.

Brent's blow-up in the locker room had turned the tide in my direction, and it felt good. I'd taken everything for granted—acceptance, friendships, school, and football. Losing it made me realize what was important and what was meaningless. Maybe you had to lose something to know its value.

I had a free period before practice, so I worked out in the weight room with Rodger. Neither of us mentioned Brent or what had gone on yesterday. At practice, there were comments about the unfairness of Brent not being allowed to play, but the coaches shut that down quickly. After that, everyone ignored the fact as if it were a pimple on the homecoming queen's nose. Everyone speculated the Esker would post the team roster for Friday's game after practice. For some players, this would be their last day. My stomach was doing flips as I eyed Richard. He looked anxious too, which told me he hadn't been told he had the halfback position. That sparked an element of hope in me.

We scrimmaged for most of the practice. He and I changed positions throughout the practice. Richard made a couple of good runs, but I hit the line harder and made more yardage. Three times, Rodger brought me down for a loss. He was by far the best tackle the Raiders had on defense and the best blocker we had on offense, and he could play both when necessary.

As we went through the drills, I played the scenario about what I would do if my name wasn't called. I was better than Richard, but it didn't mean I would suit up or play the halfback position. Coach had forewarned me about that. There were still plenty of people around that didn't want me on the team. Lies lived long lives in Banning, and minds were hard to change. Some people couldn't admit they'd been wrong, while others wanted to believe the worst. If I didn't get a uniform, I planned to stand stoically, as if I'd expected not to be on the traveling squad all along. I'd congratulate everyone who made the team, but this would be my last day playing football. Fuck a bunch of school spirit.

We were all out of the shower, with most of us dressed, when the coaches came out of Esker's office. He was holding the notorious roster as he walked to the front. It was like Christmas, and Santa's bag didn't have a present for everyone. Esker said that he appreciated everyone's hard work and emphasized our unity as a team regardless of who was on the starting lineup and those in reserve or on the second team. He posted the list on the bulletin board and asked me to come to his office. He was standing as I entered, so I didn't take a seat.

"Danny, I want to compliment you on your sportsmanship, even yesterday when you played against Brent. You always give it everything you have, and you're one of our best players."

"Thank you," I said.

"But that's not why I asked you in here. Coach Bailer and I feel you're the best player to fill the halfback position. You're probably well aware of that. You're equally good at wide receiver, so your ability is not in question here. However . . ."

Whatever came after *however* was always the part that destroyed everything said before it. It must have made him feel better to say it because it sure didn't do a fucking thing for my attitude.

"At the last school board meeting, several parents presented a petition demanding that they suspend you and Brent from playing on the team until your cases are decided. That puts everyone in a difficult position."

"Does that mean I didn't make the team?"

"The school board decided not to take any action. Your name is on the team roster. I wanted to discuss this with you first. If you play, it might be difficult out on the field because it's a home game."

"I don't care. I want to play."

"If there's an incident, it won't be fair to the other players."

"How about what's fair to me? You said I'd given everything, and I have. You said I'm the best to play the halfback position, but in the same breath, you won't let me play because there may be an incident. How fair is that?"

"I didn't say you would not play. There's been no decision. Yet."

"So, when will you decide?" I asked.

"The same as always. We'll announce the starting line for offense and defense on game night. I was hoping you'd understand the pressure I'm under here."

"The only thing I understand is I may not play."

I left, only briefly glancing at the roster. As usual, the names were listed alphabetically. There were no surprises, at least not to me. My name was there, but Coach Esker had taken away any enjoyment of seeing it there.

Wendy was sitting on the pickup's hood, talking to Steve and Sylvia Lindell when I came out. They were all laughing as I threw my gym bag into the back.

"You are so funny, Wendy. I wish I had your sense of humor." Sylvia laughed. "When I try to say something funny, it sounds stupid."

"How was practice? Anyone crippled?" Steve asked. Steve had dropped out of practice last week. He'd not made the travel squad last year, and it was doubtful this year that he would make the travel squad.

"Not today. What's everyone up to?"

"Nothing much, just killing time with Wendy. Sylvia has to get home, but we wanted to congratulate you for making the team," Steve said.

"Thanks, but you didn't need to stay. Just leaving a gift would have been enough."

Sylvia gave me an odd look, and Steve laughed. "He's just kidding, Sylvia. You don't need to buy him a gift. Giving him money is fine."

Her eyes bounced from one to another. We were all laughing.

"I think you're all nuts," she said, grabbing Steve's hand and leading him toward his car.

"Care to get into my convertible?" I said mockingly.

"I need to get home. I have to babysit. My parents are playing cards tonight."

"I'll drop you off. I've got to get home too," I said.

As I pulled up to the curb at Wendy's house, she drew in her breath. I looked at where she was staring.

"Your dad," I said, nodding at her father, who was raking leaves in their front yard.

In an instant, her earlier smile had vanished. She pushed open the door and got out.

When I got home, my attitude had dropped to just a hair above *fuck-the-world*. Three wagons full of corn were waiting for me in the yard. I changed clothes and began unloading the corn. It was nearly seven when I'd finished with all the chores. My father came up with the last load as the sun was setting. Jim followed him up with the plow. He had almost finished plowing the west eighty. My father parked the load next to the elevator. I hoped he would wait until morning to run the corn into the crib, but that was not the case. As he climbed down from the picker, he pointed to the wagon. Football practice, unloading three wagons of corn, and chores had sucked what little strength I had left, but I hooked up the WD45 to the load and ran the corn up into the crib.

My father came up as I pulled the WD45 into the shed. I stubbed my toe into the dirt, bent down, picked up a clot of dirt, and threw it out toward the fuel tank.

"I got my old number twenty-five back."

A huge grin that went clear to his eyes. I hadn't thought it was a big deal to him, but his face was filled with pride. "That's fantastic. You should do a jig right now. What's wrong?"

"Nothing. I'm just tired, I guess. The coach said he wants to start me at halfback, but some people in town don't think I should play because of what happened."

"They can go pound sand up their asses. You have a right to play just like anyone else."

"But I'm not anyone else, am I, Dad?"

"This will be over soon. Just forget about it for now. You can't change people's minds, but the truth will come out. It always does."

As my father and I walked to the house, Ranger was at my heels, snuggling his nose into my hand. He made me feel guilty for not giving him any attention. I told my dad I was going to play with Ranger for a minute. Ranger's eyes told me I'd spent more time with the chickens than with him these last few weeks. I kneeled, and he snuggled his head against my neck.

"I love you, boy, and I'm sorry. I can be a self-absorbed asshole, but you always forgive me. You're the one thing in my life I can count on."

As we walked to the porch, Ranger ran circles around me, excited that I was playing with him. I sat on the porch steps and tapped my palm on my leg. He barked twice and leaped the last five feet, landing his total weight on my lap. His tongue covered my face as I hugged him. After a few minutes of petting, he relaxed, lying across my legs. As I stroked his head, I thought through my day. If this was growing up, it was overrated.

CHAPTER 19

My mother fixed a grand breakfast of pancakes, bacon, scrambled eggs, and a thin slice of ham.

"Linda, if you continue to make breakfasts like this, Jim will never leave the table," my father said.

"You should talk, old man. You'll put everything on that plate away and then steal some of mine."

"When it's this cold, you need a good, strong breakfast to ward off the chill," my mother said, enjoying the compliment.

"We have a good weather forecast for the game this weekend. They say highs in the upper sixties, then a cold front coming from Canada on Sunday," my father added. "We should be done with picking by tomorrow afternoon."

"If it rains, we can kiss that lower twenty acres goodbye," Jim said. "I'll pick it late tonight if I have to. That means you feed the cattle tonight, little brother, so get your butt home right after practice."

I got up from the table and snapped a *Heil Hitler* salute with a heel click.

My father jumped up, spilling his milk, glared at me, and said, "Never do that again, son. Never."

"I'm sorry, Dad. I didn't think."

It sparked silence at the table. We never discussed the war or watched it on TV. In our house, the war had never happened. Whatever my father's experiences were, they would always remain a mystery to the whole family.

I was on the blacktop before the pickup cab was warm enough for my breath to no longer fog the inside of the windshield. A few miles from Banning, I pulled my gloves off. I parked beside Steve's SS and hurried into the school, making it a few minutes before assembly. I was halfway to my desk when my breath froze in my throat. In the back corner of the last row sat Brent, holding court over a few devoted fans. My reaction produced a smile from him, and he gave me a friendly wave as his smile morphed into a sneer.

I sat staring ahead but could feel his eyes on the back of my head. Fantasy thoughts of walking back to his desk and pounding him stupid coursed through my mind. I glanced over at Wendy, a half dozen seats up from Brent. She gave me a wink and a smile. Thank God for her. She was sunshine on a stormy day. There were no announcements from the almighty Larson, so everyone headed to their classes.

At noon, I was walking down the stairs to the cafeteria when Ted stopped me. "How about working with me after lunch? I want to improve our timing on the long pass before practice."

He was a shoo-in for quarterback—and part of Brent's inner group. He'd been cordial to me on the field but showed no interest outside of practice. I wasn't sure I trusted him. He'd been one of Brent's close friends, but the incident in the locker room had changed that. He reached out his hand to me. I couldn't refuse it. I hoped Wendy would understand.

"Okay, I'll grab a quick lunch and meet you on the field."

"Why don't we have lunch together?"

"I usually have lunch with Wendy."

"Okay, I know where you sit. I'll meet you there."

Before I could answer, he turned away and headed down the hall. When I got to the cafeteria, Wendy was waiting at the end of the line. "You'll never guess what mouthwatering cuisine is on the menu for today," she said, looping her arm through mine.

"Let me guess. Boiled turtle on the half shell."

"Not even close. Mashed potatoes with sausage gravy, butter biscuits, and peach cobbler."

Wendy loved sausage gravy on just about anything. "You lucky girl. And it's not even your birthday."

"I know. Sometimes, everything seems to roll your way." Wendy giggled.

We moved through the line at a snail's pace. No one in school was skipping out on this meal. Ted came up from behind and cut in right behind Wendy and me. "Thanks for saving me a place, man."

Wendy looked at me, puzzled. I hadn't had time to tell her about him joining us or that he'd be working out with me over our lunch. She ignored us both as we got our food and sat at our usual table in the far corner. Ted placed his tray beside mine and began discussing what plays would likely work against Pepperdine. I tried several times to bring Wendy into the conversation, but she only answered in monosyllable words. She was upset.

Ted was picking up his tray before Wendy even took a bite of her cobbler.

"We'd better hustle, Danny, if we're going to get a few passes in."

"Go ahead, I'll be right behind you," I said.

"Oh . . . Sure, I get it. I'll be on the field." He picked up his tray and walked out.

Wendy gave me a look that could have frozen fire.

"I'm sorry. I should have told you. Ted caught me leaving class. This is the first time he showed any . . . I don't know, wanting to work with me, and the game's coming up with Pepperdine."

"And that's more important than being with me?"

"I am with you."

"No, you weren't. All you talked about was football. You're the one who got on my case; the first chance you get, you did the same thing. It's not fair." She picked up her tray and walked out of the cafeteria.

He was waiting on the practice field. As I ran onto the field, he shot a pass in my direction, a perfect spiral. I sprinted twenty yards, picked it out of the air, and tossed it back. "Take off about thirty yards and cut right," he yelled.

Ted tossed me passes from various points on the field for the next thirty minutes. He was accurate, and the passes were perfect spirals, but he was right. Our timing, when I cut, and how fast I ran needed work. As the five-minute bell rang. I stopped at the edge of the field. "Ted, I want you to be straight with me on something. All season you haven't said *boo, crap, kiss my ass*, nothing. What's the story? You're a good buddy of Brent's, and he hates me, so what's up?"

"Okay, you might have a point. Brent and I were good friends; you want to believe your friends. I don't know what happened at the Tinsley farm. I know Brent's version, but he always comes out as the hero in any version, so I can discount that somewhat, and it didn't help that he got his story out first. That's irrelevant now. What isn't is Friday night's game. I'm not an all-state quarterback and probably never will be, but I love the game and want to be as good a player as possible. Maybe I'll even pull off a scholarship to a small college. That's all this is about."

"Fair enough," I said, handing him the football. "See you at practice."

Wendy wasn't waiting at the pickup when the practice was over. I hadn't expected her to be there. I'd screwed up. I should have told Ted I had other plans. On the chance that she had walked home, I drove the route to her house, but I didn't see her. I turned back on Main Street and headed home.

After chores, I did what I always did when I was down. I lay on a pile of soft straw in the barn with Ranger, listening to the pigeons cooing in the cupola. I heard my father call my name once but didn't answer. Ranger laid his head on my chest, enjoying the attention. Wendy could put me in the clouds or drop me in a hole, and tonight, it was a hole I was peering out of.

I was up early Thursday morning, dressed and waiting for my father on the side porch. The temperature had climbed into the fifties. Jim, my father, and I walked to the barn together, and my father verbally planned his day as we walked. Going outdoors without being bundled up like an Arctic explorer was a relief. Jim and I added more bedding for the pigs, checked the steers for sickness, and fed the cattle. I finished breakfast as quickly as possible so I could catch Wendy before she left for school. I grabbed my letterman's jacket from the closet. When I'd earned my letter last year, I wore it every day until the weather turned too warm. I hadn't worn it this year, but it seemed fitting to now. It felt good to have it on again.

Jim slapped me on the back as I climbed into the pickup. "Looks good on you, and it's probably the only *B* you'll ever earn."

"Said the *C*-average brother," I replied. The pickup's engine drowned out his reply as I pulled out.

I drove by Wendy's house, but I didn't stop. The lights were on in both their living room and her room, so she probably hadn't left for school. I parked on the next block. She would have to walk by me on her way to school. While I waited, I went over what I would say. A simple "I'm sorry" wouldn't cut it. I saw Wendy in my rearview mirror as she rounded the corner. She stopped for a second, then continued toward me. I rolled down my window as she came alongside me.

"Need a ride?" I asked.

She didn't reply, just walked around the front of the pickup to the passenger side and got in. She sat for a moment looking out the windshield, then turned to me. I hadn't taken a breath since she got in. I interrupted before she could tell me I was an asshole. "I'm sorry, Wendy. I'm an insensitive imbecile. It was a mistake not telling Ted to take a hike."

"I didn't mean to be such a bitch, Danny. I was hurt and overreacted. Lunch was our thing. It was like you didn't care. I'm sorry too. I wanted to run out and tell you that, but I was too embarrassed."

"You're forgiven," I said.

"I take back everything I said."

I leaned over and kissed her.

"Okay, maybe not everything, but I thought we'd agreed that you were going to stop pissing me off."

"If I remember that conversation correctly, I said I would try."

"Then you're not trying hard enough."

"Point taken," I said, starting the truck. "We okay?"

"Yes, until you piss me off again."

I parked the truck, and Wendy and I entered through the gymnasium entrance. The cheerleaders were hanging decorations for the afternoon pep rally. We stood for a minute watching as they bustled around in their Barbie doll outfits, handing each other crepe paper, posters, and Raider pendants to place around the gym. This was their time to be center stage. Wendy split off as we entered the assembly hall. Brent was at his desk, his head down, reading. His entourage was growing smaller. I slipped into my desk without being noticed. The last thing I needed today was a hassle with him. The school was a beehive of activities, with everyone doing something and preparing for the pep rally and game. After my eleven-o'clock class, I rushed to catch Wendy at her locker. As I approached, she was putting her books away.

"I thought we were meeting at the cafeteria. Don't you dare . . ." she said.

"I've got a better idea. With the pep rally, unless the cafeteria has barf on the menu, no one will be at Mike's, and I've got enough money for hamburgers and malts."

Wendy clasped my hand. "What are we waiting for?"

I was right about Mike's. Inside was only an older couple and the cashier from the A&G Grocery. We sat in the end booth and waited for Gladys to take our order. I dropped a quarter in the slot of the tabletop jukebox as Wendy flipped through the song selections. We each picked two and agreed on the fifth. I knew her selections before she made them. The first to play was one of Wendy's, "Don't Break the Heart That Loves You," followed by my first choice, "I Can't Stop Loving You." No one on earth could sing that song as well as Ray Charles.

"I knew you would play that. I'll bet you memorized the number."

"B10," I said. "Someday, we'll start finishing each other's sentences."

"I don't think so," Wendy said. "With my vast vocabulary, I use words that exceed your single-syllable word set."

"I use big words too."

"Okay, tell me the longest word you know."

I tried to think of a big word, but my mind locked on words like "existentialism" and "sesquipedalian." Neither would be helpful in this contest. I chose *existentialism* since I didn't know the meaning of *sesquipedalian*.

"Now you go," I said.

"*Pneumonoultramicroscopicsilicovolcanoconiosis*," Wendy replied.

"That's not a word."

"It is, my vocabulary-challenged boyfriend."

"Then what does it mean?"

"It's a lung disease caused by inhalation of very fine silicate or quartz dust."

I sat back in the booth and studied her face, trying to determine if she was jerking me around again. I let it go. I lacked the mental firepower to challenge her. She was laughing while I decided what to do. When she laughed, her eyes widened with a smile that made her look even more beautiful.

"I knew that," I said. "I didn't use it because I wasn't sure how to pronounce it."

"You are so full of it," Wendy said, laughing again as Gladys arrived with our orders.

We had to run to make it back in time for Wendy's one-o'clock class. I went into the assembly hall to read the assignment for my two-o'clock. At three, the team gathered outside the gym door, preparing for our grand entrance. After the cheerleaders did a few routines on the gym floor, Principal Larson stepped to the microphone and introduced Coach Esker and the new 1963 Raiders football team. The band played Banning High's school song as the team ran out behind Coach Esker like conquering heroes to the students' applause and formed a semicircle behind the coach.

Each player raised their arm in salute to the cheers of the students as the coach introduced us alphabetically. *Prescott* and *Zimmerman* were the last two names called out. Last year, everyone in the bleachers had stood and cheered when Brent's name was called. I promptly dropped my arm when Coach Esker announced my name to only a smattering of applause and a few cheers. Rodger's name prompted a roar and stomping from the bleachers. It was like a double slap in my face. *Fuck every one of you* came to the surface of my mind, but I kept quiet. I thought it best not to share my feelings. Not until I was out of the gym, at least.

As we left the gym, Rodger came up beside me. "Don't let it get to you, Prescott. They're all dumbasses." He gave me a shove with his shoulder.

"I think they were saving all their enthusiasm for you," I said.

He turned back toward me, laughed, and gave me the finger.

I followed the team out of the gym for the ceremonial run down Main Street to the park and the burning of an effigy of Pepperdine's mascot, a wildcat. As the students descended around the team, I broke away. I stood at the corner of the parking area for a few minutes, watching as the entire high school flooded out of the building. I took my letterman's jacket off as Wendy approached and threw it into the pickup.

"It's a little cold to go around without a jacket." She pulled the jacket from the seat and handed it to me. "You deserve to wear this more than anybody. Don't let them get to you; it will tear you apart, Danny. A few cheers and a whistle. What does it matter?"

I put the jacket back on. She stepped closer, putting her arms around my neck. In those eyes, I found all the joy I needed. I kissed her as her arms tightened around me. Nothing else in the world mattered when she was with me like this. The embarrassment of the reception I'd received in the gym faded away. It no longer mattered.

"Want to go watch them burn a toy wildcat?" I asked.

"It will be the high point of my day."

We parked at the park's edge as Principal Larson used a torch to ignite a pile of old two-by-fours and rotting pallets. The cheerleaders danced around the fire with a stuffed pillowcase painted in yellow and black, and then, to the shouts of everyone, threw it into the fire.

"Rather barbaric, don't you think?" Wendy asked.

"Heathens, all of them."

"Next, they'll start sacrificing the virgins!"

"Good luck with finding one in that crowd," I said.

Wendy burst into laughter. "You're terrible."

We both saw her father at the same time.

"Oh, crap," Wendy said, and clutched my arm. "You'd better go."

I hurried toward the pickup. I didn't want to cause a scene that would embarrass Wendy even more. My hands shook as I gripped the wheel and drove from the park. I was a tennis ball slammed back and forth. We'd been laughing at the silly act of burning a painted pillow. In an instant, it had changed. Anger had etched her father's face, and I'd left her alone to face that. Had I gone because she'd told me to or because running was my habit?

As I drove into our yard, I noticed a new Ford sedan parked near the gate—too new for a salesman's car. I saw the picker parked near the equipment shed, and nobody seemed to be around the buildings. Jim, my mother, and my father were sitting around the dining room table with Merle Shagger, the attorney my father had hired to defend me.

"Good, Danny's home," my mother said as I entered the kitchen.

I took a chair next to Jim and across from Mr. Shagger.

"Danny, your parents and I were discussing some good news. I met with the county prosecutor this afternoon."

"I thought that was next week," I said.

"That's the formal hearing with the judge," Mr. Shagger said. "The county attorney will present his recommendations then."

"You said good news."

"Miss Tinsley has stated that you were not involved in the assault. That, coupled with your agreement to testify, has led the prosecutor to drop all charges against you and expunge your record. It's the best outcome we could have hoped for."

"Isn't that great, Danny? It's finally going to be over," my mother said.

"What about Brent Arrington?" I asked.

"There's a plea deal on the table for him."

"What kind of deal?" I snapped. Were they going to let Brent off with a hand slap and a lecture?

"They'll offer to give Mr. Arrington three years' probation if he pleads guilty to indecent contact with a child."

"Three years' probation for what he did." I shook my head in disbelief and stood up.

"Danny, understand. Miss Tinsley is not in any condition to testify. This way, she won't have to," Shagger said.

"So everybody wins but Loretta," I said. "Why isn't my testimony enough? I saw what he did to her."

"I'd recommended against it. You don't want to take the stand against Brent Arrington. His attorneys will smear your name and attempt to place all the blame on you. If they're successful, you'll carry that stain forever."

"He's right, Danny. This is best for everyone, even Loretta," my father said.

"It doesn't seem that way to me."

I went out to the front porch and sat down on the steps. Ranger ran up and sat down in front of me. I stroked his head and hugged him.

"Well, boy, the adults have fucked it up again. Brent walks away with little more than an ass chewing."

Jim came out and sat down beside me. "Well, sport, things could be worse. Brent's not getting off scot-free like you think. Sure, he won't serve any time, but indecent contact with a child is an aggravated misdemeanor, and he serves three years' probation."

"So I heard."

"It means he can't play football in high school while on probation. After being convicted of a crime against a child, do you think any major university will offer him a scholarship? Think about it, dumbass. What is Brent Arrington? He's a piece of shit in a football jersey. You take football away from him, and he's just an arrogant prick, just like his father."

"Football means everything to him," I said, grinning. There was joy left in the world. "You're pretty smart as big brothers go."

"And don't you ever forget it," Jim said, getting up. "Now, change your clothes. We've got cattle to feed."

CHAPTER 20

I met Wendy at her usual spot, a block from her home. She was smiling as she walked up. I hadn't expected that, not from the situation I'd left her in at the park.

"My dad wants to talk to you."

"Oh shit," I said, closing my eyes and putting my head back on the seat. Why was she smiling? My imminent demise was not something that should have made her happy.

"Come on. It won't be as bad as all that."

"Not that bad? Your father didn't look like he wanted to shake my hand in the park."

"He was a little upset seeing us together, but that's changed. We had a big blowup when we got home. The details aren't all that interesting, but the highlights are that he will not object to our dating, but he wants to meet you and clear the air."

"Are you sure it's not a subterfuge to kill me?"

"I'm pretty sure it's not."

"But you're not sure," I said.

"Come on. Don't be a chicken. I'll be there cheering you on."

"So this must be my pep rally."

We returned to Wendy's house, leaving the truck on the side street. It was better for her father not to know the location of my getaway vehicle. Howard Warner opened the door as we came up the sidewalk. He stepped aside like a doorman as we entered the living room.

"Take a seat," he said, pointing to a chair beside the couch. He continued to stand, towering over me like King Kong did Fay Wray. I took in a large breath and held it.

"Wendy feels I haven't given you a fair chance, and I agree, but I wasn't all wrong either."

Okay, was he looking for a comment? I kept my mouth shut till I was sure. Wendy cleared her throat. My head was ping-ponging back and forth between them.

"But that's neither here nor there," he continued. "My daughter is generally an excellent judge of character, and she seems to think that you're a good kid whom the people of this town have unfairly judged. They did the same to her a few years back, and that's one group I don't want to be associated with."

"Yes, sir," I said for no reason. I felt I had to add something to the discussion.

"I'm going to allow you two to see each other if that's what Wendy wants. I hope your problems work themselves out, but there will be rules until that happens."

"Sir, all the charges are being dropped against me."

Wendy looked at me in disbelief as if I'd just said I was Superman. I continued, "They will remove the earlier arrest, so I won't have a record. Sir, I just learned about the prosecutor's decision last night and didn't have a chance to tell Wendy."

"Well, that's great news, son. I guess the additional rules won't be necessary then."

"Yes, sir," I said again.

"Dad, we should probably get to school." Wendy opened the door and stepped out.

I let out my breath with a sigh. I was still alive, and I could walk.

As I got up, Howard put his arm on my shoulders with his face close to mine. "One last thing. You hurt my little girl, and you'll find my foot in your ass," he whispered.

I nodded. "Yes, sir. I'd expect nothing less."

"Then we're on the same page," he replied, tapping my back with a wink as I left.

I glanced back at him as I went out the door. The slight smile on his face said, "Don't fuck up, boy, or it's your ass." And I understood completely.

When we'd turned the corner toward school, Wendy asked what her father had said to me as we left. "He wanted to ensure we were on the same page."

She looked puzzled but didn't probe any further. It was one of those things that should remain just between men.

We barely made it to morning assembly. I hurried to my desk as Principal Larson took his place at the lectern for morning announcements. On game night, he asked students to park in the back of the lot, freeing up the closer spaces for adults. Of course, that would never happen and never had, but it was a nice thought.

Wendy and I met for lunch, and Steve and Sylvia soon joined us. Three others invaded our little lunchtime world, but Wendy and I didn't mind. Steve had just sat across from me when Ted and Richard sat down with two cheerleaders at the end of the table. Our exile table in the corner was full. Wendy and I exchanged a smile. It was like coming home. Lunchtime may no longer have served as our refuge, but now it was something better—a gathering of friends, which was what it was always supposed to be. Laughter replaced our muted conversations. Wendy was bubbly, witty, and the center of attention. I played her straight man, our version of George Burns and Gracie Allen.

On game day, football players could leave an hour early. I pulled the books I'd need for assignments over the weekend and went to the parking lot. I'd almost reached the pickup when Brent came around the car next to me. He wore his leather motorcycle jacket, making him look larger and more menacing than usual.

"Game day," he said, stepping in front of me.

"What do you want, Brent? Haven't you caused enough trouble?"

"Shit, I'm only starting, you fucking asshole. I'm looking at the cause of every problem I've got. I heard you've been lying to my friends about me."

"What is it you want, Brent? I've got to go home and get ready for the game."

"I want you to know I'm not taking their fucking deal, and you're not going to testify."

"That's where you're wrong, Brent. If you don't take the deal, then I'm going to testify about everything I saw and everything you said, so fuck off."

Slowly, with purpose, he unzipped his jacked and placed it on the hood of the pickup, then stepped closer to me. I could feel the warmth of his breath on my face as we glared into each other's eyes. There was no running this time. I waited for Brent to make the first move, and when he did, I would hammer the most brutal blow I could into the side of his ribs. From there, it was anyone's game.

"You got a problem, Brent? Come talk to me and Jerry." Rodger and Jerry stood at the back of my pickup.

"Danny Boy and I were just discussing the case. He has mixed feelings about testifying now. I'm just giving him encouragement and some advice."

"Come talk to us, Brent. Danny has to go home and feed the sheep or something," Jerry said.

"Stay the fuck out of this, Jerry. Your dog is not in this fight," Brent shot back. His eyes continued to lock on mine.

I didn't move. I wanted this to happen. At least with the other two guys there, I'd have someone to take me to the hospital.

"Oh, but mine is," Rodger said, stepping beside me. He took Brent's jacket off the hood and held it out to him. "You best be leaving, Brent. This is game day. I wouldn't want anything to happen to our halfback."

Brent took the jacket. His eyes moved from me to Rodger, and then he smiled as he put the jacket back on. "Good luck. I hear they've upgraded their defensive line. Jerk-off here—" Brent nodded toward me "—will be lucky if he has positive yards. The Raiders are fucked without me, and you know it. Good fucking luck tonight, assholes." He shoved me aside as he walked away.

"That was inspiring," I said to Rodger. "How did you know he was waiting for me?"

"We didn't. We were heading over to Jerry's car." He pointed toward a '57 Chevy parked across from the pickup.

"Thanks for joining the conversation, but I'll have to have it out with him eventually."

"You remember what I said, Danny. Don't expect a fair fight from Brent. That's not his style. We'll see you at the game."

When I pulled into our yard, it was about four thirty. My father was running a trailer load of corn into the crib as Jim pulled another load into the yard behind the picker.

"We're done," Jim said, climbing off the picker.

I was still in school clothes and said, "I'll change and help run that load into the crib."

278

"Don't bother, sport. We've got it. You've got a football game to play. Get some rest before you have to go back. Dad and I can handle it."

"Thanks, Jim," I said, but he was already walking away.

I grabbed a cinnamon roll from the pan as I passed through the kitchen.

"You'd better eat more than that," my mother said. Her back was to me. How had she known I'd grabbed a roll?

"Can't play on a full stomach. This is all the energy I need," I said, heading to my room.

I stretched out on the bed, thinking about the encounter with Brent. Even though I'd known he would probably kick my ass, I hadn't felt afraid. I felt good about that. The anger I felt tuned everything else out. I wanted a piece of him and was a little disappointed Rodger had stepped in, but knowing Brent, there would be another opportunity, and next time, I'd be ready.

I couldn't rest; I was too excited. I quickly dressed in a new pair of khakis, a navy-blue shirt, and a red pullover sweater—not bad for a farm boy. My mother complimented me as I went out the door, but she would have thought I looked good in bib overalls. Ranger escorted me to the pickup, and as I opened the door, he jumped into the seat.

"Sorry, buddy, we'll go to the river tomorrow," I said as I reached across the seat. He looked at me with disappointment. "Come on now, Ranger. You're making me feel guilty."

He backed up against the door. He had no intention of leaving. As I pulled him over to me, Jim came up and handed me his car keys.

"Here, sport, you need something besides a pickup to take that pretty girl of yours out after the game. Don't worry about Ranger. I'll get him out."

My brother drove a 1960 Chevy Impala convertible, white with a red interior. It had been my dream car before seeing Steve's Impala SS. A teenage boy's love for a car was fickle; it diminished with each new model.

"You're not coming to the game?" I asked.

"Wouldn't miss it. Becky is picking me up in her new Mustang."

"She's got a new Mustang?" I asked excitedly.

"Don't panic. It's a tin can with a motor. I'm having a hard time even fitting into it."

"Thanks, Jim," I said, taking the keys. "I'll take good care of it tonight, but I'll get Ranger out. He's had hardly any attention. I'll take him out to the river this weekend."

I got back in and pulled the dog onto my lap. He nuzzled my face and neck while I ran my hand over his body and hugged him close to me. "I promise, tomorrow we'll do something fun, maybe chase some rabbits, but tonight you can't go with me." I pulled him out and sat him down on the ground. He looked up, disappointed, then trudged into the yard, making me feel like a real shit.

I parked Jim's car at the end of the lot, away from where most people parked, not because of the principal's request but because I didn't want to risk someone dinging my brother's car. Half the team was already in the locker room. Esker motioned for me to come into his office. As I entered, he was sitting with one cheek on the edge of his desk. Whatever he had to say wouldn't take long.

"Danny, I know you expect to start tonight as halfback, but Coach Bailer and I have decided that Richard Donnelly will start tonight."

"Where does that leave me?"

"We're holding you in reserve to back up Donnelly."

"Like I did Brent," I said. It felt like a hit in the gut. All the hours of practice, working out on the weights, all of it for what? "Is that all, Coach?"

"I wanted you to know before we announced the starting lineup."

"Yeah, thanks a lot," I said, then left and joined the others in the locker room. I stood away as my teammates grouped around Coach Esker and Assistant Coach Bailer. Esker read off the starting team. Richard seemed surprised. Rodger shook his head. A minor consolation for the humiliation I felt at being sidelined.

We ran onto the field to cheers and honking horns. The starting players formed a circle, shoved their hands into the center, shouted "Raiders!" and ran out onto the field. Banning won the coin flip and chose to receive. Pepperdine's kickoff went deep. Weldon Palmer, a senior on special teams, gutted the ball on the first bounce but was slammed hard on the twenty-seven. The offense took the field. Ted completed a short down and out, putting us on our forty.

It looked like we were going to stomp all over Pepperdine. But after slamming into a block of granite named Gawronski, a tackle for Pepperdine, Richard fumbled on the forty-five. He was lucky to recover the ball. Ted tried a pass, but it went nowhere. Richard went to the left side, but their safety stripped him of the ball, resulting in a crazy bounce, and Pepperdine recovered it at midfield.

Our defense took the field. Back at the bench, Coach Esker placed his hand on Richard's shoulder and told him it was just first-game jitters and to settle down. Bullshit. He'd never tucked the ball away and then cut the wrong way. He had never seen the hole Rodger had opened. Rodger dropped on the bench beside me, pissed off. He shook his head and shoved an elbow into my side.

"When the coach puts you in, watch for Gawronski. If he digs his cleats in, he's coming straight ahead."

"What's Gawronski's number?" I asked.

"Don't worry about his number. You can't miss him. He'll be the biggest guy on the field. They put their best defensive players on the opposite side of Gawronski, so either Jerry or myself will open a hole for you. Like I say, he's slow but stronger than Superman."

"Esker isn't going to put me in."

"Remember what I said about Gawronski?"

"Yeah, maybe I'll just run out and tap Richard on the shoulder," I said, dropping my helmet between my feet.

Pepperdine hammered the ball down to our seven before our defensive line pushed them back to the fifteen. They took a field goal for three. It didn't look promising for the Raiders' opening game. We needed a runner like Brent, who could pound the line and open the backfield for the receivers. Banning snagged a short kickoff and reached the fifty. We had excellent field position to start our second possession. Rodger and Dave created a hole, allowing Richard to advance the ball to their twenty, and then Ted threw an interception. There was a moan from the sidelines as our offensive came off the field without a score. Fortunately, our defense again stopped Pepperdine short of a score on our own thirty-five as the quarter ended.

Halfway into the second quarter, Ted launched a forty-yard pass to TJ. The Raider fans were on their feet, and so was I. Richard sprinted off the line and cut right, pulling down a short pass to score. The extra point put us in the lead, but only for two plays, as Pepperdine's halfback broke up the middle, taking it over the goal line.

Our next two possessions ended in punts. Pepperdine's quarterback ran the ball in for a touchdown following a broken play to score from their twenty. We had a glimmer of hope after they missed the extra point. Our fans were not giving up on us, but another touchdown by Pepperdine and the cheers would be scarce.

We were ten points down halfway through the third quarter when Ted dropped a long pass to our tight end, putting us on our ten-yard line. The bleachers and sidelines came alive. I was on my feet cheering when they caught Richard in the backfield for a loss of twenty-five. Our balloon popped, and the crowd quieted down to a low murmur. Coach Esker called a timeout. As Rodger came to the bench, he snapped off his helmet and stood toe-to-

toe with Coach Esker. "Put Prescott in. That hole was big enough to drive a herd of cattle through, and Richard didn't see it."

"I say who plays and who doesn't, and you don't talk about one of your teammates that way."

He briefly glared at Esker, then jammed his helmet back on. Our kicker was as good as any, but he was about as accurate as a slingshot shooting apples from the forty-five.

Pepperdine took over and drove to their thirty. After stopping them on their fifteen, we ate another field goal. Now we needed two touchdowns to win. Near the end of the third quarter, their kickoff landed us on our thirty-five, but by the fourth play, it was third and five on their forty. It didn't look good for Banning. Coach Esker came down to where I was sitting. "Prescott, go in for Richard."

As I neared the huddle, someone in the stands yelled, "Rapist!" and I realized why Esker hadn't put me in. I tapped Richard on the helmet, and he headed off the field. The boos gained strength, and someone yelled, "Take the rapist off the field!" Then the chant came repeatedly: "Take the rapist off the field! Take the rapist off the field!"

Some man in the bleachers shouted, "Shut the hell up! We're here for football, not to listen to a bunch of fools." Someone else joined in, "Shut up or get out, shut up or get out," drowning out the original cries. The referee called a timeout. Rodger put his arm on my shoulder. Ted did the same. "Stay cool," Rodger said. "We're a team, and you're our halfback. Let's shove it up their ass."

My teammates grouped around me as the coaches and officials talked, and then the referee blew the whistle to resume play. Ted called a right-end sweep. Jerry and Rodger hit Gawronski one after another as Ted jammed the ball into my gut. I was in full stride when I broke through their line to a clear field all the way to the twenty. On the next play, Ted flipped a quick pass to me over the center, and I was in the end zone. My teammates slapped my helmet and gave me chest bumps. It was the most incredible feeling of my life.

Starting the fourth quarter, Banning's defense stopped Pepperdine on their forty. Esker put Richard back in but as a receiver. I faked a run to the left as Ted stepped back and hurled a perfect pass to him. We were midfield. I took a handoff, found an opening on the left between the cornerback and linebacker, and went in for six. As the two-minute warning sounded, we were ahead despite missing the extra point. We came back to our bench, circling the coaches. We were up by one.

"We hold them at their end, and we got this game," Esker said. "Rodger, how are you holding up?"

He had been playing both offense and defense to counter Gawronski. "I can play another five quarters," Rodger replied.

"Finishing the quarter will be enough."

Our kickoff was a wobbler, giving Pepperdine field advantage on our forty-six. The Wildcats had come to win. Two of their biggest players hit Rodger, knocking him off his feet as their fullback scored. Our lead vanished, as did the chance of victory.

TJ took the kickoff to our thirty. We had one timeout to stop the clock, and the play clock was down to a minute and twenty seconds. The defense was keying in on me, so Ted tried Richard on an end sweep, gaining a yard. The play clock ticked down to less than a minute.

"They're playing wide on the ends to stop a sweep. I'll open it up for Danny to take it right up the gut," Rodger said. Ted nodded, and we broke from the huddle. He took a fast count. I came past him in full stride, hitting the line with all I had. Rodger struck Gawronski hard, knocking backward. I lowered my shoulder, hitting him again, then bouncing off his right side and all the way to the ten. We called our last timeout and grouped around Esker, hoping for a miracle play. Gawronski was like a stone wall.

"They may not expect an end sweep," Esker said.

"If they catch us in the backfield, it'll be our last play," Ted said.

"Do you have anything better in mind?"

"Prescott up the middle again."

Coach looked at me.

"I can do it," I said.

Every muscle in my body tensed as I went back to the line. I glared at their defense.

Their helmets lifted, and our eyes met.

"Not one of you sons of bitches can stop me," I said under my breath.

Time slowed as the count stretched out, and then Ted yelled *hike* as my cleats dug into the turf. My eyes were on the defensive line as I felt the ball shoved into my hands. Rodger and Dave hammered the line, but Gawronski closed the hole. I hit the line to his left, twisted right, breaking the tackle, and struck their middle linebacker, knocking him off his feet as their safety hit me.

Twenty seconds remained on the clock as Ted yelled the same play, and we quickly formed up on the line without a huddle. Pepperdine hit the line with all they had, but as Gawronski came at me this time, I stutter-stepped to his right, ducked under his arms, and shot forward. Their outside linebacker and cornerback hit me from opposite directions, but I was over the goal line by two feet.

People flooded from the stands and sidelines, hugging players as we tried to reach the locker room. We had beaten the Pepperdine Wildcats. The Raiders had won, not with the great Brent Arrington but as a team. We yelled and shoulder-bumped our way into the locker room. I felt like I was riding a cloud and there was only joy in the world.

As I left the locker room, the cries of "Take the rapist off the field" seemed like a distant dream. I walked out into the cool night air to find Wendy. A small crowd remained as I went to where I'd parked Jim's car. Then it hit me. Wendy would expect the pickup. It was unbelievable how stupid I could be. I rushed to where I usually parked but no Wendy. I ran back toward the locker room to see if she was waiting there. I rounded the corner of the building. Wendy stepped out from the shadows of the doorway.

"I looked all over for your pickup. I thought you'd left to celebrate with the team."

She'd been crying. I pulled her into my arms. "Oh God, Wendy, I'm sorry. Jim let me use his car. I didn't even think about telling you. I'm sorry."

"I'm not mad. I don't know what I am right now, but you were great out there tonight, Danny. I am so proud of you."

"I didn't play that much."

"I'm not referring to that. You sat on that bench knowing you should be on the field, and when you played, you took that crap from the crowd without complaint. I wanted to kill them."

"That thought passed through my mind too."

"I'm proud of you, Danny. You didn't let them push you into reacting. I kept wanting to run out and hug you."

"I'd like to find the guy who told them to shut up and give him a hug," I said.

"That would be my dad," Wendy said, "who I'm also proud of."

We laughed till our eyes watered. What a fantastic night! We walked, arms around each other, to my brother's car.

"Most everyone is meeting at the A&W, and then there's a party at the Red Bridge," I said.

"Is that what you want to do?" Wendy asked.

"I want to be with you. I don't care where."

"Then let's go somewhere where we can be alone."

I drove to the edge of the river park. Other than one car parked far from us, we were alone. I tuned the radio to an easy-listening station that played love songs, laid my head back, and closed my eyes, enjoying the music and Wendy. She cuddled closer, her hair smelling of sandalwood. I closed my eyes and let the words of "Why Do Fools Fall in Love" spill over me.

She turned her head to me, and we kissed. I pulled her into me. My hand moved under her sweater, pressing against her breasts. Her kisses were more passionate, more wanting, as my hand moved beneath her bra. Her tongue moved over my lips, and I pulled her tighter, feeling the heat of her body. She squirmed against me, her body finding its rhythm as my hand moved down her stomach. She pulled back from me.

"Not now, not yet, Danny. I want you, but I want us both to be sure, and I want to give us time."

"I'll wait forever for you," I said.

Several cars pulled into the park. We sat up in the seat as Wendy adjusted her clothing. A minute later, Steve pulled beside us and rolled down his window. Sylvia was with him.

"Hey, hey, hey, you two watching for whales?"

"Pirate ships," I said. "I thought the party was at the Red Bridge."

"It was—until a mass of law enforcement surrounded us."

"It was one car. A deputy," Sylvia corrected.

Wendy pointed to the clock on the dash. It was 11:45.

"I need to get Wendy home," I said.

"Party pooper," Steve said, rolling up his window.

A few minutes later, as we parked in front of Wendy's house, I asked, "Do you have to be in by twelve?"

"If you don't want to talk to my dad, I do."

"I love your dad," I said with a chuckle. "I owe him a hug."

I was tired but elated as I parked Jim's car in the alleyway between the cribs. It wasn't the best place for a cool car, but the farm had only one garage, and that was for my father's Bonneville. I was feeling the exhaustion of the game as the adrenaline deserted me. The night's memories filled my mind as I walked toward the house. Jim's room had a light on, but I didn't want to rehash the game, so I went to my room. I fell asleep soon after, content knowing that life was good and even the worst storms eventually passed.

CHAPTER 21

I awoke to the sounds of my brother and father tromping down the stairs. I threw my legs over the side of the bed and yawned. Every muscle in my body seemed to revolt. I switched on the bedside lamp and inspected an angry bruise from my hip to my knee and its smaller twin under my left armpit. My room seemed uncommonly warm for a morning in late October. I slipped on a pair of work jeans and pulled an old Banning Raiders sweatshirt over my head. That would be all I'd need with highs expected in the sixties. I tromped down the stairs and into the living room, where Jim and my father talked at the table.

"Hey, sport, we were going to let you sleep late," Jim said in greeting.

"Great game, son," my father said.

"Yes, I was fabulous," I replied.

"Don't let it go to your head," Jim said. "You're still a pissant to us."

"Fame certainly is fleeting," I answered.

"Did you bring my car back in one piece?"

"The wrecker service said they'd tow it out this morning."

"Okay, now that we've cleared that up, let's get cracking," my father said. "When we finish chores, we can have the rest of our day to ourselves." He opened the door to the porch.

"That's a plan we can all get behind," my brother said, pushing me toward the door.

Something felt off as I closed the gate and followed my father and brother to the barn. Halfway to the barn, it hit me. Ranger wasn't beside me. I looked around, and a cold panic gripped me. "Dad, have you seen Ranger?"

My brother and father stopped and turned around. "Now that you mention it, I don't think he was around when we got home last night," Jim said.

When I got home, I hadn't missed him either. He should have greeted me at the gate. He was always there when a car drove in, but he wasn't last night. How had I not noticed?

Shouting his name repeatedly, I turned in a wide circle, expecting him to come running from around one of the buildings or charging off the porch. I ran to the cattle barn and flung open the doors, thinking someone might have locked him inside. He wasn't there. I ran into the straw barn and up the steps to the loft, calling his name, but there was no response. Tears welled up in my eyes as I dropped to my knees. It was as if someone had reached inside of me and pulled me inside out. Where was Ranger?

My brother entered the loft, dropped to one knee, and put his arm on my shoulders. "You keep looking for him, Danny. We'll finish the chores, then we'll help look. He's got to be somewhere. He'll show."

"Maybe he's run off somewhere, chasing a rabbit or something," my father said encouragingly from the top of the steps.

"He never runs off, Dad. I don't think he's been off this place since I got him as a pup."

"You keep looking. I'm sure he'll turn up."

Something was terribly wrong. I could feel it closing in on me. Ranger always came when I called, regardless of where he was or what he was doing. The more I called, the faster he came. In the last couple of weeks, I'd shown him little attention. Maybe he was teaching me a lesson, but I knew that wasn't Ranger. There was no vindictiveness in my dog. He loved me too much for that. I searched until there were no other places to look. I went up into the loft in the straw barn again. It was Ranger's favorite place on the farm. I lay on my back in the straw where Ranger and I had so many times. Tears filled my eyes, but my tears would not help Ranger. I got a flashlight from the pump house and began retracing the places I'd already searched, calling Ranger's name.

When the cattle were fed, Jim and my father joined the search, covering the places I had already looked, hoping a new set of eyes would find Ranger.

"I'll drive the roads," Jim said. "Then you and I will each take a tractor and search the fields. Stay here till I get back. Mom is calling the neighbors just in case he wandered off."

If Ranger were alongside the road or in a ditch, he would have been there all night suffering. The thought of that made me want to die. I pushed all possibilities of that from my mind. If he had run off, it would be because I'd mostly ignored him, and last night, I'd been too self-absorbed to notice his absence. Only having Ranger jump into my arms and feeling his tongue on my face would take that guilt away.

Jim drove down the lane, stopped at the road, and parked. Several minutes later, he U-turned and came back down the lane. He must have found Ranger. I ran to the pickup and yanked open the passenger door. Ranger lay beside him on the seat. Blood was clotted in his hair, and his skull was caved in. Someone had killed him. Someone had killed the thing I treasured the most.

All the strength went from my legs as my knees buckled. I sat down on the pickup's running board, holding my head in my hands. "No, no, not

Ranger. Not my dog. Oh God, not my dog." I fought a sob as I shook the tears from my eyes.

"Danny . . ."

"Where did you find him?"

"He was draped over the top of the mailbox," Jim said.

All my breath left me as my mind tried to grasp what my brother had said. How? Was it possible that my father and mother hadn't noticed Ranger when they'd come home? No, it wasn't possible. Our headlights would have struck the mailbox as we pulled off the road. We'd have seen Ranger.

"No, you're wrong," I said. "That can't be right. I would have seen him."

"Someone put him there after we were all home," Jim said. "As I passed the mailbox, I glanced to see if the mail flag was up. I'd put a letter in there earlier."

As I had done countless times before, I picked up Ranger from the seat and cradled him in my arms. I closed his eyes and held him tight to my chest. He was cold; Ranger was no longer there.

"Why would he kill my dog, Jim? Why Ranger? He was friendly to everyone. Ranger would have run up to him and welcomed him like a friend. Why would Brent do that?"

"We don't know that it was him, Danny."

"Who else? Who else would kill him like that?"

"I don't know, Danny. There are bad people in this world. I'll take care of Ranger when you're ready," Jim offered.

"No, I'll care for him like I always have."

I carried Ranger to the straw barn and into the loft. With the sun's warmth streaming through the doorway, I laid him down next to me, his head on my lap. He loved to lie here with me, the morning sun warming him, my hand stroking his head. I would never again feel the softness of his nose nuzzling against my neck, never see the joy in his eyes as we'd sat together on the riverbank. I would never open my arms and hold him in a hug. Ranger was gone. I lifted him from the straw and carried him down from the loft. There was only one thing more I could do for my friend. I would take him to the spot he would have wanted. He had such joy being by the river, watching turtles and frogs. It was there that I would leave his body, but I would keep his love forever in my heart.

I stopped at the barn, loaded a bale of straw into the pickup bed, then drove to the river and carried Ranger to our favorite spot. Here, beside the water, Ranger would lie alongside me, watching the river or running along the bank. Sometimes, while I fished, he would tour the area, scaring frogs into the water and turtles off the rocks. When his job was done, he would return and lay his head in my lap, and I would reward him with a pet for a well-done job.

No leaves remained on the large maples that shaded the riverbank. I fought the tears back that filled my eyes. Nothing would ever bring him back to me. All around me were memories of him. It took so little to please him: walking by my side, lying beside me as I fished, or just looking at the river together. I cleared a small patch of ground of leaves near the bank. The ground was hard, with roots interlacing the soil. I rammed the shovel into the ground, cutting through the network of roots. Two hours later, I slumped against the maple, the grave dug. If God were a loving God, He would unite our souls someday. I could at least hope for that.

I lifted Ranger's body and held him to me for the last time. Then, I laid him softly by the hole I had dug. Here, no one would ever disturb or harm him again. I carried the bale of straw I had taken from the barn and spread half into the bottom of the hole for him to lie upon. I gently lowered him into his grave, stroking his fur one last time before covering him with straw. It was the best I could do.

I stood over Ranger's grave, searching for the words to express how much

I loved and would miss him. I turned from his grave with no words spoken, for there were no words to convey what was in my heart. Ranger knew how much I loved him, as I knew he loved me. He would know that his leaving was tearing me apart. I didn't need to put what was breaking my heart into words. I left no marker on his grave, no reminder of the wonderful friend that lay beneath. His memory would always be with me, which had to be enough.

My father and Jim were pulling down the elevator from the crib as I parked the pickup near the gate and entered the house. As I went to my room, my mother was talking to Susan on the phone. I lay on the bed on my back, studying the cracks in the ceiling, but my mind was on the bastard who had killed Ranger—a fiery rage burned inside of me, pushing the grief of losing Ranger away. I welcomed it.

A few minutes later, I heard a car come down our lane, and I got up and looked out the window. The car was the ridiculous Ford Edsel that belonged to a neighbor whose farm was a mile south of Evert Tinsley's. My father and Jim stopped work on the elevator. The three talked for several minutes, and then my father and Jim came to the house as the neighbor drove off. I paid little attention to their conversation until I heard my mother gasp, "Oh Lord, no. What happened? She was doing so well."

I kneeled on the floor, laying my face against the floor register that allowed heat to circulate to the second floor from the downstairs oil stove.

"Where's Danny?" my father asked.

"He's in his room."

Their voices dropped, but I could hear their words clearly.

"It must be terrible for Ester and Evert. What could have caused her to do such a thing?"

"Howard said that Evert called him early this morning. He said they'd received several hang-up calls. Loretta had answered the phone at around nine thirty. She'd been expecting a call from some girl to find out who had won the game. When he asked her who'd won, she told him it wasn't the girl but the devil and went to her room. In the morning, they couldn't find her. Howard said he and another neighbor found her hanging by a hay rope in the barn. Thank God it wasn't Evert who found her.

"With rain expected, the corn may stay in the field for days, so the neighbors will finish picking the remaining seventy acres. It will be one less thing they have to worry about. Howard told me they have two pickers coming, and with mine, we should be able to knock it out today. I'm going to take the picker and a wagon over with me. Jim has to run over the Kesslers' for a bit, and then he'll come over to help fill the cribs. It's best we not involve Danny in this. He's got enough to contend with right now."

"You men will need something to eat. I'll bring the bread and rolls I just baked and the ham I have in the refrigerator."

"I'm sure everyone will appreciate the ham sandwiches," my father said.

"I'll check on Danny before I go to the Tinsleys'—just to ensure he's okay," Jim said.

I watched from my window as my father left with the picker, followed by my mother in the car. Jim left a few minutes later. A hollow coldness gripped me. I felt everything inside of me shriveling up. Loretta was dead. I couldn't shake the image of her hanging, her lifeless body swinging above the place that had started it all. The place where everything had been taken from her by Brent Arrington. The agony she must have felt as she walked to that barn, climbed into the loft, and placed the rope around her neck.

It was Wendy who she thought might call, or she would have never answered the phone. The devil could only be one person. The guilt I had felt was gone. This was all on Brent. He had taken Loretta's life as surely as if he'd put the rope around her neck and pushed her. He'd taken an innocent girl's life, made Wendy an outcast, and killed Ranger. He had to answer for what he'd done. He had to answer to me.

I glanced into the corner of the side porch as I closed the door to the kitchen. My mother had removed Ranger's old blankets. The corner seemed empty now, as empty as I felt inside. The furious rage I'd felt earlier was gone, replaced by a coldness unknown to me before. Maybe there was a point when nothing could be taken anymore, nothing remained inside, where a limit had been exceeded and it all had to stop. I got into the pickup and turned the key like I had that Sunday. I couldn't take it all back, but I could end it. I felt under the seat. The paper bag I'd put Steve's knife in was still there.

CHAPTER 22

I was in Banning at a few minutes after one. I drove directly to Brent's house on the corner of Euclid and Fourth Street. A narrow alley separated the backyards of the homes on Euclid from those facing the next street. I drove slowly past. The double garage door was open on the one-story ranch. The family's Lincoln was gone, and there was no sign of Brent's Harley in the driveway or garage. He was out somewhere. There were only a few places he'd be on a Saturday.

Cars lined both sides of Main Street. A handful of people stood outside stores chatting with neighbors and enjoying the last of the warm weather. At the stoplight, I saw Rick Deter leaning against the building. A cigarette dangled from his lips. I stopped at the light and rolled down my window. Rick eagerly came over to the pickup.

"Hey, dude, what's shaking?" he said, leaning into the window. I smelled the odor of beer and stale cigarettes on his breath.

"Nothing. I haven't seen you around for a while," I said.

"Yeah, I spent four weeks in County for tossing eggs at some old biddy's house." Rick laughed as he dropped the cigarette and ground it with his foot.

"Have you seen Brent around?"

"Not today, but he was around last night."

"When last night?"

"I guess I didn't see him; it was more I heard him."

"What do you mean?"

"I heard him go by about one or so. I'm staying with my grandmother. She lives out on the blacktop just before you come into town. Nothing sounds like that Harley, and he revved it up as he went by. If I see him, you want me to tell him you're looking for him?"

"No, I want to surprise him," I said as I pulled away.

I drove past the Skelly service station, where Brent sometimes worked on his bike, and then by Banning High. The longer I drove, the more the hatred grew inside me. Brent had never had to answer for what he'd done—not to Wendy, to Loretta, to me, or to Ranger. Because he was Brent Arrington, he felt he was invulnerable. Today that changed. Today would be his day of reckoning. Today he would answer for what he had done. Today he would answer to me.

I drove down Main again, U-turned at the park, and was about to drive by when Rick yelled my name. I pulled to the curb as he ran up to my window.

"You just missed him."

"Where did he go?"

"He didn't stop, but I think he was heading home."

I took Fourth and then turned on Euclid. The garage doors on the Arringtons' house were still open, and there was no Lincoln or Harley. I drove on by and turned on Fifth. I saw Jim's car cross the next intersection and pulled into the alley behind Brent's house. It was then that I heard the deep rumble of the Harley's motor. It came from the Arringtons' backyard, behind the eight-foot wood fence that enclosed it. I'd found Brent.

I opened the door, reached under the seat, and pulled out the paper bag. The knife was gone. In its place was a half-full pint of Four Roses whiskey. My father had found the knife, and he was drinking again. I sat down on the running board, holding the bottle. I'd brought this on too. If not for what I'd done, he wouldn't have been drinking. I slipped the bottle back into the bag and replaced it under the seat. It only increased my hatred of Brent. This was on him too. I didn't have the knife. There were other ways.

I walked to the corner and stopped at the gate to the backyard. The Harley was shut down, but I could hear movement inside. Brent was there. I opened the gate and went through. The Harley stood on its kickstand next to a toolbox with wrenches littering the ground around it. Brent kneeled next to the motorcycle with his back to me. I looked around but saw nothing I could use as a weapon. I watched him for several minutes, the hate building in me, images of Ranger stoking my hate. A car door slammed somewhere out in the street. Brent rose to his feet. He turned, looked toward the gate, and saw me.

He smiled as he pulled a rag from his back pocket and wiped grease from his hands. "If it isn't a yellow-bellied snitch. I thought you were all extinct, yet here you are in my backyard." He took a step toward me and stopped, looking around and listening.

"No one's with me. It's just you and me, champ," I said.

He chuckled, a sneer coming to his face. "What are you here for, Danny Boy?"

"You're going to answer for what you did. This time, you're not going to skate free."

"I already have. Haven't you heard? The bitch is dead, no trail. So what are you here for? Are you going to beat me up? You going to kill me?"

"I don't know, Brent. It'll be one of those. We'll have to see."

The sneer fell off his face as his eyes narrowed and darkened. There was nothing behind those eyes. I'd seen those same eyes on a snake. He reached down and pulled a large lug wrench from the Harley's saddlebag. Blood was smeared on the end.

"Is that what you used to kill my dog?"

Brent slapped the wrench into his palm. "The very same one, Danny Boy."

"Why did you have to kill my dog, Brent? Why didn't you break the pickup windows? Burn the buildings. Why my dog?"

"I didn't go out to kill your dog. It just kind of happened. I improvised. Wrong place, wrong time." He laughed.

"He never hurt anyone," I said, surprised how calm I felt inside. I decided then that the world was better off without Brent Arrington in it. He wouldn't need to fix the bike. He wouldn't be riding it ever again.

"Yeah, that was his problem. He came trotting up while I was putting the booze under your seat. I intended to call the police and tell them that a red-and-white pickup was weaving on the road. The cops would stop you, find the bottle, and wham-bam, you're off the team. I didn't want to leave him in the yard and risk you checking the pickup, so I waited in the cornfield until everyone was home, then sent him special delivery."

"You called Loretta too, didn't you? What did you say to her?"

"Heard about that, did you?" Brent laughed. "She thought I was Wendy. I tried a half dozen times, but her mother always answered. Sometimes, you get lucky. I told her I enjoyed fucking her, and she wasn't safe on that farm. I was going to do it to her again. It was all she was good for now."

Brent slapped the wrench into his palm as he stepped toward me.

I squared my stance, readying for his attack.

Slap, slap, slap.

He took another step, circling me, narrowing the distance between us. "I'm going to cave your fucking head in. The same way I did your dog." He continued to circle me, waiting for an opening.

I pivoted with him. If he came at me, I would have one chance to strike back.

300

"How are you going to explain this, Brent? You won't be able to lie out of this one."

"Explain what? That you came in my yard to attack me?"

"How you beat me with a wrench. The great Brent Arrington beats a younger boy to death with a wrench. How will you get out of that one?"

Brent stopped circling. He gripped the wrench tightly in his palm as he thought about what I had said. I stepped forward to rush him, but he jumped back out of reach, and he still had the wrench. I'd be lucky to land one blow before he hit me.

"You're right, Danny Boy. When you're right, you're right." He threw the wrench over by the Harley, reached behind him, and pulled Steve's knife from his back pocket. It was the one he'd taken from my pickup. He pressed the button, and the blade shot out from the carved bone handle. Brent playfully jabbed the knife at me, flicking the chrome blade back and forth near my chest.

"How's this one hit you, Danny Boy? 'Sheriff Brennan, I was working on my bike when Danny Prescott came rushing into the yard with this knife. He said he was going to kill me, something about his dog. We fought. Somehow, I got the knife and stabbed him.' You won't be here, Danny Boy, to refute anything."

Brent lunged forward with the knife. I jumped to the side, swung hard at his head, and caught him below his eye. He staggered back from the blow. He lowered the knife to his side as I charged forward, slammed into his midsection, and drove him backward. I struck him again, a straight blow to the middle of his face. I felt his nose dissolve against my fist. His right hand went to his face, inspecting the damage. Blood oozed through his fingers and down his arm. His nose was pancaked against his face. He held the knife out in front of him, but most of the fight in him was gone.

It was only starting for me. I circled him as he had me. He followed me with the knife.

"Stay away from me, Danny, or I swear to God I'll kill you." His lips pulled back in a bloody grin. "You know I got you, right?"

I felt a burning sensation in my side. I looked down. My sweatshirt had a small slit. I pressed on my side, and red trickles of blood flowed over my fingers. Brent's face tightened as his shoulders squared off. I'd seen the tell dozens of times at practice, and I was ready. He came at me full force, his head slightly forward. I spun to the side, bringing a roundhouse punch to the side of his head, half turning him around. He weaved on his feet momentarily, the knife falling from his grasp. My next punch was square to the middle of his face, driving Brent down on his hands and knees. Blood trickled from his left ear, the side of his mouth, and his nose. It wasn't enough, not even close. I slammed my knee into his face, driving him up and onto his back. He lay there, arms out, gagging on his own blood.

I picked up the knife and dropped my knees onto his arms, pinning him to the ground. I pressed the knife against his throat. He spat blood off to the side, and his eyes grew wide with fear. He knew he was going to die.

"Please, you don't want to do this. You'll go to jail for the rest of your life."

"Someone has to stop you. You're a fucking animal. You need to be put down." I pushed the blade harder against his throat.

"Oh God, don't, Danny. Please. I'll take the plea. I'll tell them you didn't do anything. I don't want to die."

"Shut up, Brent." I snarled. Blood trickled down his throat. I pressed the blade harder. It would only take a little more pressure as I brought the blade across his throat, and then it would all be over.

"Do it, or I'll take care of you both."

I looked over my shoulder. Evert Tinsley stood a few feet behind me. A pistol hung limply at this side. I looked down into Brent's terrified eyes. If I cut his throat, I was no better than him. I threw the knife off to the side. Pain shot from my wound like there had been molten iron poured into my side. I stumbled to my feet, my vision blurring as Evert leveled the pistol at my chest.

Brent pulled himself up on his elbows and pushed himself backward until his back was against the Harley. His face was swelling, and a piece of his lip hung loose and bleeding. I turned back to Mr. Tinsley.

"Go ahead, shoot me. I'm probably already dead, anyway, but hasn't there been enough death, Mr. Tinsley?"

I stumbled past him toward the gate. Death was walking with me if I didn't stop the bleeding. Doc Stansbury's office was less than a quarter mile away, but it might as well have been a thousand. I barely had enough strength to make it out of the gate. I was almost to the truck when Jim's car pulled into the alley. He slammed on his brakes and ran to me. No strength was left in my legs as I leaned against the truck. Jim grasped me under the shoulders, holding me up.

"What happened?" He pulled up my sweatshirt and saw the blood pumping from the wound. "Was it Brent?"

"Yes."

"I'll take care of that bastard later. We've got to get you to Doc Stansbury."

A minute later, we were speeding down Fifth Street. I closed my eyes. The world around me was hazy and darkening.

"Hang in there, Danny," my brother said. "You're going to be okay."

But I knew nothing was going to be okay again. I let myself drift away, away from the pain and away from what I'd done to Brent.

CHAPTER 23

The next few days were a haze of shadows and murmuring voices. The world around me was darkness and confusion. I awoke to a searing, intense light in my eyes and shimmering voices. I tried to speak, but there was only a gasp followed by a painful jolt of fire in my side.

"I'm Nurse Ransmeier. Please don't try to talk. They just removed your breathing tube, and your throat is raw. It should pass in a few hours. Just nod your head to my questions. Do you understand?"

I nodded.

"Any pain?"

I thought, *Are you shitting me?* But said, "A little."

"No talking, just nod. Is your name Danny Prescott?"

I nodded.

Nurse Ransmeier turned to my mother and father and smiled. My mother nervously twisted a handkerchief in her hand. My father looked old and tired. They watched the nurse as she adjusted the tubes and wires connected to me and raised my bed to a sitting position.

It was an effort to raise my hand and point to my mouth. I endured the pain and whispered, "Water."

"I'm sorry. You can't have water until the doctor sees you. I'll bring some ice chips, which should help," the nurse said.

My mouth was dry enough for a Bedouin reunion, and my tongue felt like sandpaper.

The nurse left, and my mother came to my side and clasped my hand in hers.

"We've all been praying for you. Jim has been here every night. You've never been alone, Danny, not for a second, and now you're back with us. Wendy has been here every day too and all last night. She was hoping to be here when you woke up. She's quite a girl." My mother tried to smile, but only a tear came to her eye.

My father said, "You had us scared for a while, but Doc Stansbury says you'll be okay."

"How long have I been here?" I whispered. My voice sounded graveled. The nurse was right; speaking was a bitch. Where was the ice?

"Three days," he said. "It's Tuesday. They sedated you so you wouldn't pull the stitches loose in your side. The knife blade penetrated your liver and nicked an artery. We almost lost you, son."

"Brent?" I whispered.

My father hesitated for several seconds. "Don't concern yourself with anything but getting better."

"Brent?" I whispered again.

My father moved closer and touched my shoulder. "Brent Arrington is dead. Evert shot him, then killed himself."

I closed my eyes, wanting to go back to where I'd been for three days. So much hurt, pain, and death, and for what? What had it all been for?

Nurse Ransmeier was back with a glass filled with ice. I opened my mouth, and she put a piece on my tongue. The relief was instantaneous and glorious. I opened my mouth for another. She placed another on my tongue, then placed the glass next to me. I tried to move my arm to get it, but the jolt of pain put a stop to that.

"Your son needs to rest. The doctor will be here in a few minutes. He'll probably need to talk to you after he sees Danny."

A few minutes later, Doc Sorenson entered the room. He looked as if he was barely out of puberty. Nurse Ransmeier pulled back the sheet, exposing a large bandage, and carefully removed the tape, leaving a pile of gauze atop the wound. The doctor snapped on a pair of latex gloves, then pulled the remaining gauze off. He might as well have poured vinegar into the wound.

"Oh, shit!" I screamed through clenched teeth. I barely noticed the burning rawness in my throat.

"Still a little sensitive there," he said, picking at the stitches.

My eyes were watering as I nodded. How had they let this psychopath out of medical school? He redressed the wound and picked up the glass of ice. He placed several chips, one after another, on my tongue and immediately became my favorite doctor.

"You're a lucky boy, Mr. Prescott. It took two surgeries to patch you up. We had to bring in a vascular surgeon from Des Moines. Everything seems to be healing well. You should be able to go home in a few days, but you'll have to stay off your feet for a couple more weeks. We don't want that wound to reopen, do we?"

We sure as hell do not, I thought. *And certainly not if you're the one who'll redress the wound.*

In the afternoon, Jim and Susan came to see me. My sister kissed me on the forehead.

I looked at my brother and said, "Next."

Jim shot back. "No way. I'd rather French kiss a pig."

"Then you're speaking from experience, I assume," I said. It wasn't nearly as funny with a raspy voice, but it brought a smile to Jim's face, making it worth the pain. My throat was better, and I could drink a small amount of water.

The morphine was wearing off; the pain was a bitch when I moved, but I was feeling more like myself. Susan was excited about being accepted into a sorority and the freedom of college life.

"I wish I could stay, Danny, but I have midterms this week. Don't do anything stupid like this again. Okay?"

"I think I can agree to that."

She kissed me on the forehead again, tears glistening in her eyes. We cared for each other more than either of us wanted to say. Family was like that. It wasn't what you said. It was that you were there when you were needed. Jim stuck around until close to three o'clock. There was still work on the farm, and it didn't stop because someone was ill or injured. He told me Mom and Dad had always been with me until I woke up. Wendy had also been there, staying with me throughout the surgery. Her parents finally came and got her, making her go to school.

"That one's a keeper," Jim said.

"I hope I'll be able to. She's the most special person I've ever known," I said.

I napped a little after Jim left. When I awoke, Wendy was sitting next to my bed. She had piled several textbooks on the table beside me.

"Hello, butthead," Wendy said. "I brought your books and assignments— no reason to neglect your education." She wasn't fooling me. Her eyes were red and puffy from crying, and she had never looked more beautiful. She wore flowery bib overalls with red suspenders. It made me chuckle. Weird Wendy was back and as charming as ever.

"You look fantastic," I said.

"You say that to all the beautiful girls."

"I do," I admitted.

She leaned forward and kissed me. "I love you, Danny Prescott, but if you ever do anything like that again, you're going to seriously piss me off."

"I love you too, Wendy Warner, and I will never do anything again to piss you off."

"Bullshit," she said. And it was—all except the "I love you."

Tears filled her eyes as her comical facade fell away. "I'm sorry," she said as a sob escaped her throat. "I came here to cheer you up."

"You are just by being here."

"It must have been terrible for you, Danny, finding Ranger and then hearing about Loretta."

"Have they had Loretta's funeral?" I asked.

"No, they haven't released their bodies . . ." She stopped and looked as if she had said something wrong.

"It's okay, Wendy. I know Brent and Evert are dead. My father told me."

She described all that had happened since I'd collapsed in the waiting room. Police cars had sealed off the entire neighborhood around Brent's home. Mason City and Des Moines TV stations were in town all weekend. So far, Wendy had avoided the reporters and the sheriff. "Danny, I need to ask you something, and I'll never mention it again, but I have to know. There was a photo of the knife in the paper. It was the same as Steve's. Was it his?"

I hesitated before I answered. I knew what she wanted to know. Did I bring the knife to kill Brent? "Brent stole Steve's knife from the pickup when he killed Ranger. He dropped it during the fight. You want to know if I went there to kill him? I don't know, Wendy. I think I intended to, and I hated him enough, but when I had the chance, I didn't. Does that make me a bad person?"

"It makes you the boy I love," she said.

Wendy stayed another hour and read me a chapter of my English

Literature assignment, Hemingway's *A Farwell to Arms*. I closed my eyes, listening to the musical cadence of her voice until her mother motioned to her from the doorway.

"I've got to go, Danny. I'll be back tomorrow." She smiled down at me and touched my cheek with her fingertips. "Do a few of your assignments, bozo. I'll hand them in for you. I don't want to marry a high school dropout."

Wendy's mother gave me a friendly wave as they disappeared into the corridor. Marriage. I'd never thought about that, but it was an excellent thought. My parents came a half hour later and stayed until four o'clock. There were chores to do.

Sheriff Brennan entered the room shortly after they left. I didn't think that was by coincidence. "I'd like to talk with Danny, if that's okay. I have a few loose ends to tie up, and then I'll be out of your hair."

"Should I have my lawyer?" I asked.

"You're a witness, not a suspect, Danny. There are three people dead. I deserve to know why." Sheriff Brennan picked up a chair and set it close to the bed. "Let's start with why you were in town."

The sheriff knew about Ranger and that I suspected Brent was responsible. He didn't interrupt until I described how I had heard the Harley and entered his backyard.

"What did you intend to do to Brent when you found him?"

"I wanted him to admit what he had done. If I had to beat that out of him, I was okay with that."

"Did he?"

"Did he what?" I asked.

"Admit to killing your dog and calling Loretta Tinsley?"

I told the sheriff that he had admitted to killing Ranger and calling Loretta and about how we had fought before he stabbed me.

"Where did Brent get the knife he used to stab you?"

"He took it from his back pocket, but Brent stole it from my pickup the night he killed my dog."

"So you didn't have it when you entered his backyard?"

"No, sir."

Sheriff Brennan looked at me oddly, as if trying to solve a puzzle. He closed the pocket pad where he'd been jotting down notes. "One more thing. Were you aware that a switchblade is illegal in the state of Iowa?"

I didn't respond, and Brennan didn't probe further. If he'd been sending a message, I'd gotten it. There would be no mention of the knife again. He pushed the pad into his shirt pocket, replaced the chair, and stepped back from the bed. For several seconds, he studied me as if trying to decide what to say.

"I'll be filing my report. It's going to say that you confronted Brent at the Arringtons' home about killing your dog. You fought, and Brent pulled an illegal switchblade from his pocket and stabbed you. He was about to stab you again when Evert Tinsley intervened and shot him. I'd hate to hear later that you were talking with your friends and contradicted me."

"That won't happen," I said.

"Good. Oh, by the way, I took that bottle of whiskey from under the seat of your pickup. With everything else going on, I saw no need to tell your dad. I'll never find another one under there, will I?"

"No, sir."

"Then I guess we're done here."

On Friday, I was released. I was feeling better, even strong enough to walk around the hospital, but they wanted me to use a wheelchair until I was in the car—hospital regs. My father pushed me, while my mother walked beside me. We'd just gotten to the car when Ron Arrington walked up.

"I heard your boy was getting out today. I thought I'd stop by and see if you were satisfied with what you've done to me and my family."

My father stepped away from the chair until he was standing toe-to-toe with

Ron. My father was four inches taller, towering over him. "Satisfied with what?"

"With all the lies you and your boy have told about my son. You've blamed me for every bad thing—first your sister and then this. You've held a grudge against me since she slammed into that bridge. Now my son is dead. I hope you're satisfied."

My father helped me into the car and then turned back to Ron. "There's been no grudge and no getting even. There never has been. That's your turf, Ron, not mine. One thing caused all the tragic things that have happened. Your boy grew up to be just like you, and you'll have to live knowing that for the rest of your life."

By the third week home, I was ready to return to school. Wendy and a parade of friends, including the football team, had visited our farm and kept me company. The Raiders had lost two games, putting the regional title out of reach, but there was always next year.

We heard later that Ron Arrington's wife had left him and that he was drinking again. A year later, his insurance and real estate businesses closed. I had no empathy for the Arringtons; neither was there joy for me in their adversity. No one had gained. There was only loss. Banning would never forget the weekend that forever linked the Prescott and Arrington names. My aunt's story and Possum Earl's were retold. Legends outlive the truth and die a hard death in Banning.

I was named all-state halfback in my senior year after setting a school record for yards gained in a single season. The Raiders brought the regional title back to Banning. All but the incarcerated were in the stands that night, but as I came off the field, I saw only Wendy. If I'd learned anything during my junior year, it was that I could do anything as long as Wendy was at my side. She always found a way to be there when I needed her.

Wendy...she received an art scholarship from Drake University in Des Moines that covered her tuition and living expenses. I was happy for her. It was her dream, but walking into the assembly hall each morning, knowing she wouldn't be there, was tough. It was even tougher having her two hours away. A phone call was no match for holding her in my arms, but we found a way to overcome the distance and the occasional spat. Weird Wendy Warner and I always would. It's what outcasts do.

THE END